Hazel Hucker is a graduate of the London School of Economics. She met her husband there and saw life as an army officer's wife in several countries with him and their children. Later she worked as an Organisation and Methods Officer and then taught Economics and History, helping to support her family as her husband changed careers from the army to the Bar. A move from Hampshire to London in the early 1990s gave her the time to fulfil her own ambition of writing. THE REAL CLAUDIA CHARLES is her fifth novel.

THE REAL CLAUDIA CHARLES

Flora Monk, a struggling novelist in her thirties, plans to make her name known with a biography of Claudia Charles, a distant cousin of her mother's, described in her recent TIMES obituary as 'an early feminist, and one of the world's finest writers of twentieth-century prose'. But this project does not please Flora's aunts, nor her elderly widowed mother, Primrose, who vehemently opposes it. When Primrose dies, Flora uncovers shattering truths, and finally begins to understand, too late, what her mother has had to suffer throughout her life, and why their own relationship was such a difficult one.

Books by Hazel Hucker
Published by The House of Ulverscroft:

THE AFTERMATH OF OLIVER
A DANGEROUS HAPPINESS
CHANGING STATUS

HAZEL HUCKER

THE REAL CLAUDIA CHARLES

Complete and Unabridged

ULVERSCROFT
Leicester

First published in Great Britain in 1998 by
Little, Brown & Company
London

First Large Print Edition
published 2002
by arrangement with
Little, Brown & Company (UK)
London

The moral right of the author has been asserted

All characters in this publication are fictitious and
any resemblance to real persons, living or dead,
is purely coincidental.

British Library CIP Data

Hucker, Hazel
    The real Claudia Charles.—Large print ed.—
Ulverscroft large print series: general fiction
1. Women biographers—Family relationships
—Fiction
2. Domestic fiction
3. Large type books
I. Title
823.9′14 [F]

ISBN 0–7089–4626–7

Published by
F. A. Thorpe (Publishing) Ltd.
Anstey, Leicestershire

Set by Words & Graphics Ltd.
Anstey, Leicestershire
Printed and bound in Great Britain by
T. J. International Ltd., Padstow, Cornwall

This book is printed on acid-free paper

In remembrance of my mother,
Violet Louise Blew-Jones
(Mrs Roy Drake)
1902 – 1983
and of
Dr Letitia Fairfield, CBE
1885 – 1978
with great affection

Acknowledgements

Grateful acknowledgements are made to Sam Elliott and Nicky Davis of BPAS, British Pregnancy Advisory Service, Twickenham, for their valuable help over consultation procedures and the discussion of terminations; to Miss Pauline Adams, librarian and archivist at Somerville College, Oxford, for her kindly help over details pertaining to Somerville College shortly after the First World War, and to my dear friends Dr John Kelly and Mrs Janet Nuboer for their aid over medical details.

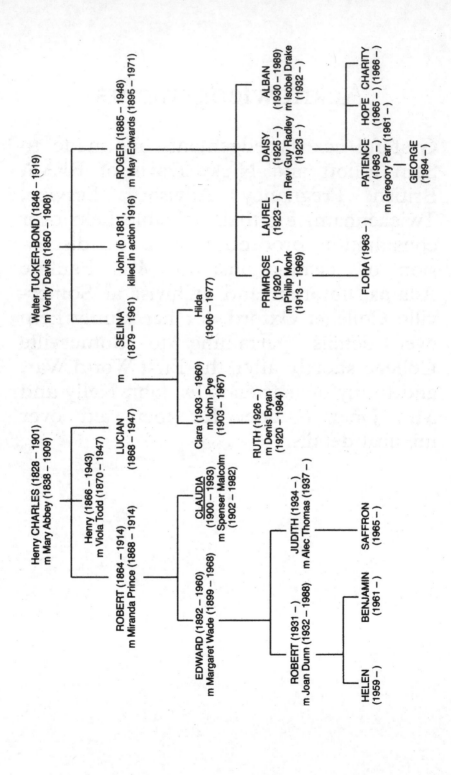

1

'I am going to write the biography of Claudia Charles.'

I have dropped a stone into the pool of the three sisters' consciousness and the ripples run out and out, rocking them where they sit. There is a silence, which somehow encompasses a conflict. They stare at me as I hand them cream and sugar, their eyes fixed.

'No,' my mother says. 'No. That wouldn't be right.' She folds her lips in and her mild elderly face is suddenly implacable.

'I don't see that,' says my aunt Daisy, running her fingers through her wild white hair. 'Claudia's one of the century's great writers. Someone's bound to eventually; why not Flora?'

Aunt Laurel, the family oracle, gazes first at me and then at my mother. Her eyes are searching. She frowns. 'It's not unthinkable, Primrose.'

'It is to me.' Mother blinks through her bifocals and will not focus on any of us. Her brown-blotched hands are clasped in her lap, the knucklebones white and gleaming through the tightened skin. She is agitated. 'I won't have it!'

It is a dark and stormy day, and beyond their heads wind-whipped snowflakes are being driven across the long windows of my mother's flat on Richmond Hill and over the landscape below, stealing the colour from the wide spreading view of Petersham Meadows and the curving sweep of the Thames as it flows past Marble Hill Park. The sight of the grey waters, the whitening meadows and the steadily blurring trees beyond sends a cold shiver through me. I switch on more lamps to brighten the room and sit down to sip the coffee and eat the mint chocolates Mother has provided as the finale to her little New Year's Day lunch party.

Mother, who is small and skinny, is sitting in her chair with the nervous alertness of a monkey I'd once seen crouching in a cage in our local pet shop, waiting to be rescued. An indeterminate nose above a long upper lip and a wide mouth increase the simian look. I contemplate her fretful face against the background of the storm, the way she is huddling her beige cardigan around herself, her shaking head. For years I have had the impression that Mother regards me as some dangerous explosive object; today the feeling is particularly strong.

2

'What's wrong with a biography of Claudia?' I ask.

'If it were to be purely an analysis of her writing and her times I shouldn't mind,' Mother says flatly, 'but you're bound to go further. Today's biographers don't just dabble their fingers in the stuff of people's souls, they sift among the sewage. And they can do as they like because the law doesn't protect the dead from libel or slander. I don't want my daughter disinterring the secrets of someone in my family, distant or not. Let the dead bury their dead.'

'Goodness, you're right!' Aunt Daisy interrupts happily. 'Lloyd George messing about with his secretaries, Dorothy Sayers giving her illegitimate son to someone else to bring up, the book I lent you about the poet who interfered with little girls — you were so cross with me about that one — quite sensational, but poisonously nasty. That sort of thing comes between us and their very real achievements. I do see what you mean, Primrose.' She casts her bright blue eyes heavenwards. 'Your novels are frank enough, Flora; Heaven help us if you put your claws into Claudia. We wouldn't know where to look.'

'There's been a biography already,' Mother pronounces. 'One's quite enough. The reviews are unkind, but *I* thought it hit the right note.'

An early memoir had been written and distributed soon after Claudia's death by a young woman called Susie Peters. When Claudia was between secretaries one summer, this English graduate from Nottingham had taken on the post (elevated in the memoir's blurb to Personal Assistant), and continued working with Claudia for the better part of a year, which she considered amounted to knowing her 'intimately and deeply'. One gathered that Claudia had liked to reminisce about old love-affairs with the famous and the notorious, yet in the memoir Susie tiptoed about these intriguing episodes, never quite bringing them to life: perhaps she could not bear to be thought a voyeur, peeping through the keyholes of the great. Nor did her perception of her subject connect with my own memories of Claudia. She quoted a well-known critic as dubbing Claudia Charles 'a baroque woman', and if this implies the disregard for mainstream concepts and the love of the opulent and the outrageous that I think it does, then it encapsulates my own view of her, yet Susie Peters made nothing of her flamboyant subject, drawing a portrait at once humourless and sentimental, lacking the depth and the third dimension that a

4

biography demands, flat and blurred as an amateur's holiday snapshot.

'That memoir?' Aunt Laurel rises from the sofa and goes to plant her feet apart on Mother's Ispahan rug, a big, stout, broad-shouldered woman, her hefty backside to the fire, her hands in her pockets like a man. 'Slipshod work,' she declares. 'No real research, just the regurgitation of a lot of magazine articles and reviews, larded over with rumour, chitchat and sticky sentiment. A hagiography, with areas of Claudia's life omitted to save the family's feelings — or so the woman now says. Rubbish. The family has no feelings any more. The scandals aren't just years old, they're history. Who cares? Not us. She outlived anyone who could really care.'

'I care,' Mother says. 'I care for what people think.'

'Oh you,' my aunt says with contemptuous affection, 'you're still living in a bygone age of Victorian morality. You imagine views that haven't existed for more than half a century.'

'Claudia Charles isn't even properly related to us,' I add. 'She's only a cousin by marriage. I can't imagine what you're having the fidgets about, Mother. In any case, I'm authorised to write it by the Trustees; my agent and my publisher are enthusiastic

— and more to the point, the contract's been signed and I have a surprisingly handsome advance.'

Silence, a deep silence. Outside the wind whips the snow across the meadows and along the road till the few cars braving the furious icy flakes seem to move in a soundless dream-world. The landmarks I identify in the familiar landscape will soon become obscured.

* * *

I take the drive back to my own flat and my live-in lover, Jake, tentatively. I put my headlights on at first, but the effect is eerily unpleasant since the swirling snow appears to be hurling all its malevolent force directly at me. I reduce the beam and the view changes, is altogether more gentle; the wind seems to drop. The windscreen wipers bat the wet flakes away and I slither and skate my way along, but thank God without incident.

A memory flits through my mind of a similarly snowy day; it is elusive and I strain to catch it. My mother is in the picture; she is driving and nervous; she complains the weather forecast has not mentioned snow and anyway it is late March, this is ridiculous . . . Ah, I have it. I was twelve, no, thirteen, and this is the first memory I have of going to see Claudia Charles that is not a brief flash, but a clear recollection of several hours' duration.

I hear Mother demanding immaculate behaviour from me. 'No showing off, no outrageous comments. Quiet dignity, please, Flora. And think before you speak. Claudia Charles is one of the most brilliant and knowledgeable women you'll ever meet and I want her to see you as the highly intelligent girl you are, not as a chattering child. Ooooch, this snow — did you feel us slide? Driving in this is man's work. God was very unfair on me when he took your father so soon. Oh, and Flora, if you're unsure which pieces of cutlery to use with which course, just remember to start with the outside ones and work your way in. All right?'

'Yes, Mummy,' I said, wondering at the sharp note in her voice. Was it the treacherous conditions or visiting Claudia Charles which made her so nervous?

The house was at the end of a country village in Berkshire; it was large and white, with pilasters here and ornamental ironwork there along its façade. Mother called it 'rather rash and overgrown Regency'. She added that it was not a truthful house, which puzzled me all the way up the drive. Mother prided herself on her architectural insights and had read Ruskin and Pevsner.

The housekeeper opened the front door to us, a little brown woman, like a nut. She took our coats and scarves, and tutted at the weather. Then a door opened somewhere in the hall and Claudia's husband, Spenser Malcolm, stooped out to welcome us with warm embraces. 'Primrose — and Flora! Lovely. How are you both?' He was a tall heavy man, dressed in a three-piece tweed suit, with a spotted bow tie strangely adorning the neck of his Tattersall shirt. His thick grey hair fell over his collar at the back and he peered through thick-lensed spectacles. Mother had told me he was a stockbroker who had made his pile early and retired to indulge his twin passions for literature and the opera, but I saw a definite resemblance to the absent-minded professor in the TV series which was my current passion, and I warmed to him. Aunt Laurel had said: 'Goodness knows what Spenser's antecedents are, but there's a lot of Jewish blood there.' She liked Jews, considering them both sharp and cultured — admirable traits. Mother had said: 'I think of him as a man of letters.' A librarian, she doted on men of literary knowledge and perception. Aunt Daisy, on the other hand, simply thought he was a poppet. 'Such a lovely cuddly man. Whatever did Claudia do to deserve *him*?'

We were shown into the drawing-room and I drew in my breath in shock. The hall had been rich with long velvet curtains and gilt-framed pictures, but this room was sumptuous. As we walked in, Claudia Charles rose from an elaborate writing-table between two long windows, where, she was swift to tell us, 'I've been frightfully busy all morning, proof-reading. My last novel, I swear, Primrose. My absolutely last novel.' She was sumptuous too, and I stared and stared, torn between admiration for the theatrical effect she made even against the tremendous background, and an awful suspicion that she might be simply magnificently farcical, even (and how dreadful the thought) vulgar. She was a heavy woman with a big strong-boned face in which the deep-set eyes were as alert as a bird's, and the wide mouth always moving — in speech, laughter, grimaces, or in savouring the chocolates we had brought her: 'One of the few sensual pleasures left at my age, so I'll indulge myself to the full. Thank you, Primrose and Flora. How kind you are.' She must have been in her mid-seventies then, having been born in 1900, but she seemed to tower above my mother and, despite the flesh that sagged and crumbled, she gave an overpowering impression of strength and power of purpose. Her clothes were fantastic, a flowing dress of some woven material resembling brocade in sombre yet rich dark reds and browns and blues was girdled mediaeval-style at the hips and clasped with an elaborate gold clasp, while over her shoulders she had thrown a silk shawl from the Far East; this was of peacock blue, embroidered lavishly with gold and silver thread. Heavy gold jewellery jangled at her throat and wrists, and her thick ankles overflowed dark-red suede shoes.

The room held me open-mouthed: an outrageous double-cube, stuffed with opulence and flamboyance, in whose chimney a roaring fire burned, its logs leaning on elaborate firedogs that would not have been out of place at Blenheim Palace. At the windows were magnificent rose taffeta curtains trimmed with deep blue ruching. The hand-painted Chinese wallpaper featured twining pink roses visited by tropical birds and butterflies, all on a dusky blue background. Vases, seventeenth-century Italian bronzes, Venetian glass and baroque candlesticks jostled each other on tables and shelves, while the most amazing clocks ticked in each corner. The contrast of this pulsating room with the untouched fields of white outside was too much. I felt dizzy. Everywhere I looked there was something breathtaking — pictures, porcelains, Persian rugs — a dazzle of light and riches. I was attracted and I was repelled. I looked at Mother in her trim grey librarian's suit and her best pink lambswool jumper, faded to the point of invisibility against this background — and Claudia — and I thought in my groping adolescent way: *This isn't fair!*

Spenser offered us drinks and Mother dithered for a moment before deciding on a small dry sherry (she sensed dry was smarter than sweet, though she sipped distastefully, like someone forced to take medicine). I drank orange juice, while Claudia and Spenser drank whisky. We talked. Perseveringly. Claudia spoke of her novel, *The Midnight Oil*, recently published in paperback. She was furious about the cover artwork, which she claimed was hideous. 'Hideous and pretentious. But when I complain they tell me with infuriating condescension that I don't understand the sales aspect. This ghastly reproduction of some unknown seventeen-century painter, so I'm told, will sell it. By the thousand. I tell them, Rubbish, it's my name that will sell it! But it's always the same.'

Mother nodded with eager comprehension.

'Yes, our local authors complain to me of the same problem. It must be infuriating.'

'Who are your local authors?' Claudia demanded to know.

Mother gave a couple of names and Claudia looked blank. Then Mother brightened. 'Oh, and there's Geoffrey Pickstone, of course. I helped to arrange a very good lecture he gave us on his novel *To Rouse a Lion* shortly after it was broadcast.' She gave a reminiscent smile. 'He's a charming man, and the lecture was crowded out. Everyone was delighted.'

Mother was always talking about Geoffrey Pickstone, who was short, sallow and quiet, as well as being at least fifty. I found it impossible to believe that someone so hopelessly ordinary could possibly know, I mean, really *know*, about love and adventure.

'How fascinating,' Claudia said, tossing back her whisky. 'Remind me what it was about, will you? I can't call it to mind.'

'The conflict between the call of duty and the call of love seen through the eyes of a chap in the SAS who is sent on various undercover missions in Oman and the Yemen and falls for a young nurse in one of the hospitals there. It was a wonderful sense of atmosphere and place. It reminds me of H. E. Bates' *Fair Stood the Wind for France*. It's been unusually popular with our readers at the library. We've had to purchase several copies.'

'Didn't he send you a copy?' Spenser enquired of Claudia.

'Oh goodness, yes, I remember it now,' Claudia said, holding out her glass to Spenser for more whisky. 'He sent me a copy when it came out, saying how much he admired my work and how it had influenced him. I suppose he hoped I'd review it. Sympathetically, naturally. But he could hardly have imagined it was my sort of thing. He isn't exactly a writer of great literary ability, is he?'

Spenser murmured that he'd liked it.

Mother looked down into her sherry glass as if her thoughts were struggling in its depths and she was painfully attempting to fish them out. Then she said, 'No, I suppose he isn't. Not at your level. But when he wrote of love and loss under fire he touched a chord in me.'

Claudia raised her eyebrows. 'I didn't know you'd ever lost someone under such circumstances.'

'No,' came the quiet reply. 'But then you've never known me closely, have you?'

Her retort shocked me and caught at my attention. I had a brief moment to wonder; I saw an extraordinary grimace on Claudia's face and then the little brown nut of a housekeeper entered to tell us that luncheon was ready, and we all found places to put down our glasses and trooped into the next room.

I remember that the dining-room was spacious and handsome, and that the four of us were spread a long way apart from one another at a big shiny table that seemed to be a mass of silver and cut-glass and out-of-season flowers, but details of the meal have fled my memory. I know only that it was lavish and the food was what Mother described afterwards as 'far too rich!' and that it made me nervous because it was strange and therefore suspect. I remember most of all how Claudia talked.

She spoke with emphasis, her voice loud and dramatic; she spoke with lucidity, so that every issue was made crystal-clear to me, something rare in my dealings with grown-ups. But when Mother ventured upon a topic of her own Claudia snatched it from her — the state of British architecture, politics, new novels — no matter what, Claudia had dined with the architect, knew the minister, had read the novels and met their authors, and *she* must tell us *all*. I saw from Spenser's wry expression that her comments were wickedly apt. She rolled her eyes, she waved her knuckle-duster ringed hands, she drew me and Mother into these people's lives and I felt I touched greatness. It was a monologue with no room for the exchange of ideas, but I was entranced. More, I was inspired. From that day forward I was certain that I, too, would be a writer, mingling with those people whose views influenced events.

My mother should have been impressed too, yet I sensed she was resisting Claudia. She was opposite me, her eyes on her plate, wearing the withdrawn, non-committal expression that I knew from experience denoted annoyance. I felt I could hear the thoughts running through her brain as clearly as if she had spoken them aloud: *I am a person, too. I may only be a librarian, but I am the deputy Borough librarian and valued in my community. Why aren't my opinions requested, why am I not part of this display?* A small part of me understood and sympathised; the rest wanted only to listen to Claudia Charles' firework display of words.

We left almost as soon as lunch was over, to my disappointment. But Mother spoke of the snow, the unsafe condition of the roads and the need to go while the light was still good. 'It's bad enough driving in the dark at any time, but snow has an extraordinary habit of turning even a familiar road into a deceptive and dangerous world.'

'Yes, I suppose it does,' Claudia agreed vaguely. 'Erg-strordinary!' She blinked, pressed her powdered and scented cheek against mine, and then unexpectedly enquired, 'What and whom are you reading now, my dear? Somebody worthwhile?'

'She's reading *Jane Eyre*,' Mother told her with emphasis. 'Her teachers say Flora has the most adult tastes.'

'Do you like it?' Claudia asked me. She looked suddenly tired and old.

'Yes, I do. It's different from anything I've read before. It's really good.'

'I'm glad you're developing a taste for literature. Very important. Early experience of the best. I read *Jane Eyre* when I was eight.' She said an abrupt goodbye to us both and vanished back into the drawing room, leaving Spenser to hug us and wave us off into the icy grey afternoon.

As our little Mini nosed its way out of the drive, the growing feeling that something had somehow been wrong all day intensified. Every nerve and muscle in my upright little mother seemed wire-tight. I didn't like it. I said with a shiver and a nervous giggle: 'Mummy, did you hear how Claudia burped as she spoke? 'Erg-strordinary!' Wasn't it funny?'

She exploded. 'Flora! For God's sake! You've been with one of the greatest minds in Britain all day and all you can think to say is that she burped. I'm appalled. I suppose *that* is the one thing you'll remember all your life!' The car slid on frozen snow and almost buried its bonnet in a hedge. 'Oh hell!' she swore again, something she never did. She backed out angrily and drove on.

I sat on my cold hands. 'She's very clever,' I offered.

'Claudia Charles is an outstanding person,' she corrected me, glaring out through the windscreen at the snow. 'Her achievements are tremendous. Books like *Shadow of a Child* and *The Fountain of Living Waters* have spread her fame worldwide. But she is too aware of it, too intent on displaying it. To my mind that diminishes her greatness. Real greatness has time for the ordinary person, for the less successful. Real greatness knows it can learn from them. She should have drawn you out. She should have drawn *me* out.'

'Yes,' I said. I was embarrassed for her. I thought for several seconds. 'Spenser was nice, wasn't he? He talked to us a lot when we were having coffee.'

'Spenser is a gentleman. He has time for everyone. Claudia was exceptionally lucky to find a husband like him.'

I hesitated. I didn't know what to talk about in case it was wrong. Finally I remarked that Claudia and Spenser had an Ispahan rug like ours. That should be all right.

'She gave me my rug for my wedding present,' Mother said. 'That and my pearls are the only real presents I've ever had from her.'

'They're lovely, those rugs,' I said. 'Lovely colours, all special.'

'Perhaps,' said Mother.

The afternoon was growing darker every moment, but the snow's whiteness, together with the rise of a full moon, illuminated the fields and the trees and an owl flying low beyond us with an eerie light of tarnished silver. I had never seen anything like it before; it gave me the same strange exultant feeling of reaching into another world that I had experienced that afternoon, and the skin at the back of my neck crawled deliciously.

Suddenly Mother began to reminisce about her childhood, about how she'd always been different from her brother and her sisters, and how hard it had been for her to get a decent education after her father had lost all his money, things I'd never even heard mentioned before.

'I was the odd one out. I was the eldest but

18

I was different from the others. Small and plain and shy. But then I was named after a woodland plant that's small and shy: Primrose. Perhaps I lived up to it. I wasn't witty, either, and I never did learn to put myself forward. When we were in the nursery or the schoolroom, Mummy and Daddy used sometimes to invite one or two of us to tea in the drawing-room with them.' A sigh. 'We went in turns. It was a lovely tea. Toasted muffins in the winter, or hot scones thick with butter. And dear little cakes, oh, so light! Cook used to make them specially. But it wasn't my turn very often; Laurel and Daisy went far more than I did, and my little brother, Alban, more than any of us.'

'Why?' I asked, shocked and indignant.

In the dark car I felt rather than saw her shrug.

'I don't know. It was never up to us to put ourselves forward. Nanny would decide with my parents who should go. Favouritism wasn't a word that bothered people then. I adored it when I did go. I could sit on Daddy's knee and smell the eau de Cologne on his handkerchief. We weren't a family for cuddles normally. Mummy said it was bad form. She liked us to have dignity.' She negotiated a roundabout with care. Then she went on: 'Did you notice the cornices in

Claudia's drawing-room? And the two ceiling roses? They reminded me, oh, so much, of the ones in our old house in Holland Park, when we were well off. Daddy used to come home quite often for tea then. Perhaps that's why he lost so much of our money. But things were bad in shipping between the wars and the 1929 Crash wrecked his investment portfolio. I heard the servants talking once about how bad things were with us. Nothing dramatic at first, but then we had to move to Golders Green. Quite a small house, only four bedrooms and all our old servants had to go, even Nanny. We just had a cook-general and she used to complain about sleeping up in the attic. Decent schools were out of the question for us girls, until Aunt Selina and her husband said they'd pay Laurel's fees, and Daisy's godmother took on Daisy's. They kept Alban at Sutton Valence School, but the bursar was always dunning Daddy for the fees, that I do know. Aunt Selina almost adopted Laurel, they took her on holiday and everything. They took Daisy, too, sometimes, but I never went.'

'Why not?' Now I was furious on her behalf.

Mummy shook her head. 'I told you. I was different. I was the odd one out.' Her voice thickened. 'I used to feel so hurt; I never understood what was wrong. I supposed it was because Mother took to her bed. She was quite a hypochondriac — that means she invented most of her illnesses. She always wanted *me* to nurse her. She said Laurel never understood her needs, and besides, she was clumsy, and Daisy was always giggling. So . . . from fourteen onwards I had to study by myself in the empty schoolroom — when I wasn't giving Mother her medicines or stroking her forehead.'

It sounded horrid, dreary and lonely. I felt furious for her, as if she were a child I'd discovered being bullied. But at the same time I felt that faint scorn one feels for the bullied child who hasn't fought back, who has failed to kick out and scream.

'We never saw Claudia during that time,' my mother added. 'She was busy making her name as a clever young writer. She never came near us.'

I sat chewing my lip. I wished I'd had a sister or a brother. The events of the day had had a strange effect on my perception of my little universe and I urgently needed a confidant of my own age to mull it over with me.

It had dawned on me for the first time that there were people who occupied quite different levels of existence and knowledge from the one that my mother and her friends inhabited. With consternation, I saw too that it was possible to view both Claudia and my mother objectively and to judge them, though I was not acquainted with that word 'objectively' yet. And there was worse: I was judging my mother, and concluding not only that she lacked the moral fibre and stiff back of women like Claudia and Aunt Laurel but also that it was possible not to love and admire one's mother. Claudia had accomplished this. Beside her wit and dazzle, Mother had been diminished to something second rate. In the Mini, on that icy cold night, I was obscurely and petulantly ashamed of her.

2

I park my car on a blanket of whiteness and switch off the engine. The snow has stopped falling. The silence is broken by the scraping of a neighbour's spade on the path, steel ringing on paving. I turn my head in greeting and see a yellow car beyond him. I know that MGF; it belongs to Saffron Thomas, Claudia's great-niece and my great rival.

I run up the stairs of the late Victorian house to my flat on the first floor. Inside, I find Saffron lounging with her feet up on my sofa and Jake hovering somewhere mid-floor; big, dark, handsome, intelligent, sexy, lazy and complacent Jake. Used glasses, plates and coffee cups are scattered about them. The room looks steamed-up and crumby.

Saffron turns her head. 'Oh, Flora, hullo!' she says, smiling. 'I came round to wish you and Jake a Happy New Year and he asked me to stay for lunch. Wasn't that sweet of him?'

'It was blowing a blizzard,' Jake says shortly. He stops hovering and comes to kiss me on the mouth, bang, an aggressive, challenging kiss.

Why should Saffron come in a blizzard to

bring good wishes? She doesn't even like me, nor I her. I say sweetly, 'Happy New Year, Saffron dear. I'm so glad Jake was able to look after you. Are you well?'

'I'm very well,' she says with a drawled emphasis. 'How's your mother? And her sisters? I often think of poor Laurel with her lonely life, and Daisy in that dreary rectory. I'm so fond of them.'

'They're all well, thank you,' I return. I'm never certain if she means the devotion she swears to the three sisters, whom she telephones really quite regularly, or whether she plans to write a satirical short story around their beleaguered antiquity — something in the manner of Somerset Maugham's *The Three Fat Women of Antibes* (*The Three Rueful Women of Richmond*, perhaps?).

I don't know why I dislike Saffron as I do, except that she too is a novelist, with four published titles to her credit against my three, and all of hers have received flattering reviews. I covet her reviews but I hate her books. They are clever, clever in a sour way, full of social perception and dry satire — the vanities disembowelled with the chilling precision of a surgeon. I think they are nasty, nevertheless I find myself jealous of her laser-sharp accuracy of attack and her

24

dexterity with words. She writes rather as Piers Paul Read does, stories of outsiders looking in and observing, but hers are arrogant outsiders. Those inside are seen as duplicitous, poseurs, ruthless competitive women (her work is ninety per cent about women), delineated with swift strokes of her pen in Gerald Scarfelike exaggerations that make their point exactly, but to me fail in credibility. Are women truly so despicable? I don't think so. My novels pose questions, I tell myself; they do not annihilate.

Aunt Laurel once said to me that the point of life is to do as well as you can *for yourself*, not to win an imaginary competition with others — meaning Saffron Thomas. She herself had pottered through life, manageress of a golf links hotel on the south coast, spending her time off at the bridge table or the local racecourse, whisky glass in hand, relaxed and unbothered. I would find it impossible to live in that way: for me, to compete and to win keeps the languors of life at bay. Besides, Saffron is in open and undoubted competition with me, and in the whole arena of life, looks, sex and influence, not just in our writing. Perhaps the characters in her books are variations on an original theme of herself.

Her first novel, *Hell Built on Spite*

(inspired, we're told, by Pope's *Essay on Man*), was Claudia's selection for the 'Books of the Year' chosen annually for *The Times* by famous writers. Despite the fact that it was the brainchild of her great-niece, she wrote, she had no compunction in proclaiming it a tremendous piece of satirical writing, mercilessly observant, the best novel she'd had in her hands this year. Naturally, Claudia's remarks were reproduced on every one of Saffron's subsequent books, and, with such an endorsement, how could they fail to succeed? When my own first effort came out a year or so later, despite Mother's cries I forbade her to send it to Claudia; I'll succeed on my own merits, thank you, I said.

As I shed my coat and boots in the hall, I comfort myself that I sell better than Saffron does, and that I have a New York publisher for two of my novels, something she has not yet achieved. But then, glancing through the door, I am reminded that while Saffron's body on the sofa beckons from beneath a svelte and flesh-caressing black jersey dress, I am clad in a dull but warm knitted suit, compatible with the old ladies' views on common sense and the weather, clothes that now seem to diminish me into insignificance. Saffron, I have to admit, has a certain predatory grandeur to begin with in her long curving body, her aquiline features and her imperious dark eyes. Lads in BMWs racing her MG across traffic lights falter at the sight of her profile; strong men turn silent when she makes her entrance at a party, they stare in the streets. Whereas me, though I am tall, I have a certain packhorse sturdiness that is not classy, and, while my hair is a glossy brown, my eyes large, my mouth full and my figure a pleasure to inhabit, all matters for self-congratulation as far as I can tell, I do not act as a steely magnet to men's eyes, or not to those tall, dark intelligent yet macho men we both fancy and for whom we are in contention.

Oh, to hell with it! She is also two years younger than my thirty-four and looks nearer ten: a forceful twenty-five, perhaps.

Age is not easy to evaluate from physical appearance. Nor is character. There is a rich sensual warmth in Saffron's appearance that is wholly at odds with the clinical detachment of her writing, indeed to her approach to the world in general. And certainly to me. Which conveys the real person? It occurs to me that I can pin no exact epoch, nor any clear and rounded personality on her great-aunt Claudia, either. Weeks of reading, annotating and analysing her eleven tremendous but often exhausting novels, and ploughing through that memoir of Susie Peters', had created instead of one person a series of figures of colossal, goddess-like proportions. I flirt with this fancy. Egyptian, perhaps. The vulture-goddess Nekhbet, or the lion-goddess Sekhmet, or even, I think, remembering Claudia's capacity for putting my mother down, the goddess Hathor, often represented as a cow. Off-handedly I had asked my family about Claudia, but their reminiscences were coloured by her reactions to them as individuals. She had relished Daisy's 'delectable malice' about men, appreciated Isobel's knowledge of her pictures and bronzes and Laurel's scorn of today's politicians: 'Not one working brain between the lot of 'em!' — and told them so. Thus on the rare occasions when they saw Claudia they in turn relished her. But they agreed that as she got older they approached her with trepidation. She was not so much rude as irascible. One would hear her muttering, 'Oh hell, oh hell, oh hell!' as she struggled to move her unwieldy and pain-filled body from one room to another, or, 'Ignorant clot, stupid fool, senseless idiot!' as she strove, half-blind, to find the passage in some article which she must discuss with you, and you must damn. At ninety visitors could proclaim her 'difficult' or her food-spattered untidiness 'distasteful'. Was this, then, the same Claudia as the young woman who had fascinated great men such as Laurence Britton, George Bernard Shaw or H.G. Wells with her 'witty, generous writing' and 'the vitality of her reforming spirit'? Or again, the woman who wrote in *Shadow of a Child* of the death of a baby, sharing her grief so that we wept with her?

How can I re-create these women and somehow fashion them into one through the flawed medium of my writing? Nervousness shivers through my skin at the size of the project. I look at Saffron, so different with the three sisters and with me, or again with her men. How can anyone know her entirely? Nobody can enter her head and investigate its thought processes with the ease of surfing the Internet. It is as I am thinking this that she reveals her thoughts by asking what I'm working on now.

Nervousness changes to guilt, unexpected and unwanted guilt. 'I'm working on a biography. Claudia Charles.'

'Claudia Charles!' She is incredulous. 'You can't be serious. You hardly knew her.'

'I knew her,' I say.

'Not as I did.' She rears up on the sofa. 'She was part of my family, part of my life.'

I watch the skin of her neck and then her face as she reddens and blotches with anger.

She thinks I have stolen something from her. I adopt a judicial tone. 'Biographers should be detached and neutral in their approach. Anyone knowing Claudia as well as you did would find detachment impossible. Think of her endorsement of your work — you owe her too much. Besides, I thought you were involved in a three-book contract with your publishers.'

'That won't take for ever!'

Jake tells Saffron, 'Flora's been working on the preliminaries of this for weeks. She's lived and breathed bloody Claudia Charles. You should have been told.'

Thank you, Jake.

'What about the Trustees?' Saffron demands to know. 'You'll need their formal agreement for access to her papers, all those letters and diaries. Unless you're aiming at a simple literary study, of course, or one of those unauthorised works that assumes what it can't prove and hopes the reader won't notice the difference.'

She is snapping. I feel my own irritation rise.

'Oh, for Heaven's sake, Saffron, of course mine is to be an authorised biography.'

'You've seen my uncle Robert and Helen?'

'Numerous times.'

These two, Claudia's nephew and his

daughter, who are in their mid-sixties and late thirties respectively, together with a solicitor make up the Claudia Charles Trust. Since Claudia died in 1993 they have administered the estate, and Helen has acted as its literary agent. Helen, like her great-aunt Claudia, is a big-boned and forceful woman. She's ferociously clever and inclined to outpourings of exasperation against those less quick-minded than herself. She cannot believe that stupidity is not wilful aggravation and there are times when I share her suspicions. She is, in fact, a literary agent by profession, and a successful one, running her own agency. She and I met infrequently, but when we do we're always surprised and diverted by our similarities. We had bumped into one another at some literary party last May, whose, I can't remember — oh God, probably Saffron's — and taken ourselves and our drinks into a corner where Helen had complained that it was time for a serious comprehensive biography of Claudia Charles, but she could not think of a soul who could tackle it. She was at a standstill. Veronica Manning was heavily involved with Virginia Woolf and the Bloomsbury Group, and Angelica Framer was only just starting on Samuel Pepys. Tom Peace would love it, of course, but could I imagine the babble of clichés that would punctuate that literary whore's liturgical effusions? 'Look what he's just done to Laurence Britton.' She sloshed down more champagne (I remember it as a well-oiled and glinting party), then started up again, lubricated to lyricism over the appeal of tackling Claudia's life, her work, her times: 'Think of it — she lived through cataclysmic years: two world wars, and tremendous social and technological changes. There could even be a case for saying she was an agent of social change; in her work she foreshadows and urges as well as records it.' And her lovers, 'sheer fascination — no minor personalities there, Flora, but mental giants, every one of them.'

Suddenly I was inspired, as I had been by Claudia at that lunch nearly twenty years before, a yearning springing up in me to take the mission on — a great work that would be clear-cut and factual, not demanding that every day I must spin a complex web of personalities straight out of the empty air, but instead permitting me to turn to libraries and historical records, boxes of letters and journals for what I had to tell. I saw myself writing a subtle, analytical and provocative assessment of a woman who was all those things herself. I raised my eyes to Helen's and in that moment she looked at me.

'Would *you* . . . ?'

'Could *I* . . . ?'

'*Why not?*'

I retreated: 'I've no experience.'

'You're a good writer, you've a Cambridge first in English and — oh, definitely yes — you went on to do that excellent piece of research into Benjamin Disraeli and his writing that you showed me. You discussed nineteenth-century novels of social purpose in a masterly fashion — weren't you thinking of continuing to your doctorate?'

'A student aspiration I soon dropped. I wanted to earn money and learn about *life*.'

She laughed. 'And write about it! Now you can write about Claudia and her life. You knew her, you knew her capacity to charm or dominate or impress, but you weren't involved with her in any way that might prevent you being dispassionate about a character, who, let's face it, was as volatile and exasperating as the English weather.'

We agreed to meet the following week; there were discussions, pleasingly positive, with the Trustees, with my agent, Carol Saxon, with my publishers, then suddenly I had at least three years' work in front of me, settled and contracted, and I was bringing boxfuls of books and dusty old papers to the flat and piling them up in the second bedroom that I'd made my study. Now I could hardly pick my way to my desk, with its Macintosh computer and its card indexes and all the reassuring clutter of my craft. But I didn't mind. It felt good.

'It's entirely settled,' I tell Saffron.

Her black-jerseyed breasts rise and fall swiftly in her annoyance. 'I can hardly believe that my own uncle and cousin would ignore me like this. You must have been extremely persuasive, Flora.'

Ignoring these remarks with their insinuations of treachery, I say, 'Perhaps the aura of success you give off intimidated them. That and the three-book contract. I had only a couple of months' work left on my own number four, so I suppose I did have the advantage of being available.'

'Robert and Helen should at least have consulted me. I should have liked the option.' Saffron stops, stoops to pick up her coffee cup and drains what must now be icy dregs to give herself an appearance of calm. 'Well,' she says, putting the cup down, and glancing through the window, 'the snow has stopped and I must move on.'

'Yes, David will be missing you,' I murmur. David is her current partner, a saturnine man who gives one interesting sensations in certain areas when his eyes do their undressing act. He is a merchant banker, and successful, we are told. 'How is he these days?'

She looks away. 'He's well enough. Bored by the meaninglessness of the so-called festive season, of course. He's with friends somewhere or other. Like me, he needs his own space.'

'Very sensible,' Jake says. He rubs his neck. 'Togetherness can be an overrated concept, especially when proclaimed by the wrong person — which it usually is. I'll see you out, shall I?'

He puts an arm round her shoulders and sweeps her off through the door, and I hear their voices as they run down the stairs. Jake admires Saffron; he likes tough intelligent women, he says, and we're very alike. I don't know what he means by this; I see no resemblance at all. I wander over to the window and look down. The wind has dropped and the snow looks docile now, a blanket softening the street's hard edges. Jake and Saffron emerge and stand together, talking. He is telling her something in some detail, she looks up, her face doubtful at first, then thoughtful. They stand by her alluring yellow car and Jake touches its gleaming flanks but his eyes are on her.

I lean on the windowsill and I ponder my credentials as biographer of Claudia Charles.

They might have worried Claudia. That she thought little of my intellect she had made clear when I met her once during that awful summer gap between the taking of my finals and the announcement of the results. It was in Bond Street. I can see why she could be there, but it escapes me how I was. She was vague as to exactly what was happening to me at that time, and I explained, adding modestly that I was certain I had done disastrously in one paper: 'So all I can hope for is a pass, a third. Anything would do!'

'Any degree is better than nothing,' she said with a kind of absent and condescending acceptance of my self-assessment. There was no doubt that she saw my future as that of a typist, a teacher, a housewife — a non-starring role.

I was immediately resentful. How dare she accept my humility without question, without understanding the touch-wood superstition that forced me to propitiate the gods with that humility? When the incredible, the wonderful results were published I rushed in triumph to telephone my mother. Then Claudia, if possible even more triumphantly. She seemed bemused that I should have bothered. She congratulated me, but there was something missing. I felt let down. I telephoned Aunt Laurel, who said she'd won a huge bet that day on a mare called Flora-Dora. 'I knew it,' she told me, 'I just knew firsts were in the air!' I mentioned Claudia's flatness. 'Her?' she said scornfully. 'Your mother'd never tell you but she was thrown out of Oxford for wanton behaviour. She says degrees are baubles for children. I say sour grapes.'

Jake comes back in, shivering and complaining at the cold. I tell him he shouldn't have stayed out so long, and whatever were they talking about, anyway? He says that Saffron was put out and he'd calmed her down for me. For me? 'New Year's Day,' he adds, seeing my face. 'It's my New Year resolution, be nice to Flora! And Saffron's your cousin.'

'Only by marriage. And she'd not admit that as cousinship.' I look at the litter of plates and cups and glasses on the floor and suggest that he might deal with it.

He looks revolted, stirs a plate with his foot. 'We'll do it together,' he coaxes, using my own formula.

'Not bloody likely. Your lunch, your mess, you deal with it,' I say and I walk away to telephone my cousin Pattie, my real and very much loved cousin, Aunt Daisy's eldest daughter. 'Be nice!' I throw the witticism over my shoulder to an unreceptive stare.

Jake is an accountant and he works with a firm of management consultants. We've been together for nearly three years. For the last year he has been away more often than not, working on projects dealing with the economic rundown of the earlier oil installations in the North Sea. Safety requirements mean he must attend courses on escape procedures from helicopters that ditch in deep waters, and on fire-fighting in horrific conditions, real live stuff, too. I don't know about Jake, he seems almost to enjoy such tests in a swaggering sort of way, but his descriptions give me nightmares. Nowadays he's away for a fortnight, back for three days, then off again. Sometimes he's living on an oil platform, other times in an hotel in Aberdeen. When he returns he expects hotel service from me. His absences give me space to write without interruption and I can bear the lonely patches, but it's become a strange relationship: long periods of emptiness punctuated by brief periods of passion in which I feel that almost any woman would do. Jake doesn't admit to this. 'Nonsense,' he says, nibbling at my ear, my nipple, my little finger. 'God, you're so hot for me when I get back! We're marvellous together.'

I sigh and pick up the telephone. 'Pattie? Happy New Year.'

'And the same to you, Flora. Oh, thank God you rang! Now that slob of a man I married will have to amuse Georgy while for once I sit down and relax. Greg! Get your backside in here and play trains with your child while I'm on the telephone, can't you?'

'Tell him Happy New Year from me,' I prod.

'Flora says Happy New Year!' I hear her yell. She adds in a normal tone to me, 'More than I do!'

'What's he done?'

'What's he done?' she reiterates with theatrical intensity. 'It's a matter of what he's *not* done! Georgy was sick in the night and Greg refused to help. Would you credit it? Here's me, six months pregnant — well, nearly, anyhow — and all that mess, and Greg goes back to sleep. *And* snores. I hurled his huge shoes at him. He wouldn't move. I had to clean up the lot. Yuk. I'm surprised I didn't go back and throw up myself, all over him!'

'Men are useless brutes,' I agree, observing the crumby mess still on my floor. Jake has disappeared to the bathroom, his sure refuge.

Her tone softens. 'Georgy was so sweet,' she says, 'he came into our bedroom all plaintive and aggrieved. He said he'd woken up feeling nasty and when he sat up stuff kept coming out of his mouth, and it made his bed and him all yukky and he didn't like it.'

'Oh, how sad and comic. Poor Georgy.' Georgy is three, tough and healthy like his father and I have a weakness for him that shocks me. I tell myself it's a biological weakness I must repress. A child would wreck my well-controlled life.

'He's gorgeous. But I'm exhausted. But then I'm always tired. Don't ever get pregnant,' Pattie instructs me. 'I feel like I've elephantiasis. I look vile, I feel vile, I am vile. And my boobs are a disaster. Vast? I don't need a bra, I need major lifting equipment.'

I laugh. I love Pattie and her moans.

'How's you?' she enquires.

'Surviving. Saffron was here. Pattie, I told her I'm to do the biography of Claudia Charles and she's spitting vipers.'

'Oh Christ. That's tactless of you. Just when David and she have split. She'll be devastated, pulverised.'

'What? What do you mean, she and David have split? She said nothing of that to us. Are you sure?'

'Of course I'm sure. She came round for coffee and sympathy at our dump. She's finally flipped and flung him out.'

'But what happened? Why?'

'Well, you know David. He's always been knee-deep in women while she shrugged and

40

got on with her life. I'd supposed she'd decided to be . . . well, what she'd call modern and civilised. You know what that means. Overlooking his escapades as long as their own personal world wasn't aware what he was up to, and thereby falling into a trap of pretence that was humiliating for them both, with him having to croon over and over 'But you're the only woman who really matters to me' so that he could deceive her yet again.'

'I don't believe it. Saffron would never accept such a situation.'

'You'd have thought that, wouldn't you? But her love was stronger than her pride. Or do I mean it was the other way round? Her pride wouldn't let her leave the man and betray the betrayal.'

'You mean there's no such thing as invulnerability, not even with Saffron?' I am incredulous.

'She's a tough, dangerous woman,' Pattie responds. 'I imagine she took her reprisals. But she's never been as tough as you make her out to be. She can hurt and bleed like us, you know.'

'I'm beginning to see that,' I say thought-fully. 'I think she's bleeding over Claudia. She perceives her own family as joining me in a treacherous game.'

41

'Her family, our family,' Pattie says crossly. 'I've never managed to sort out the exact relationship. Ma's tried to tell me, but she hasn't a clue how to draw up a family tree and we get lost every time. You tell me how it works.'

'It's very simple. Our grandfather's sister, Great-aunt Selina, married a Charles, Lucian Charles, and it was his brother who fathered Claudia Charles. So Selina was our mothers' aunt, *and* Claudia's aunt by marriage.'

'But Claudia was years older than our mothers,' Pattie objects.

'That's because her father was older than his brother, who was older than his wife Selina, who in turn was older than Grandpa — who was well into his thirties when he started his family.'

'Christ.'

'Simple. Great-aunt Selina links us all through her marriage to Lucian Charles. But that's no blood link. Hence Saffron's pride . . . and fury.'

3

Five-thirty a.m. and Jake's alarm shrills. A large bare shoulder heaves from beneath the duvet; the alarm is silenced. He slides out of bed; I grunt with annoyance. 'It's got to be,' he says and pads off to the bathroom.

Outside, rain is drip-dripping. It's an improvement on treacherous snow. In half an hour the taxi will come. Soon Jake will fly from Heathrow to Aberdeen and from Aberdeen to the Shetland Isles, making the final long hop by helicopter to the oil platform deep in heaving icy seas. He will be in a man's world: I shall be alone. Writing is a lonesome affair. I love it, love the characters who teem in my head, become involved in their complex lives and rarely find myself bored, but when the day's stint is over and reality returns I want to plunge back into my own life: I crave companionship, I want Jake for talking and teasing and loving. The pain of being without him infuriates me, and most of all because it's clear he's not suffering in the least. I discovered last summer from the comments of one of his colleagues that he prefers this nomadic life, that his hugs and murmured regrets into my neck are false; an inner need drives him. Once, I suppose, his sort would have joined the Army, but the opportunities there have dwindled: this is today's alternative. Already his company is priming him for his next project, and it's in America, something to do with cement factories. I sigh, but Jake murmurs of Alabama, Georgia, Colorado, Arizona, and his eyes light up.

The doorbell rings, the taxi throbs softly beneath the window. I call Jake, who has been dressing in the bathroom. He gives me a kiss, and is off.

I try to sleep, but my mind is overactive. Today, I remember, I start serious work on the biography of Claudia Charles. The new year, the new project. Excitement rises and I fling my legs over the side of the bed and sit there for a moment thinking happily of all those tantalising boxes and bags of journals and years-old love-letters awaiting me.

I decide on a shower. The water splashes over me, hot and stimulating. What do I know about old Claudia thus far? I run a mental video of her life: the death of her parents in 1914 in a carriage accident; the upbringing largely by her brother, Edward, eight years older, and her aunt Selina, both so bitterly resented; the genteel poverty that had left her

44

feeling she was 'a floating person, attached to no class structure whatever and never truly belonging anywhere'; her early writing, described by Susie Peters as 'an extension of the rebelliousness she had shown at school and which she struggled to contain throughout her life'. Then comes her first novel, her clever, incisive reviews of books on feminism and socialism and her early love-affair with the many-years-older Laurence Britton, that brilliant but unstable writer whose erotic letters to her survive in one of those boxes, and whose encouragement led to her experimenting with new forms of writing, as well as flaying critics who dared to suggest that fiction was incompatible with the development of ideas. I view, too, her greed for food, her collector's mania, her passion for foreign travel where few would venture, and many later lovers and admirers, all in their varying spheres men of brilliance and intellectual certainties. She needed to be among such people, for the scope and scale of her thirst for knowledge was prodigious and she demanded their certainties to bolster her own. Then at thirty-eight there appears her husband, Spenser Malcolm, the gentle charmer we called 'the poppet', with whom she spent her middle and later years swinging wildly between affection and exasperation, but with whom some said she had produced the best of her writing.

I turn off the shower and grab a towel. Does Claudia Charles require an orthodox chronological biography? No, too restrictive. Hers had not been a plodding life. I dry between my toes and think. Not a linear biography, then, rather a series of essays on aspects of her life ... themes perhaps inspired by those of her novels? I know little yet, but ideas seem to swirl, like mountains half-seen behind mists. I dress for working in a thick knitted top, snug trousers and ankle boots. I remember Monet's series pictures where the same subject is shown again and again in the different lights and colours of a changed hour, a changed season. I reflect. Humans are changeable and the impressions we have of them are subjective, dependent on the perspective from which we view them. I'm bound to hear contradictory tales. Do I tell them all? Again, do I treat her as essentially a woman who was a writer, or a writer who happened to be a woman? Violet Trefusis said of Rebecca West that she was 'brilliantly clever, with the only true conception of cleverness — namely, that it is of such secondary importance, and that one's emotions matter infinitely more'. Cleverness secondary? Was that Claudia's view? I think not. Where do I begin to find out? With her letters, her journals, her books, with the insights of her oldest friends? Those few who are alive, that is.

In my study I tug the nearest cardboard box towards me. It is packed with dusty thick exercise books. Marbled covers, leathercloth spines, and, as I dig more deeply, real leather protect them. These were precious items. I blow away dust, sneeze, and open one. *Journal, 1922*, I read, in Claudia's strong flowing handwriting, less scrawled then, more youthfully rounded, but unmistakable. I sit cross-legged on the floor and look at *January 1st*.

Such a sad grey day after a bleak evening alone. Edward called this morning to wish me a Happy New Year, but the effect of his presence was to blight me like frost on a rose. I have been drooping ever since, nipped and sapless. Sometimes I believe he hates me for not conforming to his joyless views. Instead of bringing me chocolates as a loving brother should, he parades a sense of guilt before me as if that were some special gift. It isn't and I won't accept it. Yet still his voice drones on, while I am transfixed by his eyes, reproachful as a kicked dog's . . . except that dogs have a cheerful unconsciousness of our taboos on sex, dear creatures, copulating in public to the horror of old ladies and nannies who hide their charges' eyes. God's gift of sexual love is wonderful, he intends us to revel in it — and not with the lights out! I shan't parade my love before the world because I believe that even fools have a right to their own persuasions, but I'll hold to it for ever.

After Edward had gone I stood by the window looking out over wet slate roofs and soot-darkened chimneys and I was alone. There were no people in London, no dogs, no pigeons, no spiders spinning webs. Nor was anything growing, no shoots in the ground, no buds on the trees. Nothing. The dead of winter. But then the grey mists thinned away from the sun and a brief watery beam struck the wet roofs and made them sparkle and gleam. I was aware then that I had this new year, this something that I seemed to hold in my hand. And I felt tender of it, like a child with a bird's egg warm from the nest, fragile yet full of potential. I thought of the novel which I shall be writing over the next twelve months: Symphony in Blue. In places the plot's as shadowy as the future, but for me it's the theme that is important, and it's a theme that will weave its way through my year, that of a young woman discovering her own purposive self through love and loss, in the comings and goings of her soldier lover throughout the Great War.

Laurence approves thus far but scolds me that I shall never be more than a minor novelist until I plan my work as he does. Each of his novels has the feel of a tapestry that has been designed inch by inch; every character in it is analysed in depth and it's all intended to illuminate some philosophical or social notion, every part set down in notebook after notebook. I, on the other hand, write to discover myself, in the belief that the act of writing will form my ideas from the hidden workings of my mind, instinctive and intuitive. I tell him I am a salmon, leaping great waterfalls, and I won't be pinioned in his net. Oh, how we argue and oh, how we enjoy ourselves. And this is what Edward would kill for us. Will this new year see the end of us? I am a resolute Free Woman but sometimes there's fearful unhappiness and muddle inside me and I know that repels L.

January 2nd. Laurence is here, and so happy, like a schoolboy blessed with a Royal Person's gift of a special exeat. He came from lunch with his editor to discover me in bed with a horrid headache and an attack of the glooms, caught from Edward. He jumped in beside me full of laughter and mockings and soothings, and soon my body was vibrating with purrs beneath the caresses of his hands and my head cleared and all of me was content . . . Oh lovely lovely love. What can Edward know of our joys in his own womanless life? A virgin man? A contradiction in terms. He praises our poor grandmother, so repressed that she flinched from approaching the lavatory door lest someone might see her, as a modest and womanly woman and asks why I can't be like her. He has a sick horror of anything the least fleshly. And as for Free Love, enjoyed with a Married Man (even one whose wife is forbidden intercourse), well, hell opens and sulphur belches out.

Laurence laughs at Edward as I can't do, saying that he is a study in thwarted desire and I must immediately turn myself into a sturdy English version of the oriental Go-Between and find him a wife. Today he made me see the pity of him. Poor lonely Edward.

January 3rd. Another day with L, a day of early frost followed by brilliant sunshine — and that's how it was with us. In bed in the dark cold early hours he lurched upon me with a lust that had nothing to do with the essential me, deeply asleep and crudely awakened. I bit his nose in fury and shook him off, accusing him of wanting to rape me. He flung away in a temper. 'Always you use these stupid exaggerated terms,' he stormed. 'You believe that only you can define the relationship between man and woman, and always you must put the man in the wrong.' Later I challenged him to justify that and he ripped back that in The Power of the Dog I'd written of amorous conflict, amorous warfare, laying siege, images implying that sexual attraction in a man equates with domination, brute force, mastery, forcing the woman to yield. He said it was a stupid view, a feminist view, and he rejected it. Men were not like that — not enlightened ones like him anyway. I said: 'What about this morning?' He looked at me and said: 'I was selfish and greedy, craving your body in that impatient way, but loving lust is not rape, Claudia; rape is hate.' Then he hugged me and apologised and asked me why I was so often antagonistic, and I shook my head and said he must find out and tell me. I hate the distrust that's inside me and the itch of emotional unease. I vow a New

Year's vow to fight to live in a bowery happiness. Why does one dwell so much more on the wrong in one's life than the right?

After lunch we went out to Richmond to walk in the park and the sun shone on the frozen grass and the stags' breath was smoking as they stood sentinel guarding their hinds in the silvered remains of the bracken. L told me he feels as primitive and defiant a care for me as the stags do for their females, but at the same time he admires and reveres me both as a dear delectable woman and a ripening mind that reaches into the infinite.

With the coming of darkness he went back to her, but today I didn't hate her; rather I glowed all evening.

I read on. Sometimes I am absorbed by lengthy passages vibrating with rage or excitement, sometimes the day's entry is no more than a note — 'Lunch with Emmeline Pankhurst — discussed the different competences of women' — consuming me with frustration. Half an hour later I come to myself with a jerk and a strange feeling of being watched, a feeling that Claudia Charles, reincarnated, might suddenly manifest herself in the doorway and enquire by what right in hell was I investigating her most sacred moments? I tell myself that the dead have no feelings, and that Claudia had been nothing if not robust, both in her fiction and the emotional quagmires of her life. Accurate biography can't allow for sensitivity, nor take account of Mother's rules: 'Personal questions are rude, Flora. We leave it to our friends to confide if they wish. And we never, never, let ourselves overhear others' conversations.' What I'm doing, I reassure myself, however enticing, is serious research. I'm not peeping through windows nor listening at doors. Hell, I'm stiff and the floor's hard; I stretch and shift to kneeling. The events of Claudia's life and the feelings they inspired in her are inextricably involved in the themes of her writing. I have to know her.

These diaries, I decide, must be my evening reading while Jake is away. I shall curl up on the sofa and read and make notes, with Beethoven as a background. There is other work for the daytime. Hold on . . . I sit back on my heels and frown. Beethoven's powerful symphonies seem valid for Claudia Charles, whose love of music resounds through her own powerful writing, but what provoked the thought? I recollect the memoir of three years ago and laugh. 'Claudia's young enthusiasm for socialist and feminist ideas,' Susie Peters had gushed, 'had in its own way echoed Beethoven's obsession with egalitarian and revolutionary ideas, while her tempestuous life had followed his in its desire for independence, in the recurring quarrels with critics and friends, and in the hot-blooded but cataclysmic love-affairs.' Help! The last thing I want is for the overheated air-inflated emotional persona of Susie to descend upon my shoulders. But I can still listen to Beethoven.

I sort the journals into their years: 1918, 1919, nothing for 1920, then 1921, 1922, and on to 1930. The diary for 1931 is missing (the year of her lover Archie Pope-James' death?), then 1932 and on until they stop in 1937. Claudia married in 1938. Had she nothing more to say then, and what of the records of those missing years? Had she destroyed them because they were too revealing, too intimate? More prosaically, are they still hidden away in some dark corner of one of the Trustees' houses, and, in which case, whose: Robert's, Helen's or even the solicitor's office? Robert was Edward's child, born in 1931. Since Edward had been born in 1892, I calculate that he must have been thirty-nine before he produced a child. He'd married a year earlier. (If he'd possessed anything like his sister's sexual drive, the

54

years of celibacy must have been a torment for him: no wonder he resented Claudia.) I go to my desk and make a note to discuss all this with Robert and Helen.

One box down, thirteen more to go. I squat beside the next bulging carton, cursing the dust that makes my skin prickle. Letters here, in an unfamiliar hand — Laurence Britton, I discover. I extract one and read a page to judge its value.

In spite of my bruised feelings I crave your dear presence. You say you were emotionally starved in a childhood that contained no mother or father, but only the cold Edward and your horrid aunt Selina. But please don't starve me when you are cross. You forget that I pour emotion into you and that is not, I repeat, not, a synonym for desire. Oh yes, when I'm away from you I do lie in my bed searching for you with empty and aching arms, sniffing about for the soft warm smell that is you and having tantalising, unrealisable dreams about your dear orifices, but those are not the only ways I remember you. Whatever our pastimes — a punt on the Thames, a visit to that exhibition of vast Cubist compositions, a shopping foray to Bond Street — they are all made glorious by your spirit, when your spirit is gay. I tell you I have every loving emotion imaginable for you, in all the colours God made and more . . .

I force myself to stop reading and I remember Jake's few letters which are of the 'I'm looking forward to getting home and giving you the best fuck ever' variety. I sort the elastic-banded bundles into date order. Chronology has its purposes. Heavens, there are a lot; did Claudia keep every letter she ever received? And every newspaper cutting?

Tomorrow I am to have tea in Sonning with Laurence Britton's daughter, a Mrs Amy Carrick, who must be in her mid-eighties. She dislikes the thought of talking to me about her father and Claudia Charles, but has accepted: 'So that I can make sure the truth is told, no sentimental ramblings romanticising what was always a stormy relationship, nor any of that blindingly obscene muck some of you modern writers wallow in either.' Apparently she views me rather as a fool than a villain, as others of my potential witnesses seem to do, and she hasn't refused to give evidence — which is a relief seeing that I'm in no position to issue a subpoena in the matter.

Mrs Amy Carrick, b. 1910, daughter of Laurence Britton and widow of Alfred Hunter Carrick, Reader in Botany, Reading University

Yes, I did once meet Claudia Charles, with my father when I was about eleven. It was in Regent Street and we were Christmas shopping. I believe it was an unplanned meeting, they both kept looking at me and then at each other, and laughing.

. . . Yes, we went for coffee in Swan and Edgar. They talked and I felt excluded; I suppose even then I sensed something wrong in their intense breathy conversation. She was dressed in a crimson . . . costume we called it then . . . that lit up the room on that dark day, and I wanted to say thank you. But she never gave me the chance.

. . . Yes, it was unusual. Ladies wore serviceable greys and browns and navies, red was thought rather fast. Miss Charles was well built, too, with dark wild hair and dark expressive eyes. Yes, I suppose she was attractive if you liked that sort of Bohemian look. Tea? Milk? . . . Before we continue, would you please tell me what you intend to say about my father?

. . . You don't know until you've found out all the facts? You mean you haven't decided on a theme the facts have to suit?

. . . Sorry, yes, that was uncalled for.

. . . Well, they say any publicity is good publicity, but I'd rather not read a sludge of sentimental trash like that silly woman produced . . . wait a minute . . . Susan Peters, that was her name. 'She was his muse, he was her father-figure.' Sickening. Biographical fiction, you might call it, and like all fiction it involved travesty. If I'm to talk to you in detail and give you papers, I want to see the chapters in which he's involved *before* publication, to check the facts. I want to see the balance redressed between him and her. He was a great writer, too, and he's mentioned in any work on English literature of his time.

. . . Your biography could regenerate interest in Laurence Britton's work? Literary obscurity? Never. Several of his novels are still in print, forty-five years after his death. But I agree with you he deserves better.

. . . He wrote on the sadness and waste of women's mere existence, like her? *Like her?* What rubbish! She latched on to him as *the* original male voice in that field and he inspired her in everything. She was far from being the original Free Woman, you know. Nor had she any voice until she met him, her work lacked structure. He introduced her to dozens of people who could be of use to her, publishers, journalists, other writers — and he taught her, he *made* her.

. . . Yes, we all knew about the affair. Not from the beginning, they kept their relationship quiet for a few months, but then he was away such a lot, it didn't take my brother long to work out why. And of course my mother knew from the start. And it lasted for seven years.

. . . We hated her, if you really want to know. Claudia Charles was never content to share him. She grudged every minute he was away from her and we children never entered into her calculations. And what about the sadness of my mother's *mere existence*? Do you think Claudia ever thought of that?

. . . Yes, Father was torn. We'd hear him and Mother arguing in his study, and he'd be pleading, pleading. Then he'd cry, sobbing and sobbing — but soon he'd be shouting again. I'd lie rigid in my bed hating them both for all the embarrassing emotions I couldn't understand. He was greedy, like *her*, no doubt about that. But she had him where she wanted him. She was a young girl, your Claudia, sensual and attractive and twenty years younger than Mother, and Mother'd had such a terrible time bearing my younger brother, Eric, she was told she must never risk intercourse again, another child would kill her. So it was easy for Claudia to mesmerise him and seduce him, and twine herself into his life like poison-ivy through a tree. And then our world went dead. No bedtime stories with Daddy, no help with maths prep, Mother white with sadness. How would you feel about that?

. . . You lost your father? Cancer. I'm sorry to hear it. But I have to say this, Miss Monk, death is final; you grieve, you cope and you have sympathy while you rebuild your lives. But my father wasn't dead, he was very much alive — just that so often, so obviously, he was elsewhere. We lived in a right little, tight little world of respectability in Putney and, far from sympathy, we suffered ostracism. We could have had some loathsome contagious disease. No one should suffer for another's sins, but we did; we suffered for Claudia Charles'. Mother had no social life, nothing to console her. And Father wasn't there when Eric broke his leg badly, he wasn't there when I won the English Literature prize at school, he wasn't there when a drunken

60

burglar broke into the house one night and frightened us half out of our minds. He'd promise amends, then break his promise. For *her*.

. . . She was a great feminist, we're told, fighting for women to live the same full and satisfying lives as men, to share their place in the sun, but she didn't cede my poor mother any fullness of life or any sunshine, did she? Here's the difference between her literature and the truth of her life, the gap between preaching and practice. The hypocritical Victorians lavished praise on their great men for their work, but kept quiet about their private lives, and that continued until Lytton Strachey debunked his 'Eminent Victorians,' but now every word they ever spoke, every body they ever embraced, every damnfool thing they ever did — and God knows we all have our moments of folly — is recorded in intimate detail and sniffed at and pawed over for the salacious or the just plain nasty. I'd say, Right! You haven't yet chosen your scheme, or the angle of it, for your portrayal of Claudia Charles. Well, if your public demands to know all, never mind fawning. Choose the hypocrisy gap, why not? Show the gaping honesty and decency chasm for the sake of

61

people like us who suffered to make her art great.

I transcribe the interview with Mrs Amy Carrick from my miniature tape recorder on to my computer the following morning. I feel I have something of the flavour — the sour taste — of the Britton children's lives. I am surprised by her openness for she is a cautious person and suspicious of my motives, but hatred impels her.

The printer spits out the finished pages of Amy's words. I take my red pen and note on the first page: *Claudia as vulture-goddess*.

★   ★   ★

I see Mother once a week for lunch. Today, a frosty February day, it is in her flat and my aunt Isobel, widow of my uncle Alban, is there, and so is Aunt Laurel. My mother loves all her family with a meek and tremulous affection. There is no question with her of drawing a line between in-laws and 'real' family. Once the ceremony is over the new member belongs, as if it has never been any other way. Presents on birthdays and at Christmas are no less than to blood relations; letters and telephone chats between them are as long and confidential. As a child this did not strike me as odd, it did not strike me as anything. I did not know until I was in my teens which were the real, the blood-members of the family, or which the outsiders. Mother adores my aunt Isobel, who is fey and psychic and funny, and when she and Alban separated, staunchly took her side, which struck her friends as strange. 'Blood's blood, after all!' one of them said to me. 'You'd think she'd support her own brother.' But Alban had been in the wrong (the wrong bed), and Mother seethed with anger and refused to speak to him. She still hadn't spoken to him when he was killed by a drunk driver whose car mounted the pavement one evening two years later.

In the same way as Isobel, I suppose, Claudia had been family to Mother too, her natural inclination to adulation of the great and worthy warring with her instinctive distrust of Claudia's flamboyance and dubious behaviour. At the least they exchanged Christmas cards, Claudia's being photographs of Spenser and herself on their rose-smothered terrace or in the South of France. Their names were printed inside, not signed: 'So show-off, so vulgar, so shallow!' Mother would say with a look compounded of annoyance and an odd bafflement. Isobel gave Mother cashmere cardigans which were kept wrapped in tissue paper for special occasions that never arose.

'Flora, my dear,' Isobel says, kissing me on both cheeks. 'Primrose and Laurel are telling me you're to write Claudia's biography. Congratulations. What a prize!'

'Thank you,' I say, and return her kisses. I, too, am devoted to this aunt, who in my childhood gave me wonderful extravagant presents no one but she could ever have dreamed up. In Isobel, Alban had married a woman of wealth, who not only ran her own successful London gallery but also was prepared to pay his gauche adolescent niece to 'help' her whenever she held an exhibition, and in her gentle offhand way give her a considerable education in the fine arts. Her moving-in present for my flat was a stunningly handsome bronze vase with a stylised scroll design, a showpiece.

'I'm ignorant about the details of Claudia's earlier life,' Isobel says. 'I gather it was what the French call *une vie mouvementée*! I shall look forward enormously to your telling us *all*, Flora. What a woman! What a character! I loved her penchant for elaborate display, her big-hearted wallowings in richness and magnificence, whether it was in her writing or her clothes or those eccentric seventeenth- and early eighteenth-century pieces that filled

64

her house. It's positively baroque, isn't it, her concept of grandeur as an ethical category? One sees it in her later writing.' She leans back in her pale gold knitted silk suit and waves her long-fingered hands in a gesture of exaggerated admiration.

I laugh, Mother purses her lips as she pours me a glass of wine, and Laurel says dryly, 'Myself, I'd say her writing was a Christmas pudding — packed with the best ingredients, intoxicating, overrich, and indigestible in all but the smallest portions.'

A good simile. 'I'll quote you,' I tell her.

'I love Christmas pudding,' Isobel says, leaning her elegant white head thoughtfully to one side, her big sunken eyes surveying me. 'I shall reread those novels, then I'll be ready to appreciate your assessment of her work. And put in plenty of sexy bits about her love-affairs, won't you? At my age, that's the only way one gets one's kicks!'

Laurel chortles, but Mother pushes the glass of wine into my hand and says abruptly, 'If it hadn't been for Claudia's love-affairs, Daddy might have let me go to university. My headmistress recommended I should go to Oxford and read English. But he wouldn't hear of it because she'd been thrown out and he didn't want me ending like her, he said — a socialist and a Wild Woman and a slut.

So that was that. Denied the education I wanted. Doomed to a job Claudia despised — because of *her*. And there were only two men in *my* life and they both died young: I lost the man who loved me at twenty in the war, and then my husband had to die when he was only in his early fifties. I'm old now and I look back and I think I've done so little, been so little compared with her — '

'Better than me,' Laurel interrupts, as bracing as the wintry air. She lives in a flatlet in Twickenham that is little more than a bed-sitter with cupboards posing as kitchen and bathroom. 'You had a decent job and a husband and a child. And Philip left you this flat.'

'Yes,' Mother says, staring down at her veined and bony hands. 'Better than you, but you've never cared.'

I hold my breath and wish I could block my ears. I don't want to hear this. I'm annoyed with my mother for the revelation of her envy and bitterness. Isn't my grandfather in fact the one to blame? Normally I admire Mother for having fought on in her own quiet way, for keeping the family in touch with one another, for forcing a younger lazier me to study. Now I cringe from the nakedness of my mother's soul, from the resentment she is revealing for the subject of my biography, a woman whom I want to admire — a woman whose work I *do* admire.

My eyes avoid Mother's only to focus on her room, so different from any of Claudia's. It's dull; no bad taste, but lacking in style. Pale walls, pale grey chairs and sofa, a charcoal-grey cord carpet. Nothing to make a statement about her own past life or her family's. No photographs, no pictures on the wall except two watercolour sketches of country scenes, she's never said where. The furniture is elderly and nondescript. She has some charming old photographs of her family in the 1920s that she could frame, but won't.

The room seems to say, after her, Don't look at me, I am no one, I count for nothing. Only the Ispahan rug, her wedding present from Claudia, strikes an unexpected note of colour.

Aunt Laurel mutters, 'Daisy heard from Pattie that Saffron is highly put out that she wasn't offered the Claudia Charles biography herself.'

Mother forgets her own grievances in deriding Saffron's. 'She could never write it. She could never be objective, never criticise or in any way diminish the greatness of the woman who had praised her. She'd be diminishing herself. It's a ridiculous notion.'

'You couldn't be more right,' I say and drink my wine.

'Hmm,' Mother says, finishing her sherry and rising to her feet. 'I'll tell you this, Flora: both of you are too young to have known the real woman deep inside Claudia. Neither of you should do it. What's more, even the most brilliant of writers can't re-create the dead subjects of their biographies without distortion, any more than an artist can take a likeness of a dead woman from old photographs and her friends' descriptions. Either their visions are bland, vague likenesses seen through mists of sentimentality and supposition or they are crude, garishly coloured pop-art interpretations, appealing only to the sensation seeker. So if you must do it, Flora, stick to what you can be sure about — her novels and her other writings, together with what people like us remember, and put them against the background of her class and her time. Then you'll have a fine piece of work. Don't try to dig up the stinking body.' And with this she herds Laurel and Isobel across the room to her circular mahogany lunch table and instructs me to deal with the soup.

4

March, and my evenings are still being spent with the young Claudia whose journals and letters are so compelling and so disturbing. I feel I have been staying with her in the little house in Highgate that became for her 'the happiest house in all London'. It's not a comfortable visit — the happiness was intermittent and won at the cost of struggle and pain — but I can't leave it. I lie in front of my fire, reading until I feel quite sick; I stir my solitary supper on the hob while Claudia's long-dead voice speaks to me from the book propped on the pasta packet; I crouch on the sofa till the small hours, making notes.

She has little discretion in what she reveals. Surprisingly, her diaries are not the self-conscious revelations destined for posterity that I'd have expected from someone so aware of the importance of written testimony, and certain, even then, that she had a destiny. Instead, like her novels, they are her efforts to understand herself and stretch that free mind she celebrates — and they depict her at once loving Laurence Britton and hating his guts. And telling him so with gusto, either way, and recording her outbursts. Sometimes she would pour out a torrent of defensiveness: *Why shouldn't I spend my weekends with friends when he can't promise to be here? I'm not some inanimate object stuck on a shelf for him to pick up or leave to the dust as he chooses!* Other times the torrent would be of anger, bringing rocks and boulders down on Laurence: *Your particular genius lies in consuming people like me to feed your own art and pleasure. I see I'll never be anything more to you than an amusing bauble.* Claudia brooded over what she endured and what she had renounced. The entry for All Fools' Day holds the pathetic sentence: *I'm no sort of Free Woman at all.* Yet at other times she wrote of him with an extraordinary vividness of delight, as she did when he flayed a reviewer over his words: 'Claudia Charles writes with the mind of a man, masterly and muscular . . . ' Laurence had reacted with fury: 'The patronising brute. You have the mind of a great woman, perceptive, incisive. If you allow him that sort of comment you agree that the male is essentially greater and that is not your thesis. I shall write to tell him so.' Moments like this uplifted and enheartened her. She was tied to him; she loved his 'huge swelling mind', she relished 'the way he's taught me to observe my environment to

70

see what chances of spiritual progression it offered me', and the passion they shared for the theatre, art and sculpture, 'which produce progression through pleasure of ear and eye and soul'. He was too, above all, her 'wonderful, strong, sensual, sensitive lover'.

'You can't imagine it, though, can you?' my cousin Pattie says to me over the telephone. 'A young girl like her and that middle-aged little man with his perky moustache.'

'He wasn't that small,' I say mildly. 'He was five foot eight.'

'But Claudia was a big woman. And she was nothing if not forceful. Physically, Laurence was damned ordinary. As Sylvia Plath said of one of her lovers, she'd have felt like Mother Earth with a small brown bug crawling on her!'

'For God's sake, Pattie, a man's height has nothing to do with his sexual capacity.'

'But it does with his sexual attraction. I've seen it demonstrated on television animal and bird documentaries; the females of the species go for the big dominant males. They promise the best hope of survival. We're the same. Look at Jake and Greg, our hunky men!'

'Oh God, how awful, so we do.' It's true, I do crave macho man, arriving home at night triumphant as from some primitive hunt, blazing with certainties and rampant with lust, and Jake is typical of the genus, as is the six-foot rugger-playing Greg. 'How Neanderthal of us. Clearly Claudia had evolved further than we have — she was thrilled by Laurence Britton: brain, not brawn.'

We laugh, but I think: Jake's due back tonight; he'll boast to me of his triumphs, arouse me with his achievements but my work on Claudia Charles will never fire him with excitement. 'Oh yes,' he'll say, parroting me condescendingly as he moves towards the kitchen, 'you've made real progress? The journals are fascinating? Good. Great. What's to eat, then?'

For Laurence Britton, as for Claudia, life had to be a progression, a quest for values, a development of the mind. Sometimes I yearn for a similar search and awareness of progression in my partner, as well as sexuality. Do I ask for too much? Probably. Jake is fun, he's good in bed, and there's plenty of intelligence there. Just that it's a different kind from mine. Cars and computers attract him, never the abstract, he's not concerned with ideas. He's down to earth, hard-edged, dominant, driving, wholly male. But Claudia was dominant and driving, too, as well as searching. There *were* aspects of maleness in her mind. Do all strong

72

creative minds have those two sides to them, the male having a modicum of the female, the female a little of the male, and is it that which gives Laurence and Claudia's work their universality?

'Sometimes,' Pattie says crossly, her mind in tune with mine as it often is, 'I think I'd like a more creative, more sensitive man. And a touch of empathy from time to time would be great! But a man like that would have to have something of the female in him and females and I don't generally get on. Except for you. I can stand you.'

'Thanks.'

Pattie's the sister I never had. It's true she doesn't get on with women, she's too direct, too scornful of polite evasions, too full of herself. And yet she is female. No one would call her feminine, not when she's painting her big bold canvases up in her converted loft, dressed as she almost invariably is in Greg's old checked shirts, with grubby jeans and clumpy shoes. But she has a female affection for her son and her husband, and a delight in gossip that's all woman. In this she resembles her mother, Daisy.

Aunt Daisy is a connoisseur of gossip, collecting it and retailing it with glee throughout her husband's parish and on into a wider world. She and Pattie share a sense of humour and an enjoyment of the ridiculous, particularly Daisy, whose dull, poverty-stricken life is redeemed by it. It was in mischief that she'd called her daughters, not by the sentimental flower names of family tradition, but by the Puritan virtues they'd need to have in life — Patience, Hope and Charity — names they loathe. Her husband is a retired clergyman, for many years rector of a sprawling Surrey parish only twenty miles from us in Richmond. God knows why she coupled herself with Guy Radley, they could not have been more different. Pattie says it was an attraction of opposites; she so frivolous, he an earnest Oxford graduate. Aunt Daisy maintained it was his sermons: 'His parishioners didn't value him, but I did! A man who could compare Plato and Aristotle's philosophies with Judaeo-Christianity in a way that I could understand had to be a fantastic genius. I became Guy's pupil and his fan, all big-eyed with an intellectual crush I didn't know how to handle. He was flattered, he was frustrated, and his parishioners told him he needed a wife. So he married me with a broad gold ring all engraved with flowers. Look at it now — the symbol of our marriage — the flowers obliterated and only scratch marks left.' They had fought their way through the years. She resented his failure to rise in the Church, the endless grinding poverty. He detested what he called her lack of sense: when Daisy took a rival clergyman's wife for a drive the car was bound to run out of petrol miles from anywhere, or she'd forget to do the altar flowers when it was her turn, leaving a previous week's stinking remnants to brood like bad fairies over an important christening. Uncle Guy would roar, Aunt Daisy would giggle. I giggled too. I loved her for being so funny and easy-going, so different from my strict mother.

After my father's death when I was six, Mother had had to return to full-time work. She put me into a boarding school as a weekly boarder so that I shouldn't be a latch-key kid, but her brief weeks off in no way took care of my long school holidays. So then Daisy took me over, and Pattie and her sisters and I ran wild over the rambling rectory and played in its overgrown garden, gorging ourselves among the raspberry canes, rolling in the warm, shabby grass. There were pets there that I wasn't allowed at home: cats that were always having kittens, equally prolific rabbits and guineapigs and parakeets. 'Have them put down!' Uncle Guy would roar as yet another half a dozen squirming and enchantingly vulnerable bodies joined the menagerie. His daughters would sob, he would rush off to the sanctuary of the church, and my aunt would offer the creatures for sale (usually unsuccessfully) at her next bring-and-buy sale. In that haphazard house I learned about sex and birth the natural way, and if there was anything I didn't comprehend, Aunt Daisy would explain it with more hilarity. I learned other things too. Uncle Guy's study was as packed with dusty tomes as any second-hand bookshop, and, while mostly he locked himself away from us to read or write those amazingly erudite sermons that I, too, came to relish, he would from time to time as I grew older beckon me in to recommend some great work. Then on wet days while Pattie painted I would loll on a battered sofa near her, the latest kittens curled up on my lap, and read. From Jane Austen, the Brontë sisters, Dickens and Thomas Hardy, I moved on to Tolstoy and Balzac and Proust at Uncle Guy's urgings. I remember those childhood holidays as unsullied bliss.

I say to Pattie, 'Your mother fancied your father as a brain, you know. She thought he was fantastically clever and that really got to her.'

Pattie chuckles. 'Strange, wasn't it? She had no way of communicating on his level. She was simply content to glory in him, which drove him to ridicule her as a fool. And she isn't, you know, however much she plays at it. She's shrewd. But at a very female, intuitive level. She could have been an illustrator, or even a cartoonist; those pen-and-ink sketches she used to do of Dad's parishioners were terrific fun.'

'I know.'

'She wasted her life in the parish and on us children. God,' furiously, 'the frustrations of that generation were horrific. Sometimes when I'm trying to paint and then I'm torn away to deal with Georgy's needs and awful things like cooking for us all, I know just how she must have felt.'

I sense that Pattie is working herself up to some huge complaint. I brace myself. 'Painting? Are you able to do any still?'

'With only four weeks to go and me as big as a tank — and as clumsy? Christ, no. I've all sorts of ideas and visions looming through the maternal smog in my brain, but it's not being communicated to my fingers and I can't even paint a blob that looks right. Besides, when I stand up for more than five minutes my back aches. It's the way the baby's lying. I swear it's got its shoulder blades jammed into my lower spine.'

'Oh, poor love. How maddening. But

couldn't you perch on a stool?'

'No. Not with what I'm doing. Not with my big canvases.' Pattie is painting her own version of the seven deadly sins. The ones I've seen so far, *Envy* and *Gluttony*, are forceful and thick with pigments, paint swirling round opened greedy mouths, narrowed eyes and swollen contours; near ugliness subsumed by magical colour. She's struggling to express in paint what Saffron and I try to express in words. The canvases are not enormous, but they are large. I see her point. 'Anyway,' she goes on. 'I'm all hormonal, I know I am. That's a killer of creativity. Like the PMT days and the start of a period. Can you work then?'

'No,' I say promptly. 'Not as I want to; the fluency goes. I sit cursing in front of my computer and I ask myself what's wrong? And then I think, Oh, God, yes, of course, one of those days, and I curse some more and turn to writing boring letters, or doing research.'

'Exactly,' Pattie pounces. 'Well, I'm in *one of those days* all the time now. It isn't fair, it isn't *fair!*' Her perennial cry against being a woman. 'I want to carry on and feel that I'm pushing myself forward. What I'm doing is good and it's exciting me. I don't want to be one of those damned Madonna images, breathing ineffable love over my brats and looking for nothing more.'

'You won't be,' I assure her. 'You couldn't. But right now you probably feel you'll never paint again, that inspiration's cleared out, deserted you — '

'Hell yes!' she interjects.

' — the inspiration that makes you feel so good, somehow specially blessed. Well, it hasn't. It'll be back when your hormones have stopped rioting.' Pattie conceives of hormones as evil spirits inhabiting her flesh in droves and responsible for all that's out of true in her body and soul. 'And you *are* moving forward. You're having a baby, that's being creative.' (Why am I saying this, when it runs counter to what I believe myself?) 'Pattie, shut up and shut off your pictures. For the next six months, a year, whatever it takes, just for once stop swimming against the current. Be productive in a different way, with your children.'

Pattie growls: 'I don't want to. I want to have it all. Like Greg. Like any man. I feel so torn, so exasperated, so *deprived*. I *hate* not being able to paint. I'm right in the middle of my sequence of pictures — '

'You did it! You got pregnant.' I interrupt calmly. This is no good.

'It was pure unselfishness,' she wails. 'We

thought Georgy ought to have a brother or sister. I must have been mad. It's a horror story — pregnancy, breast feeding, screams in the night, Greg never waking. I'm tired now and then there's the birth to go through . . .'

There's a note of real anguish. I try to coax her out of it. 'It doesn't last for long. Think of the pleasure Georgy gives you. It's worth it.'

'He's lovely. He's gorgeous. But I could never love another child like I love him. It's all gone to him.' Panic in her voice now.

'Nonsense. Love isn't limited, it's infinitely elastic. You'll wallow in it doubly. I know you.'

'Do you think so?' Pathetically.

'I know so.' I know nothing of the sort, but I have to calm her. 'Tell you what you should do, read Claudia Charles' novel, *The Shadow of a Child*, about a woman who was never able to bear another child after her first had been stillborn . . .'

'I remember, the doctor then was ignorant and messed up the birth.' Pattie lets out a reluctant giggle. 'Don't tell me, Flora, I know, I know — I should be grateful I'm not in her position. I read the book years ago and it was a tremendous tear-jerker. The woman went on against opposition from her husband and his family to become not only a doctor but a gynaecologist and introduced a new attitude to childbirth and its dangers among the medical profession, didn't she? God yes, it's flooding back. But despite the praise and fame lavished upon her there was always this sense of deprivation in her life. She had no child.' A pause. 'And I feel a sense of deprivation that I can't paint during pregnancy. Nothing, is it? Comparatively. But it's there, and I'm hating it, and I'm certain I'm locked into pregnancy for ever. Everything that's meaningful seems . . . well, dissipated into nothingness and waiting. It can't be just coincidence that great women writers of the past like Jane Austen and the Brontë sisters and George Eliot and Mary Mitford were all childless. Or Claudia Charles.'

'No,' I agree. No, I think, it isn't. And that's why I don't intend to be caught in that particular net, not ever. We both live intensely, Pattie and I. When my writing is going well I feel uplifted, certain that I've broken through the old boundaries of my mind into a new and special area. Energy rushes through me, my characters reveal novel facets to their personalities and my plots leap to unprecedented life. Then I'll happily work all the hours God gives to achieve the maximum I can before the inspiration fades. Other times my surroundings are grey and narrow and I plod, achieving an approximation of the effects I want through concentrated effort. The difference is the difference between two worlds, the world of creativity and the world of everyday. I hate the grey times, terrified they'll never end. Pattie, I know, is the same. I see for her what I mightn't do for myself — that the habit of seizing on one segment of time as embodying the whole is a reaction that could confound and destroy us. When the body is creating a child, it seems, other forms of creativity wither. We had been through similar conversations before Georgy's birth, Pattie and I. I understand how locked in she feels, and try to reassure her.

'Not long now,' I say lightly. 'Time will pass, I promise you. Like it did at school before the holidays. They did come, didn't they? We did get to the sea and the sand.'

She laughs reluctantly. 'Eventually. Yeah. I know. Don't mind me, I'm just pissed off. Hey, Flora, thinking of that book, do you reckon Claudia ever did lose a child? Have a late miscarriage, perhaps? She wrote as if she had that sort of knowledge.'

I have achieved something; Pattie is distracted from her depressed state. 'Could be. Or it could be careful research,' I say. 'That's something she believed in; she liked to have the ring of authenticity. But the real theme of her novel was to show how much a

82

woman was capable of contributing when she was allowed the opportunity to concentrate her mind.'

'Claudia made certain she had that,' Pattie says crossly. 'She put her work first, last, and in between. But she'd submerge one tenet of her beliefs to illuminate another without compunction. When you think about it, you see how clever she was to start her novel with that sad childbirth, rather than have her heroine the saintly sort who renounced marriage and motherhood in order to work for others. At a stroke she created a sympathetic character she could deploy as she needed, to illuminate her points. But she herself never had children. Wily old trout, wasn't she?'

'Oh, always.'

'How are you getting on with her?'

I think about this. 'Well,' I say lamely, 'I know her, in theory at least, from the diaries and letters she wrote when she was young. That's up the age of twenty-eight so far and it's all from her angle which, to say the least, is coloured as she wants it — the sensual and generously giving heroine, too often betrayed. I know her from her novels, which are rich and satisfying, but show her surprisingly differently, often as the perceptive narrator in the background. Then I knew her as an old

83

lady, as you did, and she was all lurid clothing and poses and that tremendous voice of hers swooping up and down, always provocative, and what was underneath I've no idea.'

'Nor I,' says Pattie. 'She was a huge great icon set up to be admired, and everyone said how brilliantly clever she was, and frankly, Flora, I was mostly too terrified to speak to her. Besides, I suspect she hadn't much interest in children. They're for the future and she had none left. She wanted to speak knowledgeably about the past, her past.'

'And so she did. And, oh God, I wish I had listened more. Now I have so many images to blend into one, and how I'm going to do it I don't know.'

'Don't even try yet,' Pattie advises me. 'You'll find many more on the way.'

$$\star \quad \star \quad \star$$

Friday evening and it's time Jake's back. I ponder whether I dare put the final touches to the meal and the telephone rings. Perhaps he's at Heathrow.

No, he isn't, he's still out in the North Sea. I'm furious and tell him so. I'm cooking him a special meal, special to celebrate the three years since we first started living together and now half of it will be wasted. He says he's sorry, he couldn't get through before; he mutters something about telephones not being available and appalling weather preventing the helicopter lift to the Shetlands for the plane to the mainland. It's clear the date means nothing to him. Then he's saying he has a ton of work to complete before he addresses a special meeting in Aberdeen on Monday. He makes it sound like an Intergovernmental Conference at Heads of State level. It's news to me. I ask, what about tomorrow? He sighs. Gale abating, should be OK.

He's about to hang up, but if I'm not to have him here tonight, I must have his voice a little longer and I want to know about the helicopter journey. Takes about an hour, he says. Often the weather's foul, the helicopters dodging round the storm clouds towards open air. In turbulence they get buffeted. His voice says he hates it.

The Shetland Islands must be bleak, I remark, and try to picture them. Barren mostly, Jake tells me, stony places of rocks and snow and ice with the few houses mere pinpoints as they fly over. And gloomy. Like the oil platform, where there's light of a sort from ten in the morning until two or three in the afternoon and nothing to see but heaving grey waters.

He's terse and reluctant to talk. Poor Jake. I tell him I'll see him tomorrow and he can feast his eyes on Richmond Park and the deer, that there's frost here at night, but sunshine in the day. He needs the light and me.

He grunts, I make kissing noises across a thousand miles and hang up. It occurs to me that Jake has freely chosen his ultra-male role in the North Sea just as Pattie has freely chosen her absolutely female role of pregnancy, yet both are moaning at me. Why me? As I scrape Jake's meal into the bin, I feel grumpy too.

5

When I hear Jake's key the next day it's a lot later than I expected. I find him booting the door shut with his heel. Bang! His hands are swinging great bulging bags of kit and I can't get near him. His face is set in bleak lines of aggression, his eyes bloodshot and avoiding mine. There's stubble on his chin. If we had a cat he'd be kicking it.

'Problems?' I ask.

'What d'you think?' he snarls.

'I don't know until you tell me,' I reply equably.

He flings his bags down on the floor. 'Helicopter was late. Planes were delayed. Don't ask me why or how, I don't know. They boom things at you you can't hear. Snow. Ice. Fog. God! And I'd had to work all night, I wasn't in the mood for it. And don't you start telling me you're hard done by, because I don't give a highly coloured shit!'

I take a grip on rising anger. 'Don't be bloody, Jake, it's a bore. Have you eaten?'

'Plastic sandwich. Sawdust apple.'

'I can shove a lamb chop or two under the grill,' I offer.

He looks wary, surprised. I feel that he is expecting antagonism, demanding it even, as an excuse for venting his own internal pressures. 'If you want. Up to you.'

I put chops under the grill while he has a quick sluice-down under the shower. He's been like this recently each time he's returned from his bleak punishing world of work; he can't make the transition to me and my life, the otherness of its softness aggravating rather than enticing him. Space is what he needs, though I need him. He must wash and change and eat and read his accumulated mail, and only then will he sit back and shrug his shoulders to loosen the knotted muscles and at last, almost reluctantly it seems, stretch out a hand to me.

Today it's worse than before. I remember back to the start of our loving, three years ago; I want him to grab me as he did then, eager, greedy, groping in my clothes for the soft places beneath, raking my hair with his fingers, kissing me till we're laughing, fucking, gasping for breath and the world's lit up. It's neurotic to relive the past, I tell myself, and I push it away. But out of nowhere comes panic. Why the change? Is he stressed at work? Ill? Perhaps I expect too much. Light-heartedness can't last for ever; middle-age lurks. Jake's chops spit and hiss beneath the gas. My stomach does a dive and I tremble.

Mother sees me as an independent-minded modern girl, one who shrugs off difficulties, takes life as it comes. To a degree that's true: I've my own highly desirable flat halfway up Richmond Hill, bought with money left by my paternal grandparents; I'm successful enough that my income is adequate, and I've the looks to ensure that I've never had to live alone except by choice. But even the strongest of women has her fears. With me, it's loneliness. Not being alone, I don't mind that. I was alone after Paul left, after Magnus went to Canada, after I'd pushed Will out, alone and relieved. But loneliness is different. I feel lonely now. Jake insists he's tired, but I remember sculptor Paul drawing in a long cold breath at the flaw suddenly apparent in his marble, and that coldness is in my chest and my arms are aching and empty.

I shred salad and slice tomatoes and smother them in dressing; I fry mushrooms; I butter a crisp roll. Jake slouches at the kitchen table, I push the food in front of him and he eats without acknowledgement, scowling at the wall.

Afterwards he watches the news to a growling mutter of contempt: yet another government minister's been sexually indiscreet and the media are revelling in the details. We go to bed in silence, a cold gap between us and, while I wait for sleep, sentences from one of Claudia's diaries drift in and out of my mind:

A bad day on Sunday. Squabbles, petty but painful, made me feel lonely even when Laurence was beside me in bed.

Tough and dominating as she'd appeared in her later years, she'd had her hurts and anguished over them like every other woman. I warm to her for admitting her vulnerability.

Every week he returns to that dull house with the sexless Hermia, sacrificing me to her, his goddess of respectability. And that's where he works. There are no distractions there, he says. Why is work a thing apart for men?

Why, indeed? I feel the parallels between us. How I resent Jake's distant oil platform — and how I despise Laurence for his failure to commit himself entirely to Claudia.

But on the verge of sleep, I jump to wakefulness. What nonsense. Jake knows almost nothing of my work, no more than I of his. I've never seen him open my novels. Claudia and Laurence, on the other hand, had huge areas of shared affinities. He wrote her letters that lovingly acclaimed the importance of her vigorous mind to him as well as the infinite ecstasy of their embraces. He praised her novels. Claudia had more of Laurence Britton than I have of Jake. It is on this nasty thought that I succumb to the enveloping grey folds of sleep.

In the morning everything's changed. The sun is shining through chinks in the curtains, birds are singing, Jake's naked body is pressed against mine. As he stirs, sighs and nuzzles the back of my neck I remember that it's the first day of spring, and with the thought something springs in me. The bed is warm and it smells of Jake's sleep and his rumpled hair and his maleness. Soon he's kissing me and his mouth is hot, his hands insinuating and demanding.

'Adorable Flora,' he mumbles, moving his head down, lipping a nipple.

'No,' I say. I won't respond automatically. And I try to lift his solid head.

It rises two inches. 'What is it?'

'Last night you ignored me. Now you want me. What is it with you?'

He gives me a contrite look, kisses the nipple, blinks. 'I was tired.' A deep breath. 'Stuck between two worlds.'

'Yeah,' I say caustically, 'you felt like an alien. An enemy alien.'

'I'm sorry,' he grunts, so softly I can hardly hear him.

I hold him at arm's length. Do I feel sympathy for him in the stresses of his work, or am I still offended? Somewhere a blackbird is singing to his mate in lyrical cascades of notes. Jake's grunts are unacceptable. I shove at his chest. 'I don't like you!' I say.

He smiles at me almost mockingly in his male certainty that my refusals are meaningless gestures. He whispers, 'I may be a bastard but I'll always like you, Flora.'

Like? This isn't how we should be, how we used to be. But clarity of thought vanishes as Jake is suddenly all over me, caressing me with strong delicious strokes of his hands, moving my limbs, his lips and his tongue tangling with mine, and while my head is saying no, no, my body is panting yes, yes, yes! It is a fortnight, after all, I tell my reproving head as my body meshes with his.

When the telephone rings two hours later we are still in bed, the duvet littered with the Sunday papers and magazines, and us dizzy and panting and entwined again. One of us has pulled the curtains back, and one of us must have made coffee because as I wriggle free of Jake and grope for the telephone a shaft of sunlight illuminates the cold dregs in two mugs.

'Hello?'

'Flora! We wondered what had happened to you.'

My friend Penny, who lives with her hefty and dull husband, Henry, at the other end the road and declares herself one of my fondest fans. We're due to see them for lunch . . . oh my God, today! I glance frantically at my watch and fall back in relief against Jake.

'Sorry?' I say. 'Something wrong?'

Her laugh has the sound of breaking glass. 'Only that it's well after one, darling!'

'No, it's not,' I say stupidly, 'it's twelve fifteen! We're not due with you till twelve thirty . . . ' My voice fades. I gasp in realisation: 'Oh hell, the clocks . . . They've gone forward . . . Christ, Penny, we forgot. I'm sorry, sorry, sorry!'

Beside me Jake is grinning idiotically as he plays with my breasts. I knock his hand away.

'Well, are you coming?' The voice is sharp. 'I'm about to put the soufflé on!'

'We'll be with you in five minutes, Penny. Promise!'

I drag Jake from the bed and we collide in a scamper for the shower. 'I'm not shaved,' he says as we soap each other vigorously, water cascading from our noses and chins.

'No time. Call it designer stubble. We've got to dress and go.'

We fling on clothes and I ladder my tights and swear. Grab skirt . . . brush hair . . . minimum of make-up . . . grab shoes . . . snatch up bag. We tumble from the house, Jake in an unironed dark red shirt and jeans. I bend to pull on my elegant shoes but he tugs me upright.

'In this life-and-death hurry we'll have to run — and you can't run in those. Come on!'

He takes my hand and pulls me down the road, and I run in my stockinged feet, yelping at the harsh paving stones, breathless from the rush. And suddenly we're both giggling crazily, stumbling and holding each other up, and Sunday strollers are looking at us and laughing as well, and everything's fun again.

It's a lively lunch, too.

There are eight of us. We eat straight away: 'Because of my soufflé,' Penny reminds me reproachfully. We're squashed round a table in her tiny basement dining-room, made intimate and cosy as a bistro at night by the antique brass lamps illuminating her assorted guests. There's an assertive couple I know by sight. He's from the world of television and it's clear Penny's invited them because he might be useful to me. But she's picked the wrong man. Martin Carpenter is a producer of current affairs programmes, and what he doesn't know about our leading politicians

94

and our media tycoons isn't worth knowing. But he knows nothing of my world; he and his groomed and glossy wife, Elaine, have heard of Claudia Charles, but never read her. 'I don't have time for *books*,' she says, and seems to think this a matter for self-congratulation. And why not? We hear that she's a fashion designer and partner in a highly publicised shop in Beauchamp Place. She insists, 'You must know it — of course you do!' and her nightfire-red lips part in shock when I say I don't have time for shopping in Knightsbridge. 'How dreadful!' 'How dreadful not to read,' her husband says in mock reproach. 'Oh, but I do,' comes her riposte, 'I read *Vogue* and *Tatler* and *Harpers & Queen!* Just not story books. I'm in the real world.' She grins triumphantly and everyone laughs. The perfection of her appearance and her great good cheer tell me that she is making huge amounts of money and thrilled with her own acumen in doing so. She's seated next to Jake who rubs his stubble with his fingers and seems to be regretting it. Beside her he looks rough stuff, but his voice is smooth as they chat. Henry's sister is on his other side, hefty and moon-faced like him. Jake nods at her and looks away. He is not given to social kindnesses.

Then Penny says, 'You *must* meet each

other,' and I am introduced to my neighbour, a bespectacled man who I'm told is a landscape architect and an admirer of my writing. Freddy Gulliver, he's called. Apart from the singularly sweet smile with which he praises my latest, *A Nest of Brambles*, he appears unremarkable. Moderately tall, medium build, fairish hair, quietly dressed, the sort ancient ladies would gaze up at in trust as they asked for directions, the sort younger women would like but ignore for something more flamboyant.

We talk and I discover he's unusually well read. He's livelier than his looks lead me to expect, too, discussing the psychology of my dubious characters with dry humour and a perception I can't help but find flattering, since clearly he remembers every word I wrote.

'Tangled dysfunctional families and dark thickets of intrigue,' he murmurs over the veal. 'Fascinating — and how apt your title. Did your um . . . Jake, is it? Did he contribute his views?'

'No,' I say. 'No, he's not a novel reader.'

'Not even of yours?'

For a moment we both look at Jake and then the blood is in my face and I feel unravelled and cross again.

Around the table the others are listening to

Martin Carpenter's inside stories of those who rule over us. Scandalous and witty, he has them choking with shocked laughter over their food, Jake louder than anyone. His tension of yesterday gone, he's noisy with relief and spite against the politicians. He hates stupidity, he says, and he hates sleaze and they are given to both. He adds a story of his own, leans back to let Penny deal with plates, and grins at the applause.

My neighbour raises an eyebrow. 'Are you interested in the gossip of the great and not so good?' he asks.

I shake my head. 'Are you?'

'Not particularly.' His mouth twists itself at one side, quirky, slightly mocking. 'We can do better.' Then he leans an elbow on the table, turning to me, shutting out the others. 'I heard you lived in this area. I hoped I'd come across you. Tell me about the Claudia Charles biography. How did you achieve such a prize? Did you know her at all?'

His eyes look directly at me and I feel something stir inside. At times in company I've found myself baffled by the unbridgeable distances opening up between me and fellow guests, strangers with whom I've struggled to find topics of mutual interest only to cringe from the void. To find any sort of soul mate is unusual; today I feel this man Freddy is reaching out to me, and my grumpiness evaporates. I respond. 'Claudia? Yes, I did know her, we're almost related.' He demands that I explain this and we embark on one of those conversations where there's an excess of intriguing points and every topic suggests another: 'Yes! Oh, yes!' we say, pouncing on it before swooping back to a previous point. He has recently read an earlier Claudia Charles' novel, *The Fountain of Living Waters*, and asks whether I think the central male character is based on a mythologised version of her own unstable visionary father.

'Was she trying to re-create him as she wished he'd been or did she invent this tremendous character? What do you think?'

'I think it's an allegory based on a father she considered Godlike. She was given to building people and events into fables.' I laugh, remembering her vigorous voice and my mother's blinks of amazement. 'She couldn't even talk about her previous night's dinner party without hurtling off into some flight of fantasy. One fact would be instantly recognisable: 'Julius and Iris were talking to each other of the Uffizi and the Galleria Palatina in Florence . . . ', the next wickedly fantastic, ' . . . they're code words for their illicit rendez-vous, you know!' She loved to embroider the facts. She maintained that poetic truth was what mattered, not the sordid details of reality. Unlike me.'

Freddy laughs too. 'A different generation. And yet you're not unalike.'

'Now how can you say that when you know my novels? I'm down to earth and minimalist.'

'Yes. But your simplicity is deceptive: those tangled relationships of yours are in fact ingeniously interwoven. And your writing's colourful, like hers. Painterly.'

Coffee is served. He looks at me thoughtfully over his cup and I look back, liking him, contrasting him with Jake, and not to Jake's advantage.

He enquires, 'And which bears the most weight as you delve into Claudia's life, the outsize personality or the analysis of the work?'

'Oh, that awful question! One's supposed to insist that it must be the work, that a biography which concentrates on a wayward life in preference to the real achievements is squalid, and almost invariably directed by a search for scandal to boost the sales — '

He interpolates with a grin: 'Oscar Wilde said that every great man has his disciples and that it is Judas who writes the biography.'

I hear my shocked laugh. 'Oh God, what a fearful thought!' It occurs to me that

Mother's views aren't so far from Oscar's.

'Well?'

'But when you're faced with someone as explosively vital as Claudia it's not so simple. I'm picking my way through the minefield.' And mixing my metaphors: 'I'm not a Judas nosing about for the one-night stands, but it can't escape anyone who is genuinely interested that lovers like Laurence Britton must have influenced her work, and it's those influences that I have to explore — '

Jake interrupts, hovering big and dark behind me in the lamplit room, saying, 'Not Claudia Charles again. Heavens, Flora, you're becoming obsessed. Listen, I don't care if you want to stay on and chat but I've got to go. Back north, I mean.'

'Why? Oh, hell, Jake, I thought you'd be flying back tomorrow, as you usually do.'

'Changed my mind. After the recent fiasco I want to make sure I'm back on time. I've too much work to do to mill around airports all day.' Impatiently he adds, 'Well, are you coming or not?'

I swallow coffee, pondering certain matters, resentful. I say, 'You don't need me to hold your hand while you pack. I'm enjoying myself. I'm staying.'

He lifts one shoulder in a shrug and walks away.

Freddy raises an eyebrow. I tell him about Jake and the oil platform and how we've been together for three years but hardly see each other these days.

'That's no good,' he says.

I ask about him. He shakes his head and says little, but I do discover he has a place in The Alberts, so he's quite a near neighbour. The Alberts are terraced and picturesque one-time workmen's cottages, much in demand by young couples. 'You live with a partner?'

'I did. We parted a year ago. And yesterday she married a wealthy banker.' He pauses. 'A dull affair, but the champagne was good.'

I conclude they must have parted on good terms for him to have been invited. Then I think of my own partner and unease replaces enjoyment. I get up, say my goodbyes and leave.

Jake is on his way out. He zips his bags as I enter the bedroom and looks tense.

'Right, I'm off. All this bloody travel. I'll see you in a fortnight, Flora.' He picks up the bags and heads for the bedroom door.

I open my mouth to say, What about a kiss? and instead, snap, 'What about this mess you've made packing?' The place is littered with grubby socks and shirts and gaping shoes.

'You'll have to sort it yourself. I haven't the time.' As an afterthought he adds, 'Sorry.'

I shrug and he walks off. Then anger gusts over me. I grab a heavy shoe and hurl it after him but he's moving too fast — the door shuts a nanosecond before the shoe hits it. What's happening to us? Why don't we talk? There's more than the mess on the floor to clear up. I remember Claudia's fury each time Laurence leaves her, so often in a sullen mood himself, and I feel resonances from the past vibrating in me. In a strange, unthought-of way I'm in touch with her anguish. Outside the window the sky is the colour of old grey socks.

6

Christabel Pierce, b. 1906, poetess and travel writer, widow of Caspar Pierce, dramatist

Yes, we were tremendous friends, Claudia and I. We spanned the century. I was a lot younger than her, but then I was more mature, coming from the background I did. Her family was nothing much, you know, and her father was quite raffish, a speculator in funny little publishing ventures producing fiction and poetry so avant-garde no bookshop would stock them. Anyway, he'd died.

... We met at the Gardners, in their Cheyne Walk house in Chelsea, and I remember Virginia Woolf being there. It must have been towards the end of the 'twenties. A lunch party, my first true meeting with great literary minds. I couldn't begin to tell you how appealing — how intoxicating — such occasions were to me then. But I didn't let the greatness of the company overwhelm me. I'd just had my first volume of poetry published, *The Seeking Soul*, and Claudia

103

had praised it as 'masterworks from a pen that does not shirk the radical issues', and other reviews were equally encouraging . . . Sorry?

. . . I was particularly struck by that fine-honed mind of hers. She cleaved through the second-rate like a Cossack with a sword, fierce and forthright.

. . . Let me think . . . Yes, I remember we discussed the influences affecting our contemporaries' vision of modern society, writers such as Britton, Forster, Wyndham Lewis, Lawrence, Katherine Mansfield — you know. Claudia had read widely and retained what she read, so her arguments had the stuff of truth about them. Many of us were fascinated by Freud and the theory of the subconscious. It's all in my diary of the time.

. . . Claudia understood the thrust of D.H. Lawrence's work and supported him as a genius, but that didn't stop her from agreeing he had defects. On the other hand, his vision of the nature and importance of sex and of the body's life as a source of vitality ran far closer to her own vision than anything that emanated from the Bloomsbury Group. She told me once she found them physically bizarre. And I agreed with her. I was happily married in every respect for more than half a century, myself.

. . . She complained that most of the Bloomsbury Group assumed that humane values and intellectual understanding were the purview only of a small elite of the leisured classes, a snobbish assumption that dismissed women like her out of hand. She found it insulting.

. . . No, she couldn't fit into Bloomsbury, nor did she try to. They weren't working towards the same ends — or if they were, it was from a different standpoint.

. . . Yes. Social acceptance eluded her at first and she felt left out. People were wary of her, of all that raw and intense intellectual power. She dressed badly in those days, too, not so much Bohemian as muddled. She had no style. Laurence Britton was the same, nor did he have any social manner, either. However brilliant his ideas, he was essentially an awful little man. They'd parted by then, but I knew most people and I knew him. She spoke of him having swallowed her whole, teeth, hair and all. She was bitter at how she'd been used. I told her she needed to re-create herself with a new persona, dashing and glamorous. Her writing was flamboyant and she was developing a theatrical extravagance in her new flat in Chelsea that reminded one of Edith Sitwell; I told her she should dress with some of that baroque opulence also — what could better suit her big-boned body and that strong, almost masculine face, so different from my own soft femininity? Of course, I was petite in those days . . .

. . . Laurence Britton? I only know what she told me, that he'd first been unfaithful to her when he went on a lecture tour in America without her.

. . . In 1925, I think. But what can you expect from a man like him? They say he had gross appetites. Claudia wasn't the first or the last of his mistresses, but he took her youth and left her nothing in return. But then, she'd rather laid herself open to it, hadn't she?

. . . Yes. She'd hoped he'd leave his wife for her; for years she went on hoping it. She said she'd longed for him to be beside her every night, so that when she was troubled in the darkness he'd hold her and say, 'What is it, my love?' He called her his Muse but she wanted to be the mother of his children too. And what about the effect of their instability on her Muse?

. . . Essentially, she was a romantic. She saw Free Love as romantic. Not to me, though. You have to be madly stricken to put up with being loved in the shadows, to weeping alone at Christmas. Because Free Love was unacceptable then — people felt it as a threat to society.

. . . Yes, and her too. Oh dear, yes. She'd broken the strict social rules and she was damned for it. She had servants who tried to blackmail her. Imagine the strain, at a time when she should have been happily in the public eye, establishing her career.

. . . She wanted someone of her own — and respectability, whatever she said — but who'd have wanted her, with that past? The upper classes could afford to ignore their friends' peccadillos, never the middle class. Besides, she was too successful. My husband Caspar relished my brilliance but there weren't many like him. Most women who wanted a career had to forsake marriage and children because in those days they meant domesticity and submission.

. . . And as you say, so few men of our generation remained alive for us to marry. Ah, those poor crabbed spinsters.

. . . We went on holidays together, travelling across Europe in an open tourer, my lovely old Lagonda. The Dordogne, Provence, Andalusia, Tuscany . . . Oh, the beauty and the poetry of those long, sunny, unspoiled days, writing in our rooms in romantic *albergos* in the morning, then motoring between the poplars with the wind in our hair or taking siestas in the olive groves. Free, when so few women were free. Free and frivolous. Poor Claudia had never had much chance to enjoy young fun, growing up as she did during the terrible war years with that repressive Puritan brother of hers and the awful aunt — and then that secretive affair with a middle-aged man. I taught her how to play. We went on gambling trips and shopping sprees to Monto Carlo, and we had introductions to wellknown writers and artists with villas in the South of France. Eden Roc . . .

. . . No, she met Archie Pope-James in Avignon. Her father's side of the family claimed to be descended from one of the schismatic popes, so there she was, enquiring into the past, and there he was deep in some erudite research of his own. He was an academic, you know.

. . . They met on a hot, breathless evening and fell into each other's arms and minds. It was instantaneous. I simply ceased to exist while Claudia sat with this dark-haired and grey-eyed man beneath a pergola of grapevines and they talked and talked and looked — and I didn't know where to look! Normally I'd have been terribly annoyed at such manners, but I could sense that some exceptional idyll of sensual and intellectual passion was taking form. I sat out three days as a gooseberry, writing up my travel notes and saying nothing. Years later she told me my silences had been thunderous. Finally I left them and motored on to my friends near Cannes and a damned unpleasant journey it was in those days when everyone thought the worst of a woman alone . . .

. . . Yes, we joined up again in Cap d'Antibes and when the holiday was over we all drove back to England in my Lagonda and they had about nine months of happiness, though it was a broken time. I remember she had to go to New York for the launch of *The Fountain of Living Waters* there, followed by a lecture tour, and then Archie went back to France for some weeks to complete his research. But every moment they could be, they were together. She wrote to me of her realisation that her feelings for Laurence Britton had been as much those of a child for the brilliant father she'd so badly missed as of a passionate woman's for her lover, and how

109

confused she'd been. She saw this as the cause of much of the conflict between them. She'd been fond of him, infatuated, but, she saw now, never truly in love. With Archie she was all feeling, glorious and real, and compelling and devastating. Her writing had direction, her words had significance, every breath had a reason. I remember her words vividly.

. . . No, I'm sorry, it's never occurred to me to keep old letters, it seems such a dusty thing to do. But I can assure you my memory's excellent.

. . . Archie died of an insect bite at Bournemouth. Or it could have been a dangerous spider. Whatever it was must have been infected with something particularly vicious and of course there were no antibiotics then. It was so sudden, so shocking; Claudia was no self-pitying weakling but she cried, she howled like an animal that's being tortured . . .

. . . Yes, she was ill. She had to go to a convalescent home in Switzerland to recover. The grandeur and the beauty of the Alps restored her.

. . . No, I don't think so. Theirs was a classical great passion. They were living for the moment, but they believed it would last for ever. I don't think men and women

commit themselves, lose themselves like
that, not these days, not as we did. Do
you? It's something that's disappeared, like
the innocence of childhood. Sexual attraction is reduced to animal levels of
performance and young people are disparaging about the opposite sex where we
were appreciative. They become sexual
campaigners instead of enjoying the divine
nature of the difference. It's sad, isn't it?
There's nothing transcendent or uplifting
left to the young of today, no other-worldly
experiences, no glory of deep feeling.
Lovers don't write poetry as Claudia and I
did, instead they read *Cosmopolitan* on
oral sex.

. . . I don't know. She had other lovers,
and she married dear old Spenser, but I
don't believe it was ever the same again for
her.

. . . You'll have a hard job trying to
record the largeness of Claudia's soul for
the contemplation of the public. I'd say it's
impossible. How could a young person like
you understand the capacity of her mind or
the aspirations and the objectives which
inspired her? No one could. Not without
having known her closely and shared the
dramas of her life as I did. Poor Claudia, to
be dressed up, watered down, predigested

and presented in glossy format for the mass market.

. . . No, I'm sure that's not what you intend, my dear, but it's what will happen once your editor gets her hands upon it, isn't it?

. . . I suppose some purpose will be served if you lift her work from the trough into which it has fallen recently. I don't like to see her flame dimmed; she deserves better, I'm sure you'll agree.

When I arrive home from Christabel Pierce's crammed and cosy Belgravia mews cottage my flat seems very empty. The work aspect of my life is good; the Jake side lacking. I type up the interview, make myself a light supper, then telephone him. I need conversation, I need company. I can't keep up squabbles; his disembodied voice from the North Sea is better than silence. When he answers I chatter to him about my work, tell him what fun I've been having talking to fascinating people about Claudia and milking them for their knowledge of her. 'Yes,' he says. I also tell him Mother was disappointed not to see him when she came to supper on Sunday. 'Yes,' he says to that, too. They don't get on, Mother and Jake. She likes men, but prefers gentle tenors

112

who've read her friend Geoffrey Pickstone, and who'll discuss aromatherapy and reflexology with her. Jake is at the ultra-masculine end of male. He lolls on the floor with his head in my lap and his silences make her nervous. She asks him, 'How's that car of yours?' as if his BMW were some dangerous pet. He stares and growls, 'Running!' and their conversation stops. She turns to me. When Geoffrey lunches with her, she says, he'll mend her doorbell or replace the washer on a tap. Jake rises then to prowl the room. I am grateful when he's away at these times but Mother clearly believes his absence to be an insult to her. I laugh, reassure her: Jake's on the oil platform in the North Sea.

Next time he's due back, I remember, Helen's having a party. Helen who suggested I should write Claudia's biography. I remind Jake. He groans.

'It'll be fun,' I say. 'Her parties always are. Good food, good booze.'

'They're all right,' he says. 'But she invites writers and poets, and they're not.'

Really? 'And me?' I enquire wryly.

'You're all right,' he concedes. 'It's the men I can't stand. Poseurs.'

'Saffron'll be there, I suppose.' Something uneasy stirs in me. I'm remembering her angry face and how I haven't seen her since New Year's Day.

'Oh, uh,' he grunts.

Oh, for God's sake, Jake. 'What's the matter?' I ask. 'What have I done? Or not done?'

'Whaddya mean?'

'The grunting. Not talking to me. Why?'

'I'm tired. I was up working half last night to move the project on.'

'It's not just today, it's been weeks. Our relationship's slipping away, we're not happy together any more. I sense resentment in you and I don't know why. Tell me. Please.'

'I don't know what you're talking about.'

'Us. We used to be loving. We used to have fun. Well?'

Silence. I struggle.

'Look, Jake . . . ' Words are there, feelings nudge me, I want to express my discontent, but what's the point? Men like him can't discuss. Talk of emotions (if they have any other than sexual) is taboo. 'Oh, to hell with it. Go to bed then,' I snap, and add sarcastically before slamming the phone down, 'Sweet dreams of love, Jakey. If you know what that means.'

★ ★ ★

114

In bed that night I look to our past for communication. A singular absence. So why had I welcomed Jake into my body, my flat, my life? He was fun, I think, yes, fun. We went to lively parties, to the theatre for the latest satirical comedies, to the pub with noisy convivial friends; we ate at venues where even the food had crazy aspects. And afterwards, alone together, he'd tell me that I was the most gorgeous thing ever in his life and make exuberant love to me, and we'd laugh and kiss and struggle and cry out with pleasure — and then laugh again. I remember Mother asking me, 'Why Jake?' and looking blank when I told her about our diversions. Life to her was a serious matter; fun never featured among her priorities.

Yes, Jake had been sexy, lively, differently intelligent in a way that intrigued me. I turn over in the big bed. The fact that I can so swiftly list the qualities, no, the factors, that attracted me is ominous. But fun is how it was. Writing is a solemn sedentary process, performed in isolation; Jake had been the antidote to the depression that notoriously dogs poets and novelists, a stimulant to revive me when I switched off the computer and returned from creating fantasies about others' lives to living my own. And what, I ask myself, had I been to him? Had I made him happy, at least for a while?

I lie on my back and listen to the distant snarl of traffic, an occasional voice, a car door banging. How absurd to ask myself how he'd felt. Only he could know that. And what constitutes happiness, anyway? Nothing worthy, not to Jake. The euphoria of a night out followed by super sex, was that his happiness? Living with me without responsibility for regular bills, relishing our light-heartedness? Did success at work, despite the pressure, give him this warm undefinable thing? And how can it be assessed? Like wine, it's fluid, not to be encompassed between one's hands or measured in metres. It shifts, giving out gleams of light and colour but, more ghostlike than wine, it will vanish in a second at misfortune or a hard word.

Ours has vanished and, where happiness once flourished, a dark dislike is growing. There is no truth between us. When he's here, he's sourly detached from me and my life, yet making use of my flat, making use of me. Maybe the thought of moving out is too much effort for him in his pressured life. But now, suddenly, I don't care; I want him out.

Decision made. Right. I switch on the light. Half-past one. I blink and stare round the room. In its corners I see the half-grubby clothes Jake flung aside in his rush to catch the plane last weekend. Anger hits me with almost road-rage intensity. Once I hadn't minded his messiness; I'd smile as I picked up a shirt and sniffed his familiar smell. Now I want to hurl the lot out of the window.

But, oh hell — I can't just chuck him out; he's nowhere to go. Besides, we're expected together at Helen's party. And Saffron's bound to be there. She didn't tell me about her man David's going, but she'll demand to know where Jake is. I cringe at the thought of her barbed sympathy. I reflect and my mood changes. I'll be calm and civilised; I won't tell him till Sunday, then I'll give him a month to move: after all, he's not around much. There'll be no shouting, none of the banality or brutality of the classic break-up. I remember that my period's just finished. It's the end of an era. I'll never have sex with him again. And I'll stop the Pill. I hate the unnatural thing.

Relieved, I turn on my side and sleep obliterates all thought.

7

Jake arrives just before lunch on Saturday, tired but calm. We exchange news stiffly, like childhood playmates who've long since lost touch and wonder why they're bothering. He's sorry he's late back but work pressed. I suggest lunch out. I've had a hellish busy week too, and I reckon he owes it to me. We often eat out and that he does pay for. I watch him fork succulent lamb into his greedy mouth and I make a further resolve: I'll never cook for him again. Cooking's for those you love. In the afternoon he flops across the bed to sleep, loose-jointed as a puppet, his mouth open, while I discover a bundle of Archie Pope-James' love-letters to Claudia in one of my dusty boxes, curl up with them on the sofa, and yearn for just such an intelligent thoughtful man in my life.

★　★　★

The first person I see at Helen's party is my cousin Pattie. She's an extraordinary sight, vast, distorted, apparently tied up in old sacks, heaving herself with a defiant look up the steps of the Hampstead house where Helen and her partner share a flat.

'God, Pattie,' Helen says, appearing at the door and looking appalled. 'I hope you aren't going to pop here! I thought you and Greg weren't coming. Are you all right?'

'No,' Pattie responds crossly to this cousinly candour. 'I'm a week overdue, I've nothing left to wear, and there's not enough room inside my carcass for this baby *and* my own bits. It's got its feet in my stomach, its knees in my lungs and I'll swear it's using my bladder as a punchball. Ouch!' She waddles across the hall to the loo.

Helen's own big-boned body is clad in casual clothes, for the occasion has been announced as ' . . . something casual and intimate for very old friends', but these shapely garments, unlike Pattie's, come from designer boutiques, and she is immaculate from the top of her well-shaped dark head to the gleaming Ferragamo shoes on her feet. Beside her is her partner, Sam, a lean, nervously intelligent man with a long nose and sandy hair cut boyishly short. Helen embraces the rest of us, blinking. I sense annoyance.

'Don't worry,' Greg says, returning her salute with enthusiasm, 'Pattie took thirty hours to give birth to Georgy. Even if her waters break right here and now there'll be time to get rid of her before she produces on your gorgeous rugs!' Bony fingers rake back a mop of dark hair and his eyes laugh in his gaunt, handsome face.

I say, 'She's hoping for dancing to startle the little one into action.'

Sam hugs me and tells us to stop winding Helen up. 'Babies make her nervous.'

'They make me nervous too!' Jake says, looking irritable. He heads away from us and into the party throng.

New arrivals are piling in at the door. While Helen turns to greet them, Sam murmurs in my ear, 'Pop your coat in our bedroom and I'll give you a drink before I start on this mob.'

There are two guests emerging from the bedroom. The first, a middle-aged woman in a purple silk suit, gives me a tentative smile as we pass; the second is Saffron. Her smile is sharp and jagged, her eyes select a point just to the side of my eyes to avoid contact. She's wearing a low-necked, figure-caressing black crepe top and flowing crepe trousers, her skin and hair are in perfect shape and she's looking sophisticated, self-possessed and scornful.

'Well, Flora,' she says, 'how are you? We

120

haven't met for ages, have we? Too busy, I suppose.'

I'm not sure whether that is a boast of her own full schedule, or a side-swipe at me over the Claudia Charles business. I respond, 'I'm certainly busy.'

'And is Jake with you tonight? That demanding schedule of his God knows where in the North Sea must play havoc with your social life — to say nothing of its other parts!'

Before I can reply she disappears in a wave of expensive scent, leaving a grin behind her like the Cheshire cat and me somehow knocked off-balance. In the bedroom I childishly place my coat at the other end of the bed from hers.

The drawing-room is large but rapidly filling to capacity. Sam is pushing a glass into my hand when guests surge round him in a clamorous bunch. A flailing female arm scatters wine on my skirt and my feet. 'Oh God, sorry!' shrieks a voice that isn't. I mutter curses (it's an expensive skirt) and search for a tissue. I bend to mop and bump heads with a man who's already wielding a handkerchief on my left thigh.

'Ouch!' 'Oh!' we yelp in chorus. Then: 'Freddy!' 'Flora!'

Freddy presses his handkerchief against my leg one last time. 'No lasting damage.' He straightens and plants a kiss on my cheek. 'Flora,' he says, 'how lovely to find you here.'

'Freddy,' I say, returning his kiss and pleased too.

Sam looks across his clamorous friends to ask how we know one another. I tell him of my friend Penny's lunch party and return the question.

'Helen's his agent,' he tells me. 'Her firm's handling his book on modern landscape design. They believe it's going to be hailed as a classic of its genre.'

'No!' I am incredulous and jolted with pleasure. 'Congratulations! Freddy, why didn't you tell me you were a writer?'

He shakes his head: 'Publication's only just been agreed. How could I boast before that all-important point? But I've been wanting to tell you!' Elation is springing in him like bubbles in champagne. 'Here.' He puts an arm round my shoulders and together we work our way to a corner where the decibel level's bearable.

'Don't tell me Helen's your agent also?' he says.

'No. She's my cousin, you see. That would be too much in the family! Well . . . ' I laugh and correct myself, 'not real family, but we're linked by marriage. Did you know she's Claudia Charles' great-niece and her literary

Trustee? We work together there.'

We talk in our corner, insiders' talk of writing and research and the four years grinding spare-time slog it took to complete his book; we laugh about problems of fluency and he says how wonderful modern technology is: 'I revised every paragraph on my computer screen until I was dizzy with the search for perfection. And once I reprinted an argument over design concepts for children's play parks in inner urban areas a dozen times before I felt I'd got the balance exactly right.'

As Sam appears to refill our glasses I respond that I've heard of P. G. Wodehouse once writing and rewriting a sentence — by hand — twenty-two times before he felt he'd achieved its maximum potential for comedy. Freddy utters, 'God, how great that makes me feel!' and Sam joins in our laughter. I feel the strangest sensation of alertness and relaxation combined, a lightness suffusing my whole body.

I relish parties where men treat me as an intelligent being rather than a target for provocative remarks. I like Sam and Helen's parties; I like Freddy particularly. That's not to say I don't enjoy provocation now and then, it's good for the morale and the skin, but Freddy blends the two with subtlety. His eyes make it clear he appreciates me in one way; his conversation, purposeful, veering on the intellectual, confirms the other. For a moment I remind myself of Claudia: she despised social chitchat. You couldn't have a conversation with her that wasn't purposeful, yet her interest in the opposite sex never abated.

'Is that man of yours here tonight or on his oil platform?' he asks.

'He's here somewhere.'

'Uh. Pity.'

'Why?' I ask, foolishly flirtatious.

'He's a show-off bastard, not worth two minutes of any woman's time.'

I redden with fury at the casual way he's condemned not only Jake but me for associating with him. I return coolly, 'I'm binning him tomorrow. And your remark was uncalled for.'

His eyebrows shoot upwards. 'Tomorrow? Are your partings always timetabled?'

Ouch. I try for a cynical smile. 'I loathe parking in a dark street alone. The man does have some uses.'

'Mmm.' A long look. He's about to say something further when Saffron arrives to probe edgily at my life and tell me I'm looking tired.

'Strain,' she says. 'You've taken on too much and Jake's taken on too much.'

124

'Nonsense,' I say, and introduce her to Freddy. Her eyes size him up in one comprehensive flicker ending in rejection. She waves over his shoulder to an acquaintance. 'Freddy's a fellow writer,' I tell her and she is immediately wary.

'One of Helen's? Tell me your latest title,' she demands of him. When he tells her, deadpan, she relaxes visibly. 'I thought you meant someone literary,' she says crossly to me.

'Oh, but he is,' I say provocatively, 'he's particularly knowledgeable.'

Landscape architects are differently categorised: Saffron ignores my remark. 'Jake seems to be forever away,' she remarks. 'Do you *ever* see him?'

'Perhaps too much,' I return lazily, 'particularly now I'm as busy as I am. And Jake's so very much a man. Demanding, you know. Over-exposure can spoil a relationship. Isn't that what wrecked things between you and David?'

She shrugs but her face is suddenly hot. 'I must move on,' she says. 'One must circulate and I know so many people here.'

She stalks off between our fellow guests to where I glimpse the face and figure of a well-known television actor, elbowing aside his sycophants and greeting him noisily, while

Sam nabs Freddy and Helen introduces me to an actress dressed in peacock blue, which does not suit her as well as it does peacocks but certainly catches the eye, notably Jake's. He stares from across the room while this lady, whom I last saw playing an evil female in a television drama, tells me how she'd *love* the part of the leading character in my novel *A Nest of Brambles*. I tell her there's no TV contract on *Brambles* as yet and move her on to the tight-lipped Saffron, whose novels, it turns out, she hasn't read. After that Saffron heads for Jake while I am talked at by an historian (female) who tells me with breathless enthusiasm of the brilliance of nineteenth-century municipalities in using the incinerators that burned their refuse to raise steam power to run engines that then pumped away their sewage at minimal cost.

Then Sam reappears, and says gloomily that he's been working on this damned party all day and he's exhausted. 'D'you think Helen might let me eat now?' he enquires. 'Eat?' I say and see that people are holding plates. 'Damn, I'd forgotten about food.' The effect of the sewage, no doubt. We find the depleted buffet supper table in the next room and consume what's left, mainly luke-warm spiced chicken wings, limp herbal leaves and sausage rolls, while he tells me, with his mouth full and blowing clouds of crumbs, that he views Claudia Charles as a hard old cow and an intellectual snob and he hopes that's how I'm going to depict her.

'You couldn't have thought of writing anything about her when she was alive,' he points out, 'she'd have argued every sentence of every draft, the precise value and meaning of every word.'

'I didn't know you knew her,' I say. 'Not closely.'

'I wouldn't have,' he admits, 'but that her dear old housekeeper, Mrs Moffat, fell ill with flu just as Claudia was having her annual winter bronchitis. Claudia refused to go to a nursing home, said she'd die of boredom. She was coughing a lot but she wasn't at death's door, so we took her. For a fortnight. And then she stayed a month. Oh my God!'

'Bad?'

'Unspeakable. She didn't care that we were both flat out in our jobs, she wanted food at times to suit her, and that could mean midnight. And greedy? A carnivore, that woman was, a real carnivore, and her table manners away from outsiders' curious eyes were disgusting. God, how she ate! I suppose she was old and had no other way to slake her appetites, but she was critical, too. Helen and I aren't foodies, but she was a gourmandising gourmet and she complained bitterly about modern food and silly fads. Meaning us eating healthy simple diets and not smothering vast hunks of venison and beef in butter and brandy and cream, of course. And she wanted to rummage about in our minds as if they were her attics, turning out our most venerated beliefs and examining them for rot, dust and woodworm!'

'Exhausting.'

'And exasperating! Any view she didn't agree with was rubbish and she'd call up facts from that computer-sized memory of hers to crush us, exuberant with triumph. If she'd been kindly with it we'd have worshipped her, but she wasn't. And when we had guests she insisted on joining us, coughing horribly but still able to dominate the dinner table. She held everyone in thrall and we were nonentities.'

I remember again from childhood her brilliance over the lunch table and my mother's feeling of exclusion and rebuff. *Claudia as cow-goddess.*

There's a disturbance in the next room and we push our way through to investigate. The cause is Pattie, crouching like an animal on the carpet, and insisting to the guests eyeing her in trepidation that there's nothing wrong.

'Piss off, will you? All right, so I've had a

few contractions and I'm having one now. But they aren't doing anything, they aren't hurting enough. I can tell, it's my body, isn't it? And I know, I just know, that if I go home they'll stop.'

Helen arrives beside her as Sam and I do. 'If the pain's not bad why are you on all fours, Pattie?'

She levers herself up with all the grace of a wallowing hippopotamus. 'Pain's gone now. Show's over. Everybody go away.' She sits down on a sofa, leaning back to make room for her vast belly. 'I'd love a cup of tea,' she says.

Yelps of advice come from all around: 'Someone telephone for an ambulance, she should be in hospital.' 'Where's Greg? Greg, take Pattie away, she can't stay here.' 'Oh leave her alone, everyone, she's fine, the partying'll distract her.'

Helen's voice cuts through the others, high-pitched and tense. 'For Heaven's sake, Pattie, think of my carpets if things start up in earnest. I don't want your waters all over my Wilton.'

'I shan't,' she insists. 'I'll have a cup of lemon tea and maybe then I'll think about going to the hospital.' Her voice thickens childishly. 'But I won't be shoved off into some lonely grey room and made to lie for hours on a beastly high iron bed with nothing to look at and nothing to do but think about the pains . . . '

'Now, Pattie, you know they have TV and pretty curtains in labour wards these days,' someone admonishes her.

Greg is tugging at my elbow, his voice urgent. 'Flora, she'll listen to you. Help me get her to the car, will you? She's been having contractions on and off all day, though she'd hardly admit it, and that last one was big. We've got to move *now* . . . '

'Understood,' I say, 'but let me get my coat first.'

I rush off thinking I should locate Jake and tell him, then discard the idea. Sod him, he'll find out soon enough. The bedroom door won't open, it's stuck. Oh hell! I rattle the handle and push. A muffled voice mutters words that I later translate as 'Go away!' Urgency impels me and I shove at the door with my shoulder; something inside gives and crashes to the carpet. As the door opens I see a fallen chair . . . And then Jake.

Jake. And Saffron. Jake on top of Saffron on top of a pile of coats. Jake with his trousers off, his bare bottom gleaming in the half-light of a bedside lamp, Saffron's shiny shaved legs grasping his. Then the pair of them rolling apart, mouths open in shock, his erection slowly keeling over. So vulgar, I think in a cold distaste that's positively nannyish.

A moment's silence. Then anger steams through me and I try to shout my fury and loathing, but it's like a nightmare where I can't make the words come and I'm hissing instead. 'You sleazy pathetic pair. Really caught with your trousers down, aren't you? Like nasty defiant teenagers. Can't you find yourself your own man, Saffron, that you have to copulate with someone else's?'

'Shut up,' Jake mutters, scrambling hastily and without dignity into the gaudily striped Y-fronts I'd chosen for him. 'Just shut up and get out.'

'You lying cheat,' I snap at him, 'don't you damn well tell me to shut up — '

But Saffron's recovered her breath if not her trousers and she drowns my words with a triumphant shout. 'Jake's not yours, Flora. You've found us, so you might as well know. We've been having an affair for months.'

'Is that so? How tawdry of you both.' I want to hit them and I clench my fists till the nails hurt my palms. I suck in breath and search for words to inflict mental injury instead. 'But you didn't need to sneak around like thieves in the night. I'd already planned to throw Jake out tomorrow. He's a mindless bore.'

Vaguely I'm aware of people beside me, grey shadows in the doorway.

'Poor Flora, how sour you sound.' Saffron retrieves her knickers from beneath a cashmere coat.

'Only revolted by your mutual loutishness.'

'Whatever's going on here,' comes Helen's exasperated voice, 'just stop it. And Saffron, will you please stop exhibiting yourself and put on your clothes? There've been enough dramatics this evening without your adding to them. Oh, pull yourselves together!'

Her reaction sounds as nannyish as mine. I cross the floor to pick up my coat, deeply relieved it's not one of those Jake and Saffron have been wallowing on. I'm trembling with anger still and feeling sick. My emotions always demonstrate themselves in physical ways. I pull my coat on and tell Helen, 'I'm going to help Greg drag Pattie to the hospital. Thanks for a great evening. Sorry about the finale.'

'Not your fault, I think,' says Helen at her most dry. 'No need to bother about Pattie, Flora; she's already on her way. She had a shocker of a contraction that made her gasp for gas and air and epidurals, and she's gone with Greg like a lamb.'

'Right. And I'll leave you too.' I manage to croak goodbye, then I go and the floor is unsteady beneath my feet and I feel very nasty indeed, both physically and mentally, but the most important thing in the world seems to be that I shouldn't show it. Behind me I hear Sam asking Jake if he's going to pay for the chair's broken leg; I suspect he never has cared much for Jake.

In the street a sheen of drizzle creates halos around the street lamps and I can't remember where I left my car. Then horrid reality hits me — Jake drove me in his BMW. I totter a few steps, reel up against a lamp post, hang on to it and throw up my supper and my spleen.

Someone has come out of the house and is standing a few feet away watching me. I push myself away from the lamp post in a mood of revulsion. The events in that bedroom are engraved on my mind in lines that are forceful and accusatory: I have been blind, stupid and lured into a trap; worse, I am guilty of creating a scene that was all coarseness and falsity. I feel as if it is me, not Jake and Saffron, who has been exposed in all my personal nakedness to the jeers of the world.

As I straighten myself a hand grasps my arm, steadying me: Freddy Gulliver. Gulliver? my dazed mind queries. Beside him I am Lilliputian and shrinking smaller still. He'd been one of those shadowy figures in the bedroom doorway. I'm almost bawling with humiliation.

'All finished?' His voice is calm.

I nod. My throat is too tight for speech.

'Then I'll drive you home. I take it you came in Jake's car?'

Another nod.

At the flat he insists that I put my feet up on the sofa, then he finds the brandy I use for flamboyant party cookery and pours a slug of it in a tumbler. I force the stuff down and the nausea in my stomach retreats, the tightness goes from my throat. Freddy sits watching me; he says nothing yet his silence gives me support.

I finish my brandy and put the glass down. 'Thanks, Freddy. You've been extraordinarily kind. I'll be all right now if you want to go.'

He nods, but doesn't move. His grey-blue eyes study me. 'You've had a beastly evening, haven't you? Tell me, why does that not-quite cousin of yours detest you?'

The question comes like a slap and my heart thumps. 'She wanted to write the Claudia Charles biography but the Trustees selected me. We've been rivals for years; it must have been a major shock to her pride.' Other questions tumble into my head, questions I've been struggling to suppress.

How long's this affair been going on between Saffron and Jake? Recent curtailed weekends that he'd excused by pressure of work — had those excuses instead been a cover for the pleasuring of Saffron?

'Then tonight was her revenge?'

'I don't know,' I say, 'could be. Oh! how stupid I've been.'

'Trusting, rather.'

Jake's pullover lies where he flung it earlier, at the other end of the sofa. His computer magazines are strewn on the carpet, together with the remains of the newspaper and a pair of battered trainers, each stuffed with a limp blue sock. I glare at these reminders of him. They make me want to retch again. I sit up and swing my legs to the floor. Jake's due to start work on the new project in America on Monday. I look at my watch. That's tomorrow now. He's supposed to fly off tonight — for three weeks. The road-rage feelings swells in me again, the desire to lash out. Why should his filthy kit mess up my flat for all that time? Frustrated, I thump the arm of the sofa.

'What is it?' Freddy asks.

I tell him in terse sentences.

He ponders and his face lights up with a glee that's quite wicked. 'Simple,' he says, 'we shove everything that's his into our two cars and drive the lot over to Saffron's place. Where is it?'

'Chelsea. But she may not want that. She may be fucking him just to infuriate me.'

He shrugs and grins. 'We don't ask. We dump his stuff on her steps. In the rain. We ring her bell, sound our horns and go. If no one answers, the suitcases go soggy. How sad. Too bad.'

I eye him in amazement, the ordinariness of him transformed by this unexpected thread of mischief. 'We? Why are you doing this?' I ask.

He flicks me a look. 'Because I like you,' he says.

His eyes crinkle up then as if he's nervous and I know it's not liking alone that he's thinking of. I jump to my feet and start to pick up Jake's things, piling them in my arms. I can't think about anything else until I've purged the place of Jake.

* * *

We arrive back at four-thirty in the morning, giggling, tired, suddenly shy.

'I'll make tea,' I say, fishing for my door-key. 'Coffee will only keep us awake.'

'Us?'

'I can't send you home at this hour, not

136

when you've been so kind.'

Freddy blinks. His hair is ruffled, there's a dirty smudge on one cheekbone, his tie is undone and his suit is damp. As I open the flat door he leans to push a lock of wet hair from my eyes and I'm hit by the thought, God, he's fanciable. While the kettle boils we chortle over the policeman who watched us first in suspicion, then in puzzlement, as we piled Jake's goods and chattels across the pavement: suitcases, bags, cartons, portable TV, CD player, tennis racquets, an old football, wine rack plus bottles . . . His eyes had bulged. As he said, he wasn't used to folk who brought things back to people, more the other way around, like. We giggle too at the remembrance of Jake's and Saffron's yells from her window as we accelerated away from her place, hooting derisively. It was at that point that the rain had turned to hail.

'Are you frozen?' I ask, handing Freddy a mug.

'No. Been too busy.' He sips tea. 'And you?'

'Bit cold. And tired. Wow.' I curl my fingers round my steaming mug. 'I wonder how Pattie is, poor love. Perhaps I should telephone the hospital.'

'In the morning,' he advises. 'Even if she's produced her babe, they'll both need sleep. Like us.'

In bed, he makes no effort to seduce me; indeed he stays respectable in navy boxer shorts. I switch off the light. Outside, hail is battering the windows. I wonder aloud, not much caring, whether Saffron and Jake have rescued all his kit yet. Freddy puts a hand on my shoulder, his voice says firmly, 'Sleep!' and instantly I'm off, relaxed and at ease.

8

At six-thirty our sleep is shattered by the telephone ringing. I grope for the thing, growling, convinced it's Jake or Saffron being bloody-minded.

'Yes?'

'Flora? I've had my baby!'

'Pattie! That was quick. Hooray! Well, what is it?'

'It's a boy. Isn't it wonderful? I've been so frightened all these months I'd have a girl who'd have to suffer all the awfulnesses of being a woman, but it's an eight-pound boy with blue eyes and lots of dark hair like Greg.'

'Clever Pattie!' Funny sexist Pattie. I like being female myself.

'Mm. He's adorable. All long legs like a fledgling stork and he's staring and staring at me in bemusement. Poor little love, what a strange gaudy world it must seem to him.'

'It must, mustn't it?' I've never considered it before; now for a second I shrink myself to child-size and contemplate its immensity. I see brilliant lights and colours, and huge fluid figures with hard cubes and rectangles beyond, all in a meaningless jumble of shapes. I hear sounds — voices, the hospital clatter, the growl of vehicles outside. What can they mean to the newborn child, that unknowing scrap of humanity? Briefly something stirs in me, some deep-buried maternal instinct, perhaps. 'Poor souls, no wonder they wail and scream.'

Pattie chirrups, 'That's mostly colic!' and I'm myself again.

'Does this handsome lad have a name?'

'He's to be Luke.'

Luke. 'Great. Give Luke a kiss from his cousin Flora, and then go to sleep, Pattie. You must be exhausted.'

'No, I'm not. Not in the least. I don't want to lose consciousness. I'm going to float on a cloud way up near the ceiling and revel in my happiness. It doesn't happen often in one's life, Flora, does it? It's a glorious day, and I can't bear to lose one moment of it.'

When I've put the phone back I turn to wriggle back down the bed and find I'm sliding into Freddy's arms. 'Pattie has a boy and she's blissful,' he says. 'I heard.'

'Yes,' I say, and I'm suddenly shy.

He leans forward to plant a kiss on my lips, a chaste, almost teasing kiss. 'Good morning, Flora,' he says. 'Not that there's been much night so far, not in terms of sleep, but now's for other things. Perhaps we'll sleep later?'

'Shall we?' I ask idiotically as he runs his hands down my spine and on round . . . roving knowing hands. He kisses me again and this kiss isn't chaste. Heat flares and my body presses itself against his.

'Oh, Flora!' He sheds his boxer shorts.

I reach for him, then stiffen. What am I doing? Freddy's not my sort. I like my men tall, dark and demanding, the macho and magnificent sort. This bespectacled man is quiet, unremarkable, and . . . and serious-minded, not frivolous as I am. We should be getting up to make porridge. Steady, I tell my body, ridiculously aroused. This isn't the man for a one-night stand. And you'd be wrong for him in the long term. He's . . . he's the Spenser Malcolm sort, a man of literary knowledge and artistic perception, kindly, not the type for the cynical jokey life you shared with Jake. But then I remember that the formidable Claudia chose Spenser and was happy with him, his thoughtfulness calling to something tender in her. So . . .

Oh Freddy, no . . . Yes . . . Oh! I surrender to his insistence, and it's a passionate surrender, no mere return for his kindness of the night, and when we climax together and I come again and again for him, I know I've never felt anything like this before and afterwards I lie panting and dizzy and glowing, clutching his hand like a child.

★   ★   ★

After breakfast (not porridge) he drives me into Kent, to Sissinghurst to see its spring flowers. He can't believe that I've never seen great gardens; he has to show me. He equates them with famous galleries, opera, architecture, as dimensions of the human soul and the human capabilities. He speaks of Sissinghurst Castle, of Hidcote, of Cranbourne Manor. I ask why he chose his profession of landscape architect and he tells me about his father, an architect who inspired him with interest in his profession, and his mother, who was and still is, a gardener of imagination and sensitivity. She began, he says, when the couple bought a manor house on a south-facing slope in Buckinghamshire, at the time when their two sons went off to school. The garden filled an emptiness in her; a need to be creatively occupied. She designed and saw to its upkeep with the holiday assistance of her sons, unwilling at first but swiftly beguiled by her assurances of their natural genius. 'She made it fun and I loved it,' Freddy says simply. 'We paddled about making a stream

142

garden. We experimented with statues and vistas and made colourful and sweet-scented borders full of shapes and contrasts and subtleties. Today its charm hasn't faded. And the ancient trees Alex and I climbed and hid in are still there.'

Then in his teens he and his father were saddened when the centre of their nearby elderly market town was spoiled by inapposite restructuring and landscaping that was all staring red bricks and concrete, a cheap and crude following of a vogue of the time. Freddy wanted to intervene and put it right. 'It's a unimpressive little town with few buildings of any merit,' he tells me, 'but it could have been made pleasant. I knew I could have made it so, retaining the old Victorian fountains and softening the brick-work with trees.' And so his future was shaped.

The spring day is flawless, sunlight winking from raindrops on bud-tipped hawthorns, a bloom of primroses beneath. Its beauty mingles with the afterglow from our sex, filling me with a sense of heightened perceptions, so that the sound of Freddy's voice, quiet yet resonant, has the same tingling effect on my spine as an organ voluntary played in an empty church.

'Tell me about your work,' I request him,

143

and as we drive through the moist and gleaming Kentish countryside I'm roused by his tales of urban regeneration schemes banishing great crumbling chimneys and rusted corrugated-iron sheds and replacing them with lakeside business parks shaded by elegant trees, and fascinated by the word-pictures he draws of country parks and wildlife habitats being created from once neglected acres. He makes me laugh as he tells me of the effect of the National Lottery on many such schemes.

'Think of it, Flora! Lorry drivers, teachers, actors and football louts all equally lost in dreams of avarice — and contributing to the costs of many such works all over the country, whether they give a damn or not. And the possibility of getting these funds is sparking off dreams of renovating parts of our heritage that would be disintegrating and lost otherwise — mediaeval churches or ancient longhouses, for example.'

As the car travels more deeply into the countryside he shakes his head, smiles at himself and we fall silent. I see meadows with cattle grazing and villages of weather-boarded houses quiet in the sunshine; I see in its park an ancient mansion covered in scaffolding. Preservation, regeneration. It's a different world from my own close world of scribblers and publishers, and he's drawn me into it as Jake never could with his.

At Sissinghurst we find the low front range of buildings and the mellow brick tower behind, dozing in the noon warmth, looking as if they've grown there naturally. Flanking the entrance archway are bronze urns of blue pansies whose colours are echoed by the blue-flowered rosemary behind them and made exquisite by a silvery-leafed *Senecio* beyond. The scene catches me with a thrill of recognition in the way great writing does.

We climb a spiral wooden staircase to find Vita Sackville-West's tower room, the sanctum where she retired to write her novels and her articles on gardening. My eyes travel over elderly books, shining old furniture and worn Persian carpets, and I inhale the scents of hyacinths and wood fires and great age. Then we climb again, out on to the roof-leads and see as if on a map the way in which Harold Nicholson and Vita Sackville-West combined his more classical tastes with her romantic views. A scented breeze touches my cheek, while below us miniaturised people stroll along paved walks and through arches leading from one garden to the next, and Freddy murmurs of 'a succession of intimacies'. My eyes pass from magnolias brilliantly flowering beyond old walls, to cross a lawn to a yew

145

walk and thence to an orchard carpeted with flowers. In the distance the emerald April countryside fades into the blue and misty distances of the North Downs.

We've eaten a ridiculously late lunch and time is well on when we turn into the Lime Walk. I take a step and stop, transfixed. A richness of spring flowers lies on either side of us. White and cream and blue predominate, delicately spiced with stronger colours. There are flowers with trumpets and flowers like stars, and the air is thick with their scents. I clutch Freddy's elbow but it's impossible to voice what I feel. In the end all I can is, 'Oh, how lovely it is. I didn't know a garden could be like this.'

He nods. 'It must have waited for us to come,' he says lightly, though clearly moved himself. 'It's at perfection point.'

He puts his arm round my shoulders and together we walk the length of the alley. Bees murmur and a blackbird is singing beyond the yew hedge. I feel a sense of infinitely extended time, of oneness with the people who had come to live here five hundred years ago. I know it's only in this century that Harold Nicholson created this lime walk, but I know too that the origin of pleached alleys lies deep in the Middle Ages and who can say that there was not one here then, similarly garnished with simple spring flowers? Seize and preserve this moment, I tell myself, so unlike everything else I've been mixed up with in my life. All else persists — the betrayals, the jealousies, the unforeseen elements, the irrationalities of life — yet here, now, is paradise.

⋆ ⋆ ⋆

On the way home I'm struck by an oddity and I ask Freddy, 'Why does someone like you who loves gardens live in a cottage in The Alberts which has virtually none?'

A quick look. 'It's just my London place. I took a short lease while I was working on a docks development and I've gone on using it to save commuting. Our head office is in Hammersmith, in one of those rather handsome new buildings near the A4, so it works well. Haven't I told you of my house in Sussex?'

'No.'

'It's in a village near Petworth, Wisborough Green.'

'Why not live permanently in London?'

'Many reasons. Because I'm fond of the house. Because I'm frequently involved with sites in Surrey or Sussex or Hampshire. And when I'm working on designs it doesn't matter where I am.'

'Is it inherited?'

He nods. 'From a childless great-uncle. When I was small its brick symmetry was my ideal of the perfect house. We'd drive over for lunch and I'd draw it over and over again, with its great horse chestnuts behind it. I couldn't believe my luck when I inherited it.'

'It sounds as if it's old.'

'It was built in seventeen seventy-two, typical of that era, and with an outstanding fanlight over the front door that's put it into books on classical English architecture. And the garden's full of old roses. I'll take you next weekend. My great-uncle was a homosexual and like many of his type he was fascinated by furniture and *objets d'art*, and in addition he was a knowledgeable gardener. Another influence on my upbringing, though not sexually, as you'll have noticed. And thinking of sex, Flora, isn't it time we made love again? I've been yearning for you all day.'

Saying this, he swings the car off the road on to a country lane and then off again into a woodland track.

'Freddy,' I say. 'Freddy, steady on. What is this?'

My heart jerks with misgiving; I'm being rushed along the road of his emotions. Do I want involvement again so soon? If this . . . this welling of feelings between us is something real it should develop at its own pace. There should be pauses, breaks for secret smiles, for the other parts of life, for movements backwards and forwards in the game between the sexes.

But Freddy's agenda is different: he wants it all now. He brakes. 'I'm going to love you,' he tells me, jumping from the car and looking around. 'This seems a suitable place, don't you think, this woodland dell? The bluebells aren't out yet, but it's definitely select!'

There's a quietness in the beech wood that's like the quietness of a church. Insects dance their silent rituals in the last slanting rays of the sun, ignoring us. Overhead the trees reach out to form a ribbed roof of burgeoning branches above a living green floor.

He tugs me out, laughing. His fingers undo my buttons and touch my breasts, and I catch his hands and hold them away from me, disturbed, combative, at the beginnings of arousal. I can't give in to this oddly beguiling man, can't allow him to direct my body, my timetable, my life, when we're still practically strangers. Why not? moans my body, while my mind warns me I'm on the rebound from Jake and easy prey. 'No, Freddy.'

His hands drop. 'Don't you want to? What is it?'

I shake my head, make excuses. 'I'm tired. I need food. I want to go to the hospital to see Pattie and her baby. I'm sorry, Freddy, I'm sorry . . .'

A fawn-coloured moth flits between us. Somewhere in the wood a bird — is it a nightingale? — is singing with great sweetness.

It's then he says it: 'I want to do what you want. I love you, you see.'

I jump. 'You can't. You don't know me.'

'I do. I know your books and I know you. Quite enough.'

Thoughts ricochet around my head. But I'm not for loving, not the serious sort Freddy means. I'm a woman who has affairs, not love-affairs. I don't want involvement, couldn't face commitment. Mother used to say, 'Why are you such a hard little thing?'

Rooks fly homeward across the fading sky. I look at them and then at him. He stares back with a look that's something between solemnity and an affectionate mockery, and then he's holding me. 'My love, my love,' he whispers, moving his lips about my face to kiss my eyelids, my nose, my hair, and I feel a rush of warmth for him, and following hard upon it the grip of stronger feelings. In a moment we're locked together and trying, laughing and breathless, to peel off each

150

other's clothes, and while the sun goes down in a haze of gold we're lying on a bed of crushed bluebell leaves, and the nightingale and the rustling trees and the dancing insects are all part of some magical place and the air is sighing with our delight.

We hardly speak again until we're in my flat and eating cheese omelettes that I've thrown together. Then Freddy puts down his fork and says, 'Look, I've a hellish busy week next week, there'll be little time to meet . . . But we'll spend next weekend at my house, won't we? I'll look after you. I can cook pretty well.'

I suck in my breath. Men don't look after me; I'm too self-possessed, too tough. Jake never did. For a moment words won't come. Then I tell him I have a Sunday lunch party planned for Mother and her sisters.

'No problem,' he says. 'We'll drive down to Sussex on Friday evening and I'll return you early Sunday morning.'

I can say nothing and he takes this as acceptance.

* * *

Pattie is euphoric, sitting up in bed clutching her new son with her husband, her parents, her sister Hope and my mother, all cooing 'Sweetheart!' at little Luke, who is awake,

151

but, thank God, silent, staring big-eyed at his new world. We shriek happily at each other, exchanging numerous kisses, and I introduce Freddy. Aunt Daisy and Mother assess this unknown male, eyes brightening with elderly approval.

'I remember you,' Pattie says to him. 'You were at Helen's party last night.' Then before I can stop her she says, 'God, what a party. I don't think our family exactly distinguished itself, do you, Flora?'

Daisy is immediately attentive. 'Why, what happened? Apart from your nearly giving birth on the carpet, I mean?'

Greg mutters, 'Shut up, Pattie, you weren't there then!' out of the corner of his mouth, but Pattie is not to be stopped.

'Shut up yourself, you weren't either, you were going green over me in the delivery room. I got the gossip over the phone from Helen this morning, Ma — she was furious. Saffron was chasing Jake — she's always fancied him — '

I interrupt with a bald: ' — And now she's got him — for what he's worth.'

'What d'you mean? Have you and Jake split? Well — I suppose that's obvious after they were found bonking on Helen's bed together — '

'*What!*' says Aunt Daisy, eyes wide with

152

delighted horror, while Mother purses her lips and gives her and Pattie a look of withering severity.

'Yes, it's true, Ma.' Pattie turns to me. 'Sorry, Flora, but it was bound to come out and now we can all sympathise. Greg says he'll go and thump Jake if you like. And if you want to throw all Jake's trash out of your flat he'll help you.' Greg nods, exuding embarrassed sympathy.

'No need,' I tell him with relish, 'Freddy's already dealt with it. We dumped the lot on Saffron's doorstep at three-thirty this morning — in the rain.'

'Oh, well done!' my mother says with prompt approval. 'I never did like that man, Flora. Can't think what you thought you were doing with him. Hard as nails. Shallow. Self-obsessed. Boring too. He never read any of the intelligent new fiction I suggested to him.'

'Well, that finishes him!' Pattie mutters. 'I thought he was quite a fun sort of bastard.'

'And what sort of fun?' Mother points out derisively. 'No fun for Flora.'

Freddy examines the new arrival, peering at Luke's fingers, toes and ears. 'I've never seen anyone so new before,' he says. 'It's amazing. Isn't he neat? And look how alert he is, Flora.' Daisy, distracted from my affairs,

swells with grandmotherly pride and, summoned as it were by Freddy's interest, I look
more closely, curious, a little wary. God, he's
tiny, is my first thought, and then, but he's
flawless. I see what Freddy is seeing — the
gazing blue eyes, the minute perfection of his
features, those incredible fingers and toenails.
I touch his soft cheek and my eyes prick.
Blinking, I think, This isn't me, not this
sentimentality. Exhaustion must be affecting
me; I'm overwrought or something.

Aunt Daisy demands of Freddy how he
and I met, and Mother stiffens with interest
and annoyance that Daisy's asked first, while
Pattie wants to pour out the horrors of her
delivery to me, and somehow simultaneous
conversations break out and I'm trying to
respond to Pattie and listen to the others in a
strange state of drifting unreality.

Pattie's saying, 'You can't imagine how
awful it was driving to this place last night.
Greg put me in the back of the car and I was
on all fours on the seat, so every time he
braked I was slammed down screaming
between the seats . . . '

Mother's enquiring, 'Landscaping? You
mean you put rockeries and water features
and things like that into gardens, do you?'
and Freddy's explaining that he's not a
landscape gardener but a landscape architect

and Uncle Guy says, 'Oh, are you one of these people making pedestrian precincts out of old high streets and filling them with those dreadful concrete containers of dying palm trees?'

' . . . So I demand an epidural straight away and my cow of a midwife tells me it's too soon and anyway the doctor is with someone who needs her help far more than I do — and then when the doctor's free she tells me it's too late and I'll be giving birth any minute . . . '

Daisy mutters, 'Don't be so rude, Guy! You don't know what he does.'

Guy retaliates, 'Stupid ignorant woman! I know only too well.'

' . . . I admired a pedestrianised street in Windsor, paving sets, bollards and street signs all charmingly in keeping, but then in Milchester . . . so clever . . . ' Mother rises superbly above the swelling mumble of yet another row between them in an animated discussion of his work with Freddy. 'No! Was it really you who did that splendid work? A run-down old market site turned into a charming square? My friend Geoffrey Pickstone — the writer, you know — agreed that the transformation of the Victorian wrought-iron monument was close to genius . . . '

Pattie grabs my arm. ' . . . I yelled, I really

did yell — my throat's still sore — and all the stupid moo said was, 'If you scream like that again I'll smack you!' Greg had to hold me down to stop me thumping her! She's never had a baby herself, how can she know how it hurts?' The baby in her arms gives a squeak and at once her attention is his. 'Sweetheart, what is it? Is Mummy ignoring you? Do you want a little suck?' She pulls down her nightdress and puts him to her breast. He roots around, snorting like a questing animal, then latches on. She glances up at me and grins. 'It's awful being pregnant, and it's worse giving birth, but when I looked at him, Flora, all new and slippery from inside me, and I saw those lovely male bits on his body, well, I was so elated, so euphoric, it was worth every minute. That's something no man can ever have, that fabulous transition from pain to the ecstasy of creation. No man can give birth. And a woman giving birth to a man-child is incredible, when you think of it.'

'It is,' I say, and the sense of unreality increases. This isn't true, any of this: last night's awful party, the brilliant day with Freddy, blissful Pattie and her male child in the ugly hospital bed with the family around them, and Mother, flushed with enjoyment as she talks to a stranger; it's happening to another person in another time, it's all surreal. Greg wants to photograph the scene. For a moment silence falls, faces turn, lift — and then an image is captured, printed for ever on my memory. My family: this strange and special day. Tension gone, I drift into euphoria, smiling at Pattie, smiling at all the faces. I think dreamily of lying in bed, recollecting the pleached alley with its sparkling spring flowers. As if catching my thoughts, Freddy turns.

'Time to go home,' he says.

And as if a bell has rung the others nod. 'We must go too.' We wave Pattie and Greg and the baby goodbye and make our way to the car park. As we go Mother takes me by one elbow, while Aunt Daisy grabs the other.

'Such a nice man,' Mother says in a low voice in case Freddy should overhear. 'Really, extraordinarily nice. Clever, too. Persuade him to join us for lunch on Sunday.'

'He's a love,' Daisy agrees happily. 'Yes, do let's have him at our lunch, Flora, he'll get my hormones jigging again.'

'I might,' I say from my other world. 'Yes, I'll ask him.'

9

Despite saying he won't be able to see me during the week, Freddy appears at my door evening after evening. I greet him with a mixture of pleasure and panic. Pleasure because we get on so well together, panic because he's in love with me, which, wanted or not, gives him a claim on me. Or does it? There's pressure anyhow. I turn away and he follows me in. He doesn't want food, he's eaten at some pub; he wants me. But he won't grab. He falls in with whatever I'm doing, often reading a volume of Claudia's journals as I work my way through yet another bundle of letters.

'Flora, listen,' he says one night in an awed voice. 'I'd no idea how fervent women could be against their own advancement, I thought it was us men who fought them. But here's stuff Claudia found her father had filed away, presumably for some contrary blast of his own, and put in her journal. Listen to Mrs E Lynn Linton, writing about *The Wild Women as Politicians* in eighteen ninety-one: 'A woman's own fame is barren. It begins and ends with herself. Reflected from her husband or her son, it has in it the glory of immortality — of continuance. Sex is in circumstance as well as in body and in mind. We date from our fathers, not our mothers; and the shield they won by valour counts to us still for honour. But the miserable little mannikin who creeps to obscurity, overshadowed by his wife's glory, is as pitiful in history as contemptible in fact.' Wow!'

'Strange women, weren't they, terrified their household god might be outshone in glory? But then they were tied to the miserable mannikin for life. I've always thought good old Queen Bess right not to marry — any man chained to her sharp wit would have died of chagrin or had her poisoned. Unmarried, she could be Gloriana, and cry 'Pish!' to them all.'

'Wily old soul. And here's another that disgusted your Claudia, from Katie, Countess Cowper. 'As far as public life is concerned, I confess I should infinitely prefer that women's assistance, however useful, should be forever dispensed with, sooner than that by their admission to a share of what has hitherto belonged exclusively to men our women should lose one fraction of the nobility of their sex, or should become one jot less mindful of those womanly virtues which are the glory of a civilised country.' '

'Warped high-mindedness. Women were to be kept down by reminders of how much men looked up to them! Something of a paradox, isn't it?'

Freddy grins. 'I'm reminded of the man who said: 'I keep my womenfolk on a pedestal — I can see their legs better there!' ' He flicks over a page, then adds, 'But if that's how Claudia's brother Edward thought, I'm not surprised she rebelled.'

He reads on and I return to my dusty letters, noting meetings with well-known figures, a sharply worded judgement on a book or a writer, cross-referencing them on my card index system.

Half an hour later he interrupts me again. 'Flora! Sorry, but you must hear this — unless you've already read Claudia's version of the end of her affair with the KC, Denzil Vaughan, the chap she was with in the early thirties? It's in the nineteen thirty-two journal.'

'No, I'm not there yet. What's this particular gem?'

'It's a copy of a letter he was writing to his brother; he'd folded it in his blotter but she found it, exploded — and confided *all* to her diary.'

'Infidelity?'

'Infidelity of mind — a worse sin to her.

And condescension of the highest order. Or should one say lowest? Here: 'Claudia is restless; she demands to go with me to those houses where I am invited to spend a Saturday to Monday, and you know what some ladies would say to that. I take her where I can, but it is never enough. She believes everyone should support the new morality, and in any case, that her fame permits her to make her own rules. With those who like to lionise it does, but these are not the bastions she wishes to conquer.

' 'Alternatively and better, she feels I should ask Flavia for a divorce and marry her. At times I wish I could, but I do remember that I have obligations to my family, to my Chambers and my career, and I cannot see my way. Imagine what it would do to poor Mother.

' 'It seems to me that this new world of the career woman is leaving many of the female sex unfulfilled in their most natural way and that Claudia is one of those who feel dispossessed and discontented despite success and fame. Once she would have felt quite cheery and fortunate as a married woman among her family. She tells me that men have for centuries so governed women that they cannot be expected to abandon this superior position overnight and allow their wives true

161

freedom; yet the adjustment must soon come. I pity her expectations. I pity the brilliance that separates her from the rest of her sex as much as I admire it. I know that real equality between the sexes is impossible, and that women with their smaller brains must be naturally inferior to men, but I cannot bring myself to say so, she would be so shocked.' '

'Shocked?' I say. 'Devastated! What did she do? How did she react?'

'First it seems she roared at him, next she refused to speak to him, then there was a dramatic scene at the theatre and after that a friend named, wait a minute . . . yes, here it is, Christabel Pierce, took her off to Tuscany for a month. That's the poet, isn't it? I imagine the relationship with the pompous Vaughan was broken off.' He reads on. 'Yes. Much fury expended in letters from Siena, trying to persuade him to recant, but he goes all manly and says he cannot deny the truth, and finally all is over, with Claudia sick and a doctor hovering in attendance.'

'Sickness was always her reaction to emotional stress. Bastards like Vaughan with their head-patting pretences of sympathy were all too common then. They were one of the reasons the feminists became so embittered. Good material for her writing, though.'

'Hey, yet, wait, this makes sense! There's a

162

character in *Shadow of a Child* who's the Vaughan type, isn't there?'

'You're right — Doctor Ebbutt — the man of charm and hypocrisy! Vaughan could be the source for him. I'll have a closer look at that. Thanks, Freddy.'

'Don't thank me — I'm enjoying myself. *Shadow* was a terrific piece of writing, wasn't it? Her perception of how the place of the professional women would evolve within society was razor-sharp.'

'It was, wasn't it? She saw not just how attitudes should change — but how to bring about those changes. *Shadow of a Child* was said to have caused a surge of sympathy for women like that gynaecologist heroine of hers, and diminished the old hostility to female doctors.'

'One thing puzzled me, though. The dreadful birth of the dead child was shown with brutal honesty. Do you think she could have lost a baby, to have described it as she did?'

'Not that I've ever heard. But a vivid imagination was always one of her strengths.'

We read and chat companionably each evening until it's time for bed. Bed and sex. Sex with Freddy surprises me every time. Why is it that women connect superb sex with craggy features and designer stubble and never with round faces and spectacles? In the daylight I look at Freddy and it seems impossible he can be so great. Am I fantasising? I think of Laurence Britton with his moustache and his small stature, and how Claudia had commented once in her journal how good he was in bed and that he needed a constant source of sexual release in order to concentrate on his work. I suspect Freddy has a similar need. Sexual attraction is a strange thing, and love too; indefinable and often incomprehensible. I wonder whether attraction's simply a chemical and hormonal reaction, if love's brought about by feverish hopes allied to propinquity, or what? Pheromones? Claudia mentions in one of her journals that Laurence's skin smells of sweet apples in the autumn. Freddy smells of wild honey and I sniff him like an appreciative bear. Are we similar to animals, operating on a level of scents and instinct, or do we have the higher feelings the Victorians credited us with? Hell, I don't know, but I think about it with a secret smile. Freddy makes me feel magnificent.

On Thursday night he asks me why Claudia detests her brother, Edward, and her aunt Selina. Their names regularly occur in her journals; not only is she aroused to fury by their disapproving remarks, or even by what she infers by their silences, but they invade her dreams with a brutal nightmare quality. What, apart from the disapproval normal to the 20s and 30s of anyone living in brazen sin as she did, could she so resent, even hate, in them? I say that's what I want to find out, too. I know only what she repeats over and over again, that Selina's and Edward's warping and repressive influence over her childhood years wrecked what should have been a happy period, while Edward's disgust at her relationship with Britton shed a gloom over it that she believed was the root cause of her later bouts of depressive illness.

'Don't tell me, her Freudian analyst said so!'

'Oh yes! Having her suspicions unearthed and confirmed was a relief, according to Susie Peters' memoir. Indeed, analysis improved her health strikingly. She coped far better with Edward once the analyst showed her that it was his subconscious incestuous attraction to her that had made him so repressive over the years — the theory being that he tried to coerce her into suppressing her allure for other men since he couldn't have her himself.'

Freddy laughs. 'But unwanted allure couldn't apply to her aunt Selina. What had she done to deserve Claudia's venom?'

I shrug. 'She tried to help her as she did my mother's sisters. According to Laurel and Daisy and Mother she was a big, generous matriarchal soul, who'd have liked more children than the two daughters she had. I know Great-aunt Selina and her husband paid Laurel's school fees because Mother told me so. I've no doubt that they paid Claudia's. And would have presented her at Court and given her a Season if she'd wished. But Claudia denounced a debutante's life as no less barbaric than an African slave-market — girls put on display to be claimed by some man. She wanted to go to university, so they helped to pay for that instead, but according to Laurel, she was thrown out for immoral behaviour.'

'Perhaps a man was found in her room after dusk; it didn't need to be any more then for the Dean to assume the worst, did it?'

'No. But I bet it was more, and I can imagine Aunt Selina's fury. Mother speaks of her as a strong character with a penetrating cut-glass voice. If she censured Claudia she'd have done so full-bloodedly.'

'And only the most generous-minded can like those they've let down, especially where money's involved,' Freddy points out. 'Oh dear. In what I've read tonight Claudia denounces Selina Charles as coming from 'the vulgar rich side of the family', and representing 'everything that was dark and disagreeable in my life'.'

'That's my side of the family,' I say. 'Vulgar rich? Grandfather was the youngest son and hopeless with money, so if there ever was a vulgar plenty my family saw none of it. I'm glad Mother's never seen the journals. She's always said Aunt Selina looked like a duchess and had perfect taste. She was fond of her. She'd be most put out by Claudia's malice.'

'I have the feeling Claudia Charles couldn't take criticism.'

'Never. Why should she? She was special, a star who was above and beyond it. Anyway, Freddy, I'm seeing Robert tomorrow — Edward's son and Claudia's nephew. He should be able to tell me plenty and from a very different angle.'

* * *

Robert is in his mid-sixties, a semi-retired academic, an historian and writer. I go to see him in the little old house in Highgate he's occupied alone since his wife died of a heart attack ten years ago. Robert looks his usual fit and lively self. He's a big man with a ruddy face, bristling grey eyebrows and plenty of white hair; there's a tennis racquet in the untidy hallway as well as a golf bag crammed with clubs, and the hug he gives me is hearty.

'Flora, how good to see you!' he says, leading the way into a sitting-room that's shabby yet inviting. It's crammed with books, which are similarly shabby and festooned with strips of torn paper and thread that he uses in some strange system of page-marking all his own. They cover the table draped in an old green chenille cloth that he uses as a desk, and towering piles of them dot the worn carpet. Victorian watercolours and faded prints cover the walls. He says he's researching forces affecting marriage rates and childbirth in the late eighteenth century. Demography's his thing. He moves a heap of scholarly journals from a sagging floral armchair and invites me to sit down. 'I'll make coffee,' he says, disappears, and returns with a brew that's Turkish-plus in its strength. After one sip I dilute it to overflowing with milk while he stares in disapproval. 'That too strong?' he asks. 'Thought I'd made it weaker than usual.'

'It's fine,' I manage, depositing the cup and saucer in the dusty hearth. Beside them I put my tiny tape recorder and my spiral notebook with its prepared questions. I indicate the tape recorder to Robert. 'That all right?'

He nods. 'Of course. Professional. Neat, isn't it? Claudia would have relished a gadget like that for her researches.' Then he asks slyly, 'And have you chosen the angle yet from which you intend to portray my dear aunt? The great writer? The early feminist? Or is it to be Free Love among the literati?'

Robert's a tease, especially with young women, and he likes to prick bubbles. I lob back at him, 'Warts and all, of course, especially genital warts. Don't you know I'm determined to write a scandalous bestseller?'

A breath of amusement, but it appears that he's serious. 'Perhaps what I'm asking,' he says in his gently sardonic way, 'is how much digging you intend to do into Claudia's love life. Let's face it, she was famed for being great in more than one respect! But sex has assumed such overblown importance in recent years that biographers must find it difficult to avoid giving it a central place in their analyses, backed up by theories from whoever the guru is nowadays. Freud in her day, of course. Judith's muttering that she's concerned. Last year's biography of Laurence Britton by that fearful man Tom Peace appalled her with all he drooled about Claudia's affair with him.'

Robert's sister Judith is Saffron's mother. She was deserted by her husband when

Saffron was nine and she's always ranting on about the awfulness of men. Her life centres round her church, one of the smells and bells sort, and she doesn't care at all, I suspect, for Saffron's sharply modernistic novels, nor for her way of life. Nor does she approve of mine. Is there a threat of interference in my work here?

I say tersely, 'Judith needn't worry. Claudia was more than the sum of her affairs; obviously it's her work that is central. Besides, we agreed in writing that you and Helen should check the typescript before it went to the publishers, for anything obscene, objectionable or defamatory, or words to that effect.'

He looks amused. 'So we did. I'd forgotten Helen's competence in these matters. I'll reassure Judith.' He offers me more of his unbelievable coffee, I shake my head. He pours the thick black remnants from the cafetière into his cup, lowers himself into a wing chair and leans back. 'Well, where do we start today?'

I switch on the tape recorder. 'With your father and Aunt Selina's care for her.'

'To analyse their baleful influences on Claudia's tragic childhood?' he mocks me.

'Let's say . . . to discover where the reality lies between the kindly upright people my family talk about and the overbearing characters she draws in her novels.'

'Go on.' He drinks his gritty coffee with every appearance of enjoyment.

'The self-righteous Lennox in *The Power of the Dog* I'm told is based on Edward, and the awful disparaging Aunt Hermione in *The Fountain of Living Waters* is recognisably Great-aunt Selina. True?'

'Yes. Claudia claimed to be furious at such 'filthy insinuations' at the time, but after their deaths she admitted they were drawn from life. She justified herself by saying that all writers of fiction drew from themselves and their experiences, even when they claimed to be writing from pure imagination. 'We build in layers of perceived and hidden images!' she would proclaim. Or, 'Fiction is autobiography in fantasy form.' '

'And she believed in Freud and Breuer's theory of mental catharsis?' I say dryly.

'I imagine so. She certainly aired her own animosities and purged her emotions!'

I think: She used people and lied about her use, and she didn't care whether she hurt them. People who'd cared for her. I'm repelled, I couldn't do it, yet at the same time I've a sneaking fellow-feeling. I, too, suffered years of disapproval and checking as a child — and I can see that these unpleasant but believable characters are vital to her plots. But it's the form in which they're shown that intrigues me.

'Was Edward . . . was your father really as tormented by religion and a warped sense of sin as Lennox was shown?'

'Never,' he says. 'It's a caricature. Dad was no more than a believer who became a respected family solicitor, full of old-fashioned decency. He followed the Ten Commandments and society's commandments and expected Claudia to do the same. As you know, she didn't. She denounced God and religion noisily when she was fourteen, that was the first struggle between them — '

'About the time her parents were killed?'

'Yes. She often spoke of the horrors of that time — remember the First World War started just two weeks later. Her friends' older brothers were going out to France and being blown to pieces. She couldn't reconcile the bloody violence in the trenches and her parents' deaths with what Dad said of God's loving care. She screamed at Dad that if there were a God then He must be either blind or warped and she wasn't going to church to kneel to Him, and he couldn't make her — he was only her brother.'

'Poor man, being lumbered with her when he was — what? Only twenty-two himself.'

'Oh, impossible. Impossible without Aunt Selina's firm grip and the boarding school. Yet Dad did have some influence. Claudia was to flout the Seventh Commandment with a wicked glee, but the Bible, as history or as literature, remained important to her.'

'Of course,' I exclaim. 'Both those titles . . . *The Power of the Dog* and *The Fountain of Living Waters* — they come from the Old Testament, don't they?'

Smiling, he recites: ' 'They have forsaken me, the fountain of living waters, and hewed them out cisterns, broken, cisterns that can hold no water.' Dad made Judith and me learn great chunks too. I didn't mind, in fact I enjoyed the roll of the words on my tongue. And the gruesome bits: 'Deliver my soul . . . ' '

As he continues I join in triumphantly: ' 'Deliver my soul from the sword: my darling from the power of the dog.' Even I know that one, Robert. It's from Psalm twenty-two.'

'Lamentations and persecutions. Claudia deals with aspects of persecution — which is how she viewed her disagreements with Dad and Aunt Selina. To the point of paranoia at times. To my mind he was the more persecuted of the two — by her cruel portrait of him. He was almost forty when he married and had us, but I remember having fun with

173

him, playing cricket or building bonfires in the garden together. Claudia's vision of him as Lennox omits all the loving kindness and the playfulness.'

She was unscrupulous. She slammed him and shamed him to his world. My sympathy fades. 'Mother says he was kindly. Go on.'

'Aunt Claudia never could accept criticism. She was right and anyone who said otherwise was a liar, a bully, and probably mad. She admitted to being in constant trouble at school. She hated all authority, and she enjoyed shocking people.' He gives a rueful chuckle. 'She chucked a plateful of junket at a mistress's head to clinch a lunchtime argument over Byron. To tell how the poor woman squinted wildly upwards to see the stuff come sliding out of her greasy curls was one of Claudia's favourite stories. She locked another who was against women's suffrage in the lavatory and the poor woman had to bang and shout to be let out till half the school was sniggering.'

'Sufficient for expulsion in those days, I'd have thought,' I say, laughing myself.

'Absolutely — except that examinations loomed and the school wanted the credit for the Oxford scholarship she was bound to obtain. And did. She could always find people to support her, however histrionic and exasperating her behaviour.'

'Because of her brilliance?'

'I suppose so. My mother would say airily to her friends that Claudia was someone whose contribution to literature put her on a different plane from the rest of us. Everyone knows geniuses are difficult.'

'The standard let-out, unavailable to ordinary mortals.'

'The famous and great have it every which way, don't they? Blessed with blazing talents together with permission to indulge in every sort of riotous behaviour. She couldn't quite convince Dad, but over the years something of that notion did help him to come to terms with Claudia's behaviour and to blame himself less for her intransigence.'

'It must have been hard to accept that anyone so outrageous could be great.'

'Especially his foot-stamping little sister. But she was his family, his blood. He couldn't reject her. He struggled to believe her when she said the awful Lennox wasn't him.'

'Poor man. But honestly, Robert, what did drive her to write of him like that?'

He rubs his chin, stares past me, shrugs. 'Sibling hatred? Unpleasant, but hardly unknown.' I remember the Freudian analyst Susie Peters had mentioned in her memoir and for a second I consider some incestuous connection — but I can hardly query that with Edward's own son.

'Why was she sent down from Somerville?'

'That I can't tell you.'

'You mean you won't tell or you don't know? Come on, you must have some idea.'

He leans from his chair to fiddle with the nearest of his towering book piles, trying to ease out a book near the bottom. 'Rules of male and female segregation were ludicrously strict in those days and I suppose she ignored them. Something of the sort — you know how she was. She shrugged it off, and frankly, I can't see that it mattered. She read so widely she'd have educated herself far better than any dons could — Uh!' His tower of books collapses in a billow of dust, demolished like some old factory chimney. A tome clouts my ankle.

'Ow! Robert, must you hurl books at me?'

'Oh sod it,' he bellows. 'Christ, how clumsy! Sorry, Flora, I suddenly remembered a reference I had to have . . . ' He heaves himself forward in his chair, chucks a book up on his table, then rebuilds the tower precisely where he's bound to knock it over again.

Where were we? How can Robert work in this pig-mess? I glance at my notebook. 'How did your father react to Claudia's love-affair with Laurence Britton?'

Robert shakes his white head, settling back in his chair. 'Ah, that disgusted him. If ever he spoke of Britton it was never as the great writer of the young twentieth century, but as a middle-aged lecher who'd debauched his sister. Besides, a novelist like Britton could never have impressed Dad, Claudia or no Claudia, because the public school code of those days imbued the English male with the notion that an interest in the arts was a bit off, and a show of feeling not the thing, even unmanly. The theatre was decadent and he deplored the writers of his day. Novels were for foolish women, not gentlemen!'

I laugh at this glimpse of a bygone age. 'Poor Edward. But if he had little interest in the arts, how do we account for Claudia?'

Robert says rather crossly, 'My grandparents were highly cultivated people with wide knowledge and tastes. Yes, Grandfather lost money intermittently in his various publishing ventures and he rarely had a stable job, and that's what the family dwelt on, especially Aunt Selina, but essentially he was a socialist idealist, acquainted with people like George Bernard Shaw and William Beveridge. He'd rush to support all kinds of causes — look at the file I gave you of his letters and articles — but he'd never stoop to the sort of steady prosaic work that's essential to worldly success. Claudia, whatever her faults, combined his brilliance with a capacity for hard work and detail. And his interests were hers.'

'She was too young to have been influenced by her father, surely?'

'She was fourteen, Flora, not four. The years of our greatest learning capacity are those up to puberty. According to Dad and her, Claudia was her father's favourite and she was brought on in the most precocious fashion. They read great literature together, he passed on to her his fascination with politics, history and art. He took her to visit art galleries, museums and great houses; he encouraged her to learn languages. He was apart from his time in believing that females had minds as strong as men, and he inspired her to believe in her destiny, which they agreed was to be great. Then he died, and killed her mother, by driving a horse everyone warned him was ungovernable in harness.'

For the first time I pity Claudia. One day thrilling in response to her Olympian father; the next, helpless in loss, stunned by the recognition that narrow, decent, plodding Edward is all she has left to take her through the traumatic years of adolescence. No, not all. Behind him lurked the forbidding black-clad figure of Aunt Selina. It was a tragedy, a cataclysm.

'Time for lunch,' Robert says.

I switch off my tape recorder and while he collects our meal I change the tape. He returns with crisp baguettes, a platter of cheese, fresh lettuce, grapes and a delicious Burgundy from a case he says he picked up in Beaune on one of his wine-seeking sorties. We're about to start eating when he darts from the room to return with a tissue-paper wrapped photograph, thrusting it into my hands. I push the paper aside to reveal the Mark Gerson portrait of Claudia, a masterpiece, reproduced endlessly, taken in the early 1980s. There's a tilt to the head and a lift to the chest as if she's about to launch into speech. The fierce bright eyes stare through the wrinkles of old age; the lips, wide and finely shaped, are parted in readiness. It's a subtle and brilliant study of an old woman that subdues the age beneath the still vibrant character.

'Nearly forgot,' says Robert. 'You of all people ought to have this.'

'Oh,' I say fervently, 'that's a terrific present. I'll frame it for my study so we can converse, she and I. Thank you.'

He pushes the cheese towards me, then adds, 'Sometime you might want to look at other photographs we've got. I know Helen's given you Claudia's favourites, but there are albums galore of her with all sorts of well-known people, dressed up and posed for great occasions or simply messing about in the Mediterranean in those funny old costumes. They're social history as well as literary, most of 'em, anyway. You'd love them.'

After lunch I switch the tape recorder back on and we work on, discussing the Charles' family history, their beliefs, traditions and squabbles, and the extent to which he sees these reflected in Claudia's novels. It's good meaty stuff, and interestingly it shows how heavily her fiction does draw on her own past or family experiences. We agree that Britton's daughter, old Mrs Carrick, is wrong to say her father made Claudia: she was her own creation. I press him again over Claudia's feud against old Selina and he frowns before replying that Selina and Edward had been perhaps the only two people in the world who could make Claudia doubt herself, that their huge, dark, distorted images became permanent symbols of all that was wrong in her life, for seeming to scorn her beliefs and her ambitions. She hated them the more for their generosity, denouncing such goodness as a ploy to gain control over her during her miserable youth.

Before I leave I ask him about the missing journals, the ones for 1920 and 1931. 'No idea,' he shrugs. 'You should have the lot. There's nothing left in my attic. All right, I'll ask Judith and Helen, though I doubt they'll know. After all, Flora, they've had three-quarters of a century in which to get lost.'

He may be right, but those gaps are bothering me and I'd love to get hold of them.

As we part he asks after my mother. 'I've a soft spot for Primrose,' he says. 'She's a stalwart soul and she's had a hard life. Give her my love, won't you?'

Back at the flat Freddy has returned from work and waits to drive me to Sussex. When I ask, 'Shall we stop for a meal on the way?' he replies that there's no need, he's raided Marks & Spencer and there's a coolbox full of duck and salads and fruit in the boot of his car. His thoughtfulness seems curious to one accustomed to the idle Jakes of this world, curious but agreeable. The day's weariness is changed to a mild lassitude. I can relax in the passenger seat and retrace with him all I've learned about Claudia — and with no fear of Freddy groaning, as Jake would have done. Yet beneath the thoughtfulness I feel again the pressure of his love. It reminds me of responsibilities I'd rather avoid.

181

10

I never get things right with Mother. Always,
her reproachful eyes tell me, I have left
undone those things which I ought to have
done, and I have done those things which I
ought not to have done. Mother, Laurel,
Daisy and Isobel all arrive together for the
Sunday lunch party. 'I rounded them up in
my car,' Daisy shrieks at me triumphantly
above the flurries of greetings, hugs and
kisses and introductions to Freddy. A flutter
of pleasure passes over Mother's face as
Freddy salutes her, but disappears as she
turns to me.

'Where have you been all weekend, Flora?
I've telephoned and telephoned. I needed to
speak to you and you weren't here.' There's
the familiar plaintive note and she's frowning.

I kiss her withered cheek, cold from a wind
that's sending grey clouds scudding across
the sky. 'I was away, Mumma.'

'Away? Where? Why?' Mother's wearing a
Christmas-present cashmere cardigan from
Isobel and her precious single string of pearls
is round her neck. But beneath the finery her
skinny frame is trembling. 'You might have

told me.' She is wounded and she is always susceptible to such wounds, brooding over them for days, the general in-dwelling hostility generated by her parents' indifference and her struggles after my father's death emerging in sighs, shrugs and chidings, designed not so much to sting the guilty one (normally me), as to bring remorse and assurances of undying affection.

Laurel hugs me. 'Don't scold, Primrose. Flora wasn't to know you'd be unwell.'

'Unwell? What's wrong, Mother?'

'It's my eye,' she tells me. A hand covers the left eye, over the bifocals. 'I can't seem to see through it properly, not since yesterday morning.'

'Conjunctivitis?'

'No. It's a hazy greyness, blackness, I don't know.' Her hand drops. Her eyes, good and bad, hold mine. 'I could be going blind, Flora.'

Her sisters and Isobel cry out against this horror.

'And I don't feel well. I'm all shaky and headachy.'

Everyone speaks at once. 'Then sit down,' says Freddy, steering her to the sofa, hand under her elbow. 'I told you that you should have seen a doctor!' says Laurel. 'I'll drive you to the hospital as soon as we've eaten,'

183

Daisy decides. 'They must have someone they can call on to have a look at you.'

'Why didn't you see your doctor yesterday?' I ask.

'On a Saturday? I couldn't say I was an emergency, could I? And I don't want a fuss at the hospital, either. I'll see my doctor tomorrow.' She stares our protests down, turns her good eye back on me. 'Where were you?'

'Freddy took me to see his house in Sussex.'

The aunts pounce. 'Where in Sussex?' 'Is it a thatched cottage?' 'Do you have a gorgeous garden, Freddy? He should have, shouldn't he?'

Poor man. But Freddy smiles and pours Chardonnay for the old ladies while satisfying their pleasurable feelings of curiosity with a word-picture of a house that had staggered and bewitched me.

I leave him to it and slip out to the kitchen to finish putting together the lunch we've hurtled back to give them. But while my hands work here my mind is elsewhere, taking me along the flag-stoned hall of Allords to the big untidy room that extends across the back of that two-hundred-year-old building. 'Go on in,' he'd said when we arrived, tossing me the keys. 'Fling the windows wide, will you, while I unload the car?' I remember standing for some moments holding the china knob of the door, observing in the fading light a profusion of jumbled and delightful things — sofas and chairs loose-covered in country chintzes and heaped with cushions and magazines and books; books everywhere, in fact, and a whole wall lined with them. There were dusty Bow figures on the marble chimneypiece, old snuff boxes on a Sheraton side-table and piles of half-finished sketches and plans on a mahogany work-table, while beside it stood a wine-cooler holding an empty bottle over which were draped a discarded jersey and tie — and the sight of it all was bringing bubbles of delight surging up in my chest while my tense Friday-night self unwound. I opened the long windows to the shadowy garden and the distant downs and then, while Freddy brought in our bags, I explored the rest of the house. It was his house, not mine, yet I felt no strangeness there, rather a sense of identification, as with a place loved in a distant past whose exact whereabouts had been forgotten and now is rediscovered. I wanted to exult and sing and do foolish things like telling Freddy I adored him, especially when we looked from the bedroom window early the next morning to see his garden, misty and pale, with wood

185

pigeons and squirrels on the lawn and a distant stone statue standing like a ghost between shrubs arching with white blossom. It was all too much. I had to hold myself in tight against emotions so contrary to my normal feelings, turn from Freddy's arms, quell the astounded beating of my heart and retrieve my own detached persona, in danger of disintegrating into a mush of sentimentality.

I'm beating up a hollandaise sauce when Isobel comes into the kitchen. 'I'm worried about your mother, Flora,' she says without preamble. 'That suddenly blind eye. A cousin of mine had just the same symptoms and it turned out to be a thrombosis.'

'Oh hell, I hope not.'

'Make sure she sees the doctor tomorrow, won't you? These nasty little happenings are warnings to us elderly folk. And after all, she's at the wrong end of her seventies.'

I quail at the thought of Mother bedridden and dependent. She'd hate it. She's always kept busy in her retirement, what with her literary group, and being a Friend of the Royal Academy and the Victoria and Albert museum and making sure she never misses their exhibitions. And on the rare occasions when she has succumbed to illness she's been the world's worst patient. 'I'll make certain

186

she gets there,' I promise.

At lunch Mother is fretful. 'This salmon, it may be very nice, but look, here are two bones and it's supposed to be filleted. I could easily have a damaged throat as well as a blind eye.'

'But you won't, because you're careful.' I cheer her by telling her that Robert sends his love. 'He has a soft spot for you.'

Her face lights up. Her eyes check that everyone's heard. She says in a musing voice, 'I have a soft spot for him, too. He never forgets to send a card on my birthday or a little present at Christmas and he shows a real interest in what I do. He told me once he thought I'd had a hard life and it wasn't my fault at all.'

'True,' says Laurel in her gruff voice. She tells Freddy, 'Primrose was widowed when Flora was only six. She wasn't left well-off so she had to sacrifice Flora to boarding school so that she could work. It must have felt like losing her as well.'

Freddy says with grave sympathy, 'It must have been a terrible time for her.'

'It certainly was,' Mother mutters. But her attention is still focused on Robert and me. 'Why were you talking to Robert?'

'We were discussing Claudia.'

'In what aspect?'

187

'Oh,' I say, 'her relationship with his father Edward, her school-days, her reaction to her parents' deaths. Aspects of her early life, that's what I'm working on at the moment.'

'I wish you wouldn't write this damned biography.' Her voice is pinched and reproachful. 'But of course, you won't listen to me; you never have, have you?'

'You're my mother, I've always listened to you. But that doesn't mean that at the age of thirty-four I still have to agree with what you say and do what you want.' We glower, eyes locked in antagonism. Then I blink, try to smile, say, 'It's going to be a work of importance, Mumma — and I can't abandon it, I've spent half the advance already.' A pause. Mother bites into her sugar-snap peas. The thought flashes that it's better to involve her than fight her. I say, 'Something I forgot to ask Robert, perhaps you know, Mother. However did Edward escape fighting in the First World War? Was he what the Americans call a draft dodger?'

'Edward dodged nothing,' she says with indignation. 'He was a good man. He thought fighting and killing people was wrong, yet he'd have left Claudia with Aunt Selina and gone if the Army would have had him. But they wouldn't because of his short-sightedness. He was blind without his spectacles. That's what Daddy said.'

'Self-righteous women gave him white feathers in the street,' Daisy adds. 'He told me once years ago. Think of the shame. And so unfair.'

Mother doesn't want a discussion of old Edward. She wants to know about Freddy's family. She turns to him and from then on there are two and often three conversations passing simultaneously across the table. Mother is delving into Freddy's mother's gardening and fund-raising widowhood, and discovering where he and his brother, Alexander, went to school (Winchester), and whether he can understand the love of literature she and I share. His answers clearly please her, and she smiles and cocks her head almost flirtatiously as she relates sugared stories of our past to show me at my best. It's as if she's replaying a scene from another generation, the doting mother urging on the suitor from the ideal background, and I'm taken aback at my reaction to her behaviour. The Flora she speaks of is not me, nor anyone I'd wish to be. This Flora is her fantasy, and I detest Mother for deceiving Freddy with it. I'm annoyed with Freddy too, for playing up to her and listening to such rubbish.

I turn from their idiocy to Laurel and

Isobel, still musing of Edward: such an awkward relationship, they comment, to be at once Claudia's brother *and* a father-figure. 'After all,' Isobel says with a wave of her elegant hands, 'children as they grow up find it difficult to credit the notion that there is anything in a parent worth their esteem. They dare not. To reach adult status is hard: if the parent is great, how shall the child succeed? And that must apply even more to a brother. The poor lad had all the responsibility but none of the clout.'

'Besides which,' Laurel comments dryly, 'he had pigeon toes and heavy spectacles, grotesque to the scornful adolescent. But Claudia wasn't any normal rebellious teenager. She bubbled with new concepts that horrified Edward, cutting into the very foundations of his own beliefs on well-bred female behaviour. Radical feminism. He knew he was right to be revolted, but he lacked the capacity for the intellectual arguments that would put *her* right.'

I cannot help myself; I look at Mother, nodding happily as Freddy speaks, and know that she and I are silently battling across the dying tail of the comet of feminism Claudia rode so recklessly all those years ago. Mother, ignoring the changes it heralded, still dreams of bridal white and grandchildren. She deplores my changing partners; the rings my father put on her fingers are worn but still define her. But I won't have my liberty of action diminished. I've read of other women's sacrifices, I've listened to Pattie's fury: it's not for me. I'd never let a man take me over, claiming me first as Mrs Someone Else then, worse, turning me into one of those frazzled nagging beings called Mummy. I've never wanted to be anyone but Flora Monk, writer. Discussion is banned, but this is a gaping sore over which the sighs and shrugs never stop. Even as I go to the kitchen to fetch puddings and cheese I sense her interest in Freddy digging holes for me to fall into. And she is green with envy over Daisy's second grandson.

On my return Laurel demands my attention. 'Have you heard anything from Jake? Or Saffron? An apology, perhaps?'

'Nothing,' I tell her. 'Tiramisu, Laurel? Isobel?'

'I have,' Isobel says, accepting tiramisu and pouring cream. 'I ran into Saffron in Peter Jones, stamping her expensively shod feet at the thought of you. She said that dumping Jake's gear on the Chelsea streets was childish. I told her he was damned lucky you moved it for him. You could have thrown the stuff out of your windows and left it to rot.'

Daisy informs us that when Saffron had telephoned Pattie to congratulate her on little Luke, she'd said something similar. '*Pettish*, she called you. Pattie told her cheerfully that that was nothing compared with being a thieving bitch and she said, 'So what? It evened up the scales,' meaning the Claudia thing, and then she actually complained that she wouldn't be seeing Jake anyway for six to eight weeks at a time because he was off in America leading a team on a new project he'd never mentioned till the day he went. Pattie said, 'Serves you right!' and then Saffron slammed down the telephone — all pettish herself!'

We all laugh except Mother, who says with wistful mopiness how she hates to see cousins who should be friends squabbling over a worthless man like Jake, and worse, over Claudia Charles, whose biography, it's clear, neither of us deserves.

★ ★ ★

When my family's all departed Freddy gives me a puzzled look. 'Why the atmosphere between you and your mother?' he wants to know.

I explain her disapproval over the biography and add, 'Mother fights me. I have to fight back to survive. She doesn't like me as I am. Oh, she may love me in the sense that all mothers are deeply involved with the children they've borne, but she's rarely approved of me.'

'Nonsense. She talks as if she's very proud of you.'

I grimace and say, 'Yes. But there are limitations to her pride. She tells friends how close we are, and how much we have in common but, despite the love of literature she proclaims for us both, the rifts are deep. We admire different authors, different styles of writing. She criticises those I admire, claiming they wallow in sex that's gross and exaggerated, and she makes heavily ironic remarks about my own writing. She doesn't like my sharp minimalist approach, she tells me, and the issues I explore are never anything she'd want to dwell upon. When I was a child she used to say, 'Why are you such a hard little thing?' Now it's simply, 'Why do you have to be so hard?' ' I carry a trayful of coffee things to the kitchen and glare in disgust at the mess.

He follows me, piles dirty plates to make room for my tray and says perceptively, 'She knows you're the last person to gloss over Claudia's faults or conceal anything embarrassing you discover about her. You or I see that as being honest; to her it's unkind, disloyal even.'

'Oh damn Claudia,' I say. 'Anyway, it isn't just about her. It goes back years. We're so different I find it hard sometimes to credit that she's my mother. Though I suppose that's not surprising when she gave me so little mothering. She had to work after Daddy died, you see.' I pick up dishes of cream and butter and slam them into the fridge.

'Yes, I gathered that. She must have had quite a struggle.'

'She did. And I was the one she struggled with.'

'The problem of combining working with looking after you? That's any working mother's endless dilemma, isn't it?' He picks up an empty wine bottle and looks for somewhere to discard it.

'Not her dilemma. She didn't look after me. She put me in a weekly boarding school. I came out for Saturday evenings and Sundays.' I sling dirty dishes into the dishwasher.

He blinks. 'But not at six years old?'

'Six and a half, to be exact.'

'Christ! That's appallingly young. She couldn't — Oh hell!' The bottle he's holding crashes to the floor but somehow doesn't break. 'I can't believe it.' He kicks the bottle to one side and stands staring at me. 'She's a sweet and gentle person. This doesn't fit.'

I know. I feel I have two mothers: one is kindly, even sentimental, the other is resentful and coolly detached, and I can't reconcile the two. Nor can I explain this to Freddy. I stick to facts, 'As a librarian then she had difficult working hours. And since she hadn't had the education she'd wanted she was determined I should have it all.' I add with some irony, 'She didn't find it easy herself. On my first day she was so upset at leaving me she crept out without saying goodbye. She didn't want to break down in public. I don't think she thought of me breaking down. I looked up from the toy they'd distracted me with to glimpse my Mummy disappearing at the end of the drive. I didn't just cry with fright, I screamed.'

'I'm not surprised. Go on.'

I shrug. 'The staff assured me that she'd be back at the end of the week, but I was inconsolable. It was only a month or so since Daddy'd died. He'd been rushed to hospital for an immediate operation while I was out at school. Cancer. No one told me what was happening so I hadn't kissed him goodbye. In fact the cancer had reached the inoperable stage and he died within days. Young children weren't allowed in adult wards then so I never did say goodbye to him. I felt desperate about that and rejected, too. Why hadn't he asked for me? Then when Mother vanished out of sight I thought she'd gone for ever — and again no goodbye. I couldn't stop screaming and sobbing, 'I want my Mummy, make my Mummy come back!' First the headmistress told me to stop that silly noise, then she told me I was a very naughty girl to make such a fuss.'

'It's incredible.'

'It's true. I suppose they feared the noise of my screams would frighten the other children. After that I never cried. It didn't do any good. But other things arose from that day: I never quite trusted Mother, and I had this burning sense of injustice against the teachers. They were the silly people; they hadn't understood. And I'd been so devastated at my failure to defend myself that from then on I did, vehemently. Answering back gave me the reputation of being troublesome.' I slam the dishwasher door and turn the machine on. 'For Mother that word signified her struggle with me. Troublesome. I was always troublesome.'

The scudding grey clouds of earlier on have built themselves up into a dark mass. Now, suddenly, rain sweeps down outside in a storm of almost tropical proportions, lashing and thrashing — like the dishwater, like my mind as it flashes back to the impotent rages of my childhood. I hear again Mother's words: 'Flora, you've let me down . . . ' 'You're a naughty girl . . . ' 'I'm disappointed in you!' and my heart is beating faster. I see her apprehensive, resentful face and understand it. Why has she, who's had so many troubles, and tried so hard, had this argumentative daughter? But why does she always seem to be rejecting me? I shiver. I know I'm not *bad*, not really.

'How horrid,' Freddy says and I'm not sure if he means the weather or my childhood. Perhaps he despises me for not being calm and equable like him. I'm certain he'd never have been troublesome, and for a moment I almost dislike him for that.

'One of the bad things about childhood is the violent feelings you mustn't express,' he says. 'My trouble was in lashing out when people upset me.'

'Violent?' I say, scowling. 'You wouldn't know how.'

'Don't you believe it. I nearly put a boy's eye out once. Little brute interrupted me reading — I was always reading — and I thumped him a backhander with the book. It was the sharp corner of it did the damage to his left eye and it was touch and go for a couple of days. I was read the Riot Act in no uncertain terms.'

As I look at him in disbelief he propels me into the other room, where he switches on lights and puts a match to the fire, laughing at my protests that it's May and we shouldn't need it. He half-lifts, half-pulls me on to the sofa, then lies down next to me. It's cramped but I don't protest because the rain's splashing cold against the window and he's so wonderfully warm and solid. He takes my hand, looking at it as if he's never seen it before. 'Sturdy,' he comments. 'I like your sturdiness.' He places it on his thigh, orders me to continue. 'How long were you at that school?'

'A couple of years. Mother ran out of money for school fees, but she was no slouch in finding other ways and means to further my education. We didn't live in the zone of the best local junior school so I had ... I suppose you could call it paid fostering ... with a family in the right area — in Twickenham, where some City of London alderman of the seventeenth century had funded full scholarships for its poor children to a public school renowned for its academic excellence. I won one. It even provided my school uniform. Mother was thrilled.'

'I can imagine it. But paid fostering? Was

that for the hours between the end of the school day and your mother's return from work?'

'Oh no! I lived with them. For three years. In the holidays I went to Aunt Daisy — or Laurel or Isobel, or any friend who'd have me. Mother's holiday entitlement wasn't great.'

'Did you like this family?' His voice is shocked, uncomprehending. His arms tighten round me.

'The Stones? Not much. They were decent enough people, but not my sort. The father was the silent type, the mother garrulous. They had two daughters, one two years older than me — she was her mother's skivvy, silent and uncomplaining like her dad. The other was two years my junior. Betsey! A whiny brat I had to take to school every day, all snotty nose and dragging feet, fifteen minutes of purgatory. She'd wipe her snot on the sleeve of my mack if I didn't look out.'

'God, how revolting.'

'Mrs Stone used to cuddle her in a rocking chair when she snivelled. 'Mum's lovely girl,' she'd croon. I didn't want her wet kisses, but how I yearned for someone to love me as uncritically as she did the beastly Betsey!'

'What a strange tale. But I can't imagine your mother being so controlled and cold.'

'I didn't say she was cold,' I say crossly. I struggle to be fair: hers had been sins of omission, not commission 'She was stuck in an impossible position and she . . . she was pretty clueless about motherhood; she'd always worked. She was forty-three when I arrived, my father older still. And she hadn't had a good childhood herself. Her parents were typical of their time. Mother and her brother and sisters were brought up by a strict nanny. No cuddles there. Mother claims she was the odd one out. She had less attention and less education than the others; she felt rejected and couldn't think why. She still broods over that.'

'Nothing ever obliterates childhood,' Freddy says thoughtfully. 'Was she taking revenge . . . sub-consciously perhaps, through you?'

'God knows. I don't. I don't brood over my childhood, but, well . . . we never saw eye to eye. We saw little of one another, but, when we did, I didn't think she liked me much. She always seemed to be looking for the worst in me . . . as if she were afraid of what I'd do if she and my teachers weren't constantly repressing me. Unlike those mothers who furiously proclaim: 'My child, right or wrong!' mine would be more likely to sigh and say: 'I'm afraid Flora's been misbehaving again!' and look for sympathy. And so sometimes I did explode.'

'Some people might find your intelligence frightening,' he suggests.

'Rubbish!'

'You frighten me sometimes, you're so strong. In personality you and she seem opposites.' He pauses for a moment, thinking, then smoothes back my hair and asks, 'So what was this terrible struggle she had with you?'

'It was over bad reports. I didn't work at my scholarship school.'

'Really? Why not?'

'Boring. Too easy at first. I opted out, went into a dream in class or hid books on my lap and got caught reading when I should have been joining in class discussions.' I start to laugh. 'My first end-of-year report showed me top of the class. Mother showed it to Laurel: 'Read this!' she said. Laurel read, looked up and exclaimed, 'Mathematics. Position in class, first, she gets eighty-nine per cent in the exam and the beastly woman complains? *Flora contributes little to class-work.* What do they want? Blood? Flora doesn't need to do classwork. She can do their stuff standing on her head.' She'd focused on the good, Mother on the bad. Of course Mumma was right that there was a problem, but she could have mitigated her scoldings with praise. Come top and be told you're all wrong? Why work, then? I opted out more and more, shrugging off detentions and disorder reports, falling behind so badly that two years later I failed half my exams. The shame of that shocked me rigid, particularly since Mother told me Saffron was doing brilliantly at her school. I put my head down, concentrated ferociously — and achieved straight As all the next term. I liked that, so I continued to concentrate.' And besides, Claudia's conversation had shown me the possibilities of life.

'What did your mother say to your Cambridge scholarship?'

'She told me I'd done well, but what a pity I'd caused her so much worry in the past. She made me feel guilty. She still has an amazing capacity for making me feel guilty. After all, as Coleridge said: 'A mother is a mother still, The holiest thing alive.' To this day I don't know whether I love her or loathe her. She sticks in my gullet, and I can neither swallow her nor spit her out. She can be very sweet, you see, and very generous. And she's tremendously good to her sisters and Isobel — it's she who keeps the family together.' I ponder it, then add, 'I suppose for some reason I stick in her gullet, too. But

I've never seen why.'

'Oh, my poor Flora!' He gives a snort of laughter and I catch his breath on my cheek, feel his chest rising and falling against me as he pulls me close still. 'Family relationships can be hell on earth. My darling, some people seem born to rub each other up the wrong way — maybe it's something chemical between them, maybe it's of the spirit. God knows. But it's saintly that you're living in the same town and having lunches together after a childhood like that — most women would have gone long since. To Australia probably.'

I laugh too. He's called me saintly. He's blamed me for nothing. Outside, the rain has stopped and the afternoon sun is shining obliquely through the windows, lighting up my room with a glow of gold and white. I feel a great lightness of being flood through me and it's accompanied by a curious surge of belief in my own worth.

11

December 4th, 1929. May Tucker-Bond
visited me this morning, bringing Primrose
with her. She blurted apologies for
interrupting my work, assured me she
realised how precious my time was, then
talked interminably of Roger's financial
disasters, looking at me and away under
the brim of her preposterous hat, all the
time rubbing and picking at some rash on
her hands. She is pregnant again, sick and
wretched and exhausted with it. Poor
animal! as Jane Austen said. In view of all
May's child-bearing difficulties one would
think her husband could take precautions
against this situation, but 'Roger hopes for
a son!' she bleats. Why? To inherit
. . . what? His father's losses? His pretentious name? The innate stupidity and
selfishness of the male nature never ceases
to appal me.

Primrose sat stiffly beside May, speaking
only when spoken to. She reminds me of a
monkey, yes, a marmoset, skinny, large-
eyed and docile. But why this docility, why
no capering and monkeying about like any

normal child? She wouldn't chase a neighbour's cat trespassing in my garden, she didn't want to play with the yo-yo I keep for friends' children. She's a dull and disapproving girl, a marmoset in a cage of good behaviour. What have they done to her?

And why the visit? It was only after they left, with May wringing her hands over the sad Christmas they would have, that light dawned. The snobbish Mrs Tucker-Bond was here to beg. She could not bring herself to say the words but the hints were clear — successful Cousin Claudia should heap toys and clothes . . .

The doorbell rings. I rocket to the present through more than six decades, and find Mother at the door, straight from the doctor's surgery with news that it's as Isobel thought, there's a thrombosis behind that dubious eye. She accepts my kiss on her cheek, all cold and pale though it's a warm May day, and demands a cup of tea. 'I'm quite shocked,' she says and I see her lips trembling.

'Oh, poor Mumma. Here.' I sit her on the sofa and put cushions at her back. Her head tilts back and she closes her eyes.

'A thrombosis is serious, you know.'

'I do know.'

I bring the tea on a tray with a cloth and bone china cups and saucers, knowing their appeal. I even find chocolate biscuits to put on a matching plate.

Grey lids like wrinkled tissue paper still cover Mother's eyes.

'Mumma?' I half-whisper as I pour, but she hasn't dropped off. 'Tell me everything the doctor said.'

'Thank you, darling.' She sips her tea, nibbles at a biscuit, fumbles at her words. She knows little about illness, it's something she's never been bothered with. 'The doctor's certain, but I've to see a consultant anyway. It's in the vein that drains the eye. I asked him — you have to ask when it's you, don't you? — he said he'd seen fluid around the ... yes, it's the optic nerve. My blood-pressure's right up too. That'll have to be dealt with.'

She looks ravaged. Illness is most frightening to those who have never experienced it. Until now her appearance of fragility has been deceptive; today it's real and it wrings my heart. 'What's the doctor given you? What do you have to do?'

She holds her Crown Staffordshire cup before her good eye, studying the twining flowers on its translucent surface. 'So pretty,' she says. She hates my usual mugs, feels comforted and reassured by the small ceremony of the best china, a near-perfect set I picked up on impulse at an auction when no one else was bidding. 'I have some tablets,' she says vaguely. Then she brightens. 'But I'm to cosset myself and have a special private consultant. I'm to see him *tomorrow*; they're like that if you pay, you know. Things happen quickly.'

'So they should.'

The Harley Street consultant confirms what her doctor says and mutters of arterio-sclerotic changes. He prescribes more pills, tells her that she must take things easily for the next six weeks, stay at home and rest. She's seventy-seven, after all.

'I shall be bored,' she threatens me over lunch on her return. 'And who'll look after me? Perhaps I should stay with you. After all, you're my daughter.'

I gaze at her in consternation. Six weeks of my mother, day and night? She's mentally alert, she'd try not to be a burden. Why then, does the suggestion paralyse me? It's because with me she becomes a different person. 'All these unmarried mothers living on benefits, that's my money they're taking — from me, who had to struggle for every penny.' Or, 'These days young women think only of themselves. Sex, money, pleasure. Grab, grab,

grab ... The family's in decline, their children suffer, but what do they care?' They are the thoughts of thousands, but it is my own mother who utters them, and I'm distressed by the indiscriminate nature of her hostility and how often it seems to include me. In conversation together her words freeze me. 'Of course, you know that Claudia was like you and Saffron. She never committed herself to anyone, not until she was almost too old. And she never gave Spenser a child.'

I remember a passage in Claudia's journal late in 1932, a passage I'd found both sad and revealing in more than one way, and after she's gone I find it again. Claudia had been reading Vita Sackville-West's *All Passion Spent*, and pondering it in company with Virginia Woolf's *Orlando* and Rebecca West's *Harriet Hume*, novels imbued with a kind of early magic realism which she found both haunting and alarming. She could never write like those three, she admits; she was too tied to actuality, her own reality.

I'm bound by life's earthiness. How could I swoop about the sky like a swallow in summer? Besides, they're writing of people at a different level. I've no experience there, I'd make mistakes. I realise I'll never truly belong within any of the sets I know. I have to work and plan and use my cunning to enlarge the world of my acquaintance, wangle invitations to parties and dinners, seek introductions — in short, behave like some detestable social climber — except that mine are intellectual aims. My great drawbacks are that I come from nowhere and I have too masculine a mind for many — no matter what LB maintained.

On the masculine-feminine question, I do favour Virginia's view in A Room of One's Own of the two sexes in the mind, the two powers in the soul. I like to think that the creative person must combine elements of both the sexes; I know I need this masculine part of me. But essentially I am a woman and I yearn for a man who could love me for my mind as well as my body, one who would encourage me to play a main part in my own drama in addition to making me a mother.

Mother is wrong; she had wanted commitment.

That evening I consult Daisy, Laurel and Isobel on the problem of Mother's care. Is there a real need there? She's seventy-seven, blind in one eye, has high blood pressure, and could have a stroke. Of course there is. Sighs come over the line. Daisy and Isobel speak of having her to stay for a night or two, but say they couldn't cope with more. 'We're all old now,' Daisy says in her frank fashion. 'I'm fond of Primrose, and a gossipy lunch with her is great, but for weeks at a time? She'd want to reorganise my untidy house *and* my mind. No way.' Isobel sympathises but says she's off to the Italian lakes with a friend shortly. Laurel simply has no room; she could move in with Primrose, though. Mother blights that idea. 'Whisky and cigarette fumes everywhere? And Laurel arguing over the bridge table with her loud friends when I want to rest? She'd kill me off in a week.'

I look at my diary, think: And me? What about Freddy? What about my work? Freddy can retreat to his cottage in The Alberts, but my life's packed. I'm booked for a day with Great-aunt Selina's granddaughter, Ruth, hoping for new angles on the Selina and Claudia antagonism; then there are meetings scheduled with Robert and Helen; the paperback of *A Nest of Brambles* is coming out shortly and I'm being booked for radio and television then, in brief but worthwhile appearances. What else? A day in Sussex with Mrs Moffat, Claudia's one-time housekeeper ... Hold on, I remember, she'd put me off to care for a friend recuperating from an operation ... Caring. Mrs Moffat, the competent little woman with the nut-brown face ... Mother's always liked her, they exchange Christmas cards each year.

I telephone Laurel. 'Brilliant,' she says. 'Of course she's elderly, but she'd only have a bit of shopping and cooking to do. Just someone being there's the thing. Ask her.'

'I will.'

'And you could pump her on Claudia. But not in front of Primrose. Never that.'

'No,' I agree, sighing.

★ ★ ★

It's a gleaming morning full of sunlight when I drive into Kent to pick up Mrs Moffat. Birds dart from the wheels of my car, dog roses are flowering in the hedgerows, and the trees are breaking into brilliant green leaf. The air is like cider. I feel good; relieved that Mrs Moffat's happy to look after Mother for what seems to me a minute fee: 'It'll be like a little holiday for us both, with Richmond Park and the Thames nearby.' She's a woman of energy and determination who cares about others; she's interested in them, in what they say and feel and do. She'd stayed with Claudia right to the end, though she must have been nearing seventy herself. She, like Mother, has cause to complain of a sad life, her young husband killed in France on D-day, no family of her own, but she never does. I feel additionally good because Mrs Moffat's agreed to my driving over early to hear about her life with her old employer, and picked up on my hints that the biography shouldn't be discussed with my mother. 'Families can be funny about famous relations, can't they?' she says diplomatically.

She's retired to an amazing village for the elderly, built in a rhododendron wood, in the late 20s I believe. I park and look about myself. There's a central green with a big grey statue of its founder on a plinth, and from it radiate leafy roads lined with small sturdy dwellings. Mrs Moffat comes trotting out to meet me and takes me to hers, a bungalow. There are all sorts of safety features and alarms in each one, and, she says, displaying her bright and crowded sitting-room and patting her Victorian rocking chair with love, residents can bring their own furniture.

'I booked to come here years ago,' she tells me, dexterous with dishes in her tiny kitchen. 'Founded for folk like me, it was, people who'd been in service and never had their own place, so I got in easily. I've been lucky, always worked with interesting people and now this lovely village to finish my days.'

I accept a cup of coffee almost as ferocious as Robert's and a piece of lemon drizzle cake and agree that the place is special. 'There ought to be more like it.'

'Och, there should. We've our own infirmary, you know, and us able-bodied ones help run the library and a cafeteria, and I play whist and we go on such interesting coach trips — and look at those camellias still flowering in my wee garden. What more can a body want?'

Like Mother, she's small, but she has a sturdier build. Her white hair is looped back into a bun, her brown face is wizened yet extraordinarily alive and she moves with the briskness of a fifty-year-old. I visualise the tired face of my mother and the deliberation of her movements. Mother is in her mid-seventies, this woman is little less. I remember Claudia Charles, the bright hawk's eyes, the glee of living and writing and thinking that was with her into her nineties. Why do some people live with so much more gusto than others, why do they possess a quite different capacity for enjoyment? I must bring out this quality in Claudia, it's special.

We settle in Mrs Moffat's sitting-room. 'Well,' she says, 'where do we start?' My little tape recorder amazes her. 'You'll not be taking my recollections that seriously, will you?'

'Of course. I'm bound to want to quote you.'

'In a book at my age. How exciting! Go on then.'

I switch on the machine, give the name, date and time. I ask her how long she'd been with Claudia.

'Nineteen years. Longest I ever spent with anyone and longest that a housekeeper stayed with her. We got on.'

'What was it like, working for her?' Claudia's patience with her employees had been notoriously short: 'Stupidity is an unforgivable sin!' she'd rage. Spenser would retort: 'Darling, if they had your intelligence they wouldn't be doing the job.'

Mrs Moffat leans back in her chair, rocking gently. She laughs. 'Well, you knew her! Fascinating. Amazing. Impossible. Mr Malcolm, he was such a gentleman, he never fought back when she was being impossible. He'd simply potter out of the house as if she didn't exist, leaving her with her mouth open. I couldn't do that, mind. But I could feign deafness. And the moods soon passed, like mountain storms — I come from the Highlands, you know. But working for her was ... oh, I wouldn't have missed it for

214

anything. It was fun!'

'Fun?' A strange description of a house-keeper's life.

'Och, yes. Mrs Malcolm was like an actress perpetually acting a taxing part. And the part was Claudia Charles, the brilliant writer. Sometimes it was huge drama, other times she'd be light-hearted, sending herself up. And how she loved an audience! In between her writing bouts there'd be all sorts of visitors, and then there'd be lunch parties and splendid dinner parties, and visits to the theatre and the opera, and off they'd all go to London. Other times people would come to interview her, or she'd be on the radio or television. Goodness, how she could talk, how she could make you see things.'

I remember the wintry lunch party that is my first clear memory of Claudia. 'Yes,' I say, 'I know.' She'd changed my life at thirteen, formless till then, giving it direction and point, making sense of study and reading, even of homework. I'd wanted to emulate her. 'People say she could be difficult. Did you find her so?'

A wry smile flits over Mrs Moffat's wrinkled face. 'She could be. But then she was an outstanding woman, grasping at achievements beyond the reach of ordinary people. We should'nae judge folk like her.'

A familiar view. 'Everything is forgiven the great artist, the great writer? Why?'

'Ah,' she says, nodding significantly, 'they're special. Envious folk won't have that, they all reckon they could write if they just could find the time, but that's nonsense, isn't it? They want the fame without the pain. It's from deep feelings and deep passions that people like the Brontë sisters and George Eliot developed their powers and their insights. And Claudia Charles. Her books are magnificent.'

'You've read them, have you?'

'Time and again. I left school at fourteen, mind, but I always loved reading. She'd tell me about the themes of her books and the reasons she'd developed them as she did. And she'd tell me who else to read and why. There I was in my fifties and sixties, having a second education of a kind many folk'd die for.' There's gratitude in her voice and a certain surprised pleasure that such a woman should have concerned herself with her housekeeper's interests. She adds, 'She could be rude — well, let's face it, she often was, very — and she could be savage in her reviews, really nasty. But she took me on when I was getting old and she was good to me.' As she speaks something in her attitude nudges at me and I suddenly realise what it is. Mrs Moffat is a

Claudia worshipper, wry, realistic, but a fan, nonetheless.

'Which was your favourite among her novels?'

She considers. 'Favourite's the wrong word. The one that spoke to me was *Shadow of a Child*. I never had a child. She never had a child. Yet she could put the loss in a way that tore at your heart-strings, and I never could have done. It's a fine book.'

I nod. I remember the words: *Every month she mourned while her empty womb wept tears of blood.* Saffron and Helen, her great-nieces, say that Claudia had little time for them as children, but there is nothing to tell me whether this is because her own pain led her to avoid what could be wounding contacts, or whether she was simply indifferent. In which case, why that novel? Did its impact owe its force to her imaginative powers alone?

'Did she speak of having wanted a child?'

'Och no, never. But her writing told me.' Her voice is husky.

I nod and pause for a sympathetic moment before continuing. Then I ask her about the people who used to visit the house and the names come rolling from her tongue with pride: politicians, barristers, actors, artists and musicians equally with writers. In a few sentences she can paint portraits, whatever she thinks of her own abilities. 'Christabel Pierce,' she says. 'Worshipped that wee husband of hers, but I'd hear him jeer at her poetry in the billiard-room. His spirit was as mean as his frame for all his great plays! I thought her writing was just fine.' And, 'Did you ever read those novels by Meg Warren? The ones of wild country people who lived by the woods and the seasons? Lyrical, Mrs Malcolm called them, lyrical and lovely. Old Meg was like her characters, just like. Used to take a dirty old bedroll and sleep in the orchard or the woods. Gave us a fine fright once or twice when we thought we'd lost her!' And, 'Sir Robert Henslowe, the newspaper magnate, he often came. He was handsome-looking at the dinner table — fine head, big shoulders — but when he stood up? Ducks' disease: no legs to speak of, and he waddled. No manners either, never said thank you. He'd no time for people like me, I wasn't news, but Heavens, he knew all about those who were — not just what they'd said or done or produced, but how they'd acquired their wealth, who they slept with and who or what they'd be doing next. And where it all fitted in to the grand pattern of the country. I'd hear him as I served them at table. Aye, I've heard that rumour of an affair with Mrs

Malcolm in the fifties, but I wouldn't know. Not my place to know, was it?' Then she adds thoughtfully, 'And he must have been a dozen years younger than her.'

I sneak a look at my watch. I've promised Mother we'll be with her in comfortable time for lunch, a simple meal I can soon heat up. Time for ten more minutes' tasty gossip.

'I've been told that the whole house had to revolve round those writing bouts you've mentioned, that she became fanatically involved. Was it really so bad?'

She shakes her head with a snort of laughter. 'When I first arrived I couldn't believe it. She was seventy-four, then, remember, but she was working till all hours on *The Midnight Oil*. She'd scream with fury if the telephone rang, bellow at the sound of the doorbell. That drive never really left her. She was writing articles and reviews right up to the last months, and there was a novel she never did finish. Even when she was bedridden there'd be papers all over her bed, slipping on to the carpet likely as not and her yelling: 'Oh hell, oh hell, oh hell! Kirsty? Come and find this damned article for me! I've a rejoinder deadline to meet, I must fax it off today!' There was no fixed routine to her work, no concept of an organised working day.'

'Then how did she achieve that prodigious output?'

'She'd write in bursts of energy and invention, barely stopping for sleep. Folk say when she was young she needed special pens to keep up with the pace of her thoughts. Meals had to be of soup and sandwiches, forced on her when she was near exhaustion. And then she'd bellow at me not to interrupt.'

'How long did these episodes last?'

'Anything from a couple of days to a week. And longer when she was younger, they said. No visitors at those times — she'd cancel everything. Laurence Britton, her first lover, you know, she said he scolded her for it. He told her writing was a craft and she should work to a sensible timetable. But she said she was an artist, not a craftsman, and her mind didn't function in his way. She must work while the mood was on her or it was no good. A visitation, she called it.'

'How did her husband occupy himself at such times? I mean,' I give an awkward shrug, not wanting to put words into her mouth, 'didn't he feel, well, left out?'

She looks amused. '*Puir* Mr Malcolm, what a saint. He read a lot. He sat on useful committees, and he was a governor of the village school as well as his own old school. A pillar of the community, people said. And he ran the house: if the boiler burst it was he who summoned the plumber. He hated that sort of thing, but if he protested she'd sweep off from the breakfast table quoting Flaubert — always the same words — 'The more tranquil the domestic life, the more the imagination can run free.' He'd lost money on the Stock Exchange, I know, gambling to increase his capital, and he'd lost money in a West End production of a play that flopped. After he retired it was her imagination kept them both to their splendid standard of living, so what could he say?'

'I had the impression he was always very patient with her,' I say.

'Oh yes. He was a calm man, rational about emotions, whereas she flew from one extreme to another. She liked to say she was particularly sensitive . . . ' She shrugs.

I finish for her, 'But like most people who say such things, Claudia Charles' sensitivity was nine-tenths for herself.'

A chuckle. 'Och well, maybe. Take criticism — she'd brood over that in tremendous anger, dashing off letter after letter to refute critics, lambasting any member of the family who'd ever inferred she was less than perfect. But she refused to acknowledge her own power to hurt them. She was generous, very

221

generous to anyone she loved, like her husband, but she expected devotion in return. Mr Malcolm gave her that, in his own way. She missed him terribly after he died.'

'But she was able to continue working?'

'Yes, she was. She was very quiet for a wee bit, but work was a distraction from the pain, wasn't it? She even gave television interviews where she was her old lively controversial self. People said she was unfeeling, but it wasn't true. She was so involved in her work she couldn't stop. My view is she'd have run down and died herself if she had.'

* * *

Mother has dark rings round her eyes and a pinched look about her mouth when she meets us at the door of her flat; she says she feels poorly. Mrs Moffat takes control, sympathetic and firm at the same time. Mother is to put her feet up on the sofa, I'm to take Mrs Moffat to the kitchen and show her where everything is and together we'll have lunch ready in a trice.

Over our tomato and basil soup Mother tells Mrs Moffat of her sight and blood pressure problems. '*Anno domini*,' she concludes. 'I've had more than my three score year and ten. I'm of an age to go.'

'Och, nonsense,' Mrs Moffat returns with great good cheer, 'we women are living longer than ever these days. Look at the death columns in the papers, they're full of octogenarians and nonagenarians. Sensible care, that's what you need, and you'll make a full recovery. Remember Bob Hope, the film-star comedian? He had a thrombosis behind one eye, just like yours, and he kept going for years and years.'

'Is that true?' Mother reflects, and colour creeps into her cheeks. 'I don't want to live for ever, but I'd like a few more years yet.'

'And what'll you do with them?' Mrs Moffat leans forward, nodding encouragement. 'Will you travel?'

'Oh, I don't know . . . Well . . . yes, perhaps I should . . . '

By the time I'm finishing my coffee and rising to go, the room has expanded to encompass the lands of their dreams — the Holy Land and the Nile for Mother and the Brazilian rainforests and the wilder reaches of Java for Mrs Moffat — and they're on to experiences they mustn't miss. 'I'd like to fly Concorde,' says Mrs Moffat, 'that's one thing, but most of all I'd like to potter over the Highlands in a helicopter. Imagine how exciting and how beautiful!' Mother agrees, but she can't or won't miss the opportunity to be plaintive. 'My greatest wish of all is to hold my first grandchild,' she says, lifting her reproachful face to mine.

I take a deep breath but Mrs Moffat is in there first and more than a match for her. 'You'll do that yet, I'm sure,' she says, 'and how I envy you. I never shall, I haven't a lovely daughter like your Flora to do all she does for you.'

Mother has the grace to blush a little. She thanks me with unusual warmth for bringing Mrs Moffat to look after her, and doing her shopping on the previous day. 'I do count my blessings,' I hear her tell Mrs Moffat as I leave. 'Flora and my sisters are very good to me.'

12

Peter Packham of Packham & Graham, Literary Agents, b. 1933

Yes, I was Claudia's agent for — let me think — yes, almost twenty-five years. She came to me after John Fuller retired.

. . . Indeed I was pleased. She was at the height of her powers then and she commanded great reverence as well as large sums of money. And strong reactions of every sort.

. . . Wine? Good, I think you'll like this Burgundy. Well, it's my own view, of course, but I don't believe there was another woman writing fiction then, with the possible exception of Iris Murdoch, who had her muscular and tenacious mind. And in addition she had wit. And what wit! Like Jane Austen, she was by turns penetrative, sardonic or scouring as she dissected her characters, but without the detachment from the trends of her time that has been criticised in Austen in recent years.

. . . Definitely. She had a lively aware-ness of any trends — social, economic, political — that might become, as it were, force fields affecting the actions of her characters.

. . . Oh yes. Going back, take *Shadow of a Child*. It's famed as a compelling novel about the struggles women had to get themselves admitted as equals of men in the medical world, and also of the male doctors' indifference to women's agonies in childbirth, yet through the sufferings of her gynaecologist's sad patients she also illustrates the difficulties and distress of the poor in the Depression years. So it works on three levels.

. . . You're right. *The Midnight Oil* is the final great example. Claudia wasn't simply a person of her time, the time when she came to maturity in the inter-war years, but of every time she lived through. She understood the world of the seventies and eighties, though she disliked some of its aspects. The scientist she portrayed was a detached personality who rejected what he called the idea of the couple and power relations within his personal life. His career-obsessed lover didn't live with him, she lived next door instead. Their children were brought up by dubious foreign nannies whose boyfriends abused them. Of course those black eyes of hers were always observing the chattering classes in order to write about them.

... She'd speak of a wide range of contacts and friends in the political as well as the literary world and the media; she was never averse to name-dropping.

... No, no. She had her snobberies all right, but they were intellectual in the main. Social concerns she did have. She grumbled about the loss of jobs for youths from council estates. She regretted the passing of the old social controls, the power of neighbourhood disapproval and the schoolmaster's cane. But she saw the excesses of the sexual revolution as the biggest disaster of the age, and she didn't only mean AIDs. She observed to me once in her most tart voice that sexual congress between men and women at social gatherings was as commonplace as drinking a Coke. 'And how,' she added, 'can the commonplace consumer product give anyone the ecstasy of enchantment or true fusion? Everything's prepackaged and disposable, even marriage.' But while the unmarried mother lies in bed with her new lover her children are out stealing and dealing in drugs. Claudia forecast that the new millennium would be greeted not with an explosion of joy but an explosion of crime. She'd greeted the sexual revolution of the sixties with triumph as a liberation from nineteenth-century repression, but revolutions bring excesses. In this case it was the loosening of family bonds. That saddened her. Even in her eighties she could still be bitter over her own lack of close family, recognising the damage it does. She saw that damage being replicated a million times.

. . . *The Midnight Oil* was a triumph, despite its melancholy. Everyone was discussing it. In the United States it was reprinted three times in the first fifteen months. It was an exciting time for us, for me. In my hands she was still developing, you understand.

. . . Oh, definitely! She never lost her cutting edge. Those review articles she wrote for the *Sunday Times* had such punch. I remember her dismissal of Laurence Britton's last novel with the comment that it would give its readers all the wild exhilaration of a Guy Fawkes' night in a drizzle. And comparing Anthea Prince to a great lit-up ship sailing on an uncharted voyage to nowhere. She was right in both cases, of course, and acknowledged to be so.

. . . She lit up our literary scene. That

was Max Blake's verdict, and he was generally considered to be the arbiter of our tastes in the post-war period.

. . . Another glass of wine? No? Well, I shall. In my hectic life, at my age, you need it.

. . . No, she was not easy to work with. Hellish, if I'm honest. She couldn't take the least hint of criticism. The way she'd written a scene was the only way it could have been written. Who was I, or her editor — or anyone else — to contradict her? Lightning flashed from her eyes, thunder would roll and hailstones batter. One took cover and continued the argument by letter, far safer with someone like Claudia who could be savagely unpleasant at times — and would later deny all memory of what she'd said. Her secretaries frequently resigned in tears. One got her own back though; she ordered hundreds of boxes of purple personalised notepaper in Claudia's name and left just before the lorryload arrived. I imagine they'd been, as usual, all horribly under pressure.

. . . Why? Because she wouldn't turn down anything she liked and she liked reviewing the latest stuff on the literary scene, she liked to appear on television, she liked to spend a month or six weeks lecturing in America, she liked to be lionised — hell, she liked to make life hard for me. It was I who got the stick from her publishers when she failed to complete her manuscripts on time. She'd no idea of working to a timetable, hence the gaps between the novels. But I made sure we got there in the end.

. . . Yes, she endeared herself to American society with her clever, funny lectures, though John Fuller told me that in the early days the Americans were more conventionally shocked by her relationship with Laurence Britton than the English.

. . . Naturally, when she was in New York she was invited to literary lunches, society dinners, weekends in places such as Newport, Rhode Island, Martha's Vineyard, or Greenwich, Connecticut. In all of them she had old friends, many of them figures of international status.

. . . And lovers, as you say. Fletcher Mantel and Hudson Richards. A poet and a playwright. Dead now, like her. But remembered too. I disliked Fletcher Mantel's poetry. There was a feeling that he wrote it with an ironic and rather self-satisfied smile. But she'd have found his masculine assumption of superiority appealing, there was that dichotomy in her about the male that one sees in her writing. He married two or three times, but whichever the wife, Claudia would head for Martha's Vineyard to renew her animal vitality, low after the gruelling round of lectures, in flirting with Fletcher. On more than one occasion she missed lectures because the pair of them had sneaked off somewhere. All hell would break out, she'd be wide-eyed with innocence and tell the journalists how she'd castigate the organisers for letting her down over the arrangements, of course, but I knew.

. . . No, growing old didn't stop her. Nor the work I was desperate for her to finish in England. God she gave me some headaches over the years.

. . . Yes, she never ceased to relish controversy, with her publishers or anyone else. Of course, she knew I was always there to be leaned on for support.

. . . I kept in touch to the end, well, to within a few months. Her work will last, of that I have no doubt, and she'll be classed as one of the century's great. And that's what counts in the final analysis, isn't it? Not the difficulties her hard-pressed agent had with her.

When the framing's done I put Robert's photograph of Claudia on a shelf above my big cluttered desk, and immediately she dominates the room. Worse, I'm intimidated by those fierce bright eyes and those parted lips. 'Who are you, Flora Monk, to think *you* can interpret me to the world?' they seem to be asking. 'What right have you to ferret about for my innermost thoughts, my most painful secrets, you who've achieved nothing in comparison? Ninety years reduced to the contents of one small book? How flimsy your facts will be, how crude your analysis.'

I wilt at my effrontery. I look inward at the chaos and disorder of my own mental being. Life being a continual process much like the tides, my feelings tug me in different directions according to moment and mood. How can any biographer hope to penetrate the shifting undercurrents of another's existence, particularly when mortality has silenced her tongue for ever?

In the evening Freddy rejects my qualms. 'Don't start down that track, Flora,' he says, hugging me and heading for the fridge for a lager. 'That way madness lies. Be glad Claudia's dead. She can't take umbrage at your interpretation of her work or her love life. Family, friends and critics may snarl their dissent — but so what? You'll be standing on

232

the solid ground of detailed research. Cultists and groupies can take their weird perceptions to hell.'

'Freddy, I hardly knew her.'

He tips lager down his throat, lowers his glass and shakes his head. 'Most biographers write of the dead. Who nowadays knows Virginia Woolf? You're meeting Claudia every day in her letters and journals. Only last week you were telling me of your feelings of identification with her in that break-up with her chap in California, John Harley. She was writing in a flow of anguish about feelings she hadn't had time to analyse and polish for public consumption, and you felt for the first time you could touch the living, breathing woman beneath her own inflated mythology. Isn't that what you said? Right. Hold on to it.'

'*You* look at the photograph,' I say and tug him to my study.

'Hmm.' Freddy tilts his head back, squinting at it through the slanting sunshine of a hot summer evening. 'You could say she's interested, urging you on, challenging you. And when you get down to it, why all those journals, why all the letters, so carefully preserved? They're there for you, her biographer. They're your passport into her life.'

'Susie Peters' passport,' I say crossly.

'Nonsense. I've read that memoir. It's short and sugary, and it gives no indication that she ever delved into any of the stuff piled up in here. Susie says her evidence is first hand, from the lips of the great writer herself. In a nutshell, it's biased, a put-up job. It can't have been difficult for Claudia to manipulate a gullible young graduate like her, presenting her view of each episode of her life as the sole possible perspective, manufacturing for herself a piece of special pleading beside which any fresh assessment less than fulsome would seem sour, carping even. She led her into a trap baited with visions of fame, relying upon Ms Peters being too naïve to query her version of events. And it was never claimed to be more than a memoir. Yours is to be the definitive biography.'

Freddy potters off to take a shower and I perch on my swivel-chair, fanning my overheated self with one of Claudia's journals, still studying that strong-boned face. It's the face of a woman who couldn't tolerate criticism, I remind myself. When she broke the rules, the rules were misconceived, antediluvian. When she fell out with a friend, a critic, an aunt, their very souls were dark, they represented the forces of evil. When reviewers failed to praise, they were blockheads lacking in perception. The memoir was to convince the world of her greatness. Susie herself wrote: 'Within a day of meeting her I was swept into Claudia Charles' orbit, magnetised by her power.' *'Will you walk into my parlour?' said the spider to the fly.*

But as Freddy says, Claudia's dead. She can't use that magnetic power now, or interfere. Or perhaps she can. I shake my head at the lined but lively face before me. Some of your journals are missing. And I can't help wondering whether the letters have been thinned, removing evidence that fails to fit your desired image. You knew, Claudia Charles, that Susie Peters' book was bound to be a eulogy both of 'those tremendous novels overflowing with ideas and issues', and of your dubious affairs with married men, 'the dawn-glow of the great sexual revolution of the sixties'. Are you ensuring that I, or any subsequent biographer, discover only that information you want us to see? Well, mark this then: I'm not a believer, a worshipper of the goddess — lion, vulture or cow. I shall pursue you, observe, research and dissect you. Dispassionately.

Freddy pads back in on bare feet, a towel tucked round his waist. 'Don't fall into the biographer's trap of feeling inferior, my Flora, because you're not. Relax, put your mind to other things — such as me and lovely love, in the here and now.'

*   *   *

A month with Mrs Moffat and Mother is reviving fast. She's given breakfast in bed with the *Telegraph* while Mrs Moffat whisks through the flat; she's fed delicious meals and they've been for walks in the park. They've taken a boat downriver to Greenwich ('Would you believe it, I'd never done that before?' says Mother), her friend Geoffrey Pickstone's been invited to lunch, and they've enjoyed the architectural delights of Syon House and Marble Hill House. 'Like a holiday in my own home,' Mother says dreamily, 'and that's real cossetting, far nicer than being in a hotel among strangers. No one's ever taken such trouble over me as Kirsty does.'

In June I'm invited to a midweek family lunch. 'Kirsty says she's not using her skills enough,' Mother tells me.

Robert's there, as well as Laurel, Daisy and Isobel, somewhat, I feel, to his own amazement. He looks flushed, large and male beside the elderly ladies. He gives Mother a big bouquet of roses and her sallow face pinkens with pleasure. She apologises proudly for giving Mrs Moffat the trouble of arranging them, but Mrs Moffat smiles, shakes her head, bears them off, and soon two great bowls of crimson transform the room. Mother urges Robert to play host with the drinks. 'After all,' she giggles, 'you're our only man.'

Isobel's glass filled, she lifts it to Robert, giving him a flattering spirited glance. 'Such a haunting scent your roses have, quite spellbinding.'

Daisy bats her eyelids at him over her white Burgundy. 'You're a splendid man, Robert!'

Even Laurel grunts, 'I want a kiss, you haven't given me a kiss yet, old boy.'

Robert obliges, then draws me aside from all this nonsense. 'Primrose looks better than I expected,' he murmurs, 'but still not good.'

'Do you think so?' She looks fine to me, cheerful and unusually relaxed.

'Maybe you haven't noticed it, being so near her, but she's getting frail. She won't make old bones. Not like Claudia. Life's worn her, the resilience isn't there any longer.' He thrusts a glass of wine into my hands and bends his bristling eyebrows at me. 'Getting old Kirsty Moffat over is a stroke of genius, but you give her some attention, too.'

'I always do,' I retort. I feel his words as a reprimand, and I resent that.

The conversation over lunch is a mixture of

grumbles and reminiscences. The grumbles are about old age. Isobel says she can't remember people's names, Daisy complains of slowness, and Mother sighs over her diminished sight. Even Robert admits he can't play tennis like he used to do.

'Poor old love,' Laurel growls. She turns to me. 'Old age is disgusting — don't go in for it, Flora. Be warned by me — ugly specs and ill-fitting teeth at one end, and a weak bladder and piles at the other. And no fun.'

'Really, Laurel,' Mother protests, while Isobel and Daisy giggle.

'No, I mean it. If my life gets any worse I shall turn to the wall and drop off my perch. I've always enjoyed good food, but these days my gums are sore and my teeth rattle and I could hardly chew Mrs Moffat's delectable Dover sole. I'm at the end of Shakespeare's seven ages of man — *Sans teeth, sans eyes, sans taste, sans everything!* It's all pointless.'

There's a moment's silence before Robert says, 'Aunt Selina used to say that sort of thing, Laurel. For a moment you could have been her.'

'Yes!' Daisy exclaims. 'How she hated it when she couldn't eat those stupendous meals of hers. Ooh, this strawberry pudding is wonderful, Mrs Moffat. Goodness, you're taking us back to times when food was food. I do sympathise, Laurel, but Mrs Moffat's meals don't need chewing, they simply slip down.' She fills her mouth with the creamy strawberry substance and rolls her eyes with delight.

'Aunt Selina's meals,' Mother says in reminiscent tones. 'Impossible to forget. Remember how I went with her to Kent when she was evacuated in 1940? Aunt Selina produced rich, rich, rich meals that were so spectacular, I'd abandon all caution, stuff myself and retreat to throw up afterwards — and then I'd want more.'

'I don't believe it!' I exclaim, looking at her spare little frame. Mother could never have been greedy.

Laurel and Daisy laugh and nod their confirmation, however. 'It's true,' they say. They'd stuffed themselves with similar results on several occasions.

Isobel exclaims, 'Alban used to speak of it in the old days but I thought it was one of his wild exaggerations. However did the old lady do it in wartime?'

'With know-how,' Laurel says easily. 'Bribery and corruption mainly, I imagine.'

'Rubbish,' Mother says, firing up in her defence. 'That house had its own orchard and paddocks and a big kitchen garden. She didn't need the black market. We kept two

Jersey cows and hens, ducks and geese, yes, and pigs. That's what she and Uncle Lucian took me down there for, to help run the house and feed the stock with their gardener-handyman. Job, his name was.'

'Is that the one who taught you to drive?' Isobel asks, cutting herself some Stilton and consuming it with slow relish.

Mother shakes her head, chuckling, remembering. 'Job may have understood cows and carrots, but he'd no real idea of cars. I was terrified, but the only point of the Daimler for him was fast and furious driving. 'Exhilarate, miss, exhilarate!' he'd yell, every whisker on his hairy old face standing on end.'

We laugh with her. 'There were other exhilarations down in Kent, weren't there, Primrose?' Daisy enquires slyly. 'Handsome fighter pilots.'

'Is that so?' Isobel asks, eyes bright with mocking reprimand. 'Why haven't I heard of this before? Tell me now.'

The three sisters reminisce. Aunt Selina had been in her early sixties then and full of energy. Her brother-in-law and his wife had emigrated to America as soon as the war started, 'Too gutless to stay and fight it out,' Laurel says disgustedly, but old Selina and Uncle Lucian had only taken over their

240

Kentish house after being bombed.

'Aunt Selina wasn't frightened,' she maintains, 'it was the indignity Hitler submitted her to that had forced her to evacuate. I was with them at the time. God, it was funny. Even then it was funny. She'd gone up from the safety of the cellar for a quick pee and That Man caught her mid-flow, some freak of the blast to the back of us blowing the lavatory and her straight through the house and out on to the street. She was battered, she was bloody, but was she bowed? Not a bit. We heard her yelling, rushed upstairs, stumbled over the rubble to the hole that had been the front door, and there in the light of the stars was Aunt Selina, knickers round her ankles, shaking her fists and screaming abuse at the disappearing bombers like some harridan from Billingsgate fish market.'

'She was terrific,' Mother says. 'Within days of her arrival in Kent she'd inveigled herself on to all sorts of useful wartime committees; she helped to run the WVS, she knew the right people at the Min of Ag and she used to invite the entire Officers' Mess from RAF West Malling to all her parties — it was only a few miles away and she was determined the dear brave boys should have as much fun and good drink as they could hold between their bouts with the enemy.

And that I should have fun with them. It was a wild time — it was exciting and terrifying all at once. And yet we weren't terrified. We were too angry, too determined to support our lads.'

'And that's how Primrose met Harry, her first love,' Daisy tells Robert and Isobel. 'I was only fifteen then, but I thought he was the epitome of godlike young manliness, and I was wildly jealous of her!'

And now she and Laurel blow away the mists of time to tell story after story of Harry and his Hurricane plane and the warm late summer days that saw the Battle of Britain being fought overhead under endless brilliant sunshine. They were only there for part of it, yet there is about my aunts that curious air of pathos that clings to the elderly when they recollect the past. They speak of sirens and dog-fights, and the high scream a plane made in a long low dive. They speak of the shattering crump when a plane failed to pull out and hit the earth, and the sound of the fire bell as the camouflaged truck went hell for leather through the village. They remember gleefully the Dornier that spiralled down into Bishop's Copse — 'What a bonfire that made!' — and the Messerschmitt Harry claimed as his that crashed into the river. Then there was a day when there was a crackle of machine-gun fire and a plane screamed overhead, scorching away across the church tower while its empty shell cases clattered on the corrugated-iron roofs of the pigsties, and then the screams began and half the household rushed in horror to succour the wounded, only to discover the pigs having hysterics.

We all chortle and Robert pours more wine. 'Go on,' he encourages them. He can remember that time himself; he was nine years old.

Harry did brilliantly, the aunts tell us. 'Two definite strikes and a possible. And remember how he snubbed the Germans he captured?' They look triumphantly round the table and again I sense the gentle breath of pathos in the borrowed prestige of these stories of their sister's past.

Mother's not interrupted them, she's sitting with a modest smile on her lips, loving their showing off on her behalf; now she insists she tells about the captured Germans.

'Harry shot at one of their air ambulances over the Channel.' She turns to me. 'They were transport planes marked with the Red Cross, and the Germans actually claimed that they were in their rights in coming to rescue their pilots who'd been shot down. Can you believe it? Harry crippled this one and forced it to land on one of our airstrips. The German crew and doctor shouted at our boys that he was breaking the Geneva Convention, but Harry wasn't having them rescuing their fellows so that they could come and bomb us again!'

Aunt Laurel adds scornfully that the Geneva Convention had never envisaged any such thing anyway.

'He sounds a magnificent man, your Harry,' Isobel says, looking at Mother with interested eyes. 'What happened to him? Did he go on to win the DFC and be loaded with honours? I suppose if he's still alive he'd be a grandfather now.'

Mother lowers her eyes to her table. She picks crumbs from the tablecloth and puts them on her plate. 'He died,' she says flatly. 'His kite went into the drink at the end of that September. They never recovered his body or the plane. There's no grave, nothing to remember him by.'

'Oh, how sad,' Isobel murmurs. 'I'm sorry.'

'We all mourned him,' Laurel says in her gruff way. 'He was a really decent chap. It was his death that made me join the Wrens. I was so angry. For him and for Primrose. I had to hit back somehow at those Nazi bastards.'

Now real sadness replaces the pathos. The events of more than half a century ago are as

244

vivid to them as last week. Poor old loves. They had a bad time, their world collapsing just as they grew old enough to step out into it. And I think of Mother's happiness with Harry being haunted daily by the knowledge and dread of the horrors — crashes, fire, maiming, death — that hung over him and every one of those pilots.

I touch her hand, bony and spotted and trembling a little, where it grasps the table's edge. 'My poor Mumma. Life really put you through it, didn't it? Unfairly.'

She nods. 'Thank you, darling. Yes, it was hard.' A short pause. 'I'm glad you see that now. I've wondered sometimes if you ever would understand that sort of unhappiness — you're so tough yourself that emotions like empathy and sympathy don't come easily to you, do they? But then you've never known how it feels to lose someone you love and who loves you. Especially after a childhood like mine in which love was never a strong factor.'

I stare at her as Mrs Moffat begins to clear the dishes. I think: There it is again, the reproachfulness, the half-veiled accusations of callousness. Anger swells in me. There have been occasions when I've deserved reproaches but this isn't one of them; this time I was full of love and pity for her. The swell becomes a wave, one of those monster waves capable of inflicting real damage.

I draw in breath. 'Mother, I can't believe you know what you're saying. *I* haven't lost anyone I've loved? What about Daddy? He was my father as well as your husband, you know. Or don't you believe a child of six can suffer grief?' I'm cold inside, remembering. 'I suffered real grief, but after the first month you weren't there to console me, were you? You'd put me into that little boarding school — and crept out without even kissing me goodbye.' The wave of anger has broken now, it's running, foaming and hissing, over the shingle. I add with cold scorn: 'You had a bad childhood? Love was never a strong factor? You had both father and mother, you had two sisters and a brother. What did I have? I had you — and for ten years I hardly saw you. When I needed you you were never around. Is it so surprising I grew tough, as you call it?'

Mother gives me a shocked look. 'I couldn't help it. I had no choice but to work.'

Round the table I see stunned faces. Laurel is lighting a forbidden cigarette, drawing on it strongly. Daisy, her lips tight, is shaking her head. Dear Daisy; in her frivolous offhand way she's given me far more straightforward affection than Mother ever has. Isobel has lifted her glass and is staring at Mother over

246

the last of her white Burgundy, as if examining her through an eyeglass. Robert frowns. He looks as if he would say something, then stops himself. Mrs Moffat, muttering about coffee, heads for the kitchen, her face averted.

The wave has spent itself; it's receding. I say, 'I don't suppose Grandfather had any choice over losing his money. The Crash affected a lot of families, not only yours. And I know you had a hard time after Daddy's death, but couldn't you have seen that I was having a hard time too? Empathised? Sympathised? When I did see you, all you noticed in me were my faults.'

She looks lost, stunned, bewildered. She says nothing and the rest of the family look away, piling up their plates to help Mrs Moffat. I've shattered Mother's view not just of me, but of herself. Familiar feelings of guilt rise up ... she's old, she's suffered a thrombosis ... Oh God, I'm a mean bitch, I should have lashed out years ago, not now. I wonder why I spoke.

I feel wretched. I hate emotional scenes, avoid them like the plague, yet these last few days I've been edgy and oversensitive ... Is it premenstrual tension? Coming off the Pill has put my female system all out of kilter; I'm shockingly late, yes, that must be it ... and poor Mother's borne the brunt.

I say gently to her: 'The coffee will be here in a moment. Do you want us all to stay at the table or shall we move to more comfortable chairs and you can put your feet up on the sofa?'

13

Walking back home along roads familiar since I was born, I turn over memories of my father in my mind. In the late 60s society's rules had hardly begun to change: certainly the old demarcation lines still held for elderly parents like mine: Mother stayed at home, Daddy went to work at the bank. He was six years older than Mother, a grizzled, gentle, detached, rather serious man, well into middle age, sharing no resemblance with today's proactive, hands-on dads. We had one common passion, he and I, the Sunday tea-time television serials of classic children's books which we watched together, he puffing his pipe over my head as I snuggled on his lap. At other times he'd be hidden behind a newspaper, or deep in a book, usually some politician's biography. Still, he was my daddy, and one memory illuminates and encapsulates him for me. Mummy had taken me for a Sunday afternoon walk by the Thames in a brief interval between showers, and I can still feel the exhilaration of running along the old towpath with the March wind pushing me from behind, and my arms stretched out as wings, pretending I was soaring like the seagulls. Only I wasn't a seagull, I was a naughty girl running through puddles and my brown lace-ups were muddied. 'Change them, please,' said Mummy on our return. I tried, but the laces got snarled. I called for her help. 'I'm busy,' she said from the kitchen, 'I'm making tea. Go to Daddy.' Daddy put down his book and gave me a look of love. 'Yes, my treasure? Knots? Oh, nasty.' He lifted me up; I was cold from the winter wind, he was all toasty warm; he showed me how to deal with the horrid knots and as we settled to watch *Heidi* I thought I had the lovingest daddy in all the world. He didn't need to play with me all the time, just to be there and care; I asked no more. And then he was ill, and then he wasn't there, not ever again.

I'm walking above the Thames now and suddenly, inexplicably, the backs of my eyes are pricking and the sparkling water and the summery sailing boats are misting over. Poor, dear Daddy. I sniff wetly, emotional again. It's as if some other woman's inhabiting my mind. And then abruptly my vision of the world shifts — no, oh no, it's another person inhabiting my body. A baby. I'm pregnant.

As the thought hardens into certainty, my shaken mind speeds into overdrive. I can't, I won't have it. I'm the solitary sort, a writer; maternity's not my style and besides, I'd be a hopeless mother. But how do I stop this horror that's threatening my independence? I can't go to my doctor, he's Mother's doctor, too. Oh hell!

Steady on, it's not certain . . . There weren't that many times with Freddy before I asked him to use a condom . . . But there were enough, a voice in my head tells me. A test, that's what I need, and someone competent to advise me if the worst's confirmed.

For years I've seen advertisements for pregnancy advisory services above the escalators on the tube and despised the girls who needed their assistance. Silly cows! Organised Flora had it all in hand, didn't she? Now I rummage through my mind for a name I can telephone and nothing comes. Silly cow, Flora — the brilliant June day is mocking me. Sweat prickles in my armpits. I speed home to comb the telephone directory.

My fears are confirmed the next day in a small clinical room at a Pregnancy Advisory Service clinic not far from Richmond Bridge in Twickenham. 'The test's positive.' She's quiet, this young woman who's dealing with me, soft-voiced and calm, but I can't respond to her; I'm panic-stricken and tearful. 'I don't

251

want this,' I sob, 'I don't want it.' She looks at me, consults a colleague, then ushers me into a private room and closes the door. We sit in low easy chairs and I burble apologies at breaking down.

'I'm never like this,' I tell her furiously, 'never.' I grab a tissue from a box of man-sized on a coffee table and mop my face, but the flood won't stop. 'I'm sorry, I'm sorry.'

A badge on her cardigan tells me her name: Mandy Hill. 'It's all right,' Mandy says, pouring a glass of water from a carafe. 'Here. Take your time. It's common in your situation to be shocked and upset.'

'I can't do this!' I say. I'm sweating again and nauseated.

'Do you mean you can't go through with the pregnancy or you can't terminate it?'

I gulp water. I stare at the carpet. 'I've never contemplated having a baby. Well, I'm not the sort to yearn over squalling things in their prams.' But Mother will hate me for ever if I destroy her grandchild.

Mandy nods, waits for me to continue.

'I'm too busy. I wouldn't know what to do with a child. And anyway, I've never had that sort of a relationship. I'm not the sort to pick my partners for their parental capacities.'

'Does your partner know you've come for a pregnancy test?'

'No.'

'Do you want to tell him before you make up your mind what to do?'

Freddy. The suspicion hits me that he'd want it. No, keep him out of it. Don't want pressure, don't want guilt. 'No. Yes. Oh hell, I don't know. This should never have happened. It's all my fault, nothing to do with him. I'm the one to blame.'

'But would he be supportive if you decided to continue the pregnancy?'

I lift my head and look at this woman Mandy. She's in her late twenties, I'd say, dark-haired, brown-eyed, pale skinned. She's studying me with a neutral look that's not unsympathetic, certainly not judgemental. God, she's being clever; she's stopping my knee-jerk reaction, pushing me to engage my brain, weight up alternatives.

'Yes, I think he probably would. I honestly don't know.' But I do know. Of course he would, and he'd make an excellent father.

Again I'm given time to consider. I burst out, 'But I don't see ours as a long-term relationship. It won't work. He'll want different things from me than I'm capable of giving. He's too nice, too good.'

She smiles, almost laughs. 'Well, I've never

heard that complaint before. What's wrong with niceness? Do you mean he's weak?'

I turn my head away, clutching my shaking hands together. 'No. No, he isn't.' In fact, now I think about it, he radiates his own inner certainties. I grope for words to explain what I hardly understand myself. 'It's . . . he's so straightforward and decent and helpful . . . it's unnerving. I can't live up to it. One of these days I'll snap and be a real bitch . . . and then he'll despise me.'

'You're afraid the relationship won't last?'

I put my head in my hands. 'How can it?' The words echo round the little room. They sound ridiculous. But it's true, I'm not good. Mother's said so, my teachers said it too. None of my lovers have lasted more than three years in the balancing act that's the tightrope of love. What a mess I am. I shouldn't have let this thing with Freddy start, then this baby couldn't have started, the opportunity for hurt would never have arisen.

Mandy hasn't spoken the emotive words, your baby, your child — or abortion. But I'm beginning to use them to myself and I don't know where I'm at any more.

She leans forward. 'Do you need time to think this over?' When I nod she suggests a day or two's gap before I return — for counselling if I feel I need it, to talk through

254

my concerns. The sweat cools, the nausea retreats; control is in place. I'm given information leaflets explaining consultation procedures with advisors and doctors. They won't book me in until I'm sure. 'But if it's to be a termination then it's better it should be sooner rather than later. From what you've said you're seven or eight weeks pregnant now.'

*   *   *

I visit Pattie. I have to talk. She knows me better than anyone and she's not the judgemental sort either — except where Greg's concerned.

She opens the door, hugs me and hauls me into the sitting-room. 'Sane adult company,' she says, running her fingers through her ruddy-brown hair. 'Excellent!'

She and Greg live in what in Barnes is called a lion house — a rather ugly red brick terraced house with lions crouching on the gate-pillars and at the top of the façade. The enduring and endearing kitsch of a builder a hundred years ago. Inside it's all Pattie today: on the white walls, bold modern oil paintings she's acquired at her friends' exhibitions; on the floor, battered Edwardian furniture, Habitat sofas and an elderly rocking chair stand on a brown carpet, 'shit-coloured so the marks won't show,' all half-hidden beneath a swirl of newspapers, magazines, socks, strangely shaped pot plants, teddies, jigsaws, colourful plastic toys and children's books. By the French windows to the garden tiny Luke is lying naked, kicking vigorously against Georgy's efforts to hold tissues in place where his nappy should be.

'Hullo, Flora,' Georgy calls. 'Hey, I'm looking after Luke in case he's naughty and wees.' Georgy's clad in minute red trunks and his skin's caramel-coloured from the sun.

Pattie rescues him. 'Thank you, gorgeous. We'd just come in from the garden,' she explains to me, 'so we had to cover Luke's doings while I answered the door. Boys have such a long range. Sweet, but inconvenient indoors.'

She pulls a disposable nappy from a pack behind a sofa, and puts it on the baby in a few swift movements. She's wearing only yellow shorts and a skimpy yellow and white suntop herself, both tight over her still heavy breasts and bottom. She looks warm, slightly flushed, happy. She thanks me for having her and Greg to supper the other day.

'It was great being idle! And we liked your Freddy. He's something different, isn't he?'

'You think so?'

'Don't tell me you don't know so. He listens properly when you talk, not just waiting for a gap so he can tell you how great he is, the way most men do. He likes women too, really likes them, I mean, not just fancying them.'

Luke beams up at her. He thinks she's talking to him and moves his lips in reply. 'Aah, aaah!' he produces.

'Mmm,' she responds, 'clever boy, Luke. And he's interesting — Freddy, I mean. You stick with him, Flora.'

She buttons the baby into a tiny shirt and pants and rises from the floor, picking him up in one swift practised movement, his head cradled on her hand. Then she pivots, places him in my arms and pushes me down on to a sofa. She's going to get us cold drinks, she says, and Luke'll enjoy a cuddle with me.

She's gone and I'm left holding him. He peeps solemnly up at me, his little eyebrows twitching. It's as if he's observing me on a different plane from everyday, from some distant ancient world perhaps. I'm terrified by his fragility, yet mesmerised by those blue eyes. Dear little thing, he really is rather endearing. I manage a smile and tell him, 'You're all right, you know, young man. Not bad at all.' And then suddenly he's on the same plane as me and we're in communication: the blue eyes widen and he gives me a real 'I like you' sort of smile. I think, There's a baby in me, a globule of cells that's dividing and multiplying energetically moment by moment, and one day, if I don't stop this, I'll be looking after it, responsible. A baby like Luke, trusting me. Panic hits me, mingling with guilt and yearning in an explosive emotional ferment.

Pattie reappears with orange juice. She settles herself beside me and takes Luke back in her arms, cooing at him.

I open my mouth to say, 'Pattie, I'm pregnant, what the hell do I do?' but she's away.

'Isn't my Lukey terrific, Flora? God, I reject the whole idea of a baby because I hate being pregnant and it takes so bloody long. But when we get there it's just amazing. Even changing his nappy's a privilege. I love him so much I could eat him up with kisses.'

I glance nervously at Georgy, but he lifts his dark head from the wooden railway he's fitting together and laughs at her. 'You can't eat people with kisses, Mummy. Anyway, I shan't let you. Luke's my brother and he's got to grow up and play with me.'

'He will, darling. He will quite soon now.' She turns to me to add, 'Georgy's growing up fast these days. When I'm bathing Luke he hands me all the bits and pieces I need, bath oil and cotton wool and whatnot, and he distracts him when he's grizzling and I'm trying to cook us a meal. He's a good boy, aren't you, my treasure?'

'I water the garden, too,' Georgy informs me, coming to lean against my leg.

'He does,' Pattie confirms. 'He's more use than his father is. If a plant's wilting in the garden Greg says that it needs watering. It doesn't occur to him that *he* might water it. Georgy fills his own special can and deals with it. He's the thoughtful Freddy sort.'

She's a different Pattie, soft and gooey with motherly devotion. There's no sign in the house of oil paints or canvases, no smell of linseed oil or turps, only baby talc and milk. What was it she'd asserted to me all those months ago? Something about refusing to be one of those damned Madonna images, breathing ineffable love over their brats and looking for nothing more? Someone I scarcely know is smiling proudly across her children at me.

I drink, and the cold liquid chills my throat and gullet. I can't talk to this woman. I'm not sure I can talk to anyone.

★   ★   ★

259

As I enter the flat the telephone is ringing. Isobel. Aunt Isobel.

'Flora? Darling, that was an unexpected denunciation of your mother you made yesterday.'

Wearily I say, 'I suppose I'm in the dog-house now.'

'Oh no. goodness, no. We've been looking at you with new eyes. Primrose said rather pitifully that you'd always seemed so composed and cheerful a little person that she'd thought you were all right. You'd hardly cried for your daddy at all.'

'When I did, she cried too. I hated that, in fact it made me feel awful, because I didn't know how to make her better. So I had to stop crying.'

'Poor love.' Isobel's voice is warm with sympathy. 'Daisy said your mother's hard life shouldn't have blinded her to the rotten time her own child was having. And Laurel said bluntly that if she was going to die soon, like she kept muttering, then it was a good thing you'd got it off your chest. She wouldn't want you to be haunted by unfinished business like she'd been after *her* mother died, would she? Meaning your grandma May's rebuffs, I suppose. And then Laurel lit another cigarette and Primrose was so cowed she didn't say a word.' She chuckles. 'As sisters they are an extraordinary trio, aren't they? So unalike. But I'm devoted to them. They've been good friends to me over the years.'

'And so you've been to me,' I say with affection. 'As a child I loved those times I used to stay with you round Christmas. You gave me amazing presents, and you took me to the theatre and my first ballet and my first opera.' I remember *A Man for All Seasons*, and *Sleeping Beauty* and Mozart's *Magic Flute*. Uncle Alban took little notice of our doings; his wine business was on the point of failure and he had other things to think about: 'Good God, Isobel, wine's hardly one of your static commodities, is it? But then you wouldn't know about vintages, would you? I must go abroad to keep up to date.' If his exasperatingly successful and wealthy wife took his niece out for the evening, he could down his bottle unseen or sneak off to his mistress. Whether Isobel suffered over his transgressions or not, we always had fun.

'You were lovely to me,' I say in a thickening voice. 'And I still treasure the black leather brief-case you gave me for Cambridge.'

A second's pause, then: 'Flora, what is it? You sound . . . heavens, all emotional. Not you at all! But then . . . are you pregnant?'

'Yes.' Bleakly: 'How do you know?'

'Oh,' a faint deprecating giggle. 'I sense these things. Something in the eyes, the changing vibrations.' My delightful fey, psychic aunt. 'Are you pleased or appalled?'

'I don't know, Isobel, I don't know. Appalled, I suppose. How can I have a baby?'

'You could, you know. Better than many. But it's not for me to talk. I aborted the only babe I ever conceived.'

'You didn't!'

''Fraid so. I was in my late thirties, Alban was sloshed nine-tenths of the time, I didn't even tell him. I just went and had it dealt with, privately and hellishly expensively. I couldn't face it. I had to keep the gallery going, you see. Don't tell your mother or the others.'

'Of course not,' I say. I'm stunned.

'Will you keep yours?'

'I don't know,' I groan. 'I'm terrified, Isobel. I've been to see Pattie but I couldn't talk to her. She told me that even changing her baby's nappies was a privilege. I can't imagine being like that. And never on my own.'

Isobel understands. 'That's what frightened me. All the responsibility falling on one lone parent, no one to say, 'Hey, steady on, calm down!' when you're at screaming point. Listen, Flora darling, I'm the last person who should interfere, but would you be on your own? Your Freddy's the sticking sort, surely . . . ? Oh, but you haven't told him, have you?'

How does she know things like that, my odd perceptive aunt? 'No,' I admit.

'Tell him. You have to. He's no Alban, he deserves this at least. Bye, darling, and the best of luck.'

★　★　★

I wander into the kitchen for a drink of chilled mineral water. Do I have to tell Freddy? It's my body this scrap's inhabiting, me whose writing career will be mucked up. If I decide to have it. But Freddy . . . I do like him. Quite ridiculously much . . .

I'm still mulling it over when Freddy returns an hour later, clutching a large brown paper package and complaining of tiredness after a hellish journey from the Southampton area where he's involved in a big theme-park site: 'Three-hour meeting, no final agreement on anything. Miserable bastards.' He kisses me absently, then opens his package to show me the typescript of his landscape design book, returned for him to check his editor's corrections and amendments. He'd collected it from his cottage in

263

The Alberts on his way back. 'More work. I'll plod through it this weekend.' He smiles his lop-sided smile. 'God, I'm hot and cross and tired. I need a cold lager. Do you want one too? Orange juice, fine. Let me get them and then you can tell me about your day.'

Must I? My brain hurts from too much thought.

Seconds later he's back in the doorway. He says, 'What's this?' and his voice is odd.

I focus my tired eyes. There are pamphlets held out in his hands, the ones from the clinic. I must have left them in the kitchen. Stupid. Or was it? Perhaps my subconscious had decided to tell him. I look at him. I long for sympathy but I won't ask for it.

'Are you pregnant, Flora?'

I nod.

'Are you planning to have an abortion?'

'I don't know. Possibly.'

His voice has been neutral. Now it hardens. 'Possibly?'

I don't like his tone. 'Probably.' A childish defiance.

'Is it my child?'

'Yes.'

'You're sure?'

'Yes.'

He bites off each word: 'You're — probably

264

— going — to — abort — my — child?'
Pause. 'Is that what you're saying?'

'For God's sake, Freddy. I don't know. I don't know.' I can't take this intense stuff.

He glares. I've never seen him like this, never imagined it. There's no gentleness, no understanding, no quietly reasonable discussion. I'm hurt, and through that hurt I speak sharply.

'Freddy, it shouldn't have happened. It was hardly planned. If we'd been more careful it wouldn't ever — '

'But we weren't. And so we've made a baby.' Bitterly: 'What's that slogan you see on car rear-windows in the winter? *A pet isn't just for Christmas, it's for life.* You're giving my child less thought than a dog you might want to put down.'

His words catch me off-balance and I topple into anger. 'A child's not just for its birthday, it's for life, too. My life. Morning, noon and night. I'm a writer, I need peace and quiet and my own space. I never intended this. It's my life and my body and my decision. Who do you think you are to put all the blame and the guilt on me?'

'Me?' In great bitterness: 'I'm just the fool who happens to love you.' His voice is shaking, almost unrecognisable. 'And who hoped you might care about me. Seeing we

were living together . . . and loving together
. . . Oh hell!'

He explodes with fury, whirling round to
grab an orange from the fruit bowl on the
bookcase beside him and hurl it at my head.
Ouch. I duck too late, stagger back from its
force and my head flares into pain.

I can't handle this. I speak out of a deep
and lonely pit. 'I think you'd better go.'

He's already going, seizing his typescript,
banging the door behind him, crashing down
the stairs. His car starts, revs up and roars
away.

I collapse on to the sofa, staring down a
late slanting beam of sunshine to where it
illuminates the split and mangled orange. An
evening silence grips the room; no traffic
moves. Two minutes later I'm in the
bathroom retching my heart up.

14

In bed sleep won't come. Midnight . . . one o'clock . . . two o'clock . . . I lie with a metallic taste in my mouth, feeding my hurt with self-pity. How could Freddy have shouted at me, thrown that orange? Where is his tenderness now, the ready solicitude I'd thought so much him? I look back and think: it was a lovely dream but it faded to nothing. Vaporous sentimentality. Men are what they are, and I'm what I am, independent. I'm a writer, a loner; a person, not an appendage. I like my fun, a man in my bed, but I won't be taken over by some male and subordinated to his needs. That's why my relationships always fail. Too bad. This time it's happened earlier than usual, that's all.

Four o'clock . . . I'm exhausted, and my spirits, already low, plummet down a well of misery till I hit bottom, deep in the mud of my own nastiness. Mean antagonistic bitch that I am, I've ended it. Now I'm alone. No steady rhythm of Freddy's breathing beside me in the bed. Is this what I truly want? I sense retribution waiting to pounce, claws outstretched to tear at me for having cheated on nature, for having thought myself immune to real feeling. I must sleep, I must. Maybe by nine o'clock I'll feel brave enough to ring the clinic and book the termination of the pregnancy. Then I'll plod on with Claudia Charles, secure with the dead who have no feelings.

Five o'clock. Poor Mother. She was never independent minded, independence was forced upon her. She'll die thinking I'm blaming her for the sad years that made me what I am. No one's to blame, only the erratic swing of fortune, the wild unfairness of life. When I was small she said, 'Life isn't a game with rules, Flora. There's no one to cry 'Foul!' if it kicks you when you're down.' How right she was. And it's life's fault, our genes' fault maybe, if she and I fail to understand one another's ways of thought. Those irksome remarks that disparage me, half-accusing me of callousness, are cries for understanding. I sigh. I'll send her flowers by way of apology. They'll help her save face with Mrs Moffat at least. Finally I sleep for an hour or two.

I wake feeling sick, my body smelling stale. Outside there's sunlight and noise, the chink of milk bottles, car engines revving, human voices. People are heading for offices, taking children to school; they're involved in schedules, timetables, meetings. Inside the flat it's quiet, just the hum from the fridge-freezer, the sound of my breathing as I lie there listening. I'm outside their busy world: uninvolved.

I remember Pattie saying that breakfast cereal helped the nausea. I eat a little and it does. I shower and dress, order Mother's flowers from the florist. Then I work. Being in Claudia's world makes me feel marginally less displaced until I pick up mentions of Mother in the 1934 diary:

> *Roger and May's rebuffs have made Primrose into a colourless wisp of nothingness. Laurel has more to her at eleven than Primrose. At thirteen she should be developing opinions of her own as I did, but all she can do is pick up on others'. She's too anxious to please and in consequence, doesn't . . .*

I'm startled by this contemporary evidence of Mother being rebuffed by her parents. Poor her. But if she hated the drip, drip, drip of their snubs, why was she so repressive with me? I put the diary down. I feel awful again. Does pregnancy mean another seven months of this?

Freddy. He must return, mustn't he? He's

taken his typescript but his things are all about the place. Do I wait for him to come or do I dump them as he and I did Jake's? How we had giggled that night, bent double and hurting with glee, gloriously in charge of events. Now events are taking charge of me, pushing my body and my life out of shape. I don't want this baby but I don't want to dump Freddy. He's . . . well, he's my friend. I pace the floor, pace the flat. I remember a sentence from a Claudia review of an aspiring novelist's second novel: *The structure of the house appears sound, but there are rats in the cellar.* There are rats gnawing at the structure of my life. Oh Christ, can't I do better than this?

★ ★ ★

In the early evening I drive off to Broadcasting House for a radio interview on the paperback publication of *A Nest of Brambles*, feeling unusually apprehensive. But Saul Homer, the interviewer, an old acquaintance from Cambridge days, calms me and draws me out. He speaks of *Brambles* in his gentle, camp, erudite way, asking me to outline the issues involved in my intriguing plot and discussing how my family of protagonists moves from apparent security to

270

rabid conflict over revealed memories of a past bitterly denied, metaphorically hooking themselves on the brambles of the title, before fighting their way to a conclusion that allows them an escape, though not unscathed, 'For one sees, doesn't one, that your characters are snagged and bleeding still? Life as she is, leaving one thoughtful.' Lovely Saul, he's made it sound great stuff while giving little away. He comments on my novels being issue-rather than plot-led, and enquires whether I find it hard to build plots and sub-plots around such themes as sexual abuse in the middle-class family, or eugenics and the afterlife of sperm banks?

'No,' I say, 'because, look, the themes dictate the plots. Take an issue I've been pondering recently, whether the father should be permitted any rights in a woman's decision to terminate a pregnancy.' Hell, I can't believe I'm saying this. Might Freddy be listening? Well, too bad, it's a fair one. 'Plots fall into your mind like packages through the letter box: tough career woman rejects the idea of a screaming brat wrecking everything she's worked for, or girl living on benefit tells unemployed partner it's not fair to bring a child into poverty. Anguished partner cries, 'How can you destroy a child, my child?' Or the other extreme, married man afraid of blackmail insists on termination against his doting girl-friend's wishes. See? Several plot alternatives with all the necessary elements for success — innocent victim, contrasting characters giving rise to conflict, career at risk, love at risk, strong feelings.'

'You make it appear easy,' he says, sounding amused.

'Oh no,' I retort, 'it's then the difficult part begins. Creating credible characters, weaving in the threads of the sub-plots. Research. Sitting alone and writing, day after day. It's hard labour.'

'Giving birth, the image writers so often use of their work,' he mocks.

'Exactly so,' I manage gruffly, terrified as that same image relentlessly crawls over my eyeballs.

Afterwards I turn down Saul's suggestion of a whisky or two together: Freddy might call or ring, late though it is. I want to resolve things, though God knows how. I feel a tightness of oppression in my chest. What a mystery life is. In my books I play God and my characters respond as I ordain, but everyday existence is ruled by combinations of forces no one can control: transience, opportunity, rivalry, the thunderbolt of disease, the urges of sex. The Fates flirt with us in the precious game of life, sometimes, it seems, with malice aforethought. And we're tied, too, by our own personalities: I cannot struggle free from the restraints of my character to pick up the telephone and dial Freddy's number, though I'm admitting my need.

At midnight I drag myself to bed, thinking gloomily that none of us sets out to make a mess of our lives — it just happens. I pass another sweating night alone.

★ ★ ★

I wake late with my heart thumping from nightmare surrealistic dreams and feel nauseous when I get up. It's Saturday. I dress slowly in cool cotton top and trousers. While I'm forcing myself to eat a bowl of cornflakes the doorbell makes me jump. Freddy? I move fast. No. It's a large man with a small but heavy parcel for me, special delivery. My heart thumps as I sign his form. Is it from Freddy? No. The card says it's from Mother, with her dearest love. I unpack it and can't help smiling at a pair of little bronze cherubs. I touch their cool curls, run my fingers over the shiny curve of their bellies. But why . . . ? I suspect they come from Isobel's gallery. I telephone her and she agrees they do.

'Primrose wanted to show you her

affection, because she feared you doubted it, but poor old love, she couldn't do it in words, she told me, she'd be bound to sound stilted. 'Actions speak louder than words, don't they?' she said hopefully, and so we found the cherubs.'

'Oh, Isobel.'

I recognise the same impulses of conceal-ment existing in Mother as they do in me, the same rejection of emotional display. Yet behind that solemn and reproachful face there is a struggle with human loneliness, a need for contact. I telephone her, but no one answers. I don't suppose she'll be out for long. I decide in any case I must thank her in person, hugging her, for once persuading her to an unEnglish display of warmth.

I shop for food, stocking up the fridge, then make my way to her flat but again there's no one there. I walk on up Richmond Hill, past the Star and Garter Home and down to Petersham. It's hot and the air's dry with hay-dust from the meadows. In River Lane the trees and the undergrowth throw sombre shadows, but where the arches of the trees open out to the Thames they frame a blazing picture of sunlight on water with boats chugging and bobbing. Cyclists wobble past the walkers on the river path; overhead the sky is a periwinkle blue. This is how I remember it from the best days of childhood. I have a vivid summery sense of past and future mingling together. I ponder where the cherubs should go in my flat and I'm warm with the thought of such an unexpected and generous gesture.

I walk along the river bank till I'm level with Ham House and there I sit on the grass and contemplate the river. There's a change going on in my head that I don't understand, a loosening and softening of my character, and I'm confused as if all the ingredients of my personality have been put in a mixer to churn and churn and produce something quite different from what has been before, something still ambiguous and unintelligible, and yet, I feel, possibly good, even desirable. Insects murmur and buzz, and beyond their busy intensity the stifling air vibrates with its own heat. I clasp my knees and rest my head on them. Thoughts begin to take shape. It's some time before I stand up and brush the grass from my trousers, but when I do, I feel released.

No sooner have I inserted my key into Mother's front door than Mrs Moffat is tugging it open and clutching my hands, shaking with agitation.

'Oh, thank God, it's you. I've been trying and trying to reach you but you weren't there.' She swallows. 'Och, I'm so sorry, your mother's had a stroke.'

'A stroke?' A nightmare. Isobel had forewarned it. 'When? How bad? Where . . . ?'

'This morning.' Mrs Moffat draws me in with a hot and shaking hand. 'I heard a noise and found her on the sitting-room floor. Her puir face looked wrong, sagging you might say, and so puzzled. I tried to help her to the sofa but she'd no power to one side, so I just propped her up. The doctor said it was a stroke. It's bad but it's not very bad.'

'Where is she? Is she here . . . ?'

'Och no. No, the ambulance took her to Queen Mary's, Roehampton. I went with her. 'Musket Flora, musket Flora!' she kept mumbling and I was so stupid with the shock it took me time to understand. Then I couldn't get you. We worried you'd gone away again.' She points to the bowl of summer flowers on the mahogany table. 'She was wanting to thank you for those.'

'Oh, poor Mumma. And I wanted to thank her for something too.' I look at my watch. It's nearly two and I've had no lunch. Too bad. 'I'll drive to the hospital straight away. You've clearly coped brilliantly. God, I'm so glad you were here.'

I leave the house at a run, my arms clutching bags of items she says Mother must have. Have to pick up my car from outside my flat. Please God, let her be all right. As I dump the packages in the car I think to grab some fruit from the kitchen, something to sustain me, but as I take the stairs two at a time I know there's something else, someone else, I need more badly.

I telephone Freddy, praying he's at the little cottage in The Alberts. Three rings, four . . . 'Hullo?'

My knees go weak. I collapse into a chair. 'Freddy!'

'Hullo, Flora.' A cool, non-committal voice.

Part of me wants to be cool back but the other part is already pleading. 'Freddy? Freddy, come round, will you? Right now. Please. I need you.'

'Why's that?'

'I need your help,' I insist. 'Don't be horrid.' A short pause, then I flounder on in a hopeless wail, 'Freddy, everything's turned awful. Mother had a stroke this morning and I've got to get to the hospital — and I feel dreadful and I want you with me, now.' Is this me, tough, hard-headed Flora who can cope with anything? But I'm past caring about pride. 'Please.'

An indrawn breath. 'How's the baby?'

I return with childish disgruntlement, 'It's making me feel sick, damn you.'

'Oh, Flora! Oh dear. All right, I'll come.'

Do I detect a breath of amusement? I sit by the telephone, too stunned to move, my mouth dry. Eventually I force myself to the kitchen, to drink apple juice and eat a banana.

Freddy's key sounds in the front door lock; I'm in the kitchen doorway and I freeze. He appears and stops. We stare, eyes locked. Then, unsmiling and tense, he opens his arms and I stumble across the carpet and fling myself into them, clutching him ferociously.

'Freddy, oh Freddy.'

His arms close round me and I'm rocked like a small child against his chest. 'I'm sorry,' he says, 'I'm sorry.'

'I'm sorry, too.'

There isn't time for long and tender explanations or discussions.

'You haven't seen your mother yet? No. We'll go in my car to the hospital and you can tell me what's happened on the way. And we'll talk tonight.'

Sweat pours off me as we drive and there's a queue for the inadequate hospital car park. 'Go straight in, Flora. I'll find you somehow.'

After tramping along miles of dingy corridors I discover Mother in one of those inevitably chipped metal hospital beds, lying inert, her face frightened and somehow asymmetrical, its right side sagging. For the first time I recognise how old she is, how soon, inevitably, death will come for her. The intensity of my distress rocks me.

In a slurred voice she whispers, 'You wen' away again an' didn' tell me.'

I dump Mrs Moffat's bags on the floor, stooping to kiss and reassure her. 'No, Mumma, no; I went shopping and then went for a walk.' I stroke her bony blue-veined hand where it lies limp on the bed.

She moves it a little, quivering. 'My han' feels 'zo I'm wearing a . . . big glove . . . 'S all wrong . . . ' she searches for the word . . . 'clumsy. 'N my ri' leg 'n my arm won' work, all aching. Stroke.'

'I know. Mrs Moffat told me. But the doctor told her you're going to be all right, Mumma. If you're good and do all your exercises you'll be out of here in a week or two.'

Mother is distressed and cross. 'Ish too long. Bed'sh rotten hard . . . hate hoshpitals.'

I straighten and push back the damp hair that's straggling across her forehead. 'I know, but try not to worry about it. Fretting is bad for you.' I remember the bags Mrs Moffat had thrust into my hands and I unpack her clothes and toiletries into her bedside locker. 'Look, here are your pretty nighties and sweet smells, and then — oh, help — here are your flowers in this Waitrose bag, but we must give them some water.'

The arrangement of delphiniums and roses is in oasis in its own plastic bowl. I trickle water from her bedside glass on to it, splashing my sandalled feet as I do so, then I place it on the table-on-wheels thing that straddles the bed, and she struggles to tell me how pleased she was to get them. 'So priddy, sho kind.'

'Ssh. I know. And what about my lovely cherubs?' My throat constricts. I retrieve a battered plastic chair from beside another bed, and sit stroking her hand again, and telling her how I'd been so overwhelmed by the bronze babies that I'd almost burst into tears. 'It was much, much, much too generous of you, Mother, and I shall treasure them for ever. They're just . . . I couldn't think of anything you could have given me I'd like more.'

She fixes her eyes on me with a gravity that's disturbing. She attempts to say something about my childhood, but I put my finger to her lips. 'It wasn't your fault. It was one of those things. I know your own childhood was sad, and you had a hard time bringing me up, too. Fate repeated itself in a rotten way, God knows why. I don't blame you, truly I don't. I shouldn't have said anything.' And then compassion for her wrings my heart, lying there all anxious and vulnerable, and I want so much to see that little wrinkled face relax and lose its frightened look that I blurt it out, pitifully, sentimentally, and with a sense of having truly burnt my boats: 'Mother, listen to my news. I'm going to have a baby. You're a grandma-in-waiting.'

Her papery eyelids seem to quiver in disbelief, but her smile, when it comes, is almost perfect. 'Uou?' she fumbles. 'Uou an' Fleddy, a baby?'

I put my cheek against hers. 'Yes. At the end of January, I think. So you have to get better, don't you? I'll need you to babysit.'

A happy tear dislodges itself from the corner of her eye and trickles towards the hospital pillow. 'Mumma. Gran'ma.' And she mumbles something else, and I grasp that I'm not to tell boastful Daisy about it, but leave that triumph to her. If the old regress to second childhood, Mother's back in the nursery, saying: So there and yah boo! And she's half-laughing at herself and half-weepy with delight, and I dab her eyes with a tissue, and it's at this point that Freddy arrives with a well-upholstered staff nurse in tow.

Mother flutters her good hand at him and

insists that Freddy kiss her, while the Irish staff nurse insists on no excitement for her patient, and no feeling sorry for herself or weepy, because she's going to be foine, but Mother seizes her wrist with the good hand and retorts with surprising clarity that she's goin' to do the besht ever becorsh she's goin' to be a grandma. 'Schampagne,' she says, quite unlike her normal self, 'oughta have schampagne!' The staff nurse takes her seriously and says, 'You most certainly ought not.' And Freddy gives me a strange look and I giggle deprecatingly and say I couldn't keep it from her, could I? 'Because look at her, it's made her so happy.'

Buxom authority asserts her influence and insists that Mrs Monk must lie quietly. 'Afther all, she's had a bad shock and a good shock both, and though I'm shure the baby'll be lovely, she's had more than enough for one day.'

We kiss Mother goodbye; she leans back into her pillows and her eyes shine.

The staff nurse shepherds us out of the ward and I start to demand answers to the questions that are plaguing me, but Freddy wants to take me home. 'Look, Flora, I think I've discovered most of what you'll want to know from the nurse, but if I can't explain anything, well, we'll be back tomorrow and you can find out then. You're looking distinctly bleak. Aren't you going to need rest too?'

I'm on the point of launching into him for interfering when I realise that I'm feeling quite revoltingly done in. 'All right,' I concede gruffly. 'Thanks.'

15

In the car he tells me that he's spoken to both the staff nurse and a doctor on duty on the ward, and been reassured. The stroke was not severe and Mother's mind, though slow, seems clear — which is more than mine is, especially when Freddy uses words like 'cerebro-vascular accident'. 'Of course,' the doctor had said, 'the future depends on what's happening in the brain, and whether there's further bleeding which could damage more of the vital areas there. Given no recurrence there's every possibility of a fair recovery.' Tomorrow, all being well, a physiotherapist will begin exercising her arm and her leg.

Exhaustion flattens me. We drive through Richmond Park and I'm aware of the heavy living weight of my body sagging in the car seat. I shut my eyes, then open them as Freddy brakes. Half a dozen young fallow deer are hesitating by the side of the road while waiting cars pant fumes into the warm air. A stag turns his head, then, suddenly assured, trots over, a handsome fellow swiftly followed by his companions, until all are leaping and bounding over the turf on the far side. They're full of life and wild grace that seems timeless. But in the hospital Mother lies imprisoned by her weakened body, and while the doctors and nurses may speak of recovery it's clear that for her time is dwindling. Two warnings now. Will she be third time lucky? Will she live long enough to see my child, her grandchild, trotting and leaping on the summer grass? I've never seriously contemplated Mother's death; she's part of my life. Her end, as with her beginning, was connected with some mythological time; now I'm faced with a corporeal happening that's poised to occur. Death. A void. I've prized my independence from her and fought to be my own person; sometimes she's made me scream with irritation or burn with embarrassment, yet when she goes who will have her focus on everything I do, who give validity to my achievements and boast of my successes? I put my hand on Freddy's thigh, the warm firm flesh a reassurance against the disturbance of my thoughts.

His hand touches mine, then he swings the car round and out through the park gates. 'We must talk, you and I,' he says, 'talk and talk.'

'Yes,' I agree, 'but Freddy, before you take me home, do you mind if I have a word with

Mrs Moffat? To decide what she's to do. To thank her for being a tower of strength.'

'Of course.'

Mrs Moffat is troubled but practical, she wants to know how Mother seems to us, and she needs to know what to do about the flat. She looks at me distrustfully. 'Is she likely to be long in hospital, and will you want me to care for her when she does come out? Or will you send her to a nursing home? I don't want to cause expense staying on here unnecessarily.' Hers is the position of someone who has always been reliant on the needs and goodwill of others; I catch my breath at the humility implicit in her desire not to intrude. I hug her shoulders and say that on no account is she to desert us until we know sufficient to make a decision, that the expense is nothing.

'What would Mother have done without you today? You've been magnificent in a crisis that must have been frightening, and if it weren't for the fact that there's no florist on the Hill I'd be pushing a bouquet of flowers into your arms this very minute.'

The wrinkles on her brown face relax. 'Och well, I only did what anyone would. And if Mrs Monk's reasonably mobile when she comes out, I'll look after her. Just as long as she can get herself to the bathroom.'

I look at the sitting-room that she's

transformed, making it so much lighter and more cheerful with her bowls of bright flowers, embroidered cushion covers and gleaming polish that I hardly know it. I say from the depths of my tiredness: 'I'm sure Mother would like that best of anything. We'll wait for the doctors' say-so. Let me know if you want to pop back to your bungalow for anything and I'll drive you there. No, it's no problem.'

★ ★ ★

'You can be very kind when you want,' Freddy says, pushing me down on to my own sofa.

'I'm always kind.'

'Then why be vile to me?' He stands, hands in his trouser pockets, studying me.

'Because you were being horrid,' I say in a small voice. I reach for a cushion and tuck it in the small of my back. 'Typical man, you assumed the worst of me, then concentrated on your own feelings.'

'When you let me find that leaflet on abortions? Are you surprised?'

'Yes, since you ask. I hadn't decided on anything.'

'But you were considering it — an abortion, that is?'

'Obviously.'

'You didn't want my child.' A statement, not a question. A statement of hurt.

'I didn't think of it in those immediate parental terms. When I realised what had happened I was terrified, if you want to know. I panicked.'

'Why?'

'Surely you can see that?' I say. 'I never planned for a child, I've never had that sort of relationship, and anyway, I'm working flat out on the Claudia Charles biography. When I realised what had happened, it . . . well, it hit me as a catastrophic failure of contraception I'd have to deal with.'

'Didn't you think how I might feel? That I might want to stick around for this baby? And for you?'

'No. Things don't work out that simply. Partners come and go.' I shut my eyes. I know this discussion has to be, but right now I haven't the intellectual energy. Besides, Freddy's calm now, but things are likely to become intense and, remembering the resentful squabbles I've endured over the years with Jake and Magnus and the others, the thought fills me with horror: I don't want self-evident truths about my despicable self hurled at my head, I want to lie down and drift into a trance of nothingness.

I hear him leave the room and then return; a cool glass is thrust into my hand.

'I know alcohol isn't supposed to be the thing during pregnancy, but a spritzer won't hurt.'

I open my eyes. 'Thanks, Freddy.' He's poured himself a whisky.

'I'm sorry, you really have had enough, haven't you? Look, in a minute, when you've got some colour back in your cheeks, I'll take you out to dinner.'

I sip and start to laugh over my glass at him. 'You won't, you know. On a hot Saturday evening in June? With the lure of the river and the hill all the world will be in Richmond and there won't be a table anywhere. We'll have dinner here.'

'But what . . . ? Oh Flora — you couldn't have . . . ?'

'Shopped for two? Yes, I did. I was willing you to call . . . Hey, Freddy, wait a minute — that's why you aren't in Sussex. *You* were willing *me* . . . '

Then he's down on the sofa too, and we're both laughing and hugging and rocking. The remains of my spritzer are dripping on his knees and his whisky is dribbling down the small of my back. My face is buried in his solid male neck and I'm breathing in his familiar scent, and somehow in that moment it's all one in my mind with the male smell and warm security of my father's arms, more than a quarter of century ago. He's dead, but Freddy's here and he's real, more real than anyone I've ever known.

'I felt so rejected,' he grumbles after we've eaten food he's cooked (grilled salmon and crisply sautéed potatoes with a tossed green salad) and we're back on the sofa, drinking coffee. 'When I saw those leaflets it was like an almighty kick in the stomach. I thought you didn't give a damn, that I'd been a passing fancy to console you for Jake's treachery, worse, to preserve your face with your world. I felt used . . . utterly mortified.'

'Oh, Freddy.' I take his hand and lay it on my belly. 'I was mortified too. You shouted at me, you hurled that orange at my head. I was all screwed up. I felt so angry and ashamed at being such a miserable bitch, I couldn't handle it at all. And you'd believed the worst of me straight away.'

'You didn't deny it.'

'I was frightened. How could I bring up a child on my own, with my background? I'm not a fit person.'

'Rubbish. Besides, you knew I'd be there.'

'Would you? I couldn't count on that.'

'Flora, I'd said I loved you. Couldn't you believe I'd be around? I shall, you know;

you're not getting rid of me.'

I clutch his hand. 'I can't imagine *ever* believing. You'll have to keep telling me.' I can't conceive of such affection, such calm self-confidence.

'Don't you have any belief in yourself then?'

'Oh yes, I believe in me, within my own limits, just not in people. People don't stay. If they don't walk out, they die. My father, my uncle Alban. In my family only Daisy's kept her husband and there's little love lost there. They're stuck because the Church's miserable pension leaves them too poor to part.' I lift my head and say with some spirit, 'Anyway, I don't see why you should love me.'

He puts down his coffee cup. He says dryly: 'It isn't necessarily a matter of choice, you know. It happens, attraction, like lightning. You can't argue with it.'

I shake my head. 'Nonsense. You try it, you analyse it, and if the other parts aren't right, you walk away. Sooner or later. And what do we mean by love? An insurance against loneliness? A relieving of sexual tension? A warm body beside your own on a squally night?'

'Oh, all those things, but more, far more.' He's frowning now, and serious. 'What a

291

difficult woman you are, Flora. You know there is emotion in which sex isn't the only element. Listen, love is something that touches the soul, it's a delight in the essence of a person. Sex is on a different level, it's required by the sexual appetite. But if a man marries a woman who has the capacity to be a mistress — something not every man can cope with — then that love is expressed and completed by sex. For me the blend's right — and the sex was perfect from night one, wasn't it? Wasn't it?'

I can't prevent a reminiscent grin from flitting across my lips. 'Superb.'

He leans over to kiss my nose. 'Well then . . . You're sharp, tough and terrific and you've got me hooked.'

I'm silent. He's described me without restriction or qualification, giving me a value all my own. And the qualities Mother deplores are positive attributes for him. Good feelings glow inside me — Mozart and Bach and mountains-at-dawn feelings.

'I heard you on the radio,' he murmers, 'talking to Saul Homer. You spoke of pondering a father's rights, of the anguished partner. Was that directed at me?'

'It . . . I suppose it welled up from my sub-conscious . . . I couldn't believe what I was saying . . . and then I had to organise my words, and finally I was praying you were out there, connected.'

'I was. My mother heard you too. I'd . . . we've spoken about you and I suggested she should listen. She telephoned to say she thought you sounded very thoughtful, very bright. She wants to meet you. And my brother, too.'

'When?' I ask uneasily.

'Would a week's time be all right? Sunday lunch?'

I agree. How can I not, when he already knows all my eccentric family? Then it bursts out of me: 'Freddy, if we're going to stay together, give me breathing space, won't you? Equal partners. Don't ever try to dominate me. Or throw things at my head.'

He sits up, suddenly aggrieved. 'Flora, you're being perverse. What do you mean — *if?* Interdependence, that's how it'll be with us. It's inevitable we'll have our fights, but you might recognise that I went away in order *not* to bully you into agreeing with me over the baby, and that it hurt like hell.'

'Sorry,' I mutter.

He adds with a certain relish, 'And if you think that babies care for anyone's independence, you can think again. They're authoritarian and demanding to the last four a.m. yell.'

When I visit Mother over the next two days she's making good progress, her speech is not perfect but it's significantly better, and there are two matters uppermost in her mind: how soon she can go home, and — even more important, this — when will Freddy and I be married?

'We haven't discussed it. There's time enough, isn't there?'

No, she argues, from the very start we must be pledged together, dedicated to our child. If dear Freddy doesn't raise the matter, and she's surprised he hasn't, then I must.

On the second afternoon her good hand grasps my wrist and she leans quite perilously from the chair the nurse has sat her in, making her point slowly, but with clarity. 'To have the right pieces of paper ish the foundation of people's pride ... An' their confidence.'

'The birth certificate? The marriage certificate? We don't belong to the marriage generation, Mumma. Pieces of paper is all they are.'

'Don't deshpise pieces of paper,' she insists, her hand shaking my wrist. 'They ... prove loving intent. Ack ... *acknowledgement*. A child needs two parents ... jus' as much as it needs two legs . . . It hurt you not to have your father, Flora, didn't it?'

Our eyes meet. She's passionate about this and I think that it's because of my recent comments. I free my wrist and pat her arm, feeling fond of her in her earnestness. We're talking in simple direct terms as we haven't talked for years, and I wish we had managed it long before this.

''S my gran'child. I want the besht.'

'I know. But don't push us, Mumma; give us time to come to terms with it all.' Her eyes are huge in a face that looks shrunken. She's breathing rapidly, she's very tense. 'We're going to stay together, Freddy and I. Calm down, your grandchild will have all the love we can give.'

She rests her head against the shiny green plastic of the chairback, suddenly tired. A sigh escapes her. 'Unselfish love'sh what you musht have. Marry. You musht marry.'

'And you mustn't worry and fuss.'

'Quite right!' a passing nurse carols. 'Keeping cheerful, that's the best medicine!'

Mother watches with a haughty baleful look as she bustles along the ward. 'Deteshtable woman, treating ush like children, jollying ush along. Ish demeaning. D'you know, she callsh me *Primmy*? When I was a child, her sort came to the *back* door.'

★　★　★

In the evenings Freddy and I sit together at
the dining-table, he checking his copyedited
typescript, me correcting the proofs of my
first collection of short stories, *Thoughts in
Indigo*, by sheer coincidence just arrived. It's
due for publication later in the year. I help
Freddy as he struggles with proofreader's
marks, feeling capable and in control for the
first time in days. I've made Freddy show me
some of the sites he's worked on in the
London Dockland area and drawn breath in
admiration of his visual creativity in helping
to change a hinterland of crumbling mon-
strosities into a modern place of light and
shade and charm, areas fit for a new
generation to inhabit. Now this work he's
written rocks me with the sheer mass of detail
he can control, something that's demonstrated again and again by the accompanying
plans and photographs. I'm captured by two
shots of an urban scene somewhere in south
London, where, miraculously, bleak high-rise
flats are diminished by half, concrete
walkways banished, littered wastelands transformed. My eyes linger on curves of grass
and trees, on a geniality of ruddy bricks and
sturdy paving, on children playing in the
sun. I'm disturbed by the mystery of

personality. I begin to know Freddy in a different way.

* * *

The second day I've an interview with Ruth, my second cousin and Great-aunt Selina's granddaughter. We've only ever met at family weddings and funerals but she greets me with fat kisses on both cheeks, bouncing at me like her springer spaniel bitch, though she's over seventy. She's a comfortably-off widow of many years standing, and childless.

'Lovely to see you,' she says, 'just lovely. But how's poor Primrose? A stroke sounds horrid, like the knell of parting day, or something. God, I hope I shan't have one of those. She's doing well? Oh good. She'll be back home and dashing around with a Zimmer frame in no time. Watch out for your ankles. And how's her mind? I do believe the mind is of the essence, don't you? Even if it's only for gossip. I enjoy a good goss.'

'Her mind seems surprisingly strong.'

'That's it, that's the way,' Ruth says vigorously. 'Now, tell me, was it at Claudia's memorial service we last met? It was. Oh good, then my memory's not as bad as I feared. Awful service, wasn't it? Pretentious. As she'd laid down, I suppose. But then old

Claudia never quite knew who she was — socially, I mean, she knew intellectually all right — but socially she had to do a lot of pretending, or perhaps inventing would be a kinder word. Don't you think?'

'I think that's the sort of question I'm going to be asking you,' I respond.

'Oh good,' she chortles. 'What fun. Now, we'll sit outside, can't waste the sunshine, can we? And what about Pimms? Lots of Pimms? It's all ready under the roses.'

'At this time of day?' I ask, amused at the ten-o'clock start. 'No, I'd rather drink fruit juice and stay sober.'

'Up to you. I shan't. I've passed my three score years and ten, now I'm celebrating every bonus day.' Her brandy-brown eyes sparkle at the thought. She pours my orange juice, then leads me out to the tangled delights of her cottage garden in Henley-on-Thames, and, as she's said, Pimms awaits her in a bower of roses.

Ruth is not unlike Claudia, her first cousin once removed. The big, imperious sensuous face, the stocky body, the heavy legs all vividly recall Claudia. But Ruth does not have such a driven personality, and her vitality's touched with an indulgence for others' weaknesses that Claudia never had. I feel certain that her ruling passion, bridge, is played without the caustic post-mortems Claudia was said to inflict on her fellow players if they made the smallest error.

'Well,' she says, filling her glass, 'here's to the great biography. Cheers.' She places her ample behind on a wooden slatted garden chair, kicks off the shoes from her fat feet and sighs with relief. 'What were we saying about the old girl? Pretending? Inventing? Her father, old Robert, was a bit dubious, a bankrupt who never paid his debts off among other matters. You didn't know that? Oh Lord, yes. At various times Grandma Selina described her brother-in-law as a brilliant man who never found his own métier in life, a wild man, even a charlatan, to Claudia's fury. And then Claudia's own erratic and erotic past was one to live down in the thirties. So when she went all respectable and married Spenser she had to reinvent herself, her history and her background. Remember that country house in Berkshire they lived in for years and years? And made so incredible? A case in point.'

'Yes, I've never understood why they chose to live there. It wasn't a literary or an artistic village.' And Mother'd dismissed the house as untruthful. Had she meant pretentious?

'They lived there because they both envied the country gentry and wanted to be thought part of that life. God knows why. To give an appearance of solid worth, I suppose, in addition to the real solid wealth she'd achieved. And they could motor up the A4 to London. But their neighbours viewed them and their guests with amazement. In those days intellectuals were regarded with mistrust, associated with Bolsheviks and other revolutionaries, worst of all, with decadents — oh, how dreadful. Besides, neither of them hunted. The local squires stared at their brimful glittering rooms and gaped at the baroque extravaganzas Claudia wore, condescended to eat one or two of the rich dinners they were offered, then dismissed her if not him as eccentric, quite bizarre.'

The spaniel sits by my feet and paws me. 'Down, girl! Did Great-aunt Selina and Uncle Lucian visit her there?'

'Once or twice. Little love lost there, of course. Yet Claudia stayed in touch . . . as if Grandma were a hated mother, someone you loathe but can never quite break free from — because somehow you must force her to change into the person you feel she should be, the one who'll support and glorify you. At the time of her marriage Claudia insisted they should visit Wingreen Place and pay tribute to its wonders — not to mention her tremendous respectability with

Spenser — and so they did, but I imagine they must have reeled. And the next year the war broke out, and soon Grandma and Grandpa were down in Kent, entertaining RAF officers and running things, and far too busy to visit Berkshire. And Claudia was too busy to visit them. She was already fighting for her refugees and stateless persons, Jewish intellectuals who'd fled the Nazis and a Lithuanian pair who'd fled the communists and been washed like flotsam with the tide across Europe until they finally landed on her doorstep. Strange, displaced, demanding, almost paranoid men and women. Twice I spent a week of my school holidays there; naturally their conversation was way above my head, never mind their strange accents, but I do remember a man who regularly raised shaking hands to Heaven to denounce God for His blind pitiless indifference to the Nazi gas chambers, and another who got the whole household into bad odour by quietly, persistently, seducing the local land-girls. I suppose sex was all that kept him sane, poor man. But temperamental, sick or not, they were academics of real worth; they wouldn't have been landed on her otherwise, by their friends or by the authorities. Old Christabel Pierce could tell you more if you want; she loved to save on her ration books by sponging on Claudia. Oddly enough, Claudia handled these people brilliantly.'

'Why oddly?' I push the insistent spaniel away.

'Nina, stop it! Take no notice, Flora, she's on heat, that's why she's being silly. Oh, Claudia wasn't ordinarily patient with people who weren't as tough and organised as her, but these were different. She bombarded the Home Office on their behalf, she wrote letters to influential acquaintances, she published articles appealing for cash and positive action. She moved mountains.' Ruth chortles and gulps her Pimms, giving me a sideways look. 'Perhaps she had a fellow feeling for the exiles' displaced persons category. You could say she was displaced in her time as well as her background, couldn't you, with those challenging books of hers? They annoyed Grandma Selina — she feared the message would become the movement.'

'Career equality for women, sexual permissiveness, the simplification of divorce? So it did.'

'But not strongly until the mid-sixties, after Grandma was dead. Right to the end she was denouncing what she called modern views, insisting that no decent married woman should shame her husband by working, as if he couldn't afford to keep her. Those with time on their hands should do charitable work, as she did.'

'I've always heard she was a forceful character. Is that how you'd describe her?'

'Very powerful. Nowadays you'd probably find her the chief probation officer for some area, or a QC or even a judge. Criminology fascinated her. In London she worked with prisoners' wives to sort out their money and family problems.' She laughs, pouring herself another large Pimms and pressing cheese straws on me. 'And no one ever cheeked her or shoved her out of the door for an interfering busybody. Oh no. She didn't condemn, you see, she befriended. When her women ran into difficulties it was because their men had been foolish and times were bad. She said to me once: 'They find it hard to think straight. And they're so alone.' But she knew how to deal with people. Official-dom beware.' She munches a stout cheese straw, crumbs tumbling down her bosom.

'So how do you explain Claudia's antago-nism, culminating in that portrait of her as the oppressive Aunt Hermione in *The Fountain of Living Waters*? She had to be seething with hatred to do that to a woman still living who'd cared for her as a child, don't you think?'

'Goodness, yes. But then Claudia was a

great hater: her brother Edward, Laurence Britton's wife, Minna, that KC she had an affair with, Denzil Vaughan, any reviewer who dared to criticise her — while to the end she was attributing almost every vexation or sorrow of her life to poor old Grandma Selina. Why, frankly, is an enigma to me. I adored Grandma, despite her disapproval of my modern attitudes. But then I was of another generation and our views were in the ascendant.'

'Selina must have been dreadfully hurt by the Hermione portrayal,' I prod.

'Passionately so. Mother told me she was beside herself with anger. She said Claudia had treated her kindness with ingratitude and stolen her good character. And for a woman like her, bristling with lofty sensitivities, it must have been devastating.'

I nod. All novelists steal from real life, but to plunder and wound your family as Claudia had with Edward and Aunt Selina seems indefensible. And I still don't know why.

'Claudia, of course, used the old defence of: 'I didn't do it, but if I did it was justified.' Heavens, is that the time? I must bring the lunch out, Flora, you're looking tired, quite peaky. Have some Pimms, dear, do. Yes, Grandma was deeply hurt, but then Claudia and she each went into denial that she was

Hermione and for years it was all buried. It didn't become public until after Claudia's death, with Susie Peters' memoir resuscitating the stories and the reviewers and the journalists lapping it all up. Sad.'

'What was the particular event or happening that sparked the attack?'

'I've never known. We were very middle-class, very repressed in those days. Like Matilda's aunt, one gasped and stretched one's eyes at each startling new Claudia revelation, but gossip was thought fearfully bad form. Grandma wrestled with her morals when she was young but by the time of *The Fountain* she must have been habituated to Claudia's behaviour, wouldn't you think? God knows what past resentment prompted her to that. Or to portray poor Edward as Lennox, either.'

'Did you like Claudia?'

'What do you mean, *like* her? I *adored* her. She was shrewd and witty and brimful of energy. We'd laugh and talk by the hour. A weekend at Wingreen Place with her and her friends left one reeling with mental and physical indigestion, but God, it was rich and stimulating fare. I know she could be a wicked old bitch at times, but she never was with me. I do miss her, you know, quite terribly.'

★ ★ ★

When I arrive home there's a message on the answerphone, and it's Pattie shrieking, 'What's this I hear from poor dear old Aunt Primrose about you having a baby? Telephone me *at once!*'

Meekly I dial her number.

'Flora? Why haven't you told me? I take it it's Freddy's?'

'Yep.'

'I thought you weren't interested in having children, though. What's changed you?'

'The baby. And Freddy.'

'Like that, was it? Unintentional.'

'Yes. But now it's intentional.'

Pattie sucks in her breath. 'Amazing. I never thought you would.' Along with her voice comes the sound of little Luke making grumbling noises to himself. Not loud but persistent, rather endearing in fact. 'Hold on a second while I pick up Luke, he's winding himself up to yell for his next feed, so he might as well get on with it while we talk.'

'Fine.'

Indistinct sounds off are followed by distinct gulping noises. 'There, he's happy.'

'I can hear him. Greedy little fellow, isn't he?'

'Don't try to distract me, Flora, I want to

306

know everything. How long have you known? How do you feel? When's it due?'

'I've known less than a week. I feel nauseous on and off, but it's not too bad. What was the other question? Due date? I think the end of January.'

'And you're staying with Freddy? You're sure about it?'

'Pattie, must you ask such awful invasive questions? Yes, I think so. As much as one can be this early on.'

'I must say, he's a thousand times nicer than Jake or the others. Top rating for charm and decency.'

'Top rating in everything,' I say fondly.

'Including bed?' she says slyly.

'Superb. Among the classics. Like a Rembrandt to a bicycling Jackson Pollock.'

'Oh? I'd have thought you'd prefer the moderns.'

'No, I've never fancied it cycling, thank you, or soaked in formaldehyde.'

We're off into gusts of giggles.

'Are you planning to marry? Aunt Primrose is determined you shall, you know.'

This swiftly sobers me. 'Don't you start, Pattie, just don't start. My head's dizzy at motherhood. Leave marriage out of it until I've recovered my mental balance. Yes, Freddy's great and I'm willing this to stick, but there's a lot to work through. To start with, he has a house in Sussex, I love my flat in Richmond, and we haven't even begun to talk about where we'll live, let alone life-long commitment.'

'Commitment should come first, not last,' Pattie observes righteously. 'Put your priorities in order, Flora. You're not deciding on a car or a new kitchen, you're creating a new person, all dependent and vulnerable, and it should have the male angle on life and male support, as well as what you'll give it.'

I gasp at this. 'You hypocrite, Pattie. Talk about changing your mind — you're spinning like a top! Who's listened to your endless moans about the general uselessness of men and the specific uselessness of Greg? Who's consoled and counselled you by the hour through your pregnancies? You've been enough to put anyone off the family scene.'

'Oh God, I suppose I have,' she admits. 'I am a cow, aren't I, going for you? When you've been my life-line. Hey, but then that makes you a hypocrite, too, doesn't it? You were supporting the status quo all the way . . . I don't recollect *you* ever suggesting I should cut free.'

And then we're both laughing and she's going on breathlessly, 'And I'm enjoying Luke so much you wouldn't believe. Whoops,

Luke, let's sit you up for a burp. I warn you, Flora, you shouldn't laugh when you're breast feeding, it jiggles the boobs and the babe sucks in great bubbles of air.' Strange noises come down the telephone. 'Oh Lukey, clever boy. There. Other side now. Flora? Listen, love, as one who's been through the fire, I may have moaned, yes, all right, still do moan, but essentially, it's how it has to be. Greg adores the boys and I'm glad I had two parents, even if Ma did shriek at Pa, and Pa tell her she was a silly woman. That was reality and reality was bearable. It taught me that life doesn't have to be all sunshine to be enjoyable. And though you might not think it, when times are bad the two of them do come together to support one another, and us.'

When she's rung off I think about parenthood. Pattie and old Daisy agree about nothing, they argue in great screams of fury and then fall about laughing. It's a warm relationship between opposites. Mine, with my mother, would have been a frigid non-relationship if I hadn't been determined to prove that I was a nicer character than she feared. Over the years I've fought and almost thought I'd won, but still I feel the pressure of her worried disapproval, still suffer the guilt I don't believe I deserve. The warmth has been little and rare. But then Mother was never instructed in love, not in the cool communications that were all she had with her own father and mother. That's why I can't make the break that some of my friends have made from their parents; it would be cruel. I might not be the conformist daughter she'd like, but she's had enough of rejection and loss, she needs me for her grumblings. So, there she stands between me and my choices. As a child I learned nothing of how to live with a man in long-term affection. I'm not sure if I can combine successfully, and I still find it impossible to make demands on men, even in the short-term fun affairs I've had until now. I'm afraid of obligations. I wonder, as I sit with Mumma later on, can I break free from the pattern to radiate the love my baby will need, and embrace Freddy in it too?

16

Freddy's mother's insisting we come for the weekend, not just for lunch, so I nip to the hospital early on Saturday and promise Mother I'll return next evening to tell her all. She'd prefer two visits each day, but she's placated with a big golden box of soft-centred chocolates from the House of Chocolate on Richmond Green (bilberry, passion fruit, apricot and rose creams) and, more than anything, by the thought that I'm meeting Paula Gulliver.

'It's important, the day you meet your future mother-in-law. You aren't going to wear those white jeans, are you? Much too casual. Have you bought her a nice present?'

'Yes, I have; a big box of chocolates like yours.'

This seems right to her, something of a chocoholic. 'Yes, that's suitable.'

I try to discover how the physiotherapy is going, but her entire small frame, quivering and poised mosquito-like in a chair that's moored by her bed in a swamp of morning-wet floor, is fixed on the objective of my marriage. Her demands sting me.

'You must fix the date this weekend.'

Beady old eyes stare from other chairs and beds. I pass Mother a rose cream and keep my voice low. 'Mumma, stop it. That's not what we're going to Buckinghamshire for. Freddy and I will be together — but as two independent people. That's how I see it.'

A chomping on her chocolate and a furious wave of her good hand dismisses this as inconsequential. She swallows, mutters furiously, 'I'm not concerned with you, Flora, you can be as selfish as you like where your own existence is concerned; it's the child that matters. I knew a girl who used to take a friend to support her when she applied for a passport or anything similar. 'Father: *Unknown*', her birth certificate said. Without his acknowledgement she might as well have been a prostitute's child. Petty officials despised her, her employers looked down on her. She cried with the shame. Would known but unmarried parents be any better?'

'Oh, come on,' I coax her. 'You're back in the dark days of your youth.'

Mother shakes her head. 'Children's feelings haven't changed. They need the security of really belonging.'

I've never known her so adamant.

The usual nurse appears in the doorway. 'Out of that chair, Primmy,' she calls in a half-palsy, half-bullying tone, 'time you took another walk. You'll never go dancing again if you don't do your exercises, will you now? And you, Dotty, and Marge.'

Mother glares.

I seize the opportunity. 'I must go, Mother. We can talk again tomorrow.'

I help her up, hand her her Zimmer frame, kiss her and nip out, to catch up with the nurse in the corridor. 'My mother's name is *Primrose* Monk,' I tell her, 'not Primmy. But since she's not a child, couldn't you leave her some dignity? Couldn't you call her Mrs Monk?'

The nurse misses the point. In a voice of affront she says: 'These days we believe in being friendly.'

* * *

The aggravations at the hospital have soured my mood. As I step into the car beside Freddy for the drive to Buckinghamshire I say, 'Don't talk to me. I'm in snarling mood.' He watches me as I wrestle with the seatbelt, my lips thin, then with swift emphatic competence he starts the car, backs, turns and slides us into the flow of traffic.

'Want to tell me why?'

'No.' I shut my eyes.

'All right,' he says equably.

When we stop for traffic lights, he selects a cassette for the car tape-deck and switches on. It's a selection of Schubert songs, favourites of mine. The sounds swirl over me, serenity could be within touching distance. I wind my seat to the reclining position. Curling up, I mutter, 'Mother was niggly, nurse was bloody condescending. But you're the best man in the world and I love you quite absurdly.'

'Oh good,' he says, and there's a funny catch in his voice. 'Now go to sleep, Flora.'

It's a midsummer day of mature sunshine and I obey him, drowsing in my seat, giving way for once to the tiredness of early pregnancy.

I'm woken perhaps an hour later by Freddy bumping the car on to a grass verge. We're on a road running down the scarp of the Chilterns and he pulls me out, despite my sleepy protests, puts his arm round my shoulders and turns me to look at the green shimmer of the countryside below, peaceful, self-sufficient. In the near distance I see the south-facing front of a manor house, ancient and comely, with the pale lawns and dark cedars of its gardens about it, while close beyond, the sun catches on the slates and tiles and thatched roofs of its village and reflects them back to us. There are big old yews around a church, and a row of pollarded willows marks the line of a stream. 'That's where I was brought up,' he tells me.

I blink. 'That house, that village? It's like looking down the centuries.' It's the sort of place where I imagine time spinning out unhurriedly, a human place for millennia yet still intact, unsullied by traffic emissions or the detritus of crowded city streets. From above us on the hill come sheep cries, and up in the sky the spiralling larks are singing. I glance at his calm spectacled face and it's as if something's switched in my perception of him and his mother, the feeling of apprehension that's been nagging me replaced by pleasurable anticipation. My own mother and the hospital are on a different planet.

When we reach the house we walk in through its wide-flung door and Freddy calls but no one answers. 'She'll be in the garden,' he says, leading me through a huge sunlit drawing-room and out on to a wide stone terrace. There are cane chairs here and a table, sheltered by a delightfully old-fashioned striped awning that reminds me of Edwardian novels. But there's no sign of a female presence.

Freddy bellows, 'Mother!'

From a bed of old-fashioned roses to our

left rises first a large, shallow straw hat, battered but still elegant, and then a whole person who I can't conceive can be Freddy's parent, for she looks little more than fifty, her curly brown hair's showing no hint of grey, and she's dressed in a gauzy tunic of white and blue swirls over similar white cotton trousers to mine. She waves a trug above her head and picks her way out of the rosebed. 'Hullo! Just tidying these prickly brutes. How lovely to see you. Isn't it a glorious day?'

Freddy reaches her first and she tilts her face sideways under the preposterous hat brim and kisses him with enthusiasm. 'And this is Flora,' he says.

She dumps the trug, pulls off her gardening gloves and we shake hands. 'I'm Paula.' I find my gaze met by fine eyes of the same grey as Freddy's. 'You look like the photograph on your book jackets, Flora.'

'That's reassuring,' I respond. Because that photograph is nothing if not flattering.

'I've read the books,' she tells me as we walk towards the house. 'Interesting. They aren't about seductions and jet planes and muesli. They make me think, and I like that.'

'Oh good,' I say. 'Not everyone does when they read. Like to think, I mean.'

Our eyes meet in amusement and I recollect Freddy saying that the extent of her reading frequently astounds him: 'She's not the sort to glance at reviews in the Sunday broadsheets and hope to bluff her way around, she goes to the book, and ponders what she's read.'

She sends Freddy off to fetch drinks, which she says we'll have on the terrace. She asks me about Mother's stroke and seems genuinely concerned. 'A nasty thing to happen and so worrying for you. I do hope she'll make a full recovery.' Then she picks up my overnight bag and takes me up handsome stairs to a long room off a galleried landing. She tells me it was Freddy's bedroom when he was a boy and it's not been changed much since. Sunlight is dancing across the creams and pinks and soft greens of a faded Victorian needlework carpet. There's a big old bed with a cane bedhead and country furniture of a sturdy simplicity, including a desk with ink stains. On the desk, incongruous but stunning, is a white and blue porcelain bowl rampant with roses. Two cricket bats lean in a corner and the creamy French wallpaper is covered with pictures, flower prints jostling with hunting prints and faded school photographs.

I exclaim aloud, 'Oh, I like it.'

I cross to the long low casement window, lean on its wide windowsill and look south across a country garden that blends into the landscape as if it has always been there, along with the distant Chiltern hills and the fourteenth-century church behind its crumbling flint wall. Beyond the cedars I glimpse how the more formal areas below the terrace gradually blend through a long vista into a natural garden with rough grass and fruit trees — and, yes, the stream garden Freddy had described where as a boy he'd paddled and planted and experimented with subtleties of colour.

The hot air is dense with flowery scents and the strong silence of high summer. There's a certain feel to this place, a mood that I've known before, and I'm aware at once that it relates to Freddy's house and his garden, and yet also to a time before that, something atavistic from a past, less hectic and materialistic world. Relaxing, I'm lured into a fantasy of lying on just such a lush lawn, feeling the quivering burgeoning of grass and leaf and flower, and the child inside me.

'It's a place of poetry, this,' I say. On the terrace below there are footsteps and a clink of glass. I glimpse the top of Freddy's head and find I'm smiling. 'It's very beautiful. Freddy often speaks of it. He says you made it a good place to grow up in.'

'Does he? We made it together, you know, all of us. We relished it. And we had twenty-five years here, my husband, David, and I, before he had the heart attack that killed him. A long happy time.'

I turn from the window to face her, feeling awkward. 'You must miss him horribly.'

'Of course. I always shall. But he's here, you know, among the roses where he died. Literally, I mean, as well as metaphorically — we scattered his ashes among them. People say I'm mad to stay here, that the place is far too big, how lonely I must be. But I say that if I moved I'd lose my memories, lose him.' She smiles, sighs. 'Freddy's very like him. In character. A kind man.'

'Yes. I know.'

The steady eyes that are Freddy's eyes examine me. 'I hear you're expecting my grandchild.'

Her directness appeals to me. Paula Gulliver is of a sort I've met before: frank, competent, well-connected, knowledgeable, communicative — and self-assured, like her son. It's a sort I'm drawn to, so very different from Mother, with her resentments and her nervous shiftings from foot to foot in the presence of strangers. I look at Paula's strong calm face with the sunlight flickering over it, and my last tensions about the baby suddenly dissolve into relief and then from relief into liking for her.

'Yes. It's due next January.'

'How do you feel about it?'

'I was shocked to start with, but now, well, I feel good. I surprise myself. How do you feel about becoming a grandmother?'

A sudden chuckle, as if something's settled in her mind, too. 'Oh, I'm happy enough. I've always wanted grandchildren, the sooner the better, so that I can enjoy them. Now, let's go down and have some long cool drink or other.'

We've just reached the shade of the awning on the terrace when a man comes striding round the corner of the house. He's about my age, he's tall, lean and fair, he's also flushed from the heat and mopping at his forehead with a green-spotted handkerchief.

'Oh, here you are,' he grunts. 'Couldn't raise a soul at the front. For God's sake shut the front door, Ma, unless you want to be burgled.'

'Can't,' Paula says, unmoved, 'you know how oven-hot the house becomes. Flora, this is Alexander, my elder son. Alexander, Flora Monk.'

We shake hands across the table. I see a resemblance in build and colouring to Freddy, but when I look further, there it ends.

320

He's a taut greyhound of a man who looks as if he might snarl. I recognise the type whose challenges I've reacted to for years and smile inwardly at my indifference. We sit down, Freddy pours drinks, and Alexander demands whisky: 'Plenty of water and ice as well as the whisky, Fred, I'm approaching heat-stroke point.' He lights a cigarette, inhales noisily, and sits tapping ash on the flagstones while Paula, Freddy and I debate where to have lunch, listening to us with a silent, restive, caustic reserve, finally breaking in with a snapped, 'The house is oven-hot, I'm told, and it's hot here, but under the trees there'll be insects, probably biting ones. Does it matter that much?'

'Flora's the one most likely to suffer. What do you think, Flora?'

'On the whole, under the trees.'

Alexander leans forward. 'Why should Flora suffer particularly?'

Freddy and I both open our mouths but Paula gets there first. 'Because she's pregnant. Just think, Alexander, I'm going to be a grandmother and you'll be an uncle.'

He's taken aback. 'Good God, Fred a father? What an incredible thought!'

'Why?' I ask. 'I think he'll make a good one.'

Alexander flips his cigarette end on to the

flagstones and presses it out with his shoe. 'Do you? Yes, on contemplation he probably will. How horrific though — the pressure, all those broken nights. No thank you.'

' 'Tisn't you who's having it,' his mother murmurs. She pushes her glass in Freddy's direction. 'Top me up, darling, will you? I'm parched. Thanks. You know, Alexander, you were an abominable screamer at the start but you passed the stage soon enough, and you were quite endearing even then.'

'He can scream now when he's put out,' Freddy remarks with a grin.

Alexander ignores them, swivelling round in his chair to face me, leaning forward, his elbow on the table at a sharp-edged angle, an attitude consciously forceful. 'And what about your career? What will a baby do to that? Somebody told me you were working at something rather out of the way, I can't remember what.'

'I'm a writer.'

'Ah, that must have been it. Have you had anything published?'

I've encountered this reaction before and I'm ready for it. 'Ah, and I remember, Alexander, that Freddy told me you're a solicitor. Do you have any clients?'

An almost imperceptible jerk. He thrusts out his lower lip. 'Then you are published. I beg your pardon. Novels, was it? What sort of novels?'

'Contemporary.'

'What they call intelligent women's fiction?'

'Something like that,' I say cautiously. But not cautiously enough.

'With inverted commas round the *intelligent*, of course,' he says, and his smile invites me to join in his scorn, while his fingers draw the inverted commas in the air.

I'm taking a deep breath to slice him off at the knees when Freddy gets his own cut in. 'The trouble with Alexander,' he tells me with his lop-sided grin, 'is that his yen for brainless girls leads him to deny the reality of true intelligent women. It's sad.'

It's very quiet apart from the twittering warbles of swallows flying high above the garden, calling as they go.

Paula shoves back her chair, its cane base creaking protestingly across the stone; she frowns and says, 'It's too hot, sitting here. Let's move. It's time for lunch, anyway. Alex, carry one or two things out for me, please? And Freddy, put chairs and things in the shade of the cedar.'

I'm not permitted to help. I wander down to the stream garden and listen to the faint gurgle of water as it flows between banks covered in lusciously healthy plants, some gently sprawling, some, like the irises, with upright sword-like leaves, others arching gracefully above their neighbours. I walk along stepping-stones above the bank and on to the little bridge. On the far side is a dramatic plant with enormous leaves that stand quite head high, and I imagine sheltering under it from a short shower, listening to the patter of the rain on those leaves that are like huge umbrellas. This is a different world. This I could live in for a lifetime. By the water is a clump of something smaller, with glossy arrow-like leaves and a strange white flower that I find appealing. I bend to touch it, then straighten to find Alex crossing the bridge towards me. I raise my eyebrows.

'Lunch is ready, Flora.' His face is flushed, but his manner is courteous.

I nod and point downward: 'What is it?'

'You don't know the arum lily? *Zantedeschia?*'

I shake my head. 'I've lived in flats all my life with a window box my only garden. And this great plant, that looks like overgrown rhubarb?'

'*Gunnera.*' He looks it over. 'I thought it was horrid when Fred first put it there, but he was right, of course. He always is, which is a bit much in a younger brother.' He makes a wry grimace, then glances at me out of the corner of his eye. 'Look, I think I've been rather rude, Flora — no, I know I have. Fred told me, Ma told me. Sorry, you caught me on a bloody day. Not that that excuses it, but I . . . my partner — girl-friend, I mean, not the sort in City firms — she walked out on me yesterday. I'm sore, I hit out at the nearest person. It wasn't fair that it was you.'

We walk back across the bridge. 'What went wrong?'

'Fred was right there too. A lovely girl, but not quick on the uptake. I snapped at her once too often. So . . . she went, as she'd threatened. We've both got tempers, Fred and I, but his fuse is longer, and anyway, he keeps things battened down.'

'Not always,' I say, remembering the flying orange.

'Oh?' His face relaxes into a smile. 'Felt it, have you?'

'Once. I probably deserved it. Do you want this girl back?'

'In a way, yes. I am fond of her. But it wouldn't work. I need someone like you, someone with a mind. Fred was telling Ma and me about your Claudia Charles biography. I've read some of her stuff, you know. What an incredible woman . . . '

We're joining the others under the cedar tree when the telephone rings.

'Get the cordless; it's up on the terrace. Damn!' says Paula, busy at the table with food.

'I'll go,' says Freddy.

He runs up the lawn, picks it up . . . he's nodding, serious, looking at me. He walks back, slowly. 'It was Mrs Moffat, Flora. I'm sorry, your mother's had another stroke. A bad one this time.' He takes my hand and I know in a flash before he says it. 'She's dead.'

17

The world is very white, but the ground stays solid beneath my feet. Freddy is beside me, taking my hand, Paula and Alexander are standing staring, shocked. Something cataclysmic should be happening, yet nothing happens. The roses bloom on, the bees work among the lavender, the swallows wheel above us. Freddy says it was sudden, just half an hour ago. 'So sorry,' they all say, 'so very sorry.' I swallow, wait for tears to come, wait for nausea: nothing. I watch a butterfly which has perched, quivering, on the rim of a bowl of shredded lettuce. I hear the church bell strike one. I don't know what I feel.

Alexander disappears to return with a brandy and water. I shake my head. 'Drink it,' he orders. I sip and swallow. It's something to do. What does one do?

Paula is practical. 'You'll want Freddy to drive you straight back to Richmond; there'll be so many people to telephone, so much to cope with, but you must eat something first.'

Obediently I sit at the lunch table, but food seems irrelevant, silly even.

'Home-made veal and ham pie,' she says,

hovering, 'yes, and now some salad. The dressing's just a light lemony one. Take care of yourself and eat for the baby's sake, too.'

I'm touched. I chew slowly, swallow with difficulty. I think that Mother would like Paula Gulliver — but Mother will never meet her now. Oh, my poor Mumma, you won't see your grandchild. My throat aches with the pity of it.

Suddenly, I know I must see her. I have to go back to the hospital, to Roehampton where she is, so that someone who cares can say goodbye before strangers hammer the lid down on the dark box of her coffin.

★   ★   ★

She lies in a small silent room off the mortuary, a chapel of rest. The nurse murmurs, 'Take as long as you wish,' and slips outside.

I look at my dead mother, swathed to the chin and lying on a bier, and I breathe uneasily. Her eyes are closed, she's marble pale and calm, and she's at once my mother and someone unfamiliar. Death has smoothed away the lines of anxiety and resentment, leaving her looking . . . patrician. There's strength in that face. I stare, perplexed at the change. Is this how nature had meant her to look? How she would have looked had life been less unkind? I have seen much of her in recent days, furious over her stroke, happy over the coming grandchild, distressed by my indifference to the married state; I would have thought I knew her in every mood, yet in death she's a stranger.

I'm aware of Freddy near me as an area of warmth to be drawn upon. Somewhere in my mind there's gratitude that he's here, solid yet unintrusive, shielding me from the loneliness of bereavement, but I can't spare any thoughts for him, there's too much whirling about in my head.

She wouldn't have suffered, my poor mother; a stroke is a swift, merciful form of death in comparison with most others. I look back and see that she had been determined to make a good recovery from that first stroke: irritation at the limitations to her movements had been her reaction, not fear of a repetition, not the fear of death. I, too, after the first fright, had expected recovery. So I had failed to act as if each day might be her last, failed to give her the reassurances of affection and understanding she must have been craving. I should not have been irritated by her pressure over marriage . . . I should have prevaricated, teased her about her intensity, invented things to divert her. I reflect with remorse that irritation had been a part of our relationship for many years. When death snatches away someone so close, you pay for the relief of outliving her with endless stabs of guilt: none of us can look back on perfection in any relationship, we're all prone to thoughtlessness, anger, oversights; of course we could have done more, hence the regrets. Mine come from not liking her enough. As the mother of one of my friends I'd have considered her a nice old bird. As my own mother, I wanted her different: less narrow in outlook, less hide-bound by convention. More like her sisters, in fact. Why could she not have been gruff and scornful like Laurel, had the April sunshine and showers character of Daisy or the elegance and charm of Isobel? Why had I expected so much? Why could I not have accepted her as she was? Why had she not accepted me as I am? Oh, the questions. Oh, poor Mumma.

I stand by her head, bend and kiss her cheek. It's cold, deathly cold and rigid. I'm struck afresh by the knowledge that the spirit's gone for ever. 'Goodbye, Mumma.'

Freddy takes my hand and draws me from the room.

★　★　★

The nurse mingles detached sympathy with purposeful efficiency, ushering us here and there, dealing with the pitiful last belongings from Mother's locker and pushing an envelope containing the death certificate into my hands. 'That's for the Registrar and the funeral director. You can't have the funeral until you've registered the death, you know.'

We walk out into the bright, bright sunshine. The world about me is somehow surreal and I feel unpleasantly light-headed. We drive to Mother's flat and the car is so blisteringly hot, I can only sit and exist. Then suddenly we're at the flat and they're all there, my aunts and Mrs Moffat, just as Freddy had agreed on the telephone before we left Paula's house: four old ladies full of shocked and loving affection.

'Oh, Flora,' they say, pressing their damp cheeks against mine, hugging me against drooping bosoms. 'Oh, Flora, your poor mother. It's terrible, just terrible.'

Laurel is the worst, cheeks sagging, eyes like an old bloodhound's. 'I don't know how I shall go on without her, I really don't. I saw her every week of my life. She was the best friend I ever had.'

'I know.' Locks of Daisy's white hair erupt through her fingers as she clasps her head. 'She drove me mad telling me how to run my

331

marriage, but she was an outlet for all my rage and frustration, too. It was she who kept me and Guy together. Come to that, she kept us all together over the years and that matters, especially when you're old and you've no future to plan for. Then it's your past you want to dwell in, with those who remember it — and she knew me from my very first day. Life won't be the same without her.'

'She was the one you could always trust to get in touch with you,' Isobel says. She blinks her big eyes hard. 'But I wish I'd told her how much she meant to me. It's dreadful how one shies away from emotion and sentimentality. On her deathbed Jane Austen said to her sister-in-law, Mary Lloyd, 'You've always been a kind sister to me.' I should have said that to Primrose. She supported me over and above Alban, her own brother, she never made me feel guilty or an intruder. She was kind — and upright and fair.' An elegant hand dabs a real linen handkerchief at her eyes.

Mrs Moffat is busy with tea things. She pauses in her pouring and agrees. 'If only everyone could be as considerate as she was.' She adds that Daisy was right about looking back, that's how it was with Mrs Monk and her. 'We'd talk about the past because I'm old too, and we remembered the same things. Ways of thinking, behaving, even ways of loving, they were different in our time — but then the past's another country, isn't it? Strange to people who've never lived there, but we could share our nostalgia. And she'd press me for tales of Claudia Charles. She always wanted to hear of her.'

Freddy helps her to hand things round and we clasp our cups with gratitude, gulping hot tea in an English ritual that is a comfort in itself. As if by association Daisy mentions the funeral: Guy could take the service if we'd like it, with all the old words. How about that?

I remember how on her seventieth birthday Mother had spoken of her death and her Will, showing me the old deed box tucked in the corner of her wardrobe and informing me that all her most precious papers were in there, those vital certificates that proclaim us alive or married or dead, define our educational levels and our working capabilities. 'And the instructions for my funeral are there too, and my headstone. You'll carry them out, Flora, won't you? You won't let me down?'

I'd thought that lugubrious. I'd promised, told her not to dwell on such things because she'd years to go yet, and escaped, horrified.

Now I'm grateful to escape making decisions over these matters. 'Mother left instructions; I'll see what she wrote, Daisy.'

Freddy comes with me into her bedroom, where the curtains are discreetly half-drawn and the air is sultry. I open the wardrobe door on Mother's dresses, skirts and suits and feel odd: sad because she'll never wear them again, yet intrusive, as if I'm spying on her. The deed box is where I remember it, in the right-hand corner, the key, too, in the toe of an old shoe. I tug the box out, kneel beside it, pull out large envelopes once addressed to her, but now scribbled over and re-labelled — Mother with her wartime background never could waste paper. They're all there: *Marriage Certificate, School Certs, Librarian quals, Funeral Instructions* — yes, she asks for Guy to take the service — *My Will, C. Charles Press Cuttings, Aunt Selina's Will* . . . yes, I remember her saying she'd been one of the old girl's executors. At the bottom of the box are letters arranged in neat bundles and tied with worn ribbons. From my father? Keep them to look at later. No birth certificate.

I push the funeral instructions, the Will and the marriage certificate into Freddy's hands, sift the pile once more for Mother's birth certificate. Not there. I glance in her drawers, then try her bureau in the sitting-room, groping angrily around, sweat prickling out all over my body.

'What's the problem?' Daisy asks.

I explain. Laurel flexes her big shoulders, frowns. 'What do you need it for?'

'To register her death. Must prove the birth or we could be burying anybody, surely?'

Laurel and Daisy look at each other, lips pursed. 'You've the other certificates, they'll do. We can swear to Primrose as our sister,' Daisy says. 'Come on, sit down and let Mrs Moffat pour you another cup of tea.'

'No, I'm going to find it,' I say, suddenly determined. 'Mother liked matters to be processed properly and that's how it's going to be.' I start emptying the top drawer of the bureau on the floor, cash books, old diaries, last year's Christmas cards sliding across the carpet.

Daisy mutters, 'God, I'd never thought of this.'

Behind me there's more muttering, then Laurel exclaims, 'All right! Stop, Flora. If I must I think I can find it.' She heaves her heavy body up from the sofa and stomps from the room. I hear her in the bedroom. A minute later she pushes a folded piece of paper into my hands. 'Under the lining paper of her bottom drawer. I was charged to destroy it, but I didn't move fast enough, did I?' She's standing over me as I open and read it.

The shock hits me like a bolt of lightning, my heart booms as if it will burst from my chest. I hold the paper away from myself, staring at Laurel. 'What is this?'

'It's true, Flora. That's how it was. She hated it. All her life she hated it.'

Freddy's hand is on my arm, steadying me. He reads over my shoulder what I'm reading incredulously for the third time. Name: *Primrose Lillian*. Name and Surname of Father: *Unknown*. Name and Maiden Surname of Mother: *Claudia Charles*. 'God!' he breathes. 'Oh, Flora.'

A sour taste of lemons is in my mouth. 'I can't believe it. Why wasn't I told?'

'Can't believe what?' Isobel asks. 'What's wrong?'

Freddy moves me to a chair. 'Sit down, Flora. Do you want a drink of anything?'

'No. I'm all right, promise. Only pole-axed. Isobel, it seems Claudia Charles was Mumma's mother and . . . the father's down as unknown.'

I hear Mrs Moffat suck in her breath. Isobel looks as shocked as I feel. 'That can't be true. Someone explain it to me, quickly, please!'

Laurel takes up her mannish straddle before the empty grate. 'I'll tell you, but it's a sad, bad story. In late 1919, while Claudia was up at Oxford, she became pregnant, she never said who by.'

'Ahh!' The sound is jolted out of me. 'Nineteen nineteen. Nineteen twenty is a missing journal year!'

'Oh yes? Her brother Edward and Aunt Selina were shaken to the roots — but did agree to stand by her. Everything was hushed up, then and ever since. It so happened that my mother, May, was pregnant at the same time, desperately hoping for a live child. Apart from two miscarriages, bad enough for someone not . . . not very strong in health or character, she'd also lost a baby. That first child had been throttled by the cord at birth; now, in July 1920, the second was born prematurely due to a fall. Nowadays I imagine such a child would survive. But then? The son she and my father had both longed for died after two weeks.'

'Oh, poor, poor May!' Isobel's eyes brim with tears.

Mrs Moffat's eyes are round in an otherwise impassive face. Daisy pats my knee.

'She was half-demented with grief.' Laurel pushes a hand through her iron-grey hair, her eyes are filled with shadows. 'It was just thirty-six hours after that tiny boy's death when Claudia gave birth in a terrible ordeal that all but killed her. Aunt Selina, helping to nurse Claudia in a back-bedroom and rushing between whiles to the nursing home to support her hysterically weeping sister-in-law, was gripped by the thought that having Claudia's unwanted baby to love and hold might save May's sanity. Claudia had rejected any talk of adoption, but if May and Roger were to raise the child she could keep in some sort of touch with it. Edward, Daddy, the midwives, the doctor, they all connived in the scheme. Claudia . . . ' her mouth creases with downward lines, 'well, she described the horrors of Primrose's birth in *Shadow of a Child*, of course, so you'll know the state she was in — exhausted, in pain still, and in no fit state for the fight to keep her baby. She collapsed under their pressure, probably for the only time in all her life, allowing her nameless tiny girl to become Primrose Tucker-Bond.' She gulps, stops. 'Freddy, pour me a whisky, will you? I'm shaken enough from Primrose's death without all this, I need a stiffener. No, on second thoughts, pour us all a glass. Mrs Moffat, you don't have to sneak out with the tea things like that; you knew Claudia long enough, you knew my sister, you're not intruding.'

'I'll just pop the tray to the kitchen,' she says, looking shaken, 'and find the glasses.'

She disappears with Freddy and there's a deepening hush in the room. Despite the heat my hands and feet feel icy. Cold facts drop into my mind like flakes of snow, gathering slowly, stealthily, one upon another, until they obliterate the familiar landmarks of my life in the same malevolent fashion as the snowstorm had obliterated the landscape from Richmond Hill on that January day when I had announced that I was to write the Claudia Charles biography: Roger and May Tucker-Bond were not my grandparents, Laurel and Daisy are not my aunts, Pattie and her sisters are not my cousins. There's no blood relationship with any of my dear family. Only with my mother . . . who'd said to me . . . was it really only this morning? . . . '*I knew a girl . . . petty officials despised her . . . she cried with the shame . . .* '

'Oh Mumma, poor Mumma!'

The sour lemon taste gushes into my mouth again. I stagger to the bathroom and throw up. When I come out Freddy's waiting for me. He's turfed Isobel and Daisy off the sofa and he's insisting I lie down and sip whisky and water.

'Don't fuss,' I say mean-spiritedly. Everything in me is churning and distressed and

I'm sweating and shivering both at the same time. 'You can take that whisky away, ugh, I don't want it.'

He tosses back the whisky himself, then passes the glass to Mrs Moffat, who stands watching us, blinking with concern. He perches on the edge of the sofa beside me. 'What *do* you want then, Flora?'

His eyes are bloodshot, his shirt is sticking to his body in places, there's a faint but perceptible tic in his jaw. That tension's because of me . . . I clutch him. Thank God he's here.

'Hold me,' I say, shaken with desolation, 'hold me together, Freddy. Please.' His arms reach out to clasp me against the solid muscles of his body. He smells of warm hair and maleness and whisky. I lean against him, and slowly the churning and the shaking stop.

'It was the shock,' Daisy observes to Mrs Moffat. 'Upsets always go to Flora's stomach. Do sit down, she isn't going to spew again and you look shocked enough yourself.'

'*I* certainly am,' Isobel says. 'I've never been more shocked in my life. Why didn't anyone ever tell me? Why didn't Alban?'

'He never knew,' Laurel tells her. 'It wasn't something any of us grew up knowing about. On the contrary, Primrose was told nothing until her twenty-first birthday, and then our parents broke it to her. She'd been puzzling why no party or whatever appeared to be planned for her great day, but excused it on account of my parents' poverty and the war. It was nineteen fortyone — a dreadful year. They spoke to her — our parents — after breakfast. Father did it, he said he had something serious to tell her and she must take it on the chin like a man. Then it came out that she was Claudia Charles' daughter and that she'd been adopted by them and why, and that she must never speak of it to anyone, ever. Also she was never to speak of it to Claudia, she must continue to think of her as a distant relative and behave as such. There would be no fuss, no sentimentality.'

'You make it sound extraordinarily cold,' Isobel ventures.

'It was,' Daisy says sadly. 'That was a part of Primrose's shock, that they were so detached about it. That they were separating themselves from her. They gave her a little gold brooch, then suggested she find herself a job, think about leaving home. They were sorry, they said, they were fond of her, but she was grown-up now, and she knew things were straitened with them. She'd been told not even to tell us, but we found her huddled in a corner of her room, crying so hard she couldn't speak. When finally we dragged it

341

out of her we were shattered, too. Laurel was eighteen then, I was only fifteen, but we were capable of seeing the horror of her position. It set us all adrift in a world where nothing was fixed or safe. Our sensible, gentle big sister was not our sister, she was the daughter of Claudia Charles, whom we'd been brought up to view as clever, maybe, but also a reprehensible person whose acquaintanceship it might be better not to dwell on. And worse, poor darling Primrose was illegitimate, a *bastard*. In our middle-class eyes in those days it was nearly as bad as being a convicted criminal. We crouched on either side of her, hugging her, telling her through our own tears that it didn't matter one jot to us, that we'd love her for ever, no matter what, but nothing we said could comfort her. I've never seen anyone, ever, in such a state of anguish.'

'We were angry then,' Laurel tells us sombrely. 'It was only a few months since Harry's death, after all. I was all for rushing downstairs to shout at my parents for their callousness in breaking the news to her in such a way and on such a day, but Primrose wouldn't let us. She looked near fainting point so we put her to bed instead.'

'It was a complete collapse,' Daisy informs us. 'She was ill for days, running a high temperature. In the house it was dubbed influenza. We hung about, helpless, forced to pretend things were normal, hating every second of it. Then Laurel thought of Aunt Selina — '

'I telephoned her,' Laurel interrupts in her brusque fashion, 'because she was devoted to Primrose and if anyone could sort anything out she could. I had awful visions of her charging up from Kent, but for once she was the soul of tact, despite her fury at the pain they'd inflicted on Primrose. Instead, twenty-four hours later she rang Daddy to say that the library in her local town was on the verge of closing, because the male staff were away fighting, and could they spare Primrose once more? And then when it became clear the work was right up Primrose's street, Aunt Selina offered to fund any training courses she might need, to give her the chance of a career.'

'She was a great woman,' Daisy murmurs, adding wryly, 'to us, anyhow.'

'But not to Claudia,' I say. A hundred questions about the puzzling past are being answered at once, so fast my head reels. '*Now I know why Claudia hated her and Edward. They stole her child away.*'

There's a long silence. Laurel pulls a pack of cigarettes from her battered shoulder bag and lights one up, dragging on it ferociously, expelling smoke in explosive sighs. The slanting rays of the early evening sun illuminate the smoke as it curls towards the ceiling. Mother hates her to smoke ... but Mother's not here to object any more. She's in the mortuary. But she's someone I don't know: she's excluded me from a huge part of her life, deceiving me so that I misjudged her, even despised her for not standing up more for herself. I'm angry on her behalf but I'm hurt too. Oh God, my brain doesn't seem to be able to take this in properly, to fit together all the strange strands of her torn life. I feel so tired. I hate this pregnancy for making me feel so tired. Small things flit in and out of my mind.

I say, 'Claudia gave Mother her precious string of pearls. Weren't they for that twenty-first birthday? Mother said they were real and valuable.'

'They are,' Isobel nods. She'd know, of course.

'The pearls on her twenty-first and the Ispahan rug when Primrose married Philip were the only presents Claudia ever gave her,' Laurel confirms, tapping ash viciously on to the rug. 'She did, obliquely, acknowledge the important times in her life, but she never acknowledged Primrose, not even in utter privacy. I tried to raise the subject with her

344

once, but almost before I'd have believed she could know what I was driving at she stopped me with a snap and left the room.' She looks me in the eyes and adds at her most gruff that she knows Primrose had also tried to raise the subject, with the same result. Primrose as her child was as dead to Claudia as May's infant son. And Primrose the distant cousin was someone she hadn't much time for.

Unexpectedly Mrs Moffat confirms this. 'If you don't object to me saying it, Flora . . . ' she says, looking lost and shocked, 'it's true that's so. I mind things that perplexed me that now begin to fall into place. Mrs Malcolm — Claudia Charles you call her — she'd be tense when Mrs Monk came to lunch. I thought it strange because I liked her myself, she was gentle and good. But Mrs Malcolm said she didn't care for the meek of this world; they made her want to snap. Other times, she'd say in that clipped way of hers; 'She's good in a negative way because she's never dared to revolt. And she should have done, she should have fought back against the Tucker-Bonds' tiresome bourgeois preten-tions and given them hell!' ' She frowns, staring into the past. 'Och, I remember . . . Something about nature and nurture she said . . . 'In the debate over nature versus nurture I always believed that nature played the larger part in determining a person's character, but Primrose confounds me every time. There's nothing about her that I can relate to in any of our families.' '

'Well,' Isobel says softly, very carefully, 'all I can say is that they had strange natures, all of them.'

18

I can't understand why Claudia allowed herself to be browbeaten and I say so. 'A tough character like her? It's unbelievable.'

Isobel shakes her head. 'She probably did fight. But she'd no hope. She was under twenty-one, dependent on them and forced into it by their authority, wasn't she?'

'Precisely so,' Laurel nods. 'Effectively she'd neither rights nor money. Her father'd died in considerable debt, it was Uncle Lucian and his rich Tucker-Bond wife who'd helped Edward become a solicitor and stumped up the money for Claudia's education. But they were never going to take on the embarrassing burden of the little by-blow while she endeavoured to establish herself as a writer, something they'd have seen as a lunatic ambition.'

'Never!' Daisy agrees emphatically. 'These days unmarried women cope in their thousands with their babies and the poor old tax-payers support many of 'em. No support then. Heavens, no! Claudia should have been on her knees in gratitude at the amazing escape route she'd been offered, but instead she built up a steaming lava of rage that erupted first in that hateful portrayal of Edward as the censorious Lennox and then later Aunt Selina as the monstrous Aunt Hermione, massively beastly in black. So unfair.'

If I've been looking for one precise event which made Claudia hate her brother and aunt and resulted in those outstanding books, I have it now. I'd discovered when I set up a colour-coded time chart of the main events of her life that her strongest novels seemed to emerge, explode almost, from the demise of a love-affair. It's as if the torment of the lover's treachery (she could never view it as anything less) forced her to explore other women's loves and sorrows, her despair which was not quite depression moving her to singular bouts of expression. *The Power of the Dog* was written in 1920 and 1921, published in 1922. When I drew up the chart I had no substantial evidence of an affair in 1919, only the knowledge that she'd left Somerville then, coupled with rumours of a man discovered in her room. Now that certificate of my mother's birth in late July gives incontrovertible evidence of a man in Claudia's life — and treachery.

Was it the loss of her lover, possibly scared away by her pregnancy, which produced this powerful novel? Was it the loss of her child, wrenched from her arms to relieve the pain of May Tucker-Bond's loss? Or was it both, and activated by hatred of the brother who had not only agreed with the treacherous wrenching but even been behind it?

Two more questions, two huge, swelling questions, fill my mind: Who was Mumma's real father — my grandfather? And how can I, as Claudia's granddaughter, possibly continue with her biography?

I demand of Laurel and Daisy, 'Do you know who Mumma's father was?'

They shrug, gesture ignorance with open hands. 'Forbidden subject,' Laurel says tersely. Daisy nods. 'We urged Primrose to ask, but she couldn't. She became tearful at any mention of her private horror.'

I pose my question over the biography and in the stunned silence that follows I'm aware of people calling to one another in the street, of a plane rumbling towards Heathrow, a lorry changing gear. Laurel sucks in her breath and expels it sharply, Mrs Moffat coughs, Isobel mutters, 'Oh, what a nonsense all this is!' Daisy chews her lip. I sense their mental turmoil. I wait.

Freddy shifts position beside me, his voice comes harshly. 'Why shouldn't you write the biography? It's not unknown for daughters or sons to write of their parents. Why not you of your grandmother? Who better? You've already delved deeply into Claudia's life, and this extraordinary piece of knowledge will not only give you a rare insight into her writing, but allow you to show the damage she did to her repudiated daughter. And her grand-daughter.'

I hardly hear those last words. 'Mumma never did want me to write it and now I know why. She'd loathe to have her private shame revealed for the world to gasp and giggle over.'

'She's dead,' Freddy says, his tone uncompromising. 'She's never going to know. But whoever writes Claudia's biography, now or in the future, has to understand why she hated Edward and old Selina so bitterly that she portrayed them as those odious charac-ters while they were alive to be hurt by it. No good biographer, no good historian ever knowingly suppresses the truth of such situations. Besides, at nineteen or twenty maybe Claudia was defenceless and unnerved by the threat of social calamity. But later, and it can't have escaped you, Flora, she became quite simply an out-and-out hypocrite. She supported the feminists, she supported the sexual revolution of the sixties and seventies, yet she never had the guts to acknowledge her own child, who she must have been aware had been grieved — demolished — by her lack of status and love. This piece of information doesn't only affect our view of her character, it affects the truth of her work. Of her beliefs. It's intrinsic.'

Laurel looks frowningly past my head. 'I think I must find you right on all counts there, Freddy.'

'Yes,' Isobel says. 'He has to be right, doesn't he? Think of Dame Rebecca West — as time moved on she acknowledged in public her son by H. G. Wells and co-operated with her biographers. And there've been others. But Claudia never did. This revelation's shaken my view of her to the roots — and there's no way it should be suppressed.'

Daisy's nodding. 'I've never been able to escape the nasty thought that the greater part of Claudia's passion with Edward and Selina wasn't over the loss of her child, but over the injury to her dignity and self-esteem when they imposed their decision on her. Any woman with any real maternal feelings would've tried to see more of poor little Primrose, encouraging her to make something of herself, paying for her education — as Aunt Selina did for Laurel and my godmother for me — but Claudia's

351

interest was minimal.'

Laurel says sombrely, 'What maternal feelings? Isn't bonding important for that? The baby who'd nearly killed her was snatched away from her within a couple of days, she rarely had the opportunity to see her, she had no part in her upbringing and our parents had turned her child into someone else who . . . who, as Mrs Moffat says, wasn't Claudia's sort. In my opinion, the whole boiling lot of them were hypocrites. They'd left Claudia no rights in Primrose, yet when money was difficult they wanted her to assume responsibilities they themselves had torn from her, and, not surprisingly when you consider that uncompromising personality, she wasn't having any part of it.'

Mrs Moffat nods. 'She was the implacable enemy of anybody who dared put her in the wrong.'

'Then she'd be my implacable enemy,' I say dryly, 'because if I'm to continue with the biography, what can I do but dump her right in the rotten mess she made?'

Freddy rises from the sofa and gives me his lop-sided grin: 'You're capable of being dispassionate, Flora. You'll have to contact Helen and Robert and the other Trustee to ask their views, but my opinion is, you stick to it, my darling, and think with glee of the shock-waves that'll hit the literary world when it's published.'

'Think of the reviews, the publicity, the excitement!' Isobel breathes and then starts to laugh. 'It could make your name in a big way.'

'Remember,' Freddy adds, 'you do have a contract and that's going to lead to a strange legal argument if they should want to rescind, isn't it? But right now, my angel, you're looking exhausted and it's time we went home.'

He tugs me up and then I sway and clutch at him as my once solid world rocks again beneath my feet. 'But hang on, Freddy, this revelation makes Helen and Robert my cousins . . . oh God, and Saffron, too! Hell! No, don't you dare laugh, this is the most unprecedented snarl-up I've ever heard of . . . And what's the betting Robert, at least, knows of the relationship? He is Edward's son. Yet he's a party to the contract.'

'You can't go yet,' Isobel decides, her eyes more huge than ever. 'You mustn't keep us in suspense, you must telephone Robert right now. He'll want to be told about poor darling Primrose being dead, anyway.'

'No,' Freddy intervenes as Daisy, too, nods her enthusiasm for getting hold of Robert.

'Come on. Give Flora a chance to get food and rest. Everything else must wait.'

*   *   *

He drives us twice round the seven miles of Richmond Park before turning for home. Our progress is sedate; we sit in silence with the windows open, and there's a breeze cooling my face and stirring the tops of the trees. The blue of the sky is paling and I can see the moon suspended above the trees like a pale papery disc of honesty. In the distance deer are grazing. There's calm all about us and I let the happenings of the day wash over me and through me and recede gradually, mercifully.

It's mid-evening when I leave the car and cross the pavement towards the house; the road is empty of traffic and the setting sun is filling it with light. High on a chimney pot a blackbird is pouring a stream of notes across the rooftops of Richmond. Mother's dead but I'm intensely aware of my own being and that other being inside me. I hear Freddy shut the car door and the sound of his steps as he catches up with me, our overnight bags in his hands, and then he's giving me his funny sideways smile and I'm savouring his affection with a catch of my breath. And in the turn of that moment I know my life will never be the same again; I've become someone different. I clutch the deed box with the documents that chart the essentials of Mother's life, and they're from the past. An unexpected feeling wells up in me and it's release. Possibilities sparkle from the rose bushes by the front steps. I can run my life free from Mother's goads, not always directly spoken but there in sighs, in laden allusions and sub-texts. I can write the Claudia Charles biography without the pressure of her disapproval and put in and leave out exactly what I wish. And in that moment I'm determined to reveal the whole story of Claudia's refusal to be involved with Mumma or even, remotely, to care; I have to show the world both the sadness and the damage caused by their bleak unsatisfying relationship — in a way, it occurs to me, to vindicate my own ambiguous feelings towards the burdened woman who worried over my childhood years. Mother never wanted the relationship with Claudia revealed because she was afraid her friends would despise her equivocal status, but what I write will demand for her the shocked sympathy of a different generation. My work will tell the truth and sear people's hearts.

Up the stairs with Freddy behind me and

as I open my front door I hear the blackbird start its song again. The intolerably sweet notes close my throat convulsively. The next moment the guilt and grief I thought I'd escaped are pinning me between the shoulder blades. I sob and sob, gasping for breath, tears flooding down my face. Blindly I stagger to the sitting-room and fall into a chair, covering my gaping mouth with my hand. I'm crying for her and I'm crying for myself. The deed box falls to the floor, spilling its contents.

Freddy kneels beside me, holding my shoulders. I let the weight of my body fall on his chest, locking him to me with frantic arms. 'How could they? How could my grandparents have done that to her? Burned her and stung her with those blistering thoughtless words? They stripped her of her pride. Everything she believed about herself destroyed in seconds and they gave her no comfort. It's unbelievable.'

'I know,' he murmurs into my neck.

'I wish she'd told me. She didn't trust me enough to tell me.'

He shakes his head against mine. 'She didn't tell her brother or Isobel either. As Claudia's unacknowledged bastard she was abject in her own eyes.'

I'm overwhelmed by the thought of the

pain she had borne in silence over all the years. She had lost her family and the background she's believed was hers, to be faced instead with insecurity, emptiness and shame. It must have been a shock as great as any bereavement, and if she had lost her family through accident or illness there would have been the catharsis of tears of grief at the funeral, and the consolation of loving friends, but there was nothing like that for her. Mumma's bereavement was of the unmentionable sort. Grief is part of the process of change. When people you love are taken away from you, it alters your life, forcing you to move on whether you want to or not. And it's a painful process even when you're given support. Mumma had none.

I rummage one-handedly in my bag for a tissue and mop my eyes. 'Claudia was condescending to her, and cool. We saw her every other year, if that. And she'd never come to us, we had to go to her house where it would be no trouble, because she had Mrs Moffat. She didn't care.' I let go of Freddy and lean back in the chair, where a shaft of the dying sun blinds my eyes. I jerk my head aside and frown. Black spots float in the corner of my vision and dark thoughts bob up in my brain. 'Men of Mumma's class didn't marry girls with no background. No wonder she married so late. You know something, Freddy? Mother was angry. Not just hurt. Underneath, all her life, she was angry.'

Freddy rises to his feet. 'Yes, I think she was. Very quietly, right deep down. Seething. Darling. I'm going to cook us omelettes, there won't be anything else. What do you want to drink? Orange juice?'

'Yes, fine, thanks,' I say vaguely, impatiently. I reach for the telephone, on the table beside me. 'I'm going to telephone Robert.'

'Leave it till tomorrow, why don't you? You're tired. Give your brain a rest.'

I dial the number. 'It won't rest. I have to sort this now or I'll never sleep. Oh, Robert, hullo, it's Flora.'

He's shocked at Mother's death. He's sympathetic, he wants to come to the funeral, he was fond of her. 'She was a game old bird in her quiet way, but she had a tough life.'

'Yes, you've said that before, and you should know,' I say and hear the hard note in my voice. 'You were her first cousin, after all, weren't you?'

A barely perceptible pause. 'We were related . . . ' He coughs politely, waiting.

He did know. I see bad faith, and anger surfaces. 'All right, Robert, you don't have to play games, not any more. I've seen her birth certificate.'

358

'Ah. Mm. Yes, I'm sorry about that, it must have been bloody for her. Flora, what exactly does it say? I've often wondered.'

I snap out the brief details.

He makes a disgusted noise. 'Poor Primrose, how grim for her. And your grandparents . . . no, they weren't yours, were they? Oh God. Roger and May — they never did get round to adopting poor old Primrose properly, did they?'

'It would appear not.' I wait.

'Flora . . . Oh hell, you aren't just calling as Primrose's daughter, are you? You want to know about Claudia for the biography, don't you?'

'Yes, I damned well do.'

He takes a breath. 'You're angry with me. Why's that?'

'I told you not to play games. Of course I'm angry. Why didn't you tell me? How the hell could you *not* tell me? It may sound naïve, Robert, to talk about discovering the whole truth or telling the full story, but that's what I thought you'd authorised me to do with Claudia — to bring home the goods. And today I discover that all the time you've been sneakily keeping the most valuable goodies of all hidden away in your darkest cupboard. I'd heard that relatives with their desire to tidy and sweeten the dubious corpse were the biographer's most persistent antagonists — but I'm not an outsider, we're related, *as you knew*, and I don't see why you should want to make a fool of me. You must have been laughing yourself silly inside.'

'Flora, stop! You've a right to be angry, but no reason. When Helen proposed you as Claudia's biographer, well, yes, it did give me considerable cynical amusement. The thought of you judging her was intriguing — but it was the gods of chance playing games with the scales of justice, not me. When Dad told me of Primrose being Claudia's child, he bound me to the utmost secrecy. In all our married life I never told Joan, and I never spoke of it to Primrose. If you found out, you found out, but I'd made a promise.'

'Didn't Claudia's death remove the bind of that promise?'

'No. Never, was the word used by my father, and it was he whom I promised, not her.'

'So Helen doesn't know.'

'No. Do you want me to tell her, or will you? Oh dear, this is going to be a major bother, isn't it? The implications are beginning to sink in all too horribly. We'll have to talk to Claudia's solicitor Trustee, too, Clifford Cumbers. Study all those ruddy questions that have to be answered. People

360

are going to be cross with me. Well, that's my problem. But you — do you feel competent to continue with the biography? Should you continue with it? Is it possible for you to be sufficiently objective and impartial?'

I'm jumping with angry fright and it's more enormously important than ever. I see an abyss of emptiness opening in my life if they take this task away from me. And with Claudia my grandmother, it's become very personal: I want to delve deep into the debris of her past to root out the truth of her feelings, and I have to discover my grandfather, not just for me but for Mumma, drawing a thick black line through the *Unknown* on that birth certificate and writing in the missing name, to bestow on Mumma at the last the dignity of a father who's more than a nameless shadow. And if they're worrying about objectivity, how the hell do you get the balance right or tell the truth about anything? Life's packed with hidden catches.

'I can't give it up, Robert, I can't,' I say fiercely, and then catch at myself, moderating my tone. 'It's all too extraordinary, too fascinating for me just to drop it. But don't worry, I'll bend over backwards to be detached. I'll leave out the loaded adjectives and there'll be no crass tear-jerking stuff.' My

361

brain's silting up with tiredness and I haven't the energy to marshal brilliant arguments. I remind him, 'In the final analysis you do have the safeguard of the contract.'

Even as I say the words it occurs to me, as it must sooner or later to the Trustees, that this has become irrelevant, since the revelations I can make are more likely to be fought over by greedy publishers than rejected, nor will a lively subjectivity do any harm. Subversion coupled with lurid gossip will always attract more readers than the uplifting literary encounter.

'Hm.' There's a contemplative silence. 'How do you feel about Claudia in the light of all this? About being her granddaughter? About her huffy attitude with your mother?'

'Oh, God knows, Robert. I'm reeling from the shock. How can I begin to come to terms with the morals of behaviour like hers? Mother used to talk about empathy. Claudia had no idea of such connections of feelings, had she? The horrors of the happenings in her life related to her alone, never to others. Her callousness towards Mother takes my breath away.' Especially now with the coming of my own child on my mind, though I don't tell him that. 'Biography or no, I'm going to have to talk to you again — about that birth, I mean. You're the one person who might have some genuine information. And you owe it to me.'

'Yes. All right, Flora, I do and we will talk — fully — I promise. And in the meantime I'll get in touch with Cliff Cumbers and Helen and arrange a meeting to discuss this. We'll keep in touch and you'll let me know about the funeral, won't you? I'm very sorry about your mother, Flora. You know that, don't you?'

Over our supper of herb omelettes Freddy and I look at Mother's Will and her funeral instructions. They're simple, clear and short. I'm to inherit her flat and its contents, and various sums of money in saving accounts, and I and her 'dear sisters, Miss Laurel Tucker-Bond and Mrs Guy Radley' are her executors. There are various small bequests such as five hundred pounds each to 'my dear nieces, Patience, Hope and Charity'. She's detailed her funeral down to the hymns and the Bach organ voluntary, even dictated the minimal words on her tombstone. She'll cause so little work, so little fuss, it seems indecent. But I intend to put her father's name on her tombstone, whatever the work involved. She couldn't claim it in life, but she shall own it in death.

Freddy puts his fork on his plate, shoves his hands into his pockets and asks, 'What will you do with your mother's flat?'

I pick grapes from a bunch and push them one by one into my mouth. The omelette and its accompanying malted brown bread and butter have made me feel steadier. I munch, contemplating him, and my thoughts move to us and our child.

'I'd like us to keep it and sell this one. I covet that lovely view across the Thames.'

'For us? Go on.'

'Yes, for us. Freddy, we did say not so long ago we were going to talk and talk. When Mother had the first stroke. But we didn't, did we? Not about long-term plans.'

'No. No, we didn't.'

'Well, I suppose it's early days. People like Robert still know nothing of us. But with Daisy and Pattie being such chatterers — well, after the funeral everyone will be talking. Can you imagine Saffron . . . ?' I put another grape in my mouth, taste its juicy sweetness as I bite into it. It's dark now, but the air's still hot in the room. A white moth, drawn by the glow of the table-lamp, flutters in at the window. 'Well, how are we going to manage our lives? Where shall we live? In Sussex, at Allords? In one or other of the flats? And then there's your place in The Alberts. And how are we going to bring up our child?' The moth hovers about the lampshade. I swallow a grape and add plaintively, 'I need to know, Freddy.'

He looks steadily at me with his grey-blue gaze, and from five feet away I know he's locked in on me and my mind. 'And you want to talk now? After the shocks of today?'

'Earthquakes,' I correct him. 'Yes, I need solid ground beneath my feet.' I look at him in all his fundamental masculinity that's somehow at the same time civilised and controlled and good, and I feel a surge of confidence, confidence that's channelling from him. 'What do you think about marriage, Freddy?' In the semidarkness outside I sense Mumma's spirit hovering like the white moth. She believed in marriage and legitimacy with such passion. And no matter how times had changed she never could alter, and it seems right that I should do this thing for her. 'Freddy?'

He looks back at me and I see there's laughter bubbling up in him. 'Do you mean marriage in general? Or marriage in regard to us?'

'Us.'

'Then I'd like it. How about you?'

'I think I might rather like it, too. Just for a few years — forty, fifty, something like that. Yes, marry me, Freddy, and cook me your delicious omelettes for ever.' And now I'm brimming with a different emotion, half-laughing and half-crying, and I move round the table and bury my head in his neck and sniff voluptuously. He turns me round and pulls me on his lap and we hold each other cheek to cheek for a long time. Maybe Mumma's spirit's still hovering close enough to earth to know. Yes, it has to be.

It's true. I've become a different person today. I've done something I'd never have dared before. Men have pulled me on to their knees, into their arms, made every sort of approach. I've been the acceptor, never the originator of the advances. Now I've changed, and the difference is trust. I don't have to fear rejection, not with him.

19

Night comes while we are sitting there, the evening turning from fading blue to the strange glow of not-quite-darkness that's London at night. I'm so comfortable that I don't want to move, but the telephone disturbs us with its insistent ringing. I slide from his knees to flop on the sofa, pulling a resigned face; he grimaces too, and reaches for the receiver.

It's Freddy's mother and it's clear from his replies that she's concerned about me and how I'm coping. He reassures her that I'm sad but calm, then he turns his head.

'May I tell her about us? And Claudia?'

'Of course. But warn her neither's for general broadcast.'

'Understood.' He takes a slow controlling breath. 'You could say that the world's revolving dizzily on its axis for Flora . . . '

Tiredness rolls over me like a fog, pressing my eyelids shut. I lie in a separate world, remote and disembodied. At one point I hear Freddy telling me that Paula's delighted with our marriage plans. 'Good . . . ' I mumble. 'So'm I.' There's more talk, something about

367

a reception in her garden; I doze, then his voice shifts to a different note and I hear the names, *Claudia Charles* and *Primrose*. I flinch as thorns of pain snag on my heart . . .

She can't believe it at first. 'Seriously,' he says and I hear her distant voice crackling with amazement, fascination, horror. It's evident that she's as aware of the effects and problems of this revelation as we are, and she'd be talking at length if it weren't for Freddy lifting an eyebrow at me and then interrupting to tell her to hold on, Flora's white with exhaustion, they'll talk more tomorrow.

Seconds later I feel him tugging me up, bracing himself against my inert weight.

'Come on, Flora, bed.'

Paradoxically, no sooner is my head on the pillows than I'm starkly awake. The heat of the day is smouldering still in the bedroom, stealing the air, leaving me breathless. And my brain has gone into overdrive, wrestling with thoughts of Claudia and Mother, Robert, Helen, Pattie, Saffron . . . I'd thought the map of my life and my relations fixed for all time, but now the earth's moved, the map's torn apart and my skin is crawling with apprehension. Where are the boundaries of my belonging now? In the dream-castle world of aunts and cousins that Mother built for my childhood, or in today's reality that doesn't seem real at all? How can I swap Pattie for Saffron? Exchange Robert and sour Judith for dear old Laurel and funny Daisy? But if I feel shaken, how can Mumma have felt? I stare at the shadowy ceiling, remembering how she had hinted at deep hurts, irritating me by never quite explaining what. I'd found her self-pitying. So she was, but with what good reason.

In the distance a police siren screams, a sound of the urgent present. I'm sweating. I shift to a cooler patch of sheet, struggle to obliterate a vision of her suffering with a mental list of all I must do in the coming days, but can't find a beginning or an end. My brain's an insect buzzing against a glass. Poor, poor Mumma. I turn on my side and wave upon wave of unshed tears lap behind my eyes.

Freddy stirs. 'Flora? Are you awake?'

'Yes,' I say on a sob. 'My brain won't stop whirring.'

'I know. Do you have any sleeping tablets?'

'Never had one in my life,' I say, and the tears recede at the affront.

He leans over to kiss my hot eyelids. 'Then we'll try something else. Tea? Milk? Brandy and water?'

We agree on tea, and he comes to perch

beside me with a mug in each hand. I sit up, take one and blow on the hot liquid.

He runs a hand across my belly and over my hip, caressing my flesh. 'You'll start to swell soon and your waistline will go.' He sounds pleased, smug even.

'Don't you dare gloat.'

'Why not? I like the thought of you growing big with my child.'

I capture his hand to hold against my skin, and I'm struck by the thought that love is not the bantering contests I'd had with Paul or Magnus or Jake, nor a jostling for position in a brief interlude in the war between the sexes. It's this, this tender friendship, the feeling I'd looked for and missed with Jake and the others. Now I have it, I know it.

'Where shall we live, the three of us?' he asks.

I drink my tea and pretend to ponder, but I know already. I used to view the country as pleasant, but equally remote from my daily life as the Greek Islands or the Italian lakes. Now I've seen the point of it. 'In your lovely house in Sussex, except when one or both of us must be in London and then in Mother's flat. We'll set things up for the baby in both places.'

'Agreed.'

I see Freddy's house as a place of

long-term belonging. Paula's house in Buckinghamshire is the same. Places of benevolent neutrality that shelter and accept you. Perhaps it was having such parents and such houses that gave Freddy his innate sense of confidence. Because he does have it, the assurance that's so attractive. While I've always had an innate sense of not-belonging. Like Claudia. Like Mother.

Mother never quite belonged anywhere. I recognise it's something I rejected in her — that desperate need to belong that she couldn't fulfil. To me it's never mattered. I've never cringed to a lover in order to belong to him. I demanded nothing, expected nothing. I never minded living alone. Mother put up with it, but only on sufferance. Like she put up with me.

'Freddy, do you think my mother loved me?'

'Flora darling, how can I say? She should have.' He removes the mugs and shifts to his side of the bed, lying down alongside me. 'I love mine, we're great friends and we share huge areas of interest, yet I do less for her, see her far less than you did yours.'

I frown. 'Perhaps she doesn't need you in the way my mother needed me?'

'No. A different kind of relationship, perhaps.'

He's being evasive. I press. 'Do you think she liked me then, Freddy?'

'She found you diffi . . . different. She . . . Perhaps, as with Claudia, you were not each other's sort. But that doesn't mean she didn't love you. She cared about you intensely.'

'She found me difficult.' I slap the bed, flame with fury. 'That's what you were going to say, isn't it? You discussed me between you. Behind my back! How dare you!'

He jerks to a sitting position, grabs my wrist, flaring back. 'Yes, I did. And don't you shout at me, Flora Monk. I visited her in hospital — and why? Because I thought she'd love it if I played out the old-fashioned nonsense of asking her for your hand in marriage. And part of her was flattered — '

He stops again, glaring, as I tug my wrist free. 'Ouch, that hurts, you brute.'

'Don't you call me a brute. I run round after you, put you first day and night . . . '

I stop rubbing my wrist and shoved its red fingermarks at him. 'You are a brute. Look at that.'

'I didn't do that. You did it, rubbing it.'

'What? I don't believe this.'

We stare at one another in amazement, our naked chests heaving.

He catches up my wrist, studying it. 'You

shouldn't rile me,' he mutters.

Silence, then: 'What did Mother say? Come on, I want to know. And you didn't propose, either.'

His tight lips relax into a grin. 'You got in first. I couldn't ask you before you'd met my mother, that would have hurt her. But I went to clear it with yours, and, well, I was going to go all romantic on Sunday evening.' He lifts my wrist and kisses the marks. 'Sweetheart. I'm sorry.'

'Hmm. So tell me what she said.'

'It was . . . sad. That she'd found you difficult as a child, and that you had very different views on life from hers. Prickly, was what she said you were. She hoped I'd find you easier than she had.'

Surely people praise their children on these occasions? 'That was disloyal,' I say.

'Yes,' he agrees quietly.

It's strange, I'm hurt but not surprised. I recognise it as part of our relationship over many, many years. Flora's difficult, Flora's hard. I remember Robert bending his eyebrows at me after the arrival of Mrs Moffat, ' . . . but you give her some attention, too.' It's evidence of what I always really knew, that I was the subject of sighing exchanges. I feel sad rather than angry, and full of pity, for her, for me, for all the mother and child love that's destined to end in heartache and regrets. I wonder why it had to be as it was. Perhaps Laurel or Daisy will have an explanation.

'It's over,' Freddy's saying. 'It doesn't matter now whether she loved you or even liked you, because you have me. For always. I want you to be sure about that. Because I've never been more sure of anything.'

I look at him, at his tousled night-time hair, at the fair stubble on his cheeks and chin and the straw-coloured hair on his chest that he's rubbing in a tired sort of way as he speaks, and the strain of the day ebbs from me as I remember his warmth, kindness and solicitude over our three months together. I take his hand and part the fingers. 'I am sure. And as for you, you're under my skin and right deep down in me.'

I bury my face in his neck and he folds me against him. This time I'm asleep in a second.

* * *

I'm wandering aimlessly round the sitting-room after breakfast the next morning when the telephone rings. It's Pattie, very emotional and shocked, and verging on incoherence. 'I can't believe it, it's impossible to believe, poor old Aunt Primrose and poor old you. Ma

374

phoned me late last night about the Claudia thing. She woke Luke, drat her, and all the time I was trying to fathom out this monstrous tale, he was screaming in my ear. I thought Primrose was getting better, but no, there's Ma telling me she's dead and then all this horror of her being Claudia's hidden brat and keeping it quiet all these years . . . Nightmare stuff. Why didn't Ma tell me before? Or Primrose you, more to the point. We're absolutely flattened here and how you feel I can't imagine. Are you OK?'

'Freddy's holding me together,' I say, glancing at him. He gives a brief smile, then, thoughtful as ever, pours me a fresh mug of coffee. 'And we've decided to get married.'

'So you should,' she says and then giggles almost hysterically. 'That's really great. Hurray for news like that at a time like this. And thank God for Freddy. Can you imagine Jake in this sort of crisis? Hell, no. And I don't know what to say to you myself. I'm so upset for you. It's not right that you're not my cousin. You're my blood, Flora; I've always thought of you as my blood. More like a sister, really.'

'And me you.' My knees are wobbling so I sit down, clutching my hot mug for comfort. We're silent for some seconds. Tears sting the back of my eyes.

'That miserable bitch, Claudia. The way she treated Primrose, it's unbelievable. And our grandparents — I mean, my awful grandparents. Oh, this is impossible. What's going to happen to your biography? This affects everything, doesn't it? Will you carry on with it?'

'Don't know. I'll have to see what the Trustees say.'

'To hell with them. You can do it anyway, authorised or unauthorised. Put it all in, the whole boiling lot. Claudia did nothing for you, did she? You can do what you like to her, the unnatural old cow.'

I have to laugh at Pattie, she's so cross. 'Oh no. I'm aiming to be considered a serious biographer, and that means being judicial.'

'Come on, who's to define where being judicial begins and ends? It's boring anyway. And for you it'd be unnatural. Why shouldn't you write with anger, with a sense of betrayal and oppression? What's wrong with real feelings?'

'They lead you to ignore aspects of your subject that don't fit with those feelings. Besides, people say there's an element of envy in all biographical writing. You know — that insidious urge to cut the great subject down to size.'

'So what?'

376

'So that applies particularly to biographers of writers because they're in direct competition. The last thing I want is to be accused of writing out of petty pique.'

'There's nothing petty about major hypocrisy,' Pattie retorts. 'I'd want to cut Claudia into little pieces and so should you too. All that sadness about the woman who lost her baby in *Shadow of a Child* when she'd abandoned her own to adoption — and ignored her when she had the chance to make amends. It's sickening. It's . . . it's like Jean-Jacques Rousseau. Remember when Pa gave you *Emile* and *The Confessions* to read that last summer you came to us? Remember how cross you were when you realised that someone who'd written so eloquently about the education of a child had actually abandoned his own children by his mistress on the doorstep of the local Foundling Hospital? Unspeakable.'

'I know. But it doesn't wipe out Rousseau's achievements. He may have been shy, boorish and paranoid, and often behaved atrociously, yet his ideas about man in society were vital to our modern concept of democracy. It's the same with Claudia; we can't ignore her achievements, can we? Biography's a balancing act, not a diatribe.'

'Then you tell the whole truth and let your

readers decide. And that's enough of that. I'll never agree with you, not the way I feel right now. You're being far too saintly. Listen, Ma's worried about Laurel. The old love's very down. She leaned on Primrose, though she'd never admit it. What's to be done about her? It's horrid to think of her grieving alone in that dreary little flatlet.'

I think of Laurel's room, hardly altered from when I first remember it, the yellow wallpaper fading in patches, the limp curtains, the sagging armchairs, the overflowing ashtrays beside the unwashed mugs on the wood-style Formica of her 1960s' coffee-table, the general cheerless mess she ceased to notice decades ago.

'She'd better come to tea this afternoon,' I decide, 'and Daisy too. There's so much I want to ask and discuss with them both. I'll telephone them.' Beside my foot are the papers that fell from the deed box last night. I stir them with my foot, notice a bundle of yellowed letters tied with a tape, then with my toes I push the box and them out of the way beneath my chair. I'll sort them later. Pattie tells me I'm being an angel over the aunts; I agree wryly, and that concludes our conversation.

★ ★ ★

378

Helen telephones mid-morning, saying in her dry, brisk way, 'Well, welcome, new cousin. We never saw that much of one another before, but I always felt comfortable with you, Flora, as if you were family — and now you are.' What strikes her as weird is how she thought of me for Claudia. She adds that she and Sam see definite resemblances to Claudia in me, that she'd discussed me once with her and Claudia had commented that I was a lot sharper than one would expect, given my background. At this point I have difficulty restraining myself from hurling the telephone at the wall. Helen's sympathetic over Mumma, says she realises my shock over the Claudia revelations but adds that she's reeling pretty violently herself — with fury over that joker of a father of hers.

'The cynical old bastard chanced his arm that Primrose wouldn't die before your biography was published and even if she did, that you wouldn't discover the truth. Now he's fallen flat on his face and tripped up the rest of us as well. I'll tell you this, Flora, the telephone saves violence. If I'd had Dad within reach when I heard this last night there'd have been another case of child abuse in the courts — child abusing father with a fist in the face. And you know what he said? That it was my fault for suggesting you in the first place!'

She's in a hurry since she and Sam are rushing off to a lunch party in Hertford, so the remainder of our conversation is intense but minimal. Yes, she understands very well that I'm determined to continue with the work and on the whole she's inclined to sympathy. We'll meet on Wednesday to discuss every aspect we can throw up of this knotty problem, and she'll arrange a Trustees' meeting for Thursday or Friday, depending on the date I arrange for my mother's funeral. In the meantime it would be better not to let my agent or my publisher know, not until we've reached some sort of agreement in principle that we can put before them. Or no agreement. She's about to ring off when I stop her to tell her about Freddy and me. She's my new cousin after all and she was in at the start.

'Sorry? You're marrying Freddy Gulliver?' She's blank. 'What . . . ? Where . . . ? God, yes, how odd; I remember you got on well at my party . . . '

I'm laughing. 'The party when Pattie nearly had her baby on your carpet and Jake and Saffron gave their very public demonstration of heterosexual lust . . . '

'Don't remind me,' she says in a muted shriek, 'just don't!'

'Well, it had great consequences for us. Freddy drove me home, he helped me dump Jake's stuff on Saffron's doorstep, we ended the night together and we've hardly slept apart since. You and Sam must come to the wedding this autumn.' I refrain from telling her about the baby; better she doesn't know about that until everything's sorted.

'You and Freddy Gulliver? Seriously?'

'I've never been more serious in my life.'

'Well, congratulations to you both. You've nearly knocked me out for the second time in twenty-four hours but he's a lovely man and it's amazing news. We'll be at the wedding.'

★ ★ ★

As usual Daisy's picked up Laurel in her beaten-up Mini (a cast-off from Mother eight years ago) and they arrive at the same time as Isobel, who seems to have appeared by celestial summons since the others deny calling her. But they're pleased she's there. Although they aren't in fact physically holding one another up, they give a potent impression of doing so. They're as woebegone as I've ever seen them, my aunts, their old age that I've scarcely noticed now heavily apparent. Laurel, always so stoutly upright, is drooping; Daisy's silver hair looks bleached and dead, and her face resembles a crumpled old apple; Isobel's lovely eyes are redrimmed and her hands shake as she reaches out to hold me. 'Oh darling, this has all been such a shock.'

I find their grief heavy and clinging. With a strange pang I realise that it's because I'm angry with Mother at her deception, a deception that not even the thought of my writing Claudia's biography could prevail upon her to abandon. As always, she'd made me feel the weight of her disapproval without a proper explanation. The anger's blocked the channel of my sorrow.

I escape to the kitchen to make tea and collect the fresh scones I've baked. It's impossible to cry while you're eating scones, I've decided; they fill the mouth too full. When I'm ready, Freddy insists on carrying the heavy tray and we find the old ladies discussing Mumma's childhood.

They speak of it as an ordeal. In the 1920s and 1930s all children were strictly disciplined, but with the young Primrose it had been different. She had always been a well-ordered, meek child with no need of the smacks administered to the more lively Daisy or Alban, and yet, Laurel says, there was always someone squashing her. Presumably to lessen her expectations of her future, given her dubious place in it, but as she came into a spotty adolescence her mind would dissolve at the least threat of being asked her opinion, and she could barely be brought to reply to the friendly questions of family acquaintances. It was her school that saved her from becoming a pathetic nonentity, Laurel says, through a kindly English teacher who happened also to be the school librarian, and thank God for Miss Potter. She made Primrose her library monitor because, she told her, she was so reliable and sensible. Primrose thrilled at the responsibility implied in controlling the other girls' borrowings. She grew bold enough to scold girls who returned books late, she was asked for her advice on what to read, she became in a small way a personality in the school. No longer was she crushed. And her own reading was guided by someone who recognised her capability.

I pass my aunts their tea and buttered scones. 'Mother must have hated being squashed at home the whole time,' I say, 'yet she was always repressive with me. Why?'

Daisy finishes her scone, licks her fingertips and sighs. 'For the same reason she was suppressed herself, I suppose. To stamp out any inherited characteristics of Claudia Charles.'

Laurel nods. 'I don't think Primrose was ever going to take after Claudia — she must have resembled her father, whoever he was — but you threatened big problems.'

'But I'm nothing like Claudia.'

They laugh — a hollow, mournful sound.

'Not physically,' Laurel says, 'or not strikingly, though you do have the same sturdy physique and not dissimilar colouring, but mentally it seemed obvious.'

'How?'

'You were exceptionally forward and demanding. Driving was the word we used.'

'You were an awful baby,' Daisy interrupts with affection. 'A screamer. You hardly slept at all and you wanted attention every waking minute. I remember Primrose clutching you one day when you were about six weeks old — screaming as usual — and saying in a despairing kind of way, 'I think she's bored, my baby, but what can I do about it?' I said, 'She can't be bored, she's too young!' but she was right. You refused to be put down in your cot or your pram, you demanded to be on her shoulder in new places looking at new things, and the constant carrying exhausted Primrose. After all, she was forty-three, not twenty-three.'

'Driving's the word,' Isobel says, putting down her cup and saucer. 'I remember having you for the day when you were about a year old, to give Primrose a rest. You insisted that I carry you round the room and tell you the name of everything in it. You couldn't say all the words but you had to know them. 'Da?' you'd say, pointing, 'da, da?' And I'd say, 'Clock, picture, flowers, window, armchair . . . ' Over and over. And then I'd ask, 'Where's the clock, Flora?' or 'Where's the window?' and you'd flourish your little hand in triumph, 'Da! Da! Da!' Not surprisingly, you were talking by eighteen months and by the age of two you were stamping your feet over long and often comic arguments. But Primrose wasn't amused, she saw only the defiance that she wouldn't tolerate, and then it was head-on battles.'

'And tantrums,' Laurel says, sighing. 'And at that age your big eyes and your big sulky mouth were startlingly like Claudia's, far more so than now that your face has grown to suit them, so to speak. Your mother felt that she was grappling with Claudia's persona in you and it had to be stamped out.'

'And she followed her parents' methods?' Freddy asks.

'I suppose she did,' Laurel agrees. 'She could never admire Flora's liveliness and spirit as Flora's father, Philip, did. She wanted a quiet comfortable child. She wasn't unkind, though, just reproving.'

Daisy frowns. 'Motherhood worried her, particularly after Philip's death. She was proud of Flora's abilities, yet any spark of defiance and Primrose was really upset.' She turns back to me, saying almost apologetically, 'You were so different from her, you see, and she was worried you'd get beyond her control.'

'She didn't have control for most of my childhood,' I point out. 'I was at boarding school or living with the Stones.'

'She did hate sending you off,' she says thoughtfully, 'yet there were times when I sensed relief that someone else was in charge. If your father had lived it would have been different, I'm certain, but he didn't.'

They're all silent. I rise and pour more tea, hand round more scones which they accept with alacrity, the doughy food seeming to comfort them.

I sit down again and remember back, details of my childhood and Mother's striking me in a different light from before. It was unforgivable of her parents not to have treated her the same as their other children. I remember her complaints about being the odd one out in her family, of being omitted from the glories of tea and hot scones with her parents in the drawing-room, of being denied a decent education: 'Doomed to a job Claudia despised — because of *her*!' comes her voice out of the past. They left her brooding over the lacks in her young life.

But then there were lacks in my own life that seemed never to have struck her: the holidays as well as the terms spent away from home that widened the gap between us, the gap of interests. I read writers she disliked and developed notions she found startling; worse, I began to question, even to ridicule, her own beliefs.

I start to see the reasons behind the strictness that drove me wild, behind the mournful looks when we argued which made me feel I was unkind, a thoughtless nasty person. She wanted to make me in her own image, but the reflections she saw were of Claudia. I wanted her love, yet felt it withheld, even after she'd driven me to apologise.

And then it hits me how much Claudia has affected us, despite the great distance she kept, in the fear through two generations of repeating the sins of the past. How far are we the creatures of our ancestral past or how much the creators of our own destiny? Have I inherited the traumas of their cold childhoods? Will the details of her daughter's and granddaughter's repressed upbringings, along with her own adolescent pains with Aunt Selina, be relevant to Claudia's biography or not?

20

We bury Mother late on the Friday morning and it's raining. Needles of tepid July rain spatter on to the coffin, into the grave, on to shoulders and hair and dripping sharp-pointed umbrellas. The grave is up in the lee of a hedge and sheltered by a huge tree with a trunk like a pillar from the church we've just left. With one hand I hold Freddy's arm, with the other, a trinity of the crimson roses Mumma loved. Beside us the lumpy khaki-coloured clay soil is open to receive her. This is death, this is the end, black-clad Uncle Guy intoning the words of the burial service, the air around him seething with silence.

Then the sound comes, a creaking, drumming sound in the tree; a spotted woodpecker proclaiming his territory. I look up and find him just as he drums again, vigorous, assertive. I look down and men with ropes lower the coffin. ' . . . We therefore commit her body to the ground, earth to earth, ashes to ashes, dust to dust, in sure and certain hope of the Resurrection to eternal life . . . ' I throw my roses, my last gift to the woman who gave me the gift of life; my head pounds and I shudder for breath as earth spatters on the shiny wood deep in the hole.

The woodpecker darts away. Over the hedge a pair of bearded joggers pound past the cemetery, oblivious to our little ceremony, grumbling of the weather. We say the Lord's Prayer in a murmur of familiar words and I wonder at my mother's desire to be buried here rather than cremated in a secular, modern way, when she'd proclaimed that since Daddy's death she'd lost all certainty in a God so casual and cruel with people's lives.

Then clouds part to let out a gleam of sun, a blackbird sings, the woodpecker drums in a different tree, and all at once there's light everywhere, gleaming from every droplet of rain on the hedge and the grass, shining from the lowered umbrellas and the bright flowers on the coffin. The rain ceases, a rainbow arches beyond the tree and I see a pattern and a beauty that's part of an absolute, an ancient holy meaning embracing all of us: me, Freddy, the birds, the joggers, the family, even old Judith and her daughter Saffron scowling across the gravel at Robert, furious that he's kept the secret of Mumma's birth from them through all those years.

It bursts upon me that Freddy is right in contradicting me when I demur at the big church wedding and reception in her garden that Paula's offering. 'Family christenings, weddings and funerals, they're special occasions with rituals whose meanings date back centuries. Life's so short that it's good to be linked to the before and hereafter. Let's celebrate in the old ways with everyone who's ever meant anything to either of us.' For a moment the meaning of everything is straight in my head, I can tell him I agree, I can tell them all. I understand Mumma, I understand Claudia, who both wanted more than was given them. I feel for them in their grievances. The ceremony, linking us all, comforts me.

★ ★ ★

We crowd into Mother's flat, where Mrs Moffat sets out the funeral baked meats for us, except that they aren't funereal, but colourful, appetising, ruddy slices of cold roast fillet of beef with crisp salads; fresh salmon and seafood delicacies and her own home-baked brown rolls. 'Like I did for Mrs Malcolm's funeral,' she'd suggested when offering this as her final service, then stopped and looked uncomfortable. 'Yes,' I'd agreed, ironical, 'as you did for her mother.' But Mother wasn't invited to her mother's funeral, nor mentioned in her Will. 'I'll never understand it,' Mrs Moffat muttered. 'Nor I,' I said.

The old ladies reach out for glasses of wine, their colour returning as they sip. Others head for Freddy, who, grasping the essentials as always, pours whisky for Laurel, Robert, Helen's Sam, Uncle Guy, Mother's writer friend Geoffrey Pickstone — and Saffron.

Geoffrey Pickstone, a short, elderly man with rope-like muscles in his neck and a bald shiny pate like a priest's, rumbles at me that my mother was a woman of real generosity of spirit. 'She had a wide knowledge of literature, which wasn't surprising when you think she was related to Claudia Charles, but still she could praise my work — and with genuine understanding. I shall miss her shockingly.'

He pauses for a gulp of whisky only to be interrupted by Saffron, who pushes him aside to tell me without care for time or place that she can't believe what she's been hearing from Robert and Judith. 'But clearly if it's true it makes it impossible for you to write the Claudia biography!'

Geoffrey mutters, 'Bad-mannered young woman,' jostling her out of his own way and stomping off, all but colliding with Aunt Daisy, whose eyes hold him with the most hopeful and inviting of glances before falling in delicate embarrassment.

'You're Geoffrey Pickstone, the writer, aren't you? How extraordinarily kind of you to come to my sister's funeral.' She flickers up another look from under the white hair that's light as thistledown, breathes, 'Do tell me what you're working on now,' and he pauses, stammers, and succumbs.

I giggle, further exasperating Saffron who snaps, 'There's nothing funny in this. It's an appalling situation. Uncle Robert says there's nothing he can do because of the contract, but I've told him such circumstances must invalidate it.'

'How? He knew of the relationship at the time.'

'But you didn't — and he didn't know you would come to know. Now you can't hope to be impartial or objective.'

I ask provocatively, 'Are any biographies truly impartial? Those of us who write them choose our subjects because we believe them to be important, and preferably among the great. So we're bound to be fascinated by them and that's a bar to the impartiality of our theories from the start. In the light of Claudia's treatment of my mother perhaps I'll be more objective than most!'

'That's a ridiculous statement. Helen and

the other Trustee aren't at all happy.'

'And that, Saffron, is an unprofessional remark. What's happiness got to do with it?'

I'm waiting to hear the Trustees' decision. I've taken legal advice from Annabel Bateman, who lives just up the Hill, and is a barrister and a friend. Her advice was in my favour, so that makes me less apprehensive — but I still hate waiting. Annabel had telephoned when she saw the announcement of Mumma's death in *The Times* to say how shocked and sorry she was. I told her of recent disclosures and asked for her opinion. She gasped, considered, said she was no expert on intellectual property but that if this was a straightforward contractual dispute she couldn't see that I had anything to worry over. The three Trustees had authorised the biography, and in turn my publishers and I had contracted together in good faith. It was Robert who'd concealed vital information and any dispute would be with him, not me. Then she gave a snort of laughter and repeated pretty much what Freddy had said of shock-waves hitting the literary world: 'Your book'll sell like hot cakes and everyone concerned will make huge profits. Who'll object to that?'

Saffron, naturally. She can't leave the subject alone and she takes no more interest

394

in logical argument than politicians, simply slamming the opposition as hard as she can.

'Of course, I can't accept that Claudia was your grandmother in the same sense that she was my great-aunt. It's a matter of knowing a person, recognising the bond that grows over the years, feeling of one blood with them. You had none of that, did you? Having genes in common is only a small part of the mystery. The input into the relationship over the years . . . '

'You're destroying your own arguments, Saffron,' Pattie puts in blithely as she arrives at my side with Luke draped over her shoulder. 'If Flora's shared no bond of recognition over the years with her granny Claudia then she can be nonpartisan and simply tell the truth.'

'That's the most naïve statement I've ever heard,' Saffron snaps. 'Flora's bound to be partisan with her rejected mother, bound to produce sob stories. But since it's clear neither of them affected Claudia one jot, what's that sort of slush got to do with the truth of her writing?'

Freddy joins us, malt whisky in one hand, Highland spring water in the other, eyes dancing behind his spectacles. 'Truth?' he enquires, and I can see that he's in one of those wind-up frivolous moods that tend to follow hard upon funerals and similar momentous occasions. 'Come on, there ain't no such animal — except in fiction. And that's what you write, isn't it, Saffron? Fiction can never be untruthful because it's pure invention. It writes its own rules, and what it says, is. Biography, more solemnly, attempts to portray reality. But here's where the world pounces on the biographer, for what is truth to one observer, is a false image to another.' A wide gesture with the whisky bottle. 'A dozen interviews give a dozen different pictures of your subject. Is each one revealing a different facet of the whole and therefore in itself true? Or is each subtly distorted and thus veering away from truth? How can one tell? It's philosophy's oldest dilemma, the truth. And who's to say where it lies? But Flora, unlike her predecessor, Susie Peters, has the percipience to see the hidden snares.'

'I think you're lovely,' Pattie says, 'the way you put things. And one truth is that it's up to Flora if she wants to say that Claudia was an uncaring cow . . . '

'And who are you to pontificate?' Saffron snaps at Freddy. 'I don't even know you.'

'Yes, you do,' I say, 'you met at Helen's last party. Freddy also had the displeasure of seeing you and Jake disporting yourselves on that bed. It was he who helped me clear out

Jake's rubbish on to your doorstep. Remember?'

She scowls, momentarily speechless.

Freddy replenishes the whisky in the glass she shoves at him, remarking at his most urbane, 'I'm Freddy Gulliver, and I'll shortly be your new cousin by marriage.'

'What *are* you talking about?'

'Flora and I are to be married this autumn.'

Now Saffron's completely nonplussed.

'You and Jake can come to the wedding if you like,' I say kindly. 'And Aunt Judith, too. My new family.'

'They're going to have a baby,' Pattie contributes. 'In January.'

Saffron recovers herself. 'Marriage and a baby? How suburban,' she sneers.

Pattie, Luke asleep against her shoulder, glares. 'God, you are a bitch. What's so trend-setting smart about *you*, waiting around for globe-trotting poseurs like Jake? And anyway,' as Saffron opens her mouth once more, 'this is Flora's mother's funeral and Flora's upset, so go and see Mrs Moffat and fill your mouth with something more pleasant than spite.'

She blinks, shrugs and goes. There's something unsteady about her usual hip-swaggering walk. Has she drunk that much of Freddy's whisky? So swiftly?

Hands clink forks against plates, bottoms sink into chairs, voices buzz in the overcrowded room. I help myself to mounds of salmon and prawn salad under Aunt Judith's basilisk eye, while she notifies me that she won't have any long-dead scandals revived to discredit her aunt Claudia, and that she's always said it was utterly wrong I should write the biography. I refer her to the Trustees and escape to perch on a sofa-arm beside Helen and Robert while I eat.

Helen's tall young brother, Benjamin, comes to sit at my feet, cross-legged. 'I hear you're my new cousin,' he says, chewing pleasurably at his beef. 'Isn't that just mind-boggling? Do you like being this new person, or do you prefer you as you were?'

'What do you think?' I fence, smiling. I like Ben. He's a mathematics lecturer at the local university, and, unlike most men, never takes himself in the least seriously.

He sucks in the hot air of the room and exhales noisily. 'Ooof, I don't know. A Charles or a Tucker-Bond by descent? Raffish, foolish, which is worse? I'm happy to have you as a cousin, though, I'll tell you that. I enjoy your books, you see. Now I can boast about you — and boost my image as well as your sales.' He forks more beef into his mouth. 'Wow, I'd forgotten what a good cook Mrs M is. She made visiting Claudia worthwhile.'

'Wasn't it otherwise?'

'Over my head she was — I nearly drowned in boredom. I struggled through one of her books as a teenager — under duress from Dad — but I didn't see the marvel of it. Or her. An over-the-top word merchant; a literary snob with a one-track mind.'

'Does that matter? You have to have singularity of purpose if you're to reach her position of distinction.'

'A pity some of her distinction couldn't have been relieved by good humour — or basic kindliness. She made it clear she thought I was a waste of space. A mathematician? How could such a person have subtlety or depth? I could have been a car salesman. So there you are, Flora. Something for the old peacock's debit column: she lacked the wider vision, she lacked humanity.'

'And Mumma and I prove it?'

'I didn't say it.' A pause. 'Poor Primrose. But yes, of course. Ruthlessness Claudia certainly had.' A frown. 'God, I can't imagine how you're feeling.'

I shake my head. How am I feeling? That

I'm a fraud. It's as if I've assumed a false identity, an invented persona that doesn't belong to either family, and when all these people leave the flat I'll shed the disguise and become — what? Terror seizes me as the void gapes. I look at the families in the room and suddenly they all seem strangers, strangers with their backs turned to me. I've no blood link with the Tucker-Bonds, no feeling of being a Charles. Then I remember: soon I'll be Flora Gulliver. For once it's easier for a woman than for a man; women are used to assuming new identities. But I'll still be Flora Monk, the writer.

Beside me Helen shifts from her conversation with Robert to tell me, in a voice she's careful not to make generally audible, 'Flora, the Trustees met yesterday and I think I should tell you now that we've concluded you should continue as Claudia's biographer. Your strange relationship with her has taken us all aback, and,' dryly, 'it's hardly what we'd have stipulated, but on consideration we feel that we can rely on you to be scrupulously careful in assembling the evidence and evaluating it and we do — as you and Clifford Cumbers have both commented — have the watching brief that our agreement gives us. I'm glad, needless to say.'

The velvet glove of flattery concealing the

iron hand? I reply that I'm relieved by their sensible decision. To myself I add that I'm damned if I'm going to be self-deprecating or fall on my face with gratitude. If I want to expose Claudia as a fatally flawed person, then that's what I'll damned well do, grandmother or not. I take breath and tell Helen, 'I've taken legal advice and from what I'm told you are following the only course open to you, since I signed in good faith and any bad faith was on your side.'

'Don't rub it in,' she says without conviction.

'But I trust in turn that your grip on the final production — your watching brief as you call it — won't turn into the sort of pressure that other biographers have been subjected to. You know what I mean, Helen: the pressure to be anodyne, to ignore the unpleasant truths of scandal and callousness and write something that will upset no one — including Judith. I can see that it's hellish for her, or for anyone affected by a transformed vision of the person they thought they knew. But I can't let that deflect me. And if you or Robert, or any of you recollect anything or come across any other document that could shed light on the past, I want your assurance that you won't suppress that either.'

'You have it so far as I'm concerned. You'll have to speak to Robert yourself.'

'This extraordinary situation has put me on my guard against indulging in any fanciful assumptions. Some biographers assume too much when facts are not plentiful enough regarding certain aspects of their subjects' lives — particularly dubious aspects. I'm more likely to do the opposite, but I don't want that to happen from reasons of ignorance. Nor do I want any of you Trustees telling me how I should view Claudia.'

She blinks, looking discomfited. 'Certainly not.'

I drive my point home. 'Robert mentioned photographs of Claudia and her set that you and he have, and possibly Judith also. I'd like to have them now, please. There may be shots of her with Somerville friends, or London friends, or at various functions or parties. I'm going to comb the nineteen nineteen diary for the names of any men in whom Claudia might have had an interest and if I should have a suspect to follow up, then a photograph, well . . . perhaps I'm grasping at straws, but a likeness to Mumma could be additional evidence.'

She senses my urgency and rises to her feet. 'I can't resist Mrs Moffat's puddings and I must have a coffee, but then I'll go and

402

collect my boxes of albums and portraits and bring them straight back here.'

'Thanks. Oh, and Helen, help me out, will you? I'll need to search all your cupboards and filing cabinets for Claudia's missing diaries. And Robert's and Cliff Cumbers' too. I'll find them if I have to search every nook of every house she ever lived in. You see, I've a suspicion that she loved her own writing, however incriminating, too much to have destroyed them. They'll be at the bottom of some box, somewhere, I just know it.'

'Well,' she says, slightly huffy, 'if you want to get dirty and dusty in dark corners that's fine by me. But I doubt we've a thing you don't know about already.'

★ ★ ★

No sooner has Helen departed than Aunt Daisy plants herself beside me. 'Nice man, Geoffrey Pickstone,' she says complacently. 'Cheered me up. Now, Flora darling, how are you?'

'Fine.'

'You're going to keep this place on, I hear. That'll be good for our lunch parties, won't it? Not such a wrench for poor darling Laurel and Isobel. We'll miss Primrose terribly, but we could invite Geoffrey, couldn't we? I'm sure he's lonely for female company.'

I admire her assumptions and manipulations. What next?

'Shall you keep any of the furniture and the other things?' An innocent look from the bird-like eyes.

'No idea. Why? Do you want anything in particular?'

'No, no, dear. It's for Laurel I'm asking. It might be kind to offer her a piece or two to remember Primrose by. You know what her dreadful place is like.'

'Apart from the mahogany table and chairs she can have what she wants. How's that?'

'Darling, that's most kind. You're a very nice person underneath, you know. I was always telling Primrose so. Well then, you know how saggy our sofa is, could we . . . ?'

★   ★   ★

It's half-past three in the afternoon and nearly all of them have gone.

'I have an idea,' Freddy announces from the kitchen doorway.

'What idea?' I am helping Mrs Moffat clear up after the party, putting away the plates, cutlery and trays, polishing the glasses till they sparkle. I shall keep the glasses, a superb collection that were Mumma's wedding present from Aunt Selina and Uncle Lucian.

'We'll spend the weekend at Allords and Pattie and Greg and the babes will come too.'

Tension flows out of me as if a cool wind has blown across my hot tired head, freeing me from sad thoughts, from sticky, humid, horrid July London. It'll be wonderfully quiet there, a retreat for us all. If we stayed in Richmond this weekend, I'd be driven by an awful restlessness to sort through my flat and decide what to retain or discard in the move to Mother's. And then I'd prickle with guilt that I now own what was hers. Someone, sometime in the last days (was it Laurel?) said there was always guilt at a death. Guilt at being in the light, at being able to carry on with the interests and enjoyments of life. When we arrive at Allords the hall will be shadowy, but we'll be able to look through to the garden beyond, where the late sun will be gleaming on a lawn that's more than two centuries old, and the silvery evening trees hanging down leaves like tendrils. There'll be ghosts there, but nothing to haunt me.

'Yes,' I say. 'Oh yes. Ask them.'

Mrs Moffat chuckles and says getting away's just what we should do, and right now; she'll finish cleaning up. She's having her closest friend from her retirement village to stay for the weekend at my suggestion.

They're going to revel in Kew Gardens and take a boat down the Thames and visit Richmond Theatre. Then on Monday I'll drive them both back to Kent. She's been such a stalwart friend to us.

My brain races. Between us we can collect clothes and children's clobber and food, load up the cars and be there by dinner time. Pattie can feed her children before we leave. Heaven.

Pattie appears in the doorway where Freddy was. 'Count us in,' she says. 'This is an excellent idea. We're off to collect nappies and things right away.' She turns, then turns back. 'Hey, Flora, you ought to know, Judith's found Saffron locked in the bathroom, drunk, and she's trying to get her out. Saffron drove her here in that exciting car of hers, but she won't be fit to drive it for hours and hours, so poor old Judith sent for a taxi. For them both, I mean. But now Saffron's refusing to communicate and she doesn't know what to do.'

'What's the problem? Why's Saffron behaving like this?'

Pattie pulls one of her comic faces. Lowering her voice, she says, 'In a word, Jake.'

'Should've known,' I say disgustedly.

In the hallway Judith is calling through the

bathroom keyhole, her purple-clad backside enormous as she bends. 'Saffron, I repeat, do you want me to go or stay?'

'But not quite like you think,' Pattie adds softly and rolls her eyes. 'Seems Jake's been head-hunted in America, offered some exciting job with vast earnings in some corporation his firm's been doing work for, and he's accepted it. Poached, in other words. By the Texans. Couldn't refuse, he said. Before you leap to conclusions, Flora, this part isn't what you'd think either — '

'You don't know *what* I'm thinking — but I'll tell you. Jake's determined to move to America, he's said Saffron should abandon her life here and join him, and she's said, 'Like hell!' Right?'

'Right. Here, she's an established writer. There? Nowhere. So she's desolated, furious, miserable, all those things, and then there's this funeral. She was fond of Primrose, you know; she said she was much nicer than her own mother — and on top of that, the Claudia and you thing, which she can't get her head round at all.'

'Saffron!' Silence. Judith calls to us. 'Flora! Pattie! She could have passed out, you know . . . I can't see her. It's your friend Jake's fault, Flora. He let her down. I told her he would.'

The doorbell goes and it's Helen pushing four big boxes of photographs at me. I thank her fervently, she nods and disappears again.

Outside the bathroom Pattie is coping with Judith. 'Is Saffron waiting to spew? I mean, I never open my mouth to speak to *anybody* when that's in the balance, you know, anything rather than let it out.'

'She's never sick,' Judith retorts, sniffing disgustedly. 'Flora's young man — Freddy, is it? — encouraged her to drink far, far too much whisky.'

'She sneaked it when he was looking the other way.' Pattie refuses to compromise. 'She's having a hard time so she sloshed it back like a lunatic.'

The doorbell goes again. Freddy says that Judith's taxi is here. He's trying not to laugh.

'This is impossible.' A little vein throbs in Judith's temple. 'Now what do I do?'

'Take the taxi and go,' Pattie says. 'We'll sort out Saffron.'

In the bathroom Saffron sneezes in a muffled sort of way. Once, twice, three times.

'She's not dead,' Pattie giggles.

'That's it,' Judith decides. 'Goodbye, girls, I'm off.' She slams the front door.

Three minutes later Saffron emerges. She's unsteady, but basically compos mentis.

'How did I get a mother like that?' she asks.

'Job's comforter? She swallows me up like the whale. Why couldn't I have had one of yours? I loathe the nagging old bitch.'

'Mine's batty,' Pattie shrugs. 'And she embarrassed me at school.'

'I didn't find mine easy to love,' I admit.

Suddenly Pattie's off in one of her giggling fits. Saffron and I first look at her blankly, then we catch the mood and start off ourselves reeling around the hall, doubling up helplessly.

'Weren't they impossible, our families?' Pattie gasps. 'Aren't they impossible? But they do make life interesting, all the same. You'd never think that Judith was Claudia's niece, would you, Flora? Not with that bad smell under her nose all the time. God, Saffron, I'm surprised you're as sane as you are.'

Saffron gasps, 'Stop me laughing, for God's sake. Or I really shall throw up. I suppose I'd better leave after that exhibition. Just someone call me another taxi, please.'

'You should come for a country weekend with us,' Pattie says light-heartedly. 'At Freddy and Flora's place. Better than drinking yourself into a stupor alone in your flat.'

Saffron's suddenly very still. She looks awful, her sweaty skin the colour of scummy pond weed, her eyes all big and bloodshot — and needy. They look at me and away.

'OK,' I say, surprised at my magnanimity, 'you are my cousin, after all, aren't you, Saffron?'

21

Saffron's in another world when we arrive at Allords, passed out, or simply asleep, I don't know. She's lying across the back seat, her head lolling, her mouth open. I touch her and she opens her eyes to give me an alien burnt-out stare, then the lips close, she sits up abruptly and the old imperious look returns.

'Where are we?' She looks about herself and shakes her head. 'Ouch. This house . . . why are we here? I thought we were coming to someone's country cottage.'

'House. This one.'

Even with a hangover she can emerge from a car with elegance. She stares at Allords' façade, mellow in the fading light. 'Is it borrowed for the weekend or something?'

'It's Freddy's. Inherited.'

'Is it indeed? Well, a place like this is something to marry for,' she says with a kind of wan cynicism.

For a moment I think that's a standard Saffron bitch, but then I see that it's more an oblique compliment. 'Allords is a bonus,' I tell her, smiling. 'I'm marrying Freddy

411

because I want to spend the rest of my life with him.'

Greg and Pattie's estate car pulls up behind us in a shower of gravel. They gesture good cheer as they lift their drowsy children from the car.

★ ★ ★

Over our informal supper of summery foods washed down with Pimms, Saffron bursts into a diatribe against her mother, Judith.

'She's so awful, you'd think she'd worked at it day and night, like a student slaving for a first in Monstrosity. She sees snares and devious plots in every aspect of one's life; it's never possible that anything just happens. Her view of Jake and me and the break is that he'd insinuated himself with the corporation hierarchy in Texas in an underhand way, deceiving his own company and deceiving me with a view to dumping the lot of us when he'd signed the offer he wanted. Obvious, she says. It's no use my pointing out that he's been pleading with me to join him there, she simply retorts that no man with a modicum of intelligence could possibly imagine me in Dallas; he knows I'd never abandon London and its social scene and the English manners that I satirise in my writing, and he doesn't give a damn.'

We murmur vague somethings.

'Like a fool I offer to drive her to the funeral — and what do I get in return? A head-shaking denunciation of the beastly ways of the male, and a lecture on my credulous nature. I know she only wants to stand guard over me, but when I'm in trouble paranoid thoughts dart from her like shoals of ravenous piranhas and she makes me paranoid too. I end up prowling the house at four in the morning, shaking with anger and dread.'

'I know,' I say, remembering certain past times, 'I've been there too.'

The others agree, but it's me she gives the long sideways look. 'Ma's rabid over you and Claudia and the biography, of course. You manipulated Helen. If the piranhas could strip your flesh, she'd cheer.'

I shake my head. 'I've no doubt. Only she's wrong. No manipulations, not with Helen nor any of the Trustees. Quite simply, it was proposed, I accepted.'

She gives a grimace, and there's more than a suggestion of age and weariness about her.

A second later, the difference between our respective mothers' reactions hit me with a shock: when Saffron confesses to problems,

Judith's convinced the world is plotting against her; when I had difficulties, Mumma suspected I must be in the wrong. Which is the more unnatural? And then I think of Claudia — a woman who'd experienced her own purple paranoid patches, yet took no account whatsoever of her own daughter's sufferings when she reached twenty-one and found herself rejected by the people she'd believed were her parents. How strange and warped the mother/daughter relationship can be. I feel relief that I've not been alone in my struggles with my mother. She wasn't guiltless towards me and my uncertain feelings over her aren't abnormal. I return my attention to Saffron.

'I was horrid to Jake when he came back to take final leave of his company,' she's saying. She prods her fork in brooding fashion at her food. 'I wish I hadn't been. But he does want me over there. He wouldn't have rung me all the dozens of times he has without being genuine, would he?'

'No,' I agree, 'not Jake. Besides, he's always liked you.'

She frowns. 'Why do you say that?' There've been too many years of deep-rooted antipathy between us for her to credit a kindly phrase or two from me.

'When he was with me he'd be pleased

414

when you came round. He'd say that he liked clever, intense women, that you and I were alike. If you really want to know, it annoyed me.' I pause, pondering. 'That he saw us as similar, I mean.'

Pattie grins. 'The Claudia Charles genes.'

'That's what everyone's going to say.' I shrug. 'And I suppose there must be something in it. Both of us choosing writing as a career.'

Saffron and I exchange stares with the stiffness of rival cats clashing over territories. Then she gives up. 'What's in all those boxes Freddy brought in from the car, Flora?'

I relax, pass round a bowl of fruit. 'Claudia's photographs. And I've brought her nineteen nineteen journal, too. I'm intending to comb through everything I have for hints of Claudia's admirers in the period around my mother's conception.'

'When would that have been?' Greg asks, peeling a banana.

'She was born in the late July of nineteen twenty. No mention of her being premature, so nine months earlier, which gives us late October, early November in nineteen nineteen.'

'Claudia must have been in her second year at Somerville,' Pattie comments. 'That would give her a choice of chaps who were up that year, or given her early inclination to the more mature male — look at Laurence Britton — possibly a don.'

'Or a newspaper magnate or a journalist — she published her first articles under the assumed name of Clarissa Smart around that time.'

'Or someone she met on holiday that summer.'

'Hell, it's impossible.'

We're discussing whether Susie Peters might know something of this era when a wail from the direction of the stairs make us all jump. Georgy staggers in, clad in a shrunken T-shirt and tiny pants. 'I'm in a wrong bed and it's not in my own room,' he says as he rushes at Pattie and buries his head in her chest. 'I want *my* bed, now!'

She lifts him on to her lap, laughing. 'Can't be done, sweetheart,' she says, 'your bed's miles and miles and *miles* away. But this one's a very nice bed and there's a lovely rocking horse in your room to look after you.'

He raises his head suspiciously. 'I haven't seen it.'

'I did show you, but you were very sleepy. We'll say hullo to him now.'

He turns his head, weighing alternative inducements. 'Can I sit on Flora's knee first and have some purply grapes like she's got?

416

I'm hungry, Mummy.'

'No, Georgy, bed.' She slides him from her knees as she rises. 'But you can have one, one, little ride on the rocking horse, before you go to sleep.'

He's pensive, but this appeals. 'All right,' he tells her. And then to Freddy, 'Is it your rocking horse?'

'I used to ride him when I was little, but he was my great-uncle's once. He's a hundred years old, you see, and that's very very old.'

Saffron wants to know if he's a dappled grey. 'Then I'm coming too.'

In the end everyone but me goes upstairs and I hear ripples of amusement and delight at the horse. I pat my tummy where I imagine my baby is. 'It'll be your rocking horse one day, little one,' I tell it, as I clear the debris of our meal and push the plates and glasses into the dishwasher.

Upstairs I hear them deciding to join Georgy in going to bed and I'm grateful. Every bit of me's heavy with tiredness. Bereavement and pregnancy are an exhausting combination.

★ ★ ★

I wake at six to a young and tender day, full of pale sunshine. Freddy's sprawled beside

417

me, warm and rumpled. I ease myself from the bed slowly, to avoid waking him, and return with the bundle of my father's yellowed letters I've been meaning to read for days.

Only . . . they aren't Daddy's; they're the young Harry's, half a century old.

And they're amazing. So loving and sweet and naïve protective male where Mother's concerned, so full of murderous hate for the German pilots his life is geared to shooting down.

August 21st, 1940

My dearest Primrose,

I've just sent you a silly card and now I can settle down to getting off a rather longer cheerio! The Mess was in a bit of a muddle when we got back tonight with enough dust to give your tidy mind the jitters. No vital damage done, though. We went after Goering with everything we have but no luck, no damage in return. How we cursed. I have to confess I'm glad you can't hear me when I'm up there shouting and hating and demented and blaspheming in the fight. It isn't me at all, some other person takes over, but it's a person who wants to protect you above everything.

418

Darling, I loved you so much last night for being so brave and cheerful. When I was coming in to land a great peace came over me just at the thought of you and I realised that I love you with a depth of feeling that cannot be described. I know you love me, my wonderful woman, and there is nothing else that really matters. When this beastly war is over we will be together for always.

Forgive me if I can't tell you when I'll see you next but believe me it will be the soonest possible.

All my love,
Your Harry

I put it down, lie still for some moments, then slip another from the bundle.

September 6th, 1940

My own dearest girl,

It was heaven to feel your dear arms around me again on Sunday. I was so bucked that you'll have noticed I even managed to take an interest in what your Aunt Selina is doing to the vegetable garden and the conservatory. She has so much energy.

You know, darling, I think that it would

be quite amusing to keep the letters we are writing to one another at this time to read over together in the future, perhaps on some winter evenings when everything is sane again and we sit together on a sofa that will be ours and gaze into our own fire. Thank you for your last sweet letter.

Hours of stooging around the last day or two which I hate, it's all so peaceful and false and boring, then at last we were scrambled and then it was the usual frenzied cartwheeling around the sky with my earphones crazy with yells and commands and suddenly I hardly realised what had happened but there was a burning Jerry plane plummeting down near the river and it was mine. A Messerschmitt! Blasted to hell. I can't explain the feeling it gives me.

I'm glad we write to each other like this, it's more private than telephoning and we can both say things we can't when there are other ears listening. Like how lovely that evening was in the orchard when we saw the glow-worms in the cracks in the old wall, shining with that soft light, and you'd never seen any before, you Londoner, you! And the moon came out very sweetly and the searchlights were distant things many miles away and we whispered sweet *nothings in each others' ears.*

I remember laughing at you for being unromantic when you told me about the piglets' progress and how noisy they are, but I shouldn't have laughed. Yours is a world of sanity and you tether me to what's real and long-lasting and right. I love you and I am yours to command for ever.

Dearest, it is getting late and I need sleep badly.

Many loving kisses from your
Harry

Tears blind my eyes. I don't want to read any more.

Freddy sighs and turns to hold me. His lips caress my cheek with kisses. Then he stops, pulls back his head to study me. 'What is it?'

I hand him the letters, tell him what they are. He reads them in silence.

'You didn't know it was like this?'

'It wasn't spoken of.'

'Never?'

'She closed the shutters, she must have done. And it was less than a year later when the grandparents told Mumma about her birth and then she'd lost her family, too, hadn't she?'

He's quiet. 'Her Harry. All the early wonder of being loved and valued — gone.'

I grope in the box for a tissue and wipe my eyes. 'She had a sad life.'

'So did millions; something that could never be put right. In those days they were living on an erupting volcano.'

I look outside at the shimmering trees against a morning sky that's bright with the possibility of heat. But I'm inside, looking back at history, at violence, at the different rules of a different age. In my mind it's all dark. I'm on edge with her unhappiness but, as Freddy says, I can't put it right. Somewhere a strange bird calls, a plangent, protesting sound that repeats and repeats. There's a dialogue inside my head of similar sounds, offended, mournful. The shuttered darkness of her unhappiness stayed with her all her life. With Daddy's death it thickened and came between her and me. I should have been a comfort to her, but I was too determined, too different, too similar to Claudia. Besides, she sent me away. Why did it have to be like that? The seconds pass and I know that there will always be this roller-coaster feeling inside me, leaving me swooping between alienation and sadness for her.

★ ★ ★

Mid-morning coffee in the sun on the lawn. We sit on elderly rattan chairs, stick our bare legs out in front of us and stretch luxuriously. Purple and blue spikes of delphinium reach for the sky, phloxes buzz with bees. Luke grizzles and Pattie opens her shirt to feed him, her white-fleshed, blue-veined breast hanging like a bellflower. Saffron averts her eyes.

'Oh God, must you?' she grumbles.

Pattie opens mocking eyes at her. 'I didn't know *you* were a prude, Saffron.'

When Luke has finished Pattie announces that she must go for a pee and dumps the baby in Saffron's arms. 'Burp him for me, would you?' she says, and disappears, grinning.

Saffron glances across at me, but I'm burying my head in Claudia's 1919 journal, searching for the unknown lover. She looks for Greg, but he's pig-in-the-middle in a game of ball with a delighted Georgy and Freddy. 'Daddy's a pig,' Georgy shrieks, hurling the ball at him rather than past him. Greg jumps it neatly, and Freddy fields it from a distant rosebed. Saffron sighs, puts Luke against her shoulder and pats him awkwardly. 'Sprogs should be kept out of sight until they're at least two,' she observes. I pretend not to hear. Luke belches and then succumbs to huge hiccups. Saffron is appalled and looks for help that isn't forthcoming. I try not to laugh.

When Pattie reappears she rescues Saffron, puts her hiccupping son tummy down on a rug at her feet and asks me how my researches are going. Nowhere so far. The entries in Claudia's earliest journals, those of 1918 and 1919, are often mere cryptic jottings: *November 24th, 1918: Tutorial with Miss Jebb. Valuable discussion on Milton. February 12th, 1919: Met two poets at D's, Osbert and Sacheverell Sitwell. Clever gentlemen and, excellent company, the sort I need. June 3rd: Musical evening of Schubert, etc. TW full of perceptive whispers.* By mid-1919 the comments are more developed, for example in early July: *Went to tea with Norman F and graced the Balliol barge. It would have been fun except that he thought so highly of himself for giving me such a special treat that his repetitions of its wonders and my privilege made me grind my teeth to prevent myself shouting Stop. Condescension is man's most prevalent social vice. Why do men have at once to lift us up with kindness and put us down with arrogance? It prevents us from enjoying their company on any intimate level.* But I'm not finding what I want. It's annoying that she had not then discovered the mental release of confiding in her journal. By 1921, the first year of the Britton affair, she was using her journal as a special place where she could analyse the pains of her struggling, striving life in a balancing act between irony and anguish that's highly revealing, but it's the one for the previous year that I'm after.

'But what about the time round your mother's conception?' Pattie demands to know. 'Come on, you must have delved into those weeks.'

'God, yes, but there's nothing I can pin down. Claudia has a lively social life for the time, but she's secretive, damn her. She will use initials. There's a TW who's come up several times and who's around in the vital October and November period. I suspect TW to be male, but I can't be certain. She visits the country with him or her, commenting on the autumn colours and, perhaps cryptically, on 'revelations of beauty'. Then there are two or three others escorting her to a concert or the theatre, but nothing, just nothing, that directly indicates a sex life.' The sun's so bright on the page it hurts my eyes and Saffron's looking bored. Sighing, I put the journal down.

Freddy brings drinks and *The Times*. Greg starts the crossword and Saffron snaps out the answers in seconds. She's in her element, being impressive. On the downs in the afternoon she outwalks us all. I give Georgy a piggyback and the others fuss that I'll strain myself. Georgy asks if I'm really going to have a baby: 'You haven't got a big big tummy like Mummy had!'

'Give her time,' Saffron says, 'and she'll be as big as an elephant, God help her.'

* * *

I read the journal in bed, escaping there early with pleas of pregnancy tiredness. Again I scrutinise the entries of the late autumn of 1919: if I don't know any details of Claudia's friends, I do know that she's full of tension, seething with ambitions and frustrations she hasn't mentioned before.

'*I'm aware of regions of my individuality that I've had no chance to fathom,*' she writes and it becomes clear that she's thinking not only in Aristotelian terms of the rational soul and her rational powers that must be exerted to the full, but in highly modern terms that would have shocked Miss Penrose, the Principal at that time. '*It is the duty of women like me to broaden our outlook by experiencing absolutely everything as men may do; that way only can we achieve full* self-realisation.' She feels like an explorer determined to become intimately acquainted with some new wild area of country whose feet are kept to well-worn paths by her guide. The atmosphere of a women's college does not suit her. '*We cannot challenge lest we are challenged. Even after many years our position here is precarious and the professors who examine us are men too often prejudiced against women students. I've written articles that slay those men who proclaim themselves sympathetic to feminism, yet still consider the idea of the independent woman farcical, but I'm told I cannot have them published for fear of undermining women's colleges in the struggle to be awarded our degrees. Here only the highest standards of social decorum and propriety will succeed. Are these qualities essential to great minds? I think not. They are to keep us in our place, creeping at the heels of men to be awarded the crumbs from their table. I feel I have a man's mind, a mind I must be free to use in battle and I find Somerville's feminine atmosphere hard to stomach.'*

Claudia identifies two sorts of feminist: one with a strong sense of identification with other women in broadening their lives; the other craving to become an equal participant in the world of men. Clearly it was the second to which she belonged and now the journal reflects it.

That Michaelmas term, the start of her second year, had meant moving from the Skimmery quad of Oriel and back to the Somerville buildings, which had been requisitioned for use as a military hospital in 1915. This was when her social life widened, became eventful. Her most impassioned concerns were with literature, history, politics and, of course, feminism. Music was also important in her life. In her journal, concerts and the theatre feature frequently, but so do debates with the debating societies of New College and Oriel, in which she takes part, to huge applause and success, she records. There is a lecture on the industrial conditions obtaining among women, which rouses her to furious indignation. TW is present at many occasions, but D and RP figure as other escorts. I tentatively identify TW with a 'dear clever Timothy' who is at Oriel and D as Dorothy, a close friend at Somerville who is fanatical about the theatre. RP must be Robert Prince, a distant cousin, newly up at Balliol. '*He is,*' she notes, '*the man I have been needing for months to keep my reputation unsullied; decent, dull and utterly safe, the sort of escort the sillier dons and Aunt Selina beam upon with benign approval.'* Comments are being made, it seems, upon her penchant for *'the frequent company of the male sex'.* She writes with indignation of talking to a man on the loggia, not even flirting, and being taken to task for it. As well as TW at Oriel she has several friends at Balliol, one introducing her to another and then another. Could one of these have been the man rumoured to have been found in her room? She is stimulated by their company, commenting in curiously laconic fashion upon their degrees of maleness or the sharpness of their discussions. *John FB,* she notes, — *a fine-honed mind,* or of Basil East, *a slim male animal, brilliantly amusing. Norman F. perseveres ... no lion but a lumbering bear. A kind bear, though.* Which? Who? Could my mother have been the result of a one-night stand? Doubtful then, surely. But — why no marriage when she found herself pregnant ... ? In mid-December she goes to stay with Selina ...

Freddy lifts the journal from my hands; too late I try to clutch on to it, and he's laughing as he drops it on the floor on his side of the bed.

I come back from a great distance to shriek, 'Careful!'

'I'm always careful.'

I peer over him for the book. 'No, you

aren't or I wouldn't be pregnant.'

'That was your doing as well as mine!' He pulls me back against himself. He's very strong. I wriggle, but it's an interested wriggle and he knows it. He turns, pinning me down with kisses.

I surface for air. 'Give me back that journal, Freddy.'

'More important things first, sweetheart.'

I give his chest a shove, protesting, 'I want it now!'

'You're getting it now!' he says, laughing breathlessly and so I am and it's blissful. Lovely demanding Freddy.

Who was it demanded and impregnated Claudia? Who was my grandfather?

★   ★   ★

By the time we've all disposed of a late breakfast of fried bacon and eggs and mushrooms there's a wafting drizzle of rain obscuring the hills and the garden, the distant stone statue on its grassy path under the trees is wreathed in it and looks more like a ghost than ever. We're all comfortable enough, though. Freddy's nipped to the local shop for the newspapers and Saffron and the men are now sprawled on chintz-covered sofas and chairs, reading them and passing jokey or caustic asides to one another, while Pattie and I are sitting on the floor scrutinising Claudia's old photographs in their dusty albums and big old manilla envelopes, to Georgy's great interest.

Having picked out the ones that matter, those for 1918 and 1919, we search for clues, meaning possible men, but most of the photographs are of women. There's a group taken at Somerville College with Claudia in the centre of the front row. I recognise her immediately — that strong-boned face, those full lips — but I'm surprised that she's little taller than her contemporaries. She looks in fact not much taller than Mother, yet I've remembered her as a considerable presence. Pattie agrees. It must have been the effect of the outsize character, we conclude. And in later years her unabashed enjoyment of good food and drink did load on the weight.

'Think of the chocolates!' Pattie says.

'They were both mad about chocolate,' I muse, 'Mother and her. Coincidence or inheritance?'

'Don't ask me,' says Pattie. 'I still can't connect the two of them at all! Careful, Georgy, with your sticky fingers.'

We persevere. June 1919 sees a faded group of young men in punts, another of young men in the Botanical Gardens, a small group in front of the Bodleian Library. Again the exasperating Claudia identifies them largely by initials. BE is presumably Basil East, RP Robert Prince; both, like TW, figure many times. Basil is slim, as she says, and quite a young blood with his sleeked-back longish hair; Robert looks stoic and heavy, as if he finds his present company a touch too much; TW has a moustache. TW is dark-haired, not tall, and he's more casually dressed than the others. Leaning against a palm tree, laughing into the photographer's eyes, he looks outgoing, fun, the full-of-himself demanding male.

Scores of snapshots in albums pass our eyes as we push the pages impatiently over. Unknown and long-dead relations, friends, admirers. We turn to a filing box where there are larger sepia photographs. Claudia appears in a family group with Aunt Selina and Uncle Lucian and their two daughters: the girls' hair is elaborately arranged, and they sit gracefully on the floor at the feet of their elders, who are in padded basket chairs, the five of them posed in a handsome conservatory among aspidistras and potted palms. Several groups by Aunt Selina's tennis court come next — how did the girls play in those long skirts? Then comes Claudia with two self-conscious young females sitting on a rock by the sea, then again the trio tripping into the sea, their heads turned to us, smiling and waving. *Dorothy Marriott, Ivy Manners and Self, I o Wight, August '19*, says the caption. A beach photographer took these, perhaps.

'Why are they wearing those funny things?' Georgy asks, pointing derisively at the highly decent swimming costumes that half cover their thighs.

'It's what they wore to swim then,' Pattie says absently, brushing his hand away.

We're about to put them back in their dilapidated filing box when Georgy seizes from its base an old envelope we haven't noticed before because it's unlabelled and fits the box so neatly. 'Hey, there's a big one in here,' he says triumphantly, fumbling with the flap with his little fingers.

'Careful,' Pattie warns as he tugs it out.

It's a studio portrait, of which we see the back first: *Timothy Burnham Wright, Sept. 1919*, is written large across it in Claudia's unmistakable sloping scrawl. Georgy turns it over on the floor and my heart jumps. It's Claudia's friend TW, minus the moustache and grave, as was the mode for such portraits then, though there's an eyebrow quirked at an unknown audience and a look of suppressed laughter. The features are oddly familiar: the indeterminate nose, the long upper lip, the wide mouth — I know them all.

'Look, Pattie,' I say, breathless. 'What do you make of that?'

She's staring hard. 'Your mother. There's a real resemblance to your mother,' she says. 'Wow, Flora, Timothy Wright — TW. Do you think he could be, you know, her father?'

22

I shift my bottom backwards across the carpet to lean against Freddy's legs. 'Look,' I say, pushing the photograph at him, 'could he be the man we're looking for?'

The *Sunday Times* falls to the floor. Lips pursed, he studies it; takes off his spectacles and peers again. I watch him, mesmerised. The increasing rain beats upon the window panes; upstairs in his travel cot Luke grumbles.

'Could be,' Freddy says on an upward note of awe. 'There is a likeness.'

'There is, isn't there?'

'But it's in features rather than character. Primrose's look was mournful marmoset, he's more mischievous monkey.' He's careful not to sound excited, but I sense he is.

Luke revs his grumbles up to full-bodied yells of protest.

Pattie scrambles to her feet to stare over Freddy's shoulder. 'He must be the man, they're so alike. Greg, fetch Luke, do! How can you be so deaf to your own son?'

Greg flourishes the *Observer*. 'Pattie, I'm busy reading an important article. Anyway,

Luke's due for a feed, isn't he? I don't possess the necessary apparatus.'

'I'm engaged in important research with Flora,' Pattie snaps back. 'You might bring him down at least.'

'Having changed his nappy first,' Saffron drawls at him. She agrees with Pattie that Greg is a lazy sod.

'Good thinking, Saffron. Change his nappy first. Thanks.'

Greg chucks his paper on the floor. 'Female solidarity is a revolting thing, it really is.' He stomps off.

'Let me see,' Saffron says, clicking her fingers at Pattie for the photograph. She holds it in a gesture that's somehow disdainful. Then her glance sharpens, the fingers stiffen. 'Ahh. Well, if you don't object to an ape-faced grandfather, then yes, go for this fellow, Flora. I thought you were probably all imagining things, but there is a resemblance between Primrose and him, isn't there? In the lower half of the face, that long upper lip.' She turns the portrait over. 'Timothy Burnham Wright. I seem to think . . . yes, the Burnham Wrights appear on the periphery of literary society in Edwardian times and in the twenties. Fashionable society people, and interested in the arts. Blooms-bury's hangers-on, one might say.'

She'd know, of course, she would know. Genealogies, old families, the great or the fashionable from all periods, they've always intrigued her and she has the memory of an elephant for their sayings and their doings. 'Do you know any more?'

'Not that I can recollect. I don't mind seeing what I can find out though.' She ponders. 'This is a Bassano, which would tie in. Bassano was court photographer to King Edward the Seventh, and for years he did superb portraits of the society of his day. Timothy's tie says Harrow from what I can see of it. Any other photographs of him?'

'Several,' I say, and show her the dusty albums.

'Hardly good-looking, is he?' She looks from one photograph to another, concedes judicially, 'But there's a certain animal vitality about him.'

'Quite,' Pattie concurs with a grin. 'He looks the fun-in-bed sort. Claudia's sort.'

Greg returns with Luke. 'Dirty nappy. Got out of that one all right, didn't you?' he comments, and dumps his son in Pattie's arms.

Pattie says sweetly, 'Thank you, darling, so much!' and unbuttons to feed him. Over the sounds of Luke's avid sucking, she asks, 'So where do we go from here?'

'We find her nineteen twenty journal,' I say grimly.

'You could check Timothy through Oriel's archives, and Harrow's,' Saffron suggests. 'There's bound to be something about him at one or other if not both places.' The search is beginning to intrigue her.

Freddy says thoughtfully, 'I wonder if Somerville would have any record of Claudia being sent down?'

'I doubt they'd have recorded the hows and whys,' I say, 'not then, not with the question of women's degrees pending.'

'Christ, yes,' Saffron says. 'What a moment for Claudia to pick on for her escapade! The authorities must have despaired of her, poor earnest ladies. They would have buried anything like that.'

'I want the nineteen twenty journal,' I repeat. 'It's the only way I'm going to discover the truth of what happened. If it's still in existence, I'll find it.'

I'm gazing absently at Luke, tugging at his mother's nipple, when suddenly he lets go to beam at me, milk drooling everywhere.

'Oh help, Lukey, do you have to?' Pattie exclaims, seizing a paper hankie and mopping furiously. 'Now you've soaked my shirt.'

'He was smiling at me,' I say fatuously. 'He's so gorgeous I could hug him to bits. He reconciles me to having mine.'

'You didn't pick a good time to have your own offspring, did you? In fact you must be mad,' says Saffron, and she pats the silk that covers her own breasts with nervous fingers.

'You deal with the next dirty nappy, Flora,' Greg suggests. 'Learn the true basic stuff of parenthood.'

'Oh, shut up,' Pattie tells him with affectionate rudeness. 'You know you don't mind really, it's just a macho pose. We all know you think your sons are great.'

I gather up the faded sepia photographs and sift through other years, but Timothy Burnham Wright features nowhere. He's vanished as if he'd never been. No proud parenthood for him and Claudia. If he was the father of her child, did he desert her? Was he under twenty-one and forbidden to see her? Was he sent down from Oriel? The answers to many literary biographers' questions are to be found in famous libraries' collections of papers, the archives of international institutes and so on. They're recorded, catalogued, available on request to the genuine scholar. I'll apply to see and check through any records, any papers, that could be relevant. But there's nowhere I can go to *prove* Mumma's parentage. Everything's hidden, suppressed.

In a burst of generosity Saffron says she has a box of Claudia's books at her Chelsea mews cottage that she doesn't want and she'll let me have them. 'The family divided them up but I haven't room for all I've got. Throw away what you don't want.'

'Thank you,' I say, remembering that Saffron's share of Claudia's money paid for her Chelsea place, that Mumma and I received not one solitary object. Why not? Was she afraid that even a small token each might cause questions to be asked? Questions that might reveal the link between us, revealing also her startling callousness over so many years? Or had she long since buried all recollections of our relationship?

I sigh. When we return to London tonight I'll telephone Robert; he may know more than he realises. And it wouldn't surprise me to find both the missing journals secreted somewhere in the untidy book-piled recesses of his house. But I'm not holding my breath.

★ ★ ★

'Don't ask me, I don't know a thing,' Robert says with a kind of jocular defensiveness, ushering me into his sitting-room. 'And no, I haven't got those diaries. Waste time looking for them if you must, but I've never ever seen any of them, nor do I possess hidey-holes where they might lurk. I doubt our super-efficient Helen does either. You could try the various libraries' archives but my bet is Claudia burned them.' He moves a couple of abstruse journals from his sagging floral armchair and pushes me into it. 'I will tell you what I can, but frankly it won't be much. Coffee?' He flourishes an ancient Thermos jug over a mug.

'Please.' I switch on my tape recorder, take an unwary mouthful of coffee and wince. I've forgotten its horrors. 'Robert. Any idea as to who Claudia's lover was?'

'None. No one knew, Dad said. Sorry.'

'You knocked a pile of books over my ankles to distract me over her leaving Somerville. Now how about the truth of what happened there?'

He spreads his hands. 'History doesn't relate any more than that she was sent down in disgrace. The details were never revealed. To Great-aunt Selina a birth unsanctified by marriage was something abominable, dishonourable and guilt-ridden. The period was a black hole for the family, the facts were sucked down into its depths. Into oblivion, Flora.'

'Damn.' I push on, but after a while I wonder why I've come. He's had enough of

Helen's scoldings, he's wary I'll start, and he's nothing to give. Only one line of questioning produces useful information.

'Where was she during the pregnancy? With your father or Selina, or where?'

He shakes his white head at me almost theatrically. 'It's forty years or more since I was told, Flora . . . but hold on . . . Yes, it's probably the one bit of fresh knowledge I can supply. She was sent to Switzerland, to Berne I think, with some paid companion. She was to stay in a tiny pension as a widow, give birth abroad, then leave the child there for adoption.'

'But she didn't.'

'No, she claimed to be overwhelmed by the tedium and loneliness, flounced back shortly before the birth and Aunt Selina had to cope.'

'With Claudia almost dying.'

'Yes, well we all know that. She described it graphically enough.'

'Then the baby — *my mother*, Robert — was passed to May Tucker-Bond. Take a minute and think back carefully. Surely you know something of this? Did Claudia agree to giving her up willingly or not?'

The eyebrows twitch; he sighs. 'I wish I could tell you. I perceive that it's going to prove central to your hypothesis about her life and her nature — to whatever you'll want to write. But Dad told me only the bald facts; feelings weren't discussed. I can only guess at how badly he suffered himself. However, let me say this: whatever Claudia felt she'd have been damned as society saw it — because if she'd kept Primrose she'd have been an outcast and a pariah and so would the child — whereas the abandonment of her child condemns her now as callous, unnatural and for ever to be despised. You can never win over this, Flora, you should understand. If you dwell on this part of Claudia's life you turn her into an unsympathetic character. Yes, people will buy the biography, but for the wrong reasons, for the lip-licking glee of finding long-hidden scandals revealed, for the malevolent secrets that change the face of the great. Is that what you want?'

'I don't know, Robert, I don't know,' I say in exasperation. 'How can I tell at this point? I've a hell of a lot of work to do before I even *start* writing. And a hell of a lot of thinking about a woman whose early life was nothing if not anarchic. I know nothing of Claudia's motives in abandoning her child and until I do how can I come to any conclusion on how to show her?'

'True.'

'Her predicament was dire, but viewed from today's perspective it could be that the way she reached her decision will reveal her as a sympathetic character. But stop thinking of me as the biographer for a moment, will you? I want to know for Mumma and me.'

'The answer's still the same. I can't tell you.'

*   *   *

Helen says she is certain she hasn't overlooked the two journals.

'Don't you believe me?' she asks in exasperation when I turn up at her busy offices unheralded.

She lets me search, though, as she'd agreed at Mother's funeral, sighing as she directs one of her staff to help. At this girl's age I'd have been enthralled by the detective work, but Karina is cynical and overburdened, thinks Claudia Charles is overrated herself: 'All those old writers are, the contemporary scene is where I'm at!' and after half an hour of rooting in cupboards and cabinets stuffed to bursting point with files and typescripts and books, she's running black-lacquered finger-nails through her hair and declaring that this sort of thing is not what she took her degree for.

'And anyway dust makes me itch.'

I plod on alone, but Helen's right, there's

nothing resembling the journals here.

'And no, you can't search my flat, Flora. I don't remember there ever being anything of Claudia's there, and besides, Sam and I have checked.'

It has already taken me six hours of slogging to verify for myself that the diaries aren't in Robert's chaotic house among all those books of Claudia's that he's inherited, and I know Sam's the meticulous sort, so I give up and leave for home and a long soak in a hot bath.

★ ★ ★

I'm having ultrasound: 'To check that the baby's got all its bits and pieces!' my doctor says with horrible jollity.

Freddy not only comes to the hospital with me but supervises me in drinking one and a half litres of water beforehand. I snap at him as I await my turn. This is because my moods fluctuate from day to day and today's is bad. All that water is making me feel sick and the pressure on my bladder is unbelievable. Besides, while I don't actually hate being pregnant, like Pattie, there are aspects of it I find pretty intolerable. I get a sinking feeling when favourite clothes no longer fit, when I tire unexpectedly or feel yucky, like now. He's done this to me and I could hit him for looking so well and pleased with himself when by rights he should be suffering too. Besides, I'd hoped to get to Wingreen Place today to remind myself of how that eccentric old house of Claudia's looked, and also, if the people now living there were willing, to search the attics for the journals that might, just might, have been left hidden in some shadowy recess. Now I'm losing time sitting around waiting, which is what pregnancy seems to be largely about.

'Flora Monk?'

I lie down, expose my tummy and a blanket is draped over me. More waiting, then a dark-haired woman of about my own age appears and introduces herself as the radiologist. Questions, then my belly is smeared with an ice-cold gel that makes me jump, she picks up some sort of sensor, a transducer, she calls it, directs my attention towards a screen and utters something about ultrasonic waves which are bounced back and converted into pictures. 'Solid areas are lighter, fluid darker,' she adds and moves the sensor around. I hear Freddy's indrawn breath as grey and white shapes appear and shift like clearings in a fog. Something throbs. The radiologist murmurs and Freddy repeats in a hushed voice: 'The foetal heart's pulsing — look, Flora, you can see it.'

'And that's the spine.'

I'm glued to the screen. That's my baby there and it's alive and growing.

The radiologist clicks and checks. 'Full size for the gestational age given . . . ' and then in an endearing burst of layman's language, 'and everything's present and correct as far as we can tell.'

'Is it a girl or a boy?'

Freddy's concentrating, and as the radiologist says, 'I'm afraid I can't tell you,' he cuts across her with, 'It's a girl.'

'Is it?' I demand. 'I don't mind which it is, but I would like to know, to make it real.'

For a moment the woman won't speak, then she pushes back her dark hair and says to Freddy, 'Most people wouldn't have a hope of making that out.'

'But I'm right, aren't I?'

'We just can't be certain.'

He laughs at her. 'But you wouldn't contradict me?'

She purses her mouth in mock primness and says nothing.

'Ah!' I say, delighted. 'I wanted a girl.'

Claudia, Mumma, me, and now this little one.

'Me, too,' says Freddy, his voice incredulous.

The fuzzy picture shifts in images that remind me now of old black and white films. I think I see a limb move upwards. A click and an image is held. Later, when I've had that urgently needed pee, we pay for a photograph that I clutch like a talisman.

Outside, a thought strikes me. 'Freddy, could you honestly see what sex she was?'

He shakes his head and his spectacles sparkle in the August sun. 'Pure bluff.'

★ ★ ★

The thought of my daughter accompanies me throughout the day like a Christmas wrapping of happiness. In the evening I unpack boxes of books from the old flat on to smart fresh shelving in my new study in Mother's flat, the room which once was my bedroom. Freddy insists on helping, but he's more a hindrance.

'What shall we call her?' I muse, ranging Elizabeth Gaskell and George Eliot alongside Aphra Behn and Mary Mitford.

'Ermentrude? Rosebud?' He dumps my big two-volume dictionary on my desk and smiles his quirky teasing smile. He puts his hands on my breasts and he's concentrating on me, not names. 'Let's celebrate her first and decide later.'

'No, sort names and books first, sex later.'
I prise his hands off, find the baby's names
book that I use for the characters in my
books and we kiss and wrangle and laugh
while slowly the shelves fill. Names are
important, I insist, but it's impossible to
settle whether your child is more likely to be
a Euphemia than an Ernestine, and it's a
perilous decision. I'm almost lured into
naming her Henrietta Alice Gulliver before
Freddy points out with a yelp of glee that
the initials spell HAG. I throw the book at
him and he ducks.

'We could go through the entire A to Z of
names and still be here at midnight.'

'That's it,' he exclaims, retrieving the book
with a pounce. 'She'll be the alpha and the
omega of our lives so we'll have the first and
the last — Abigail . . . Abigail Zoë! How
about that?'

I want to say, Don't be ridiculous, but I
don't. I start to laugh. 'I like it.'

He drops the book and grabs me. 'So do I.
Now for the celebration.'

**Ms Susie Peters, b 1959, writer and
one-time secretary to Claudia Charles**
I'll be very glad to help you with anything I
can, you know I will. Of course, you've
landed the major work, mine was just a

little memoir, but I think it has its place, don't you?

. . . Oh, thank you, you're very kind. I enjoyed your own last novel, thought-provoking, I'd call it.

. . . She was brilliant to work with, Claudia. Demanding, of course, very demanding. I didn't have this lovely place of my own then, I lived at Wingreen Place so I was perpetually available. She'd expect me to work with her all day and even into the night when she had one of her visitations, as she'd say.

. . . Oh no, I didn't object, not formally. I'd get exhausted, I hadn't her tremendous reserves of energy, but I'd make myself go on. After all, it was an exceptional experience for me, a raw graduate as I was then, becoming the confidante of a great woman writer, a literary lion, as they say. There was nobody like her before, was there? Well! My friends were ever so admiring and envious. And I couldn't let her down by complaining, not when she was so much older than me.

. . . No, I don't think of her as selfish. Selfish means thinking only of yourself. She thought of her readers, her public, and put them first. That's what she'd say to me.

. . . Yes, it was an education. She jolted

my mind into action as my lecturers at university never did. She had a genuine and deep knowledge of the literature and culture of so many societies and countries, and that would burst through in any conversation; she'd compare or quote, but absolutely naturally, not for admiration. Then, 'You've never read Proust?' she'd say, or 'You don't know your Virgil?' She'd make me take the books from the shelves and I had to concentrate hard on what I'd read because she'd want to discuss them in detail.

. . . Yes, very sharp. If I did a piece of research for her I had to look for the information in depth and from every angle or she'd savage me like a dog shaking a rat — and I'd feel a rat for letting her down. That's part of what I mean by her educating me. She forced me to focus because she had a kind of anger in her against women who failed to realise their potential, who settled for second best because it was easier for them that way.

. . . Yes, she could be wistful sometimes about her effect on men. She knew she terrified them, that many of them resented her. It's not easy for the brightest among us even now, but for her it must have been a hellish struggle — to gain acceptance both as a brilliant brain and a real woman. In those early days of female emancipation university women had to be spinsters and celibate. Awful, wasn't it? My partner often says . . .

. . . No, she found the hen-house atmosphere at Somerville hard to take. She was determined to improve the position of women, but she was always more at home in the society of men.

. . . She left because she wasn't gaining what she wanted. There was an aridity about the teaching, that's what she told me. She was forced to concentrate that great brain in areas determined by others, and she was balked from following up fresh areas of interest by the demands of what she considered a narrow syllabus, and it made her irritable and rebellious.

. . . No, oh, goodness, no, I never heard that rumour. A man in her room . . . ? Well, I could believe it of course, from what she told me of her love life, but it doesn't fit. She spoke to me very honestly about her past, her lovers, I mean, and she often reminisced about old pranks she'd played, but not there. Well, if you've read my memoir . . .

. . . No, I'm certain. As I said, she left Oxford because it was too constraining.

. . . She did once say she learned public speaking from her debating society experiences against other colleges, and she'd occasionally reminisce of punting on the river and how novices would fall in. She could tell a story so wittily, couldn't she?

. . . She mentioned a few names, men who grew famous, like . . . well, like the Sitwells or . . . or Robert Graves. He left without taking a degree, too, you know.

. . . Basil East, no. Robert Prince? Wasn't Robert Prince the cousin who was killed in the Blitz? I seem to remember her saying he'd survived the horrors of the First World War only to be killed in the Second . . . yes, that's right, a genuinely good man, she said, and wasn't it a pity that the truly good were invariably boring? She could be very dry, too . . .

. . . Timothy Burnham Wright, Timothy Wright. Well, she did once mention a Timothy who . . . yes, who was at one of the Oxford colleges. Would that be the chap she said was a brilliant satirist? I think he was the one she said was her first experience of love, but you know, I'm so bad on names and it was some time ago, I couldn't be certain.

. . . Look, I'll try, but I doubt it. I only recall him because my first boyfriend was a

Timothy and it seemed a coincidence. Love then didn't necessarily mean sex, did it?

... No, how could I press her in my position? It was up to her to confide those sorts of details. She could be brutally frank about her liaisons when she chose, especially at two in the morning, and that was another sort of education for me. She was cynical about men despite liking them. People said she was tungsten-tough, but with a life as complex as hers she had to be, didn't she?

... No, she rarely spoke of that period, she said it was a dead time brooded over by her awful Aunt Selina, a doomed time she'd rather forget. I saw it as one of those limbo periods adolescents suffer when they're really rather depressed. You know, when they don't know who they are, or where to direct their lives. Nineteen was a dreadful year for me ...

... No, Claudia's preoccupation was always with her aunt Selina's snobberies and how she'd cringed at her crass remarks. She found her brother Edward loathsome too. She'd say terrible things about them, that they were monstrous sadists who'd used mental torture to enforce their domination over her.

... She felt there was something inside

her that awoke all their bourgeois fears, and that they wouldn't allow her to develop her own personal dynamism because they found her views on socialism and feminism threatening. She was beginning to write on social and literary topics but she hadn't the income to install herself elsewhere as she hankered to do.

. . . And then came Laurence Britton. She had to escape from her isolation in that bullying family before she became intellectually impotent, and he seemed to offer everything she needed. But they'd affected her in a way she couldn't escape. She said once that the pains of growing up had left her with an enduring heartache.

23

Freddy's mother, Paula, tells me that a party is needed to celebrate our engagement. She offers to host it herself, saying wistfully, 'It's a shame to waste my garden.' We decline the offer, pacify her with the assurance that we are throwing a flat-warming family supper party, then distract her with the thought of a granddaughter called Abigail Zoë, which she finds enchanting. 'I wanted a girl too,' she declares.

Paula is organising our wedding in October with vigour; each time we drive over to see her the guest list is longer and the marquee on order larger, while the musicians have increased from trio to quartet to quintet. I point out that I shall be larger, too, but that doesn't faze her as it would have my own mother. 'In earlier centuries a bulging belly was fashionable as a sign of fecundity,' she informs me. 'In fact it was thought rather beautiful.'

Almost all our guests arrive together for the supper party, crowding up the stairs, Pattie and Greg, Helen and Sam, Ben and his latest girlfriend, all introducing themselves to

Freddy's brother, Alexander, on our doorstep. 'We're the old-time family, they're Flora's new-found family,' I hear Pattie clarify as they pile in, 'but you'll be even newer family.'

Alexander is stunned by the view from our window. I join him and look out at the panoramic sweep of river and meadow and trees that Joshua Reynolds loved and painted. White boats shimmer on the Thames, rooks are returning to their trees, the shadows are long. In the gently fading opal light I sense the first breath of autumn.

'It's unbelievable, Flora. But I suppose you've seen it too often to be affected.'

I deny it. I start to tell him that there's never been a day when this view from Richmond Hill has not affected me with its beauty, or failed to convince me of my luck in having been brought up here, but stop when his attention swings to a different vision.

It's Saffron, standing in the doorway and collecting eyes. She's wearing a silk trouser-suit in a colour that resembles dark grapes with the bloom on. She looks magnificent. For a moment I scowl and think that it's never been anything but unfair competition between us, and that now I'm pregnant, I'll become even more handicapped and damn it, couldn't she simply look ordinary for once?

Then I remember that I'm my Freddy's wonderful woman and she doesn't have a man and I go to welcome her.

She presents a cheek for a kiss and explores the room with her eyes, acknowledging her cousins in varying degrees as she does so. Somehow Alexander, without seeming to move, appears beside me. I introduce them and they murmur, 'How do you do?' unsmiling and staring.

'I'm Fred's brother,' he says. 'You're Flora's cousin?'

A nod, but no reply as she examines his fair hair, his height, that taut greyhound look.

'Saffron Thomas. I've heard the name. Don't you write?'

A faint smile, a raised eyebrow. 'I do. Me and Flora both.' Grammatically flawed, unusual for Saffron. Without taking her eyes from Alex she tells me, 'That box of Claudia's books I mentioned is in my car, Flora. D'you think some man might lug it up here for me?'

A pause. I expect Alex to offer, but he's smiling faintly, watching her and waiting. There's some power game starting here that I'm precluded from entering. I think of checking on my honey-glazed rack of lamb. Sex is purling through the air, setting up a force field of attraction, an excitement, a teasing.

'Would you be so kind?' Saffron asks of Alexander.

'Well, yes . . . ' he says, spinning the words out in a drawl, 'I think I could manage that. How about showing me your car?'

It's a big carton of books he's carrying when he returns, some of them hefty volumes.

'Where do you want it?' he asks as he shifts its weight uncomfortably in his arms.

I've seen a rough-cut copy of T. E. Lawrence's *Seven Pillars of Wisdom* at the top. A first edition? Could be, Claudia collected such things. 'Put it to the side of the sofa, would you?' I should be rushing round the kitchen, doing women's work with the usual nagging feeling that I'm missing something, but the food must wait. I squat down to check the early pages.

'No, not a first edition,' comes from Saffron behind me. 'I'm not that generous.'

'No,' I agree with regret. It's the second edition. A pity. I put it on the carpet and see next a big old Bible, its cover of battered leather tooled in faded gilt. I release brass fastenings and discover a Charles family Bible, bought by Henry Charles in 1863 when he married Mary Abbey. My great-great-grandfather and grandmother. Births and deaths for the next four generations are entered in copperplate writing in different hands. I see *Edward Henry Ernest, born 10th November, 1892* and *Claudia Miranda Mary, born 20th March, 1900.* The Bible is profusely embellished with maps and pictorial illustrations in chromo-lithography. The first is 'Pagan Rome', all prettily coloured ruins. 'Don't you want to keep this?' I ask, taken aback and clutching it.

'No.' Saffron shrugs. 'I'm no traditionalist, nor a sentimentalist, either.'

'Well, thanks.' Something that's genuinely of my real family. And an unexpected gesture from my cousin.

I lay it on the sofa with reverence, and paw my way through the rest; elderly books dating back to the 1920s or before. Lesser-known works of Virginia Woolf, Scott Fitzgerald, G. B. Stern, D. H. Lawrence, Evelyn Waugh . . . mostly signed by the authors, too, with affection. Never mind that they're of minor value, they were Claudia's. She's handled them; they breathe an aroma of her down the years. Two more, something to do with gardening. *Window Box Gardening* by Quintella Gloster, I read from one faded jacket.

'I don't remember that,' Saffron frowns as Alexander chuckles. 'Throw it away.'

Pattie's looking over my shoulder. 'Why on

earth would Claudia want it?'

Sam joins in, 'She had window boxes at that flat she had in Kensington in her last years. She had the strangest plants put in, herbs mostly, that grew far too big. I remember a rosemary that leant out, then over, and finally fell on some toddler in its buggy, scattering dirt everywhere. There was quite a row with its mother. History doesn't relate who won, but I bet it was Claudia.'

'Window boxes with pretty herbs wouldn't be a bad idea here,' I say absently to Freddy. I open the book to glance at it and hear myself scream just a second before my brain consciously deciphers what's there. 'Aah! Oh my God. It's the journal, it's Claudia's journal. Look, Freddy, Pattie, Saffron — her writing! That year. She hid it. Not in a dark corner but under a silly cover. I don't believe it!'

'I do. She always was weird,' Sam says with conviction, then yells, 'Helen, we've found one of those lost diaries!' making me jump.

Pattie grabs it from me, breathing, 'It is, it's the one for nineteen twenty!' while I snatch up the last book, labelled: *The Scented Conservatory*, and flip it open, with Helen staring over my shoulder.

I'm so overcome I feel giddy. I manage to say: 'And this is nineteen thirty-one.' Freddy's arm comes round me and I lean against him. 'I've found them, Freddy, we've got them.'

'Yes. I can see. Pattie, Helen, move some of those books to let Flora sit down, will you? She's gone white.'

'I'm fine. Don't fuss.' Nevertheless I'm urged to the sofa and forced to take a sip or two of wine before I can escape to rescue the lamb.

It's a splintered evening, not at all the smoothly run occasion I'd intended. I hate everyone crowding for an opportunity to snatch up the precious books, and I'm so desperate to shove all these people out of the door and then delve alone into the secrets of Mumma's birth that I can hardly be polite. They are mine, those journals, mine. But I have to look after my guests. En route for the kitchen I detour to the bedroom and hide the two journals beneath my pillows. If I can't read them, they damned well won't either.

Normally on these occasions I get carried away, becoming happily garrulous and indiscreet, but now, caught as I am in a haze of preoccupations as we eat, I'm barely capable of speech.

I hear Sam admire the way Freddy and I have transformed Mother's old room. 'You've introduced colour and an appealing Pattie picture. It was always so grey before, a room that almost made a statement of having no statement to make. A leaden shell. But recent revelations explain that. Your mother grew a shell to cope with that nasty non-relationship with Claudia, her natural lack of background. Such resignation! Her own mother! God, I always thought Claudia was an old witch, but I can't say I relish being proved so right.'

'No,' I say, wondering whether Claudia'd been as slow in realising that she was pregnant as I was, and passing garlic bread. I thank God the lamb's all right.

Alexander, on my right, who has been talking to Saffron nonstop in an intent and provocative sort of way, turns to ask when my collection of short stories is due to be published. 'I know Fred's great work is coming out next February, but how about yours?'

'Mid-November, in time for Christmas, thank Heaven.'

'What a productive pair you and your cousin here are,' he says. 'She tells me she has another title coming out in late October.'

The thought of reviews so close in time to each other flashes through my mind, while he looks at me with a calculating eye as if to fathom the levels of competition between us. I point out sweetly that I vary my wares while Saffron is simply a novelist, but she swings in to say that she does not care for short-story writing. She prefers a wider canvas, one capable of illustrating the larger themes and producing analysis in depth — though as I already know she's not been unsuccessful with those few she has written.

This promising start to one of our rounds of shadow boxing is interrupted by Helen, abstracted and fractious, complaining that she's only this minute heard of the baby, and how do I propose to combine motherhood with authorship? I press her to take some more avocado and yellow pepper salad and tell her I shall work till I feel the first labour pangs. 'After all, research and writing are hardly physically demanding, are they?'

'And when it's born?' she asks crossly. 'What about your commitment then?'

'Oh, Helen, stop looking for problems. I shall be a thoroughly modern mum and read while I breast feed. Research: plenty of that still to be done. Mumma read *Gone with the Wind* while feeding me — such a suitable title, she said. And then there'll be a nanny.'

Pattie leans across to me. 'Please can't I just have a quick look at the nineteen twenty journal, Flora? I could read bits to you, maybe discover who your grandfather was for certain. I can't bear to wait.'

'Yes!' Helen agrees. 'Don't be selfish, Flora, we're all of us longing to know.'

'No,' I say, feeling suddenly horribly distraught as I gather up plates to make room for more food. 'I'll tell you when *I* know. It won't take long.'

But the evening's extending into infinity. Will my families never leave?

$$\star \quad \star \quad \star$$

They go at last, probably waking the whole terrace with shouts of: 'Telephone us when you know who, Flora!' and banging car doors. Saffron offers Alex a lift. He ignores his BMW just down the street and climbs into her MGF, waving to us in triumph. How does Freddy fancy her as his sister-in-law? I ask him as he shuts the door.

He gives me his sidelong smile. 'It'll last one week or one year. That's Alexander's pattern. If she holds him for more than a year, well, she'll be the first — and then maybe she'll be family twice over. Oddly enough, I see the attraction. They're both tense, bright characters who find the rest of the world bothersome, she more so than he, but her antagonisms can in part be explained by her awful mother. They'll either end up scrapping abominably or adoring each other's percipience — which we know can be very pleasing.'

'Ugh!' I grunt, contemplating the mess of coffee cups and crumpled cushions in the aftermath of the party.

He grasps my waist and kisses my ear. 'Right, bed,' he says.

I protest and he responds with laughter, propelling me. 'You impossible suspicious woman. I mean, get into bed before you start consuming Claudia's diaries. Otherwise you'll be groping about undressing at four in the morning, hardly able to stand. I'll clear the worst of the dishes and switch on the dishwasher, then I'll join you. I'm fascinated too, you know.'

★ ★ ★

In bed, clutching the book, I pause for a moment, heart thumping, hands shaking, blood swirling with a mixture of excitement and guilt. Here is the record of the most terrible year of Claudia's life, the year from which arose those fermenting hatreds which she later distilled into her most powerful novels. It's a real life, and my task as her biographer is to assimilate and examine every piece of available data. Yet this particular journal, that of the year 1920, she had hidden, along with that of 1931. Was this to keep her past from her husband, Spenser, from prying friends, from her secretaries, from everyone? Had she intended to destroy the books before she died, yet, never quite convinced of the imminence of her own oblivion, failed to do so? Am I poking into areas she wanted buried — or was Claudia in her sardonic tantalising way taking a long shot that they'd surface for her biographer? In this case did she consider her daughter's feelings? I doubt I'll ever know. However, it is my job to pry into Claudia's life, and hence into the life of her daughter, my mother, and the journal lies unresisting in my hands.

New Year's Day, 1920

A brave new year? How incongruous a thought. A new journal at all events. I shall break the emotional fetter I have kept on my pain and use it to release my feelings, more, to help me to a resolution of my fearful dilemmas. One thing I must do and that is disguise it in the most unlikely way. Still more necessity for concealment and duplicity. How I hate it — and those who force me to it.

Oh God, I have nothing and nobody and my life with all its lovely plans lies in broken shards. We thought we had control over our destinies, Timothy and I, but it was a false assumption. Life is a game of chance: a turn of the wheel, a flick of the ball, and all is ended. At times Aunt Selina pretends sympathy, speaking with a horrid form of unctuous sorrow of her brother John's death on the Somme and the pain that had caused her, but her chilly seagull's eyes betray her. Oh, how she squawks. Today I heard her tell Uncle Lucian that if she had been me she believed she would have killed herself. But of course she would never have been in my position, she's incapable of knowing the emotions that drive me. To her the reckless love I gave is a barbarous offence. Love should be regulated, sensible, expedient, the sort that fits with the dictates of society, else where should we all be?

My condition, as she calls it, must be hidden and dealt with. I can never tell the Wrights; it would break them in their grief to know that their dead son had foisted a bastard on to a decent girl. No one must know, appearances matter, not actuality. She and Uncle Lucian plan to send me abroad to await the child's birth in some secret place, then hand it over for adoption like a parcel of unwanted clothes to the poor. Edward agrees to it all, something *else that lacerates my heart. I thought he was my brother and my friend, but now he betrays me hourly.*

I feel totally adrift. Sometimes I think I should brave an illegal operation, reach for my freedom and continue my studies, but when I picture the physical details nausea rises acidly in my throat and I'm reduced to a turmoil of indecision, fear and moral confusion — the epitome of the weak women I despise.

Yes, Timothy is indeed my grandfather, but he's died, should she abort his child? Claudia has plunged to the heart of the matter, for once without bravado, her defences down. I stir with discomfort. Yes, I think, that's right, that's how it was with me, but how different our cases. If my nights were sick with sleeplessness and indecision after Freddy had left, in an earlier age she suffered at another level. Her lover was dead. I've been penetrating into Claudia's life, but now suddenly she is penetrating into mine, claiming my sympathy and my understanding.

I read on, although the pain that rises from the lines of her slanting writing brings me near to tears. She is, she says, sodden and ugly with anguish. Timothy is gone; as a

469

widow the child might have given her back a life, yet under these conditions it's destroying her life. '*Oh, the irony of the paradox.*'

Their love was a huge force, he had filled the bleak empty space left by her brilliant father's death. The man who had been the light and air of her life had been lost and then restored to her in Timothy, she had been radiant in all the intimacy of mind and views and interests regained: '*He caught at my heart and my understanding.*' He had suggested a country retreat before the winter came in a cottage belonging to a cousin.

How all-conquering we were before each other there, naked and unashamed. I remember the big bed lit by the early sunshine, the coos of the wood pigeons, the scent of the apple-wood fires, the friendly books . . . our companionable selves loving each other and talking about that love in endless happy contemplation of our future. I felt myself translated, reborn, made free in this culmination of my dreams. I had never known anything like it and there never was anything like it before.

The things my uncle and aunt and Edward say hurt so dreadfully because they don't understand its beauty. Free love between two people who are independent of society's trammels has nothing of the sordid or the furtive about it. God, how meanspirited and intolerant they are, and always that note of condescension as though I were a scullery maid pushed against the pantry wall by the butcher's boy. Their putrid minds disgust me. I tell them Timothy and I planned to marry and that he knew nothing of the baby. They say all men make such promises to have their way ... they recognise only stereotypes and know precisely what to say to hurt most.

Noises of cutlery and crockery in the kitchen. It's two-thirty in the morning. I read so fast it makes me feel sick, but I can't stop. I must know how Timothy died, what happened. I skim over the words, skipping some, other times picking up sentences that send a shiver through my skin: '*I had hoped my fears of pregnancy were not true, that fear had caused the hiatus, but with the nausea I knew. This child should never have been, a random trick of nature defeated our precautions.*' Yet through all her lamentations that her life was ruined and over, she preserved a healthy respect for it: she rejected the dubious lure of abortion as dangerous.

My eyes race on. I come across the name of

Miss Emily Penrose, the Principal of Somerville College. In the 1918 journal Claudia had mentioned being enthusiastically congratulated by Miss Penrose on an outstanding performance in Responsions. She described her then as scholarly, shy, given to speaking in succinct and laconic fashion. On this occasion Miss Penrose overcame her shyness to deal with the matter directly.

> *She could not conceive how I could have demeaned myself to do such a shocking thing. Her view of love resembles Aunt Selina's, but for her, rather than love shaping itself to the dictates of society it must fit with the needs of an academic community, upholding a vision of rational woman, not the lustful creature of temptation which is the last thing the university wants within its colleges. And this was her only consideration, that my behaviour, if known, ' . . . would give ammunition to those men, and indeed many women, who oppose education to degree level for females, supposing that having the two sexes together in lectures would lead to just the sort of licentious behaviour of which you, Miss Charles, have been guilty.'*

It's another world, a world I'm grateful I never had to inhabit, condemnatory, harsh, unforgiving. Freddy appears and begins to shed his clothes. I rest my tired eyes on him. There's something endearing in the dip of his spine down his back, the male swell of his biceps and thigh muscles, his neat bottom. I imagine Timothy with a similar supple physique.

Freddy turns, lifts an eyebrow. 'Made any discoveries?'

I sigh and nod. 'Timothy *is* my grandfather, Mother was conceived on an idyllic country weekend and he didn't desert Claudia, he died, I haven't found out how yet. She's beside herself with grief — and rigid with horror over the coming child. Those who know condemn her. She's obeying Aunt Selina's dictate that she flee to a foreign country because she sees no other way out.'

'I can't wait to read it. What an exotic and fascinating background you come from, my Flora.' He pulls on the oversize T-shirt he wears to sleep in and asks if I want anything to drink. 'Tea? OK.'

Nauseated but engrossed, I plunge back into Claudia's life and three pages later discover it was virulent influenza that had wrenched the life from Timothy.

'Influenza?' Freddy hands me a cup of clear amber tea. 'Yes, there was an epidemic which killed many thousands in nineteen nineteen. People weakened by the war I suppose. Dreadful.'

'She had barely come to concede that she was pregnant. She hadn't told him.'

The sadness of it wrenches at me. My skin crawls and my senses undergo a sudden transformation. The fabric of my cotton nightshirt is coarse against my arms, Freddy's breathing sounds laboured, the distant plane descending into Heathrow is overloud, the screech of a car's brakes outside fills me with dread. Life hangs by a strand as fragile as a spider's gossamer thread. Freddy could die, I could be left pregnant and alone, as she was. My breath catches in my throat. If I were to lose him I'd break, disintegrate. I never knew this panic was the price of love, but I've done it now, I'm inextricably involved and every nerve in my body is vibrating with terror. Unexpectedly I find myself in tears.

'I know, I know,' he says. 'It's sad, isn't it? Life in those years was intolerably hard. War, disease, loss, inflexibility.' He sits on the bed beside me. 'Here, sweetheart, drink your tea.'

'Hold me,' I say between obedient sips of tea, the tears trickling. 'Hold me and tell me you'll never leave me.'

I'm a snivelling mess but he puts his face against mine. 'I promise you I'll do my bloody best to live for ever,' he says, and holds me against his warm rumpled T-shirt, so close he's breathing in my ear, so close I can feel his heartbeat, thump, thump, thump.

★ ★ ★

At six-thirty I'm awake and reading again, turning the pages with stealth to avoid disturbing Freddy. Claudia's entries in Berne are brief. Her room in the pension is big enough but overfilled with dark and cumbrous furniture. She's existing like a person in prison, counting the days to her deliverance. The weeks pass, she requests Edward, if he cares for her at all, to send books, books of every sort. She reads Katherine Mansfield, who she's discovered became pregnant by a man other than her husband, lived in a pension in Bavaria and gave birth to a stillborn child. She recognises in her an original and experimental writer whose history gives her some hope for herself. She comments on the works of Thomas Hardy, Laurence Britton, Virginia Woolf, Proust and Kafka. She embarks on a study of Freud. There are English people in the town but she

avoids them, her self-imposed social ostracism, she states, the solemn advice of her
awful family. With a touch of self-mockery
she records that she has darkened her hair to
black to match her garb of mourning
widowhood and changed its style to something quite Quakerish. '*No one passing
through could possibly recognise me.*' She
works to improve her French and her
German and in turn gives English lessons to
those who will converse with her. Her
self-education compensates for nothing.

She lives with despair and anger and the
bitterness of the thwarted.

> *I am wasting my time, my life, my talent.
> Oh, the misery of all this, the boredom, the
> lies. My life is a desert of grief and
> emptiness. I am without money, without
> family, I have no one to love who loves me.
> My son will be taken from me. How could
> Timothy have left me like this? He should
> have fought the influenza, not let it kill
> him.*

By the end of June her anguish is extreme.
She is at one with the earlier English
travellers who loathed dramatic scenery and
gaunt lonely peaks; she craves England's
white cliffs and gentle meadows; she needs

intimate friends to console her. There is no way she can resolve these needs with her family's insistence on secrecy, and finally, deeply though she hates them, she returns, huge, defiant and unannounced, to the house of her aunt and uncle.

I'm unaware that Freddy's even awake until I smell coffee and hot rolls. He dumps a tray on my feet, instructs me to eat, then climbs back in beside me, taking the 1931 diary to read himself after he's licked his fingers free of butter.

I drink my coffee and skim on, almost choking as Claudia tells of her reaction to producing a daughter.

> The midwife said in coy tones, 'Why, we've a little lady here!' and I felt plundered. I was so sure I was carrying a son for Timothy. I wanted to yell, 'Throw it in the river!' Perhaps I did; I don't remember. I was befogged by exhaustion, wanting only oblivion. Reproachful eyes again. They showed it to me, so ugly, so pathetic, I could hardly bear to look, its face like a dented plum from the forceps, its mouth a dark cavern of screams.

My mother's first moments. I feel Freddy studying me. I swallow and turn the page.

Thank God I hardly see Aunt Selina. When she's here she murmurs false sympathy with my torn body and my unfortunate wracked baby, but her time is all for May Tucker-Bond, who has just lost the son she bore prematurely two weeks ago. Poor wretched woman, to have such agony of mind salved by the syrupy flow of Aunt Selina's pity. Unendurable! My aunt tells me of a previous dead child and two miscarriages, and that she is sick with grief, so wild they fear for her reason. Why should poor timid May be inflicted with such suffering? Once in my deepest thoughts I would believe I had glimpsed a pattern to life that made sense, now I see only cruelty and no reason to anything.

The baby is crying, it cries and cries. I dread the sound of it. The midwife says it will not take the milk from the bottle properly. She is in on the secret but contemptuous of us all. She believes I should feed it and keep it. She dare not say so, but she looks at me through the desperate wailing, and I, I look away.

This is Timothy's child, it is unbelievable.

My brain whirls, a dust storm of blasting thoughts. The coffee sits on my stomach like

478

lead. Hot and sticky, I shift to a cooler patch of sheet, long for a cold shower, but despite my storming mind I can't break free. I have to understand it all for Mumma. I turn to the next day.

This morning the midwife gave me the child to hold while she prepared to bath her. I was afraid she would reject my awkward arms with screams, but she was quiet and our eyes met, seriously, warily. For a moment she seemed ages old and penetrating my mind, judging me. Then she moved her baby mouth as if sucking, her upper lip lengthened and in a flash of shock I saw Timothy in her. I tightened my arms, she stirred, and the look was gone. The woman took her from me and washed her, but the tiny thing hated the water, and her cries were heart-rending. I couldn't bear it, I had to hold her afterwards, putting her quivering little body against my shoulder. She quieted then, her head leaning into the crook of my neck, warm and damp, curiously a person. I wanted her to like me, I wanted her to trust me, and she did; when the woman took her away she was asleep. I felt uncertain then, uneasy at my erratic, perfidious feelings.

I have to think but I find it impossible,

I'm so sore and tired, tired, tired.

<u>Eleven at night</u>

This afternoon Aunt Selina returned from May's nursing home accompanied by the doctor and there were others closeted with them in Uncle Lucian's study: Edward, Roger Tucker-Bond, some other man, the doctor and the midwife. Their voices rumbled all through the hot afternoon. Drifting in and out of sleep I was gripped by a nightmare vision of poor May being put away, but their intentions were quite other. They came and spoke to me, the doctor, the solicitor, Edward, all of them, filling the stifling room with their loud confident voices and their cigar and Macassar oil smells.

My child is to become May's child to save her sanity and the family's name. This is Aunt Selina's plot but they are all taken with its cunning and subtlety.

Emotion rises up and threatens to drown me as I read the reality of Selina's kindly but heavy-handed involvement in the lives of the two young women; the way in which my mother's future was settled as though she were no more than an unwanted puppy being passed to a new home. I have to break from this and return to the present.

480

It's a sun-drenched late August day, the last of the summer. I scramble out of bed, take a cool shower, dress and then we walk in Richmond Park, Freddy and I, dipping down to Pen Ponds. He's affected by what he's reading too, the love and death tragedy of Archie Pope-James in 1931, but he says little. There's something very settling about fallow deer browsing in the shade of ancient oak trees. We circle the great ponds, watch tiny children feeding the ducks, and return to a lunch of yesterday's party remnants tucked into crunchy baguettes and washed down with cold lager. Freddy gazes at me, frowns, says I hardly slept last night, so sleep now.

I lie on the bed, but sleep eludes me and besides, I have to read on, absorbed into Claudia's life despite my distaste with her curious way of thinking. The nakedness of the revelations makes me feel like a peeping Tom, but I'm a Tom whose insides are heaving.

I've ended by consenting to it all. Aunt Selina lectured me: 'You've been given a chance to escape this ruinous path of scandal and for once to make amends for your selfish indifference to others.' Edward cajoled me: 'It's a miracle of opportunity surely sent by the Lord.' I sweated in my anguish of indecision and felt sick, oh, so

481

sick and so weary. They were alternatively harsh and menacing, sorrowing and sweet, hour upon hour. I gave in. Had I had fought on I should have ruined my life, even beyond the damage I've already done. I'd have ruined that pathetic scrap's, too. I can't hope to support myself yet with my writing, let alone her; the only way I could keep her would be to live on the charity of my aunt and uncle, and that none of us could bear.

The blood rushes to my head at the thought of the child becoming the child of May and Roger Tucker-Bond. There is a gulf between us, in the depths of which they've jettisoned all that makes life fit to live: they put gold cuff links and furs before literature, rate drapes of velvet above art or sculpture, rejoice more in the roar of a motor-car than the sound of great music. People of the surface, they care nothing for the life of the mind and the soul. Still, the child will have a comfortable life, a life of the best plush. An adoption of another sort could give her far less. And I shall see her, though they warn that this is to be no more than would be expected of a cousinship so tenuous. If there should be a spirit within her that finds the Tucker-Bond social world small-minded, then let her search for *higher things as I do.*

I am moving on, I won't be a slave of the past, I shall bury it. The child will be Roger and May's. May's a soft creature, it will fill the great empty space in her heart and I've no doubt she'll love it. And as for me, caring too much has wrecked everything already. I was young, headstrong, passionate; I hated accepted ideas, I despised conventions. I loved and I lost, now I've lost again. But I refuse to admit that what I've done makes me anyone's moral or intellectual inferior, which is what Aunt Selina and Edward so detestably maintain. Oh, how I hate them. I hate them for reducing me to this, I hate them for their hypocrisy, I hate them for their social cowardice and second-rate values. One day, I swear, I shall hurt them as they have hurt me.

24

The ferocity of her emotions makes me shiver. I actually put the journal down and rub my arms. I look around; for a second the bedroom looks odd, smaller and slightly unfamiliar, the way it does when you return home after an absence. Then I blink my eyes and it's back in focus, intimate, homely and reassuring. But there's an unstable environment in my mind; I've been absent on a journey into Mumma's and Claudia's past, and that's another country, another culture, that's prompting a variety of responses. Thoughts of Claudia's terrible quandary and her reactions to the decisions she was compelled to make, thoughts tinged with sympathy, give way to other emotions — melancholy, disgust, anger. They all (and I can't exempt Claudia) cared more for appearances than for that tiny girl, and their sole altruistic action had been to hand the baby to May Tucker-Bond to be clutched like a comfort rag — and then ignored when at last she produced a child of her own. They buried the problem. But Mumma never could.

I leave the bed and pad into the front room to Freddy. He's put the 1931 journal down and he's standing at the window looking down at the Thames; when he hears me he swings round. He looks as I imagine I look, troubled and sad.

'Did you manage some sleep?'

'No, I couldn't sleep. I read on.'

He shakes his head. 'I thought you might. Tell me then.'

I lean my arms on the windowsill beside him. I tell him, briefly and loosely, because I am tired, how it was Claudia allowed the baby that was my poor mother to be passed to the sad neurotic woman I believed was my grandmother and who died, unlamented, when I was only eight. I say, thinking it out aloud, 'Freddy, Claudia was angry as much as grieved. In reality she gave my mother away because she couldn't bear to be beholden to Aunt Selina for money or help. Besides, while she was superbly scornful of her family for caring about society's values, she backed off from the scandal of rearing a bastard.' I look down at the sunny Petersham meadows, where the grazing cows are unconcerned with the agonies of the human spirit. 'She put *her* sensitivities, *her* wants, *her* needs first.'

Freddy says gently, 'She shunned public humiliation, that's natural enough. But she must have carried the pain of that separation through life like an old wound.'

'Hmm.' I search for the words to express feelings that are still only half-formed, search the past for evidence. 'If she did, it was for a theoretical child, not that real little girl. It's odd to say it, Freddy, but I think she saw my mother as an irrelevance, something neither planned nor wanted. Claudia's fury was over the personal insult of the family's disapproval. That was her lasting wound. Later, however she managed it within herself, not only did she show complete detachment from Mumma, but I've no doubt that it was genuine.'

'Primrose was taken from her too soon for any bonding to occur between them.'

I nod. 'I think that's right. There are just two flashes of feeling she records in the journal: when she sees a likeness to Timothy in the baby's face, and when she holds and comforts her after her first bath, which apparently the poor little thing hated. Claudia detested the thought of her child going to the Tucker-Bonds, but she concedes that she'll have a plush life. Then she resolves to move on and it's already clear that writing is to be her life. And that she'll revenge herself on Aunt Selina and Edward.'

I stare gloomily down at the Thames. I feel

that Claudia's holding back on me, crushing all evidence of genuine grief beneath her rage. If indeed she felt any. But it's a singularly unpleasant thought that this ferocious, ambitious and, on the face of it, compassion-less woman was my grandmother. My grandmother, who lived until I was thirty, took minimal notice of my mother or me, and whom I remember only once coming to this flat. And my sole memory of that occasion is her raptures over the view I'm gazing at now. It was the evening, and a full moon was shining on the river. I concentrate, struggling to re-create the historic past of Claudia, and suddenly her shadow's there beside me, statuesque in some flowing garment of rich fabric, saying, 'My God, Primrose, however did you and Philip manage to acquire a place like this? One of England's most loved views. An unexpected flash of genius.' Even in appreciation she put Mumma down. Yet if she had never had compassion for my mother, how do I account for the years of sorrow she describes with such tenderness in *Shadow of a Child*? There's a strange dichotomy here. I put it to Freddy.

He turns to me, the slate-grey eyes gentle behind the spectacles. 'There was another child,' he says, looping strands of hair back behind my ears. 'In nineteen thirty-one, stillborn at almost eight months. That was the child she wanted, the child who cast the shadow over her life.'

'Another child?' I stare at him in shock, my hand flying to the bulge that's little Abigail. 'Oh how dreadful.' I push away a murmur in my head of *served her right*.

'It was Archie Pope-James' child, and it was a boy. Do you want me to tell you or would you rather read — '

'No, no, go on,' I urge him. 'I've had enough of wading through her writing and anyhow my eyes are hurting.'

'I'll make you a mug of tea and then we'll sit down.'

I follow him to the kitchen. 'How, where, when? Christabel Pierce said he died in Bournemouth of an insect bite, so this baby must have been born after its father's death. A second horror story.'

'It was. As you told me Christabel said, Archie's death was sudden and Claudia howled with misery. They'd only discovered her pregnancy shortly before he was bitten by whatever vicious insect it was and they'd been planning a swift marriage.'

'And then history repeated itself.'

He puts the kettle on. Along the terrace a dog barks; someone is revving a car engine. 'Septicaemia, I suppose, and no antibiotics to halt the spread of the infection. This time, not only did she go to Switzerland but she planned to give birth there, in a nursing home run by nuns. She wore a wedding ring, called herself Mrs James and all was highly discreet.'

'I thought she loathed Switzerland.'

'She'd loathed her nightmare situation of tedium in Berne, but this time she was staying by Lac Leman with elderly friends, near Lausanne in fact. They were a childless couple and devoted admirers not only of her writing but also of her views; far from condemning her irregular situation, they seem to have found it romantic. Perhaps she and the unborn child revived long-forgotten parental instincts in them; she calls them wise and generous. It appears they were people of a radical intellectual bent who enjoyed a busy social life with like-minded friends, and they drew Claudia into their circle. Being younger than the others and in her sad position, she was petted and cossetted.'

I say wryly, 'That must have been a comfort to Claudia, who still tended to see herself as friendless and blighted by disapproval.'

Freddy makes tea and pours me a mugful. He's so close I can smell his warm body. I'm cossetted. Poor Claudia. 'Go on,' I urge.

He leads me back to the other room and

we sit on the sofa. 'During her pregnancy she invariably worked from eight until lunchtime; there are mentions of reviews for the *Daily Telegraph*, contributions to *Time and Tide*, the occasional short story. It's clear she intended to keep Archie's posthumous baby, passing it off as the child of dear friends killed in an accident. The premature birth took them all by surprise, one of those imponderable failures of the human body. Claudia was suddenly in agony, it was a stormy night, they dared not move her to the nursing home, the doctor arrived soaking wet at two in the morning, his temper frayed by the inconvenience, and after a second nightmare of pain and incompetencies, the boy was born dead.'

He looks at me. I can't say anything. I half choke over my tea.

'She was broken-hearted. When she recovered she started writing *Shadow of a Child*, where she made use of the terrible births of Primrose and that premature baby to illustrate the ignorance of male doctors who would not, could not, accept that women might have more insight than them into what was happening in their own bodies — while at the same time pouring out her exasperation with a world governed by men for men, which automatically put limits on women's endeavours.'

I swallow and think about the writing of it. 'It would have been a cathartic exercise.'

'Yes, though it must have cost her heavily. She was never short of imagination, but she hardly needed it then, the journal and the book both welling up from the pain and frustration she'd suffered. It's all there, Flora, even to the same words in places, the reality on which she based her fiction. To me, though, the most interesting aspect is the difference in her attitude at thirty-one to the loss of her child from that at twenty.'

Along the road the dog barks again and a child is shouting.

'She'd changed?' I feel suspicious, grudging even.

'This was a wanted child, although it was unexpected, and this time she could afford it. She suffered as she describes the character in *Shadow of a Child* suffering, she said that her life had been blasted by the loss of the only two men worth her love in all the world, and now by the death of Archie's child, who she was certain would have inherited not only his passionate intelligence, but his delectable disposition, and made her life a joy. I'm sorry, Flora — sorry for your mother, I mean — but it does happen even in normal families, that one child can be accepted while another is not, sometimes for no apparent reason.'

491

I clasp my hands round my mug, feeling as heady as if the tea were whisky. I remember with unease my reaction to my own unintended pregnancy — horror at the threat to my independence. There's a mixture of distaste and sympathy in me as I stare at the 1931 journal lying on the sofa arm. I ponder Claudia's emotional condition, then and in 1920. With my mother there had been a lack of bonding; that's very clear. I suppose I should research bonding, it's not something I know about. Was Claudia's lack of maternal feelings unnatural? I remember her emphatic, intimidating presence; could so formidable a woman ever have cooed to a grizzling baby? Many mothers admit they dislike the infant months, preferring their children when they begin to communicate. Perhaps Claudia was of that persuasion. In that case I don't think I resemble her. Apart from the independence threat, I was frightened by the heavy responsibility of a baby and doubtful of my own parental capacity, not resentful of the actual child. The babies that I've known, Georgy and Luke, I'm drawn to. And yes, Claudia too, if she didn't feel for the first, too early child, who survived, did yearn for the little boy who died. How ironic life can be. Another irony surfaces in my mind: Robert, her brother Edward's first child, was born that year. Her feelings on that event are unimaginable.

Freddy murmurs, 'Claudia was young and the family took Primrose from her so soon. She was poor, ambitious, without a husband; she was in an emotional deadlock between her conscience on the one hand and the pressures of her family and the outside world on the other.'

'You're making excuses for her,' I say crossly.

'Not excuses. Explanations. For then and after. You say that Claudia saw almost nothing of Primrose over the years. How could any relationship have a chance under such conditions? Affection between them was blighted from the start. Claudia despised May and Roger Tucker-Bond and when she heard their views piped in Primrose's childish voice it must have maddened her beyond endurance . . .'

I interrupt with anger, 'What she did warped my mother.'

'It did. Or rather, the actions of the Tucker-Bonds did, particularly their unfeeling behaviour on her twenty-first birthday. But think, Flora: had Claudia brought her up herself, would your mother have been so very different? Stronger? More intellectual?'

I shrug. 'How can I tell? Everyone agrees

she was repressed as a child.'

'You can repress a child, but frankly, Flora, and this may sound unsympathetic to you, I don't believe you can change its basic character. A stunted oak is still an oak and made of hard wood. Primrose was never of the tough fibre of her real mother. She was a gentle, kindly person, as I saw her, intelligent but not intellectual, and naturally meek. The genes for her character were derived from some quite different ancestor. If she'd inherited Claudia's character and drive she'd have rebelled against the Tucker-Bonds from the age of two onwards, kicking and screaming — and Claudia would have revelled in her and supported her fight, while lamenting in her diaries the cruel fate that had put such a child with such a deadweight family. But if she'd brought up Primrose herself, well, hasn't it occurred to you that she could have done quite as much damage in her impatient way as ever the Tucker-Bonds did?'

I grit my teeth. He's right, and what's more, he's poking with a blunt finger in the tangled undergrowth of conflicting feelings that has plagued me all my life. The truth is that Mumma's lack of fibre and intellectual rigour and bouts of self-pity irritated me just as they had Claudia. More a weeping willow than an oak. Unfair, I think, castigating myself; she had a bloody hard life and she did the best she could. Yet I've never been able to come to grips with her reality and admire what was good. I wanted, and I have to admit it, I wanted her to be like Claudia.

Then, I think, that was then. But now that I know the truth of the relationship between them, the strengths I revered in Claudia and wanted to further in myself no longer seem admirable. I struggle to express this to Freddy.

He nods. 'You're angry at her differing reactions to your mother and the other child. But if you're to write about them you have to understand and forgive your grandmother and your mother.'

'Oh, for heaven's sake!' I say irritably. 'What does that sort of counselling jargon mean?'

'All right,' Freddy promptly returns, 'it means this: you've been penetrating into Claudia's life but you have to keep her out of yours. You don't want to spend *your* pregnancy in a brooding miserable state. It's all past; it can't be undone. Samuel Beckett held the view that writers were never interesting of themselves, it was their work that was all important. But that begs the question of the relationship between the life and the work. In Claudia's case her life and a vast proportion of her work are inextricably entwined; I don't see how anyone could separate the two. But you must separate yourself and cultivate detachment. If you don't not only will you get hurt, but your work will become personal rather than impersonal . . . '

'And therefore third rate, as Saffron and Judith have already been mouthing. Oh God, you're right, blast you. Claudia's work was affected by my mother in *Shadow of a Child*, and, now I think of it, in *The Power of the Dog*, but she's a minor one of many satellites circling round Claudia. She affected Mumma in a big way, but did Mumma affect her?'

'There's little evidence of that.'

'Poor Mumma, always baffled by that sublime indifference. Daisy told me she'd never stopped hoping that one day Claudia would turn to her, perhaps in some firelit moment of closeness, and they'd talk and talk and form a special bond that would be an inspiration to their later years. But Daisy said Claudia regarded Primrose as a poor thing, it wasn't going to happen and it never did. God, Claudia was a cow.' Unexpectedly humour strikes me. 'Remember my multi-faceted vision of her as the Egyptian goddesses? The lion, the vulture, the cow? She was any and all of those, wasn't she?'

★ ★ ★

The telephone calls start that evening and go on for days. First, the members of my families who were at the supper party ring to say, 'Thanks for a great supper, Flora!' and then, breathlessly, 'And now, tell — what revelations have you found in the journals?'

Pattie's in her usual gusts of giggles. 'Claudia! What a player! Two babies out of wedlock but there's always someone to look after her, she wangles her way out of all responsibility for dear old Primrose — no dirty nappies or wakeful nights for our great writer — and the world's still her oyster. Yup, OK she suffered over the dead baby — God, I can hardly bear to think of losing my Lukey — and then she lost her men too, but she made a ton of money out of *Shadow of a Child*. And don't tell me that having fame and fortune and buying beautiful objects and gorgeous clothes *and* having fascinating lovers doesn't help someone like her obliterate her memories, because I won't believe it. She revelled in all the adulation and for most of her life she had a whale of a time. And on her own terms, too, not some male's. Wow,

Flora, won't these discoveries make your book sell! Great! She'll make you rich and so she should in fair repayment for what Primrose and you never had and damned well should have. I bet she never envisaged this!' Then, just as I'm about to ring off she adds, 'I'm painting again, Flora, when Luke's asleep and I can grab a decent slice of time. My hormones have risen, inspiration's returned and it's coming good, no, more than that, it's terrific!' And the subject? 'It's Lust this time. Lovely, lovely lust!'

Helen's reaction is more sober. 'Poor Claudia, she did put herself in some impossible situations, didn't she? But they gave her a vast hoard of material that few other women writers could have had — experiences of birth and death, love and grief and hate — all brutally personal to her. It explains how she achieved the force behind her writing, all those complex emotions from her past brought under control but potent with the tremendous vitality that she never did lose, not to the very end. The outpouring of a magnificent mind was what Max Blake said, wasn't it? Listen, we were thinking of the difficulties for you as her grandchild in selecting the angle of her portrayal, weren't we? It's a daunting business. If it helps you, Sam and I've been playing with ideas. First there's the Lewis Carroll model narrative according to the King of Hearts: 'Start at the beginning and go on till you come to the end: then stop.' That would be sex, warts and all in a huge gossipy compendium. Simple, readable, but hardly subtle. I don't fancy it and I hardly imagine you would.' (A not so subtle hint.) 'Then there's the one I think you originally favoured, Claudia as an aspect of history — an account of a Free Woman and feminist fighting her way to fame in a patriarchal society, revealing how her views have affected both the literature of her time and women's development. An encapsulation of the changes of the twentieth century. Hmm. Difficult to write a feminist hagiography in view of our fresh knowledge, though, don't you think? No, say nothing now, Flora, these are simply ideas for you to turn over in your mind. Yes. Then there's the more serious Great Writer style, where her life is revealed in detail only where it impinges on her texts. Scholarly, academic, objective, it might suit you better.'

I remember my Monet series of pictures idea and also, vividly, the hypocrisy gap that Laurence Britton's daughter, Mrs Amy Carrick, had dwelt upon. Am I an historian or a friend, an admirer or a detractor? I tell Helen, 'I've months if not years of research to do yet. I can't decide till I know all I can and I've stopped feeling dizzy.' In other words, don't push.

The next to telephone is my agent, Carol Saxon, who knows nothing yet of the events of the last ten days. She's delighted to tell me that she's sold world Spanish language rights in *A Nest of Brambles* and even more delighted when I tell her of the news on the biography front. 'No! Ooh, unbelievable, great! Some publicity! Only problem is, what about Claudia's other relatives who mightn't want these things to come out?' I remind her of the contract terms, tell her I'm in contact with the Trustees and that they've given the go-ahead. 'Excellent!' she says. 'I'll ensure they dot the i's and cross the t's on paper, but I do remember your being allowed to quote freely from family papers. No, promise, I won't tell a soul. And then Helen Charles is actually your cousin? Incredible. Hey, and you could edit and publish the diaries a year or two after the biography, couldn't you? Mine the rich seam. Flora, this has well and truly made my day.'

Next Laurel and Daisy appear at my door, informed by Pattie of all we have discovered in the journals and stunned, they say, though their fluency belies this statement. When, after half-an-hour's non-stop bludgeoning for all I know of the death of Archie and his baby, I insist on making us all coffee, they leaf through the two journals and on my return Daisy looks up to demand I read an entry from the 1931 journal.

It was twilight and I was alone in the meadow above the house. The sun had vanished behind the mountains, but the lake and the little village were bathed in a glow that belonged to neither day nor night. It lifted me so that I felt suspended, separate from my life, separate from my grief, while the memory of my last happy day with Archie shone like a beam across my mind. He was very close to me, in my head and all around me. I think I spoke his name. But the air about me was silent. The mist rose on the lake, the glow died. Then I cried out with redoubled pain, because our child was dead, because he was not with me, because I needed him so badly. 'Why have you gone? How could you have left me?' It hurts, it hurts not to be with him, but I never shall, never in all my life. The body that I held in my arms and the breath that mingled with mine are gone. He and the child lie buried deep, and I feel the dark pressure of the earth overwhelming me in an ache that will never end. Once more I am alone in my pain. I should never have taken a second risk of love. I swear I never shall again.

There are tears in my eyes when I look up, but Daisy is not in tune with my sympathy for Claudia. 'She went through terrible tragedies,' she observes, 'and she writes of her agonies of pain, yet she showed no understanding over Primrose's losses, first Harry and then your father. She should have done; it would have meant so much to Primrose. But Claudia never believed that others could have her sensitivities or suffer comparably.'

I ask her whether she believes Claudia to have been naturally hard, or whether all she went through had not been enough to cause her to develop a tough shell, even perhaps to feel that since she'd found the strength to cope in secret with her griefs, others should be equally strong.

'How can I tell?' She finishes her coffee, frowning, then puts down her cup. 'Both, perhaps. I leave that to you to work out, Flora, and explain in your own inimitable way when you come to your own conclusion. I'll tell you this, though: God wasn't fair. If he'd let Primrose inherit Claudia's writing skills, she could have extinguished her sorrows in a coded novel about her birth *and* made money out of Claudia's meanness to her.'

Laurel purses her lips and sighs in sympathy over the story of the stillbirth, but her view of Claudia remains clear-cut. 'To behave badly is easy, there's nothing magnificent about it. And while she showed remarkable insights in her writing, she showed little in real life, as Daisy says. Nor did her hurts stop her from having other love-affairs. What you should write about your grandmother is this: a great mind but not a great person.'

Isobel is staggered by the discoveries, she tells me over the telephone, but not surprised. She pleads to be allowed to read those two journals. 'They sound spectacular. Wasn't it Oscar Wilde who once said that he took his diary everywhere so that he always had something sensational to read? Interesting how many of the great have had wild private lives, isn't it? Was the sex part of their all-encompassing will to succeed? One wonders how far it contributed to their greatness . . . I mean the two do seem to go together, don't they? And not only in creative greatness — think of Lord Wellington's affairs, his 'Publish and be damned!' and Lloyd George's behaviour with his female staff. No widespread scandal in those days, though. Everything was suppressed and their talents were used to the full. The sex was not relevant to their work. Paradoxical, the change, isn't it, when you think of how today's sexual freedom is still accompanied by shrieks of sleaze where politicians are concerned? But I'm wittering. Flora, I'm glad I haven't your job. How on earth are you to explain the paradoxes of Claudia?'

Later, I dust and buff up the bronze cherubs Mumma gave me from Isobel's gallery. Two little babies. Like the babies Claudia bore and lost. I can't denounce Claudia in my work; fault-ridden as she was, she's silenced for ever, she can't reply. Nor can I explain her. I can only show her as she was, in all her inconsistencies and contradictions. I replace the cherubs and think of Abigail, her great-grandchild-to-be. I think about the duplicities involved in literary creation. I think about Claudia's duplicities, the parts of her life she suppressed. And yet, as a famous review of her last book pronounced, she was 'a superb writer who could impart moral weight, and above all, greatness of soul'.

I wait with interest for Saffron to telephone. It's almost a week before she does. 'Thanks for the dinner,' she says offhandedly, and then, 'Now tell me, what have you discovered from those two journals I let you have?'

She's not been in touch with any of her family then. She gasps at the revelations, unusually for Saffron, whose persona is built on being cool and cynical. 'Claudia did thicken her life with complications, didn't she? Not just the tumultuous love-affairs most of us knew about, but all this was almost . . . well, not a death-wish, but more like a masochistic yearning for bruising situations. Poor Claudia. I loved her, do you know that? She used to laugh when I riled Ma by playing her up. I thought she was sensational, twice life-size and so exciting. She and Ma loathed each other. Claudia used to tell Ma how like old Edward she was, and she didn't mean it kindly, either. Then she'd sweep me off to the theatre for the latest controversial play, explaining the unsuitable bits in explicit language, adding, 'Don't tell your mother I told you.' Ma made me feel unnatural, almost evil, when I wouldn't treat her with adoring reverence; Claudia showed me I wasn't.' A pause. 'But I will say this, Flora, I'm jarred by what she did to your mother. I thought Claudia was a woman of real strength, but she wasn't, neither in art or life. It was hateful of her to ignore Primrose. Where was the cultural sophistication I admired so much then? She could have made an eccentricity of her child or become an early heroine of the cult of permissiveness, but she failed the challenge.'

Irrationally I find myself explaining her, if not excusing her. 'Perhaps she agreed with the Greeks that honesty is a dangerous virtue. You have to admit her situation was impossible. Once she'd given in to Edward and Aunt Selina she was locked into the secret along with the Tucker-Bonds. Even when the moral climate changed in the permissive sixties she couldn't allow the world to know, not as Rebecca West had come to do with her son, Anthony, because the world would have been shocked by Claudia's cold non-relationship with Primrose, particularly after she'd portrayed her heroine anguishing over her childlessness in *Shadow of a Child*. Claudia had to live her lie or be condemned as a bitch and a fraud.'

'You're practising being objective,' Saffron retorts.

'I have to, don't I? You of all people, after all your criticisms, should applaud that.'

She grunts. 'That's what . . . what some man observed — '

'Alexander?' I laugh to myself. 'Tell me about him.'

'He's . . . well, he's with me.' She adds,

more resigned than indignant, 'He makes assumptions, that man. I offer him a lift and a coffee, but then he moves in on my house, my bed, my life.'

'So did Freddy with me. One's amazed, but then there's something rather endearing about such confidence in their judgements, especially when it's a warm judgement of oneself. Don't you agree?'

'All I know is he suspends my judgement. I've never met anyone like him. We talk for hours and it's real talk, Flora, you know what I mean, but . . . but it's unselfconscious. He'll explore concepts with me but laugh when we disagree rather than insisting on proving himself right. Though God knows he's sharp enough. Jake didn't need to prove himself, but then he wouldn't discuss, would he? He said it was just words going nowhere and he'd better things to do. David always stated everything as proved beyond discussion, yet underneath that saturnine face there were nasty pitfalls of self-doubt.'

I remember that previous boyfriend. 'That's why he chased other women,' I say without pause for thought. 'Opportunist elements apart, he needed to prove himself.'

'That's when I threw him out, when I saw that. I won't be any man's buttress. But he gave me some bad moments about myself first. With Alex I can relax. He knows about Claudia, too; he's read her. It's a new experience to be with an intelligent man who has one's own sort of mind and can admit to reading fiction, and enjoying it and . . . ' in a burst of confidence, 'who actually likes women for conversation as well as admiration and bed. Mind you, he's bossy. He won't let me get irresponsibly drunk — or mad over life's aggravations.'

'And you like it,' I say with a certain finality. This is the most intimate conversation I've ever had with Saffron, but it mustn't be prolonged or we might both give away private thoughts we'd regret.

'Well,' she admits, 'one does like a certain tension. When it's on the positive side, that is.'

She means he won't let her bitch. I say, 'I'm with you there!' and I'm about to say goodbye when abruptly she says something that nearly knocks me flat with surprise.

'Claudia could have extolled your books, couldn't she? She could have done it for you as she did for me. I think what that would have meant to Primrose and I'm screwed up with fury. She was kind, your mother. She had the generosity to say how she admired my work when I can't imagine for a minute it was her style of thing. And when my own awful parent picked at yours.'

'You think mine was in Claudia's style? I'm not so sure. She never said much, though she did drop the odd congratulatory note.'

'Oh, come on, we're not that far apart. She said you wrote surprisingly well, if you really want to know.'

'Oh God! The old witch.'

'That's what I mean. Well, you do, damn you.'

How is it she can admit this now when she never has before? Then enlightenment comes. 'You thought I was muscling in on your private family territory, didn't you?'

'Wouldn't *you* have? You were an outsider, struck by the wonders of publication as some people are stage-struck.'

The illusion of fame, of immortality. How extraordinary. My apparent bank-managing and city background from my father and grandparents didn't tie in, in fact was an affront, reducing her own achievements. But I was always going to write.

'Saffron, I suspect you'd prefer the literary world to resemble a select London club, membership strictly controlled.'

'What else?' she says, mocking herself, and we ring off almost affectionately.

★ ★ ★

In bed at Allords the next night Freddy tells me we're to spend the following weekend with his mother.

'Oh lovely,' I say, lazily stretching myself before settling to sleep. I anticipate her extraordinary kindness and the excellence of her food. 'We can settle the last details of our wedding, like the style of the men's buttonholes and whether the marquee ceiling should or shouldn't be garlanded with ivy looped round late roses. I'd never think up such ideas, let alone make them happen, but Paula loves being organisational, doesn't she? And I can help her deadhead things in the borders. That means I must do our roses tomorrow.'

'Mmm,' Freddy says, inattentive to such conjugal-style chatter. 'Listen, Alex is coming to lunch on the Sunday to discuss his Best Man role — and he's bringing Saffron. You've put up with her on several occasions recently. Can you bear yet another?'

In the darkness outside an owl hoots.

'I can bear it,' I say, smothering a yawn. 'She's mellowing, could be redeemable. One day we might each find ourselves forgetting to resent the other's existence. Rivalry from a cousin seems more ... more natural somehow. I wonder what Paula will make of her.'

'I can't imagine,' he says, and his voice is amused. 'But I'll tell you this, whatever it is, Alex will accept it. He says she's the most perceptive judge of people he's ever met.'

I settle on my back, my hands resting on my swollen belly. If Paula likes me, that proves me an OK person. Good.

I'm about to turn over and twine myself round Freddy when the flesh shifts under my right hand. I tense, wait perhaps ten seconds. Am I imagining things? It happens again, a distinct movement.

'Freddy,' I say in a whisper, reaching out for his hand. 'Hey, Freddy, put your hand on my tum. Yes, there, like that.'

'What is it?' he asks drowsily, his warm hand heavy upon me.

'Ssh. Wait.'

'Oh!' His hand jumps. 'She nudged me. Abigail nudged me.'

We laugh and hug each other. She's with us, making her presence felt. We curl up for sleep. 'Isn't she nice?' Freddy murmurs.

Claudia's great-granddaughter, Mumma's granddaughter, my daughter. In time she'll come to read the biography of her ancestor. I think: Claudia's own family was her Achilles' heel. Did she change and mellow after they died? I've only researched half her life so far, I've all the later decades to learn about yet, months or more of intriguing work to discover the real Claudia Charles behind the rave reviews, the hype, the adulation — and the scandals. I probe my grief for Mumma, and it's a little less strong, a little more diffuse. In my thoughts I promise her that within the pages of my book she'll receive the recognition that she never did manage to achieve in life.

The owl hoots again. The velvety blackness of the night wraps itself around us all. I roll myself close against Freddy's back, our minute daughter safe in my belly between us. I lie still, anticipating sleep, and it's impossible not to feel content in my expectations for the future.

THE END

We do hope that you have enjoyed reading this large print book.

Did you know that all of our titles are available for purchase?

We publish a wide range of high quality large print books including:
Romances, Mysteries, Classics
General Fiction
Non Fiction and Westerns

Special interest titles available in large print are:
The Little Oxford Dictionary
Music Book
Song Book
Hymn Book
Service Book

Also available from us courtesy of Oxford University Press:
Young Readers' Dictionary
(large print edition)
Young Readers' Thesaurus
(large print edition)

For further information or a free brochure, please contact us at:
Ulverscroft Large Print Books Ltd.,
The Green, Bradgate Road, Anstey,
Leicester, LE7 7FU, England.
Tel: (00 44) 0116 236 4325
Fax: (00 44) 0116 234 0205

Other titles in the
Ulverscroft Large Print Series:

FIREBALL

Bob Langley

Twenty-seven years ago: the rogue shoot-down of a Soviet spacecraft on a supersecret mission. Now: the SUCHKO 17 suddenly comes back to life three thousand feet beneath the Antarctic ice cap — with terrifying implications for the entire world. The discovery triggers a dark conspiracy that reaches from the depths of the sea to the edge of space — on a satellite with nuclear capabilities. One man and one woman must find the elusive mastermind of a plot with sinister roots in the American military elite, and bring the world back from the edge . . .

STANDING IN THE SHADOWS

Michelle Spring

Laura Principal is repelled but fascinated as she investigates the case of an eleven-year-old boy who has murdered his foster mother. It is not the sort of crime one would expect in Cambridge. The child, Daryll, has confessed to the brutal killing; now his elder brother wants to find out what has turned him into a ruthless killer. Laura confronts an investigation which is increasingly tainted with violence. And that's not all. Someone with an interest in the foster mother's murder is standing in the shadows, watching her every move . . .

NORMANDY SUMMER/ LOVE'S CHARADE

Joy St.Clair

NORMANDY SUMMER — Three cousins, Helen, Tally and Rosie, joined the First Aid Nursing Yeomanry. Helen had driven ambulances through The Blitz, but it was the Summer of 1944 that would change their lives irrevocably.

LOVE'S CHARADE — A broken down car, a mix-up of addresses and soon Kimberley found she was stand-in fianceé for a man she hardly knew. What chance had the pair of them of surviving this masquerade?

THE WESTON WOMEN

Grace Thompson

Wales, 1950s: At the head of the wealthy Weston family are Arfon and Gladys, owners of a once-successful wallpaper and paint store. It had always been Gladys's dream to form a dynasty. Her twin daughters, however, had no interest, and her grandson Jack had little ambition. And so, it is on her twin granddaughters, Joan and Megan, that Gladys pins her hopes. But unbeknown to her, they are considered rather outrageous — and one of them is secretly dating Viv Lewis, who works for the Westons but is not allowed to mix with the family socially. However, it is on him they will depend to help save the business.

TIME AFTER TIME
AND OTHER STORIES

Mary Williams

In this collection of mysterious short stories the recurring theme of 'time after time' is reflected upon with varying intensity, and in several as a haunting reminder of life's immortality. Time itself has little meaning in the wheel of eternity, and it is more than possible that the vital spark or soul of any human being could by chance contact that of another known to him or her in a previous existence on earth. Some stories concentrate on the effect of wandering apparitions about the ether and in all of them can be found love, tragedy, emotional yearnings and sheer terror.